# SOXKENDI

## A FAMILY OF DRAGONS

Dear Sarah,

Happy Year of
the Dragon!

# ALSO BY CAMILLA TRACY

Of Threads and Oceans
Of Flowers and Cyclones
Of Blood and Tides
Soxkendi : A Family of Dragons

https://geni.us/CamillaTracynewsletter

Or contact her directly at Camilla@camillatracy.com

# CAMILLA TRACY

# SOXKENDI

## A FAMILY OF DRAGONS

**Camilla Tracy**

© Copyright 2024 Camilla Tracy

Published by Pudel Threads Publishing

First Printing 2024

Tracy, Camilla, author

Soxkendi / A Family of Dragons

ISBN (paperback) 978-1-7380086-9-8

eISBN 978-1-7381915-0-5

B&N ISBN 978-1-7381915-2-9

Under a Federal Liberal government, Library and Archives Canada no longer provides Cataloguing in Publication (CIP) data for independently published books.


Technical Credits:

Cover Image: MiblArt

Editor: Bobbi Beatty of Silver Scroll Services, Calgary, Alberta

Proofreader: Lorna Stuber - Editor, Proofreader, Writer, Okotoks, Alberta

Created with Atticus

for those who couldn't quite get the cards they wanted in hand

*Soxkendi is from the Danish word, "søskende," meaning "siblings."

Centuries before Alexius met Thali ...

# CHAPTER ONE

## ALEXIUS

I T ALL STARTED WHEN my sister died. It broke my heart, and it set my family against me. I didn't exist to them for months because I reminded them of her ... and of what had happened. I was the salt in the wound that had cleaved all that was good and fun from their hearts.

Xerus, my eldest brother, tried his hardest not to ignore me, but the tension in his whole body when I was around was enough to tell me that I caused him more pain than anything else. My combat-training sessions with my next oldest brother, Jaxon, became rounds of silence punctuated only by grunts in response to my queries. Aexie, my next closest sibling, well, she left the room anytime I walked into one. So I laid low. I kept to myself and to my room, and that's when I discovered myself.

Did I mention I'm a dragon? I am the fifth born in my family. My father, Rixen, is the youngest son of the original twelve dragons. My mother, Elenex, is one of what we call the "Wild Ones." I spoke only to my parents for a hundred years after my sister's death. And then just when things were starting to look up—and my family was starting to include me again—life got worse than we ever could have imagined.

My father and mother were the only ones who didn't mind my presence, so I spent many a day with them in their throne room. There they would receive their guests, including the minor regional dragons. On this day, my training with Jaxon had taken longer than usual, so I strode in through a side door as my parents had already begun their public audience. I followed the flowing blues and pinks of the stone floor to the center, where the throne itself was outlined with a ribbon of gold. There were two seats: one for my father and one for my mother. My mother turned her head in my direction, and she nodded as I came up alongside her. I stayed standing as the next dragon came in. He was a caretaker of rare plants reporting that six of his dragonsbane plants had gone missing in the middle of the night.

"How many dragonsbane plants do you have?" my father, King Rixen, asked.

"I have only ten now. I had sixteen before. I have a license for each and a commission from the apothecary, Merwyn." The small brown dragon stayed low in his bow, obviously scared of repercussions.

"Do you know when they were stolen? Do you have any idea where they might be or who may have taken them?"

"No, Your Majesty. I know only that they went missing in the middle of the night, in the hours of pitchest black, for I was awake and watchful during the hours of light. I keep them locked in a separate greenhouse, one that is fortified and locked any time I am not inside. I have been applying for enchantments but have not yet received an answer."

"My apologies then." My father turned to me. "Alexius, go with this citizen forthwith and take note of the missing dragonsbane. Then please provide whatever enchantments are necessary—immediately," my father instructed.

I nodded and followed the little brown dragon out the main door and onto the rooftop courtyard.

"Brother," Xerus came around the corner as I exited the courtyard. "You may return. I will perform the enchantments."

My heart sank. I had been studying enchantments specifically for the last few years. However, I had to admit that Xerus was much better at them, so it made sense that he would do them if he was available, especially when dragonsbane was involved. I nodded and returned to the throne room. At my father's raised eyebrow, I leaned over to tell him Xerus had intercepted me and gone with the farmer.

He nodded and swished his tail, signaling we were ready for the next citizen.

A young purple dragon with yellow accents walked in with her head held high as if she was made of pure gumption. My heart stumbled and my breath hitched as she turned her attention to me. I stood a little taller next to my mother.

"Your Majesties, Your Highness." The dragon bowed and I couldn't take my eyes off her.

"What is your name, dragonling?" my mother, Queen Elenex, asked.

"My name is Brixelle. I've come today because my mother is sick, and we would ask for enchantments for our property so our labor could be eased."

Now it was my mother's turn to look at me. "Alexius, why don't you go with this young dragonette and provide her with the enchantments she needs?"

I only nodded because that was all I could manage while I told my feet to move one in front of the other as I followed Brixelle out.

"I am honored, Your Highness. Thank you," she said, dipping her head as she led the way out of the palace.

"The pleasure is all mine," I said. *Was that a stupid thing to say? I had been sent, after all. Did I sound inappropriate? Did I sound arrogant? Why did I care so much?* "Where do you live?"

"On the outskirts of The Gathering," she said. As we reached the edge of the rooftop courtyard, she looked over at me. "It'll be much quicker if we fly."

I only trusted myself to nod. Were her cheeks glowing? I motioned for her to go ahead since there was only room for one dragon to take off at a time. She was so graceful when she took off, I stared a second longer than I probably should have.

I took a couple steps and stretched my wings out, soaring over the balcony and quickly catching up with Brixelle. I flew alongside her and found my gaze sliding continuously to her, taking in how her purple scales shone in the light and how the golden scales bounced light onto the purple ones, making her purple glow so much brighter.

"It's not much farther," she said. "Just over the rise there."

I followed her gaze over the hillside to the last farm at the edge of the forest, then forced my gaze to remain off Brixelle long enough to appreciate the open farmlands. They were wide and hilly, beautiful with their green grass and large livestock herds.

We landed in the open grassiness, away from the livestock herds. "What enchantments would you like?" I asked.

"One to protect our livestock, some border alarms, and if you could, a weather detector would be wonderful." She smiled, raising her eyebrows.

I laughed. "I can't say I've ever heard of a weather-detection enchantment, but the others I can do. Can you show me your borders?"

"Of course, Your Highness." She lowered her eyes, and I thought my heart might leap out of my chest as my mind filled only with how beautiful those eyelashes were.

I coughed to refocus my attention. She took off again then, and I only needed to leap up and fly to follow her. We circled the edges of her land once. Her property was larger than I had assumed. No wonder she needed help. This was a lot of land to watch all by yourself.

"Would you object if I set wards up in sections? That way if someone or something triggers one, you'll know which section to attend to instead of having to search the entire property?"

"Handsome *and* smart," she said as she smiled at me.

My heart raced as I wondered whether she'd actually said what I'd heard. I felt the heat rise to the surface of my scales and knew I must be glowing. Shaking it off, I focused instead on the task at hand. "Do you have specific sections you'd like me to divide the property into?"

Brixelle nodded. "Follow me?"

*Anywhere*, my mind answered. I shook my head to focus again. "Lead the way. I'll start when we hit that rise there."

She nodded before pulling ahead of me.

I turned my attention inward and drew my light out, focusing on willing the light to be brighter than my surroundings. Then I molded the beam of magic into an alert enchantment as we approached the rise. With half my mind concentrating on following Brixelle, and the other half on the enchantment, I stretched the beam of magic along the path we flew until we finished one section. Then we did another and another. Making sections out of the larger piece of land took more time, but it would be more effective.

When we were finally done, the sun was starting its descent. "Would ... would you like to come in for a meal? I'm sure it's not quite up to palace standards, but we have quality sheep," she said.

She scratched the dirt with her claws as if she was nervous, and this warmed my insides. "That would be lovely," I said before following her back to her home. It was a basic stone house with perhaps three to four rooms, from what I could tell from the outside. Little purple and white flowers surrounded it, and I thought it looked both cozy and beautiful. We landed and she opened the tall wooden door. "I'll just be a minute if you want to make yourself comfortable," she said as she tried to fold blankets and tuck them into chests.

"If you'll point me in the right direction, I'd like to visit your mother." Perhaps I could give Brixelle a moment alone to ease her anxiety.

Brixelle looked stunned at first, so I continued. "You mentioned she was sick, so I'd like to see if my magic can help at all."

She glowed as she nodded and pointed down a wide hallway. I nodded my thanks and strode down the hallway to an open door. Brixelle's mother, a dragon the color of lavender, lay on a low bed.

"Your Highness?" She sat up suddenly, trying to quickly tidy the bed around her as I walked in.

"Madam, I'm pleased to make your acquaintance. Your daughter, Brixelle, came to my family to request enchantments for your vast property. I was lucky enough to be given the opportunity to oblige."

"I wish she'd told me before sending you in! I'm not dressed to receive royalty!"

"That is of no import to me. I'm sure Brixelle would agree that you need to spend your energy healing instead."

"Such a flatterer. And so kind! Please, please sit, Your Highness."

I pulled a stool over from the edge of the room and sat down. "May I?" I gestured for her foreclaw.

"Ohh, of course." She glowed, though dully, and gave me her hand.

"I know a little healing magic, and with your permission, I'd like to investigate your illness."

She nodded, her glow brightening for a moment. It made me smile.

I closed my eyes as I was a little tired from my previous exertions, then let my light flow through my claw to the older dragon's. I put up a protective barrier at my own claw but let the light flow to her body, checking her lungs and heart, and found that infection had invaded the old dragon's respiratory system. It looked much like sludge was stuck to her organs, and I gathered it together, moving it upward through her system. "I'd like for you to cough. Do you have a receptacle nearby?"

She grabbed a bucket she must have used previously from the floor beside her, and as I nudged the sludge upward, she began coughing. Soon, a lump of brown goo landed in the bucket. I sent my light through her claw again and checked her body once more for infection, scraping more off as I found it and bringing it up the same way.

She coughed a few more times, releasing more brown goo. Then I took the bucket from her and aimed a fierce white-hot flame at it. When I was done, the bucket was empty.

"Thank you, Your Highness. That was so kind of you!" The older dragon grabbed both my claws and kissed them.

"You will be tired, so I want you to rest tonight and tomorrow. Understand? Stay in bed for a whole night and day before you get up."

She nodded vigorously, and the door creaked open. Brixelle stood in the doorway with some soup for her mother.

"I believe the prince has cured me!" mother sung cheerily to daughter.

"Oh?" Brixelle turned to me.

"I found infection in her lungs and brought it up with magic. She should be much better now, but I've asked her to rest for another night and day before she gets out of bed."

"I'm grateful, Your Highness," Brixelle said.

"Now get him out of here so an old dragon can eat her supper in peace!" the lavender dragon said. I noticed a glint of mischief in her eye and was about to say something when she shooed us away.

Brixelle led me back toward the kitchen, where we shared a whole roasted sheep. I was exhausted but also excited to talk with Brixelle.

After we had eaten, I finished the enchantments. For them to be complete, I had to set up a warning system inside her home. "These will light up depending on which section has been disturbed." I pointed to some candles I'd set up and included in the enchantment.

Brixelle came to me and kneeled. "Thank you." She grasped my claws and kissed them.

"No, no." I drew her up to stand again. "It is my pleasure to help. If you need anything, please send for me personally."

"Then thank you doubly." Brixelle was shorter than me by about a head, so with a soft flap of her wings, she floated up and kissed my cheek.

I glowed so bright that I lit up the room around us. Brixelle smiled and glowed to match my own luminosity. Flustered, I mumbled my goodbyes and flew home, thinking as I did that the land looked a little brighter than it had when I'd arrived.

# Chapter Two

## Aexie

"W HERE IS HE?" I muttered, pacing the length of the library window.

"Do you mind taking your pacing elsewhere? Some of us are trying to read." Jaxon held his page in his book as he turned to me.

"It's not my problem you can't read, Jax," I said and raised a lip in challenge.

"You'll pay for that next time we're training, Aex."

"Well, this is the best window to see him return from that farm," I murmured to the floor before continuing my pacing.

"He'll be back, Aexie. He just went to put some enchantments on a farm." Jaxon softened his tone this time.

"That's what you said about Danxing," I muttered, turning to wipe an errant tear from my cheek before Jax could see.

"Aexie. Alexius can handle himself, trust me. I'm making sure of it. So are Xerus and Mom and Dad. He'll be all right." Jaxon closed his book and put it on his lap, careful not to put it back on the shelf in the middle of the room.

Something in the window caught my eye, and my heart fluttered as I thought it might be Alexius on his way back. It was getting dark, and a few simple enchantments shouldn't have taken this long. I had been livid when Dad had told me he'd sent Alexius off on his own to create some alerting enchantments today. He wasn't ready to be off on his own. I might still be mad at him, but what if something happened to him? That farm is on the edge of our kingdom. Tension filled me again as I realized it was a herd of pegasi flying by, not Alexius.

I went back to my pacing, and Jax went back to his reading, though I could feel his eyes on my back and wondered if he was actually reading anything. My nerves were wound so tight, I started practicing turning myself invisible just to let off some of the tension. I felt Jaxon startle when he looked up and saw I was suddenly gone before he calmed down, realizing what I was doing. He opened his mouth but then closed it, turning back to his book. But I saw him looking past me every other page or so, also checking for any movement out the large window.

I stayed invisible for the next hour, pacing as the sun set in the hills.

"If you wear out the rug, Mom's not going to be pleased, Aexie," Xerus said.

Both Jax and I startled.

"The tension in this room is suffocating. What are you both so worried about?" Xerus strode over in his human form and approached the small bookshelf in the middle of the room.

Mom's rule for this room was that one had to be in human form to enter. It was difficult to make things dragon-sized, and books were much easier to store if they were human-sized. Furniture was also easier to come by, so the library was for human forms only.

I thought about the first time I'd been allowed in the library. The first time I had changed into my human form, I'd been so excited to get in here, to be able to read the unlimited stories we had access to. I had run in here and up to the shelf, my mother following me. I'd looked around and seen that the room was filled with more furniture than books. There was a small bookshelf in the middle of the room, and as I'd run up to it, I'd seen only three books on the shelves. "Mama, where are all the books?" I had asked.

"They're all magically stored. This bookshelf will bring you the book you want to read, and when you're done, you'll put it back on this shelf so it can be stored away again. It also knows what you like to read," she had replied.

I could remember how excited I'd been to run up to the bookshelf every time I'd had a spare minute, constantly changing into human form just to run into the library to see what book the magical shelf would recommend. I shook my head to clear the memory as Xerus approached the bookshelf and ten books appeared on its shelves. "I'm clearly not the only one with a lot on their mind," I said as Xerus picked one and settled on a long chaise. He was the tallest of us all, slender and elegant, and he took his time reclining on the chaise, ignoring my comment.

"Aex is worried about Alexius," Jax said.

"Why? He can handle a few enchantments," Xerus said, folding both hands on his book.

Jaxon's gaze hardened as he tried to signal Xerus with a look, about what exactly, I did not know. But I was about to find out. Xerus looked from Jaxon to me, then back to Jaxon again before settling his gaze on me and speaking. "Aexie, what happened to Danx," Xerus stopped to swallow, and even I could tell he was fighting the emotion. "It won't happen again. It's been fulfilled."

I stopped dead in my tracks. "How can you say that?"

"I loved Danx as you did. She was full of light and fun and joy. But the tradition was completed, and she's gone now. There's a hole in my heart too, but it only happens once. Alexius will be safe."

My jaw dropped. How could Xerus be so casual about it? I could feel myself losing control over my human form, and I stalked out of the room, down the hall, and straight to the nearest exit. Once outside, I let go of my human form, and with a *pop!* took on my full dragon form, wings out. I flapped once and landed in the rock pit we were allowed to use to practice shooting fire, then let loose a fiery breath with every exhale as I tried to control my breathing. After scorching the wall with white-hot flames, each a good few minutes long, I heard a voice behind me.

"Something the matter, Aexie?" my father asked.

"Xerus is stupid," was all I offered before breathing more flames, now concentrating on narrowing the stream of flame on the corner of a boulder. The directed stream shaved off a slice of the boulder, and I continued until the boulder looked like a sliced tomato.

"That's very good control, Aexie."

My father was still behind me. I thought for sure he'd have gone back in by now. "Thank you, sir," I said, regaining some form of calm.

"What worries you?" he asked. I turned and saw that he sat, in his dragon form, at the edge of the pit on a large boulder. "I like to sit on this one, so please don't slice it." He pointed beneath him.

"Yes, sir," I said. We'd always been more formal with my father.

"So, what's bothering you?"

I clenched my jaw. Would my father take me seriously?

"Aexie, I know Danxing's death has been difficult for you. She was all the good things this world and this life have to offer. But you can't let her death taint your entire life. She wouldn't want that. She'd want you to continue on. Maybe live a little more through her eyes."

I exhaled suddenly, leaving a puff of smoke before me. I sat down in the rubble. "I'm worried about Alexius. He's still young. I know he's better than any of us were at his age, but he's still a baby in dragon terms. Yet everyone treats him like he's matured. He hasn't."

"Ahh ... Alexius will learn. I know the family I sent him to help today. They're good dragons. They'll take care of him. And it's about time he starts doing things on his own. Speaking of which, I think that's him I see on the horizon."

It was fully dark now, and I turned my head in the direction my father was looking. We both watched from afar as Alexius flew in, landed in the courtyard, changed back into human form, and walked into the palace, nodding to some guards as he walked by.

"See, he's unharmed and in good spirits. Until he sees the reports he'll have to fill out, that is." My father chuckled as he glanced back at me. "Go easy on him, all right? He may not realize how much you care when you berate him."

I swallowed and nodded. "Yes, sir." I felt the tension in my body release as I felt Alexius's presence nearby. I walked back to the palace with my father, both of us changing back into human form as we approached the smaller palace entrance.

"What took you so long, Alexius? Couldn't handle a few enchantments?" Jaxon was already on Alexius's case when we entered the library.

"Actually, for your information, I created a thorough enchantment by sectioning the land into parcels and setting alarms to light different candles for each parcel so the family knew which area had been disturbed."

I didn't hear a word he said. He was glowing and I pounced on it immediately. "Why are you glowing, Alexius? Is that the reason you were out so late? That girl—what was her name? Brinax? Were you two rolling around in the fields?" I mustered my most acidic tone.

"Her name is Brixelle. And no. I was held up because I was healing her mother. Maybe you should try helping others for once instead of carving rock with your fire once in a while."

My jaw clenched in response, but I wasn't about to let my little brother get the better of me. "Maybe you should learn to do a proper enchantment when you're told. Now all the farmers are going to want this new, more complicated alert system, and that'll triple our workload." I ground my teeth as I started glowing with anger.

"Enough," my father said. "Alexius, you should have spoken to me first. Come with me. You have reports to fill out. Aexie, you have reading to do. Remember your mother's rules."

As Alexius left with Father, I sneered and walked further into the library, where Xerus was fully engrossed in his book and Jax just looked at me sadly. I growled at him before stomping up to the shelf and grabbing whatever book was closest. I went to a corner and sat, curling myself under a blanket and opening the book. My mother's rule was that we all had to spend at least three hours a day reading a book in the library. Eventually, I let myself get lost in the story of a prince off to find his princess in a magical forest.

# CHAPTER THREE

## JAXON

I GLANCED FOR THE fifth time at Aexie as she huffed and settled deeper into the cushions and blankets. My sixth glance told me she'd finally settled into her book. It must have been one of those romantic fantasies she likes to read so much, princes and princesses or something.

I turned back to my book; I'd only read about three pages with all Aexie's anxiety. I knew Aexie would run into my father when she had rushed out before blowing up the library by taking on her dragon form, so I hadn't worried about her. I'd just been happy she'd had enough sense to get out of here before she'd lost all control. The library had been a gift from my father to my mother and was my mother's favorite place. Even though I didn't read as fast as Aexie, Xerus, or even Alexius, I still enjoyed the calm and quiet of the library, if only for its peacefulness.

My toes started to bob up and down and my leg soon followed. I was getting restless. I'd been here for two hours already, so at least I only had to put in another hour to fulfill my mother's requirement. Xerus had spent a couple hours in the library earlier to do some reading on dragonsbane, so he'd left a few minutes ago. A few plants had disappeared from a licensed farm, and he'd gone to search for clues.

"I've asked them to leave the place untouched. Will you go tomorrow morning and take a look?" Xerus had asked me after Aexie had burst out of the library.

"Yes. I'll go after breakfast," I'd said. I'd been a little surprised he wanted my opinion on it. I even felt a little flattered, so I'd do what I could. Xerus was an island unto himself, and the rest of us knew he took being heir to Father's realm seriously. He was constantly learning and shadowing Father in meetings so he could learn what he could.

My brother rarely delegated, so I was pleasantly surprised that he had this time.

I stared at my book again, reading the next few lines. Even battle-strategy books were boring me tonight. I read the same line six times before I let my mind wander to Alexius. He'd seemed stoic since Danxing's death, and he'd never been like that before. The whole family had been truly devastated by her death.

If I was being honest with myself, I think everyone had thought it was going to be Alexius we lost. He'd always been the slowest, the weakest, the one with the worst luck. But that's not what had happened. And since Danxing had sacrificed herself, Aexie had changed the most, though Alexius had walked around like he was lost for a couple months before he had thrown himself into work. He'd been training harder lately too, so I'd pushed him harder. Now he was quicker to listen to Xerus and spent more time than anyone else in the library reading about the realm and magic.

More than any of us, Aexie had become someone else when Danxing had died. She had once been as carefree as Danxing had been, as kind-hearted and joyful. Now she was moody, her temper flared quickly and almost without cause, and she was constantly anxious about Alexius—not that he knew how much she cared. Everything she said to him was laced with anger.

Xerus coughed, startling me. I glanced over at Aexie, who hadn't even noticed, before looking around for Xerus. He stood by the door and tilted his head. I quietly closed my book and put it under my arm as I walked as softly as I could to the door. We eased the doors closed before walking down the hall to the Jade Room.

"Jax, what do you know of dragonsbane?"

I furrowed my eyebrows and tried to remember. "It can be deadly to dragons if ingested and will kill a dragon slowly if they're exposed topically. But certain farmers are licensed to grow it for apothecaries. In small, diluted amounts, it's used to lower the immunity of a dragon so other remedies can work in a dragon's system. We can also drink it in micro dilutions to develop a resistance."

Xerus nodded. "It only takes ingesting a single leaf to kill a dragon."

My eyebrows shot up in surprise, but I waited patiently for Xerus to continue. It wasn't like him to confide in me, and I wanted to show him he could.

"Dragonsbane is also used to forcibly hatch dragon eggs."

"Why would anyone want to force a dragon egg to hatch?"

"I'm not sure. But we need to be wary. If there is dragonsbane unaccounted for, then someone wants to use it for illegal and nefarious purposes."

"I'll have a look tomorrow, I promise," I said.

Xerus nodded, but I could tell his brain was already racing through the many possible atrocious things one could do with dragonsbane. I breathed out a sigh; the royal family was always slowly exposed to dragonsbane through our lifetime so we'd all be immune. My family at least was safe.

"I know. I'm glad we're all safe too. I don't know if I could handle losing another family member," Xerus said quietly.

"Aexie and Alexius have taken it the hardest," was all I could manage. I bit the inside of my cheek.

"We've all felt the loss deeply, Jax." He put his hand on my shoulder, but I couldn't bear to look up at his face.

"I know you notice a lot, but I know Mother cries every night. Father has been working later than usual, you've been training harder, Alexius and I have been throwing ourselves into what work we can find, and Aexie ... poor Aexie. She's so jumpy, I'm scared I'll startle her when I walk up to her in the hallway."

I exhaled and some of the tension in my shoulders loosened. I was glad I wasn't the only one who'd noticed these things. "I think I might do some traveling," came out of my mouth before I knew it.

"Oh?"

I hadn't fully realized it myself, but as I looked around at the jade walls and floors and the sculpted dragons with their long, thin bodies in the center of the room, I knew. "You know, visit some of our relatives and learn some of their battle tactics."

"You feel the time of peace is nearing its end too then?"

"I'm not sure. I can't tell if it's my own inner peace being disturbed after Danxing's passing, but the world feels like it's shifting, choosing sides," I said.

Xerus nodded. "You should wait until Mother has settled a little more though. Aexie too. She'll be a wreck if you just take off suddenly."

I nodded. I had long thought of visiting our distant family to learn about their ways and battle strategies. I was the best warrior in our family, and I wanted the physical challenge of training in other styles. "It's going to mean that you have to take over their training." I finally looked up at Xerus.

He met the challenge in my eye. "What are you saying? That I'm not up for it?"

"I didn't say that."

"All right, *little* brother." He emphasized "little" even though I was easily twice Xerus's width and had triple his muscle. Xerus snapped his fingers, and the Jade Room filled with light. He removed his jacket, and I strode to the armory on the other side of the room and pulled out two swords and a dagger.

"Mortal weapons?" Xerus raised an eyebrow as he looked them over.

"Good weight training. And they won't scratch us, so they're good for practice."

Xerus smirked and transformed his human hand into his dragon claw and back again. "Worried I'm going to scratch you?"

"I don't need a sharp edge to bruise you," I said, shrugging. I tossed the sword from one hand to another after I tucked the dagger into my belt.

Xerus used the opportunity to slice sideways, but I'd been provoking him the whole time, so I was prepared as I grabbed my sword with my opposite hand to meet his slice and swept his sword downward. He broke away and I went straight in to jab at his middle, which he just barely avoided by hollowing himself out and turning at the last moment, pushing my sword away with his dagger.

We circled each other and I waited calmly. This was my element. While others would feel the adrenaline rushing through their system, I felt calm and ready. Xerus feigned a stab with his dagger, then swung his sword in the opposite direction, his dagger trying to draw my attention from his sword. I didn't even glance at the dagger as I blocked it with my sword, sliding my hilt toward his and catching his crossguard to flick his sword up into the air.

Xerus used his magic to grow his dagger longer and longer until it was the same length as a sword, and I frowned at his use of magic. I chopped down hard with my sword onto his newly lengthened dagger, and it shattered with the force.

"I thought we were testing skill, not strength," Xerus said as he surrendered, panting.

"You used magic. So I used strength. Magic will always weaken a blade, especially when you first create it, which is probably when you need it most."

"I know, brother. Please forgive me. You've brought to light my faults, and I'll take the time to correct them. Now, how about we practice with my favorite?"

I nodded, grabbing two staffs before collecting the swords and using magic to restore the dagger to its original state. Then I returned them to the armory and turned to toss Xerus a staff.

Later that night, I went to visit my mother. I knocked softly at her door as the guards nodded at me. I was glad to see that some of my best trained guards were at my mother's door.

My mother's handmaiden opened the door, and she nodded at me as I walked into my parents' sitting room. Xerus must have been by earlier given the fresh stack of books I'd seen him take out of the library earlier were now piled on her table.

My mother was beauty incarnate. Her human form had warm, tan skin with black hair and the original emerald-green eyes that we'd all been gifted with. "Jaxon." She smiled as I strode up to kiss her cheek.

I felt her shoulder blades through the fabric of her dress. She'd lost weight. "Mother, how are you?" I asked, stepping back to get a good look at her.

"Now, Jaxon, I know you're the observant one, so yes, I've lost a little weight, but that's not something for you to fret over. Your father's been getting the cooks to make all my favorite sweets of late, so it will all be back in no time. Now, come, let me have a look at you."

I let her walk around me, studying her gait carefully as she seemingly floated around the furniture.

"I think you have more muscle every time I see you, Jax." She pursed her lips and put one hand under her chin, the other hand supporting her elbow.

I couldn't help but beam.

"Now come, sit with me and tell me all the latest news," she said. I moved to sit next to her on the couch, and she snuggled right up to me, patting my arm. She leaned in and whispered, "Now, tell me all the things you've observed about your siblings."

I thought back to the first time my mother had said that to me. I'd been young, maybe a century or so, and she'd come to watch one of my sparring matches with Xerus. I had always been the best fighter, and even by that early age I was starting to beat Xerus even though he was two hundred years my senior.

I'd almost beat Xerus that day, and she'd given him a kiss on the forehead and sent him off after my father while taking me aside to fuss over. But instead of commiserating, she'd asked what I'd noticed while fighting.

"What do you mean, Mother?"

"I mean, what did you observe while you were sparring with your brother?"

"I observed his sword and his steps."

"And did you observe the way his right eyebrow raises before he steps to the left?"

"No, Mother."

"And what of your father, who stopped to watch from across the yard? Can you tell me what color his robes are today?"

"No, Mother." With each no, my head hung lower and lower. I had been proud that I'd almost beaten my brother, but suddenly, I'd been about to cry.

"Now, my son," She'd sat on a rock as she'd held my hands. "You are an amazing warrior. That we can see already. You will soon beat your brother, and you take to fighting like a fish to water. But you cannot be just a good fighter. There are other skills you must hone."

I remembered being confused. "Like observing the things around me?" I had asked.

"Yes, my darling. Like observing the things around you. And remembering them."

"Like a spy?" That had excited me.

"Yes, like a spy. And I will be your spymaster. Every day we will meet, and you will tell me all your observations."

I nodded excitedly. I had a new mission! So everyday since, I would meet with my mother and tell her all my observations.

Now, I sat this evening and told my mother about Aexie's anxiety, Xerus's concern about the dragonsbane, and about Alexius and how he'd been glowing when he'd come in, then had glowed brighter still when Aexie had mispronounced the farm dragonette's name. My mother and I whispered together until the supper bell rang.

# Chapter Four
## Xerus

I TRAINED FOR ANOTHER two hours after Jaxon left. If he was planning to travel, I'd be left to train Aexie and Alexius, so I had some brushing up to do. I dimmed the lights and went through the drills I hadn't gone through in a long time, reaching far back into my memory to when family members had come from other lands to visit before my siblings had been born. I had spent two entire centuries as the only child, the beloved child of my parents before Jax had hatched. Family had come out of the woodwork to teach me things back then. It was tradition for the firstborn to be gifted with knowledge from relatives and the distinguished dragons of the time.

"I thought I might find you here." My father walked in, and the room filled with more light.

"Jaxon plans to travel, so I'm brushing up," I explained.

"I can help fill the gap too. But your form is good. I thought for a moment that was Maddox in here when I first walked in."

"Thank you." I had just finished training and was now putting the weaponry back into their stands and armoires.

"Have you heard much from Thaxton?" my father asked. Thaxton was my cousin on my father's side. Uncle Maddox had died tragically centuries ago, but he'd been a renowned warrior.

"I've sent letters but haven't heard back. He seemed pretty busy ruling the kingdom all on his own," I said. "Perhaps I ought to write to him again."

My father nodded, then bent to pick up a sword and swung it around a couple times before putting it back. "I should brush up some time too," he murmured, maybe more to himself, as he looked at the rows of weapons before closing the doors to an armoire. "What did you learn of the dragonsbane?" he asked.

"Not much. It seems a mid-dragon may have taken it, though the farmer had been careful to lock the greenhouse. Unfortunately, it looks like it was a standard lock, not enchanted, so it was easily picked. I've asked Jaxon to take a look tomorrow. He might see something I missed."

"Good. You need to learn to delegate more." He peeked sidelong at me.

"I'm trying, Father. But I've been taking care of them for so long, it's difficult."

"Ouch. I guess that's well-deserved. Don't do what I did then. There was only me and your mother, so I put too much on your shoulders. You have three siblings, delegate so you can live a life of your own too."

"I will endeavor to do better." I nodded. My father was the wisest dragon I'd ever known. I would take whatever wisdom he was willing to offer.

"What kind of life do you want for yourself, Xerus?" He sat down on a couch as it appeared.

Another couch appeared adjacent to his and I sat on it. My father was feeling talkative tonight apparently. "Isn't that obvious? I'm heir to the throne."

"But what about your personal life? Have you heard from Xenon lately?" He raised his eyebrow as if he was truly curious.

"He's up in the alps of the Northeast doing something."

"Have you given any thought to what your lives will look like together?" he asked.

I couldn't believe it, but my whole body went warm, and I knew I was glowing. "No. we haven't spoken about it."

"Is he coming to visit you after he's done in the Northeast?"

"Yes."

"Well, maybe that'll be a good time to talk about it. You're obviously taking your inheritance seriously, so you should talk to Xenon about his options when he's here."

"He has options?" I asked. I'd dreamed of Xenon being at my side eventually, though in reality, I wasn't sure he'd ever settle in one place. He was truly nomadic. He was much older than I was, and I was still surprised he'd chosen me. Of all the other dragons in the world, he had chosen me.

"He could rule with you, taking on part of the responsibility of the monarchy, or he can be a prince, in which case you would always have the final say in matters of the crown. Being prince would also give him more freedom to travel if he so chose."

"Father, do you think Xenon would accept if I proposed to him?" My father sat back and thought about it. Part of me had wanted him to rush to say, "Of course, he'd be lucky to have you," but Xenon wasn't just any dragon. He was one of the oldest dragons in the history of the world. Older even than my father.

"Honestly, Xerus, I don't know. More than any other dragon, Xenon knows what marriage to the heir of the throne means. Fortunately, he's as wise as they come and not as power hungry as some younger dragons."

My whole body went cold as reality sank in. Maybe that would scare him away.

"But on the other hand, I've honestly never seen Xenon as happy as when he's with you. Love might conquer in this one, son." He shook his head. "I still think about the day I met Xenon when I was a young dragon. It's hard to believe he's the same being when he's around you, all soft and young and giddy." He barked a laugh then. "What do *you* want, son?"

"To be a wise and fair ruler and to have Xenon at my side to make the bad days not so bad and share the good days with," I said, quoting my parents' partner vows.

My father smiled. "I'm afraid your mother and I have made you all romantics at heart."

"Speaking of romantics, did you see the way Alexius glowed after he came back from Brixelle's farm?" I asked.

"Yes, and I also noticed him picking his jaw up off the floor of the receiving room earlier today when she walked in. This will definitely be an interesting season." My father went quiet then, and I was happy to sit quietly with him, each of us contemplating the many things on our own plates.

Suddenly, he sighed and broke the comfortable silence. "I'm glad to have you with me every day, Xerus. It's nice to have a second set of ears and eyes I can trust."

"I'm happy to be learning so much. Thank you, Father."

"I best be getting back to your mother. She's promised to skin me alive if I keep going to bed in the wee hours and waking her when I do." He rose and looked expectantly at me.

"I'm going to stay a little while longer," I said. I enjoyed the peace and quiet this room offered.

"Just put the couch away when you're done. If Jax breaks another couch, we won't have anything left to sit on." He waved as he left, closing the big jade door behind him.

I sat on the couch, bringing my small human feet together as I made myself comfortable and closing my eyes to try and clear my mind. I had to wipe away the thoughts that kept pestering me, the thoughts that kept floating in different directions.

*Hey, are you there, my darling?* The thought interrupted my own thoughts.

*Xenon! Where are you?* I whispered in my mind.

*In some dark cave in the frozen north.*

*Are you safe? Are you all right?*

*I'm fine. Just tucked in for the night. How have you been? I sensed you were a little distraught today.*

*Some dragonsbane was stolen from a farm.*

*Ah. That's why you were so concerned.*

*Yes. I haven't really figured out what happened to it.*

*You will. I'm sure of it.*

*Your ears must have been burning. My father and I were just talking about you not an hour ago.*

*Oh? Anything juicy?*

*No.* But warmth blossomed in me. I tried to stop it so he wouldn't sense it.

*You're blushing. You're so adorable when you blush. Must be good then.*

*My father asked whether I'd thought of your place in this monarchy.*

*And what did you tell him?*

*That we hadn't talked about it yet.*

*You didn't tell him about the blood oath?*

*No. I haven't had a chance. Aexie's still upset about Danx.*

*She was a sweet little dragon.*

*Oh, and I think Alexius fell in love today.*

*Who with?*

*A farm dragon. Brixelle. Have you ever met her?*

*No. I haven't spent much time in your area recently.*

*And will you be remediating that soon?*

*On my way back, after my business here. I'll stay for a while if your family will have me.*

I laughed. *Of course. Don't you have some lands around here to check on?*

*Shh. You're not supposed to know that.*

I rolled my eyes under my eyelids.

*I need to go. One of my enchantments was just triggered. I love you. See you soon.*

*Be safe. Love you too.*

I opened my eyes and blinked at the light. As I rose from the couch and remembered to send it back magically, I was careful to step softly. I strode through the open doors and went to the library. With my mind at ease now, knowing that Xenon was safe, the matter of the missing dragonsbane rose to prominence in my thoughts. I felt like I was missing something.

Walking into the library, I saw that Aexie had fallen asleep with a pile of books next to her. She must have continued reading after we'd all left. As gently as I could, I used my magic to snake light beams around her neck, head, and body and walked her back to her room, my light magic keeping her afloat. I tucked her into bed before returning to the library.

I sat near the magical bookshelf, pulling one of the desks over so I could spread out the books. About twenty books popped up on a single shelf, and I transferred them to the desk. I started opening them one at a time, looking for dragonsbane and skimming over the page when I found it before leaving the book open on the desk.

Most of the books I scattered across the desk were apothecary books about tinctures and preparations, safe handling methods, and dilution formulas. The amount of dragonsbane that had been stolen was enough to kill about a dozen dragons if ingested. I tried to think of a group that size that might have incurred that kind of wrath or hatred. None came to mind.

Of course, dragonsbane could also be used to force a dragon egg to hatch. Dragon eggs hatched whenever it pleased the dragon inside. My father and mother had created eight in total, but we had all hatched centuries apart. I still had three siblings that hadn't chosen to hatch yet or were never going to. But according to two of my books, if you rubbed an egg on one side with dragonsbane and laid it in a nest of dragonsbane, the dragon inside might be so offended that it would hatch early. But you also risked killing the dragon inside the egg.

I kept opening books, flipping through the pages and looking for dragonsbane. Then I grabbed a dusty, old, green book and started flipping through it. The title on the cover had long faded, so I didn't know what it was about. I hadn't flipped far before I saw the mention of dragonsbane. The book itself should have probably been called *Dragonsbane*. Each page had a table with dilution ratios with different solvents, their purposes, and the results. I started flipping more rapidly, taking care not to ruin any of the brittle old pages.

Finally, the charts ended and recipes began. Knowing it must be an old apothecary book, I glanced only at the top paragraphs, wondering what the recipes below them were for. I grew bored as I flipped through hundreds of different dragonsbane dilutions mixed with other common remedies. Again, they were all used for lowering a dragon's immunity enough for a remedy to take hold. I carefully continued flipping. Though each formulation was nearly the same as the next, I tried to read each description carefully. Eventually, they blended together and my eyes started to droop, so I decided to take a small break and rest my eyes for a minute before reading the next book.

# CHAPTER FIVE

## ALEXIUS

I HAD SLEPT PEACEFULLY, one of the few times since Danxing's death. Filling out reports after using so much magic had exhausted whatever mental energy I'd had left, and I had returned to my own chambers and thrown myself onto my bed.

After waking up refreshed and energized, I headed to the library. I had finished my current book yesterday and always liked reading first thing in the morning. When I pushed open the library doors, feeling the enchantments like a puff of air, I saw Xerus asleep on the desk with a dozen or so books strewn around him. I walked softly over to look at what he was studying and saw that all the books were apothecary books. I gently removed the book he was indelicately drooling on and cleaned it up with magic so Mother wouldn't notice the wet pages before I examined it.

Flipping through a few pages, I saw that it was an all-things-dragonsbane book. It began with charts of dilutions, and the pages Xerus had been reading when he'd fallen asleep all contained information about the various uses of and details about dragonsbane. I turned another page and read that dragonsbane, unlike many other plants, was relatively easy to grow. Instead of needing seeds, once a plant was fully mature, you could take a clipping and grow another plant by planting the clipping in dirt laced with the spores of a specific mushroom. I carefully set the book back down on the desk, safely away from the drooling dragon, and went to the bookshelves.

As I pulled out the book I'd originally wanted to read, I saw a few other books appear on the shelf below it and pulled those out too. They were books on mushrooms, so I started flipping through them to find the mushroom mentioned in the dragonsbane book.

Once I'd found it, I scanned the page and realized it was an easily attainable mushroom in my world, the world of Etciel. It was something anyone capable of getting to the marshlands could obtain. I looked at the second book, which was about mushroom life cycles, and flipped through it to learn how one could create dirt filled with mushroom spores.

When I saw the third book's title, I realized it was a standard spells-and-potions book, one I had studied when I was just starting to learn about magic. I flipped through the pages, half-heartedly reviewing the things that I'd learned as a beginner. I slowed when I got to the section about things that can influence magic, the different potions used to bolster or counter different kinds of magic. As I began to read carefully, my heart started to race. It was a shot in the dark, but if Xerus was concerned enough to have stayed up reading all he could on dragonsbane, then he was concerned it was a bigger problem than originally thought.

I shook him awake.

"What?!" Xerus sat bolt upright.

"Xerus, you fell asleep in the library. Look what I found on dragonsbane."

"When did you start on dragonsbane too? Brixelle isn't growing it is she?"

"No. I didn't see any on her farm, but when I came in here, you'd obviously been studying it, so I poked around. Anyway, look at this." I turned my book toward him.

His eyes went wide as he shook off the sleep and looked closer. "I can't believe I missed that. And that book is available to everyone, young and old," he said. "We have to show Father, then get word to the others."

I had stumbled upon a combination of magic and dragonsbane that could be used to control a dragon.

"They'd need much larger quantities than was stolen," Xerus suddenly said. "How easy is it to grow?"

I pointed to the book about dragonsbane clippings. And as he read that, I brought over the book on mushrooms I had just pulled out and set it below the one he was reading.

"You were up early this morning," Xerus mumbled as he moved to the next book.

I tapped my foot impatiently as I waited for him to catch up.

"Did you see this one here, Mr. Foot Tapper?" Xerus asked as he grabbed a book beside him and put it in my hands. It was about how to use dragonsbane to force a dragon egg to hatch.

"They'd need a lot less for this," I said. I'd read Xerus's report when I'd dropped my own off last night. Six plants had been taken. The culprit could force three eggs to hatch with six plants.

"Either way, we need to bring this to Father immediately, let the other families know, and start both a patrol and an inquiry. We need to know if any eggs have been stolen from the hatcheries, and we need to guard the remaining eggs and dragonsbane."

I nodded. Xerus rose and we stalked to the door only to come face-to-face with Father. "My sons are up early this morning!" he said cheerily before he saw our serious faces. He motioned us back into the library. "Before your sister wakes, let's discuss whatever this is."

We sat and quickly filled him in on our recent findings.

My father's brows knit together as he considered the information we'd given him—well, Xerus had given him. I'd just sat there nodding emphatically and getting the books to show him. "I think I'll go out with Jaxon this morning to take a look myself," he finally said. "Xerus, I want you to visit the other licensed farmers and place protective enchantments on their facilities and tracking enchantments on the plants themselves. Take Alexius with you."

Xerus nodded and my father strode out, still in his pajamas, leaving Xerus and me standing in the same spot where we'd run into him in the first place.

"I'll go and get a list of licensed farmers," Xerus said. "I'll meet you in the courtyard in an hour?"

I nodded.

"Alexius," Xerus said. I paused with my hand on the door. "Wear leathers and round up enough sustenance from the kitchens to last two days."

I nodded, feeling the escalated danger. I hurried to the kitchens, stealing a fresh roll and asking the staff to pack two days of food for me and Xerus. I impulsively decided to ask for another two packs for Jaxon and Father while I was there.

From there, I went out to the armory and found Jaxon there. I handed him the two extra packs of food. "Did Father find you?"

"Yes, thank you, Alexius. We'll have to train later. Father wants to head out as soon as we're ready."

"That's all right. I'm going with Xerus to enchant the remaining dragonsbane plants."

He nodded. "Be safe, brother." He clasped my elbow and nodded.

"You as well." I clasped his arm in turn.

Then he left the armory with his light armor and only half his weapons, so I ran off then too. I hurriedly dressed as requested then went to meet my oldest brother in the courtyard. My father and Jaxon were flying out as I arrived, but I was surprised to see my sister in the courtyard. "Are you coming too?" I asked.

"No. Someone has to stay behind and defend the palace." Aexie brushed her hair back with one hand. That was the first sign Aexie was nervous. After Danx, Aexie had become meaner. She got anxious first, then the mean would come out. By now, I was prepared to absorb without reacting whatever caustic words came out of her mouth. I knew she was hurting. I would still go to Danx's room only to have reality catch up to me halfway there. Then I'd feel the sharp dagger through my chest again as I realized she was gone.

"Seeing us off then?" I asked.

Something akin to a frustrated roar escaped Aexie, and she turned on her heel and stalked back into the palace.

Xerus came out then. "You really shouldn't provoke her." he said, raising a questioning eyebrow my way.

"I didn't!" I said. Xerus had always had a soft spot for Aexie, and he always thought I was the one to cause trouble.

"Well, no matter. Ready? The first farm is about twenty minutes away."

I nodded.

He changed into dragon form and leapt. With two great flaps of his wings, Xerus took off into the sky. I quickly popped into dragon form too and leapt up to follow him. He hovered in the clouds, but when I caught up, he flew off, the rising sun to our left. I was flying next to him when a movement to our right caught my eye.

In a field, three young dragons were practicing their take-offs and trying to get airborne. Their mother, in dragon form, looked on as she sat on a rock, dragon-sized knitting needles in her hands as she watched them and hollered advice while they took turns trying again and again.

I smiled at their efforts and remembered how frustrating it had been to leap and flap and leap and flap and not understand what it was to fly. It had taken me almost a full year to learn how to fly—to my embarrassment. Apparently Aexie had learned in a day, and Xerus and Jaxon in no more than a week. I'd always been the smallest, the weakest. And I knew my siblings blamed me for Danx's death. I knew they thought it should have been me.

When we landed at the first farm, I stayed out of the way. I watched as Xerus approached the farmer, explaining our presence and asking if we could check their security measures and fortify them where needed. The first farmer was surprised when we landed but grateful for the extra help. "Glad you're making the rounds now. You should go to Nixon's next. He said he saw some stranger's footprints beside the road near his setup a couple nights ago." The farmer crossed his arms as he looked Xerus up and down.

"Thank you. If anything strange happens, please send word to the palace. Address it to me please," Xerus said.

The farmer nodded and I just stood and nodded too. Xerus checked him off our list, and I saw that there were only a dozen or so names on it. We took off and flew to Nixon's farm next, even though it was a little way past the next one on Xerus's list.

We flew along the road, then walked up to the main entrance of the farm so as not to startle anyone.

"I thought their licenses stipulate they have to submit to inspection at any time," I said.

"Yes, they do, but we're not trying to scare them or step on anyone's toes. It'll make our jobs a lot easier if they like us because they'll want to tell us things instead of us trying to bully them. Besides, this is still their home. We're on their land. We need to be respectful and mindful of that."

I nodded. It would have been a lot easier just to fly directly from facility to facility.

"Oy there, Your Highnesses." A medium-sized brown dragon stepped out of the stone hut we were approaching.

I took the lead this time. "Are you the farmer known as Nixon?"

"Yessir. You must have been to see Arox?"

"How did you know?" I asked.

"You smell like clove. Arox always smells of clove," he replied.

I sniffed myself, realizing that I did indeed smell of clove.

"Arox told us you found strange footprints near your dragonsbane facility," Xerus said, getting straight to the point. Then he continued with the story of the stolen dragonsbane.

Nixon listened carefully and nodded. He led us to his facility and showed us the footprints. Only one had survived the last few days, and he'd put a wooden frame around it. "I figured you might be by to take a look. I've got a workin' farm here, so I couldn't save all the footprints, but this was the best one anyway. The evildoer didn't take anything though. I've got a pretty intensive security system, though a few more enchantments couldn't hurt if you're so inclined." He raised an eyebrow at me.

Xerus nodded. "Go ahead, Alexius, I'm going to study the footprint."

Not wanting to keep eye contact with Nixon, I closed my eyes and reached for the light within the core of my magic. I felt the magic of the land and drew a ray of its light to join my own, creating protection and vigilance enchantments around the facility. When I was done, I opened my eyes and conjured a mask and gloves for me.

"I always thought the royal family was immune to dragonsbane," Nixon said as he started opening the locks and removing his security measures.

"We are. But we like to take precautions anyway. Where is your protective wear?" I asked. Xerus was still bent over the footprint.

"I don't need any. I figured if I made myself immune it would make my job a lot easier." Nixon nodded at the open door.

"I suppose that's true," I said and donned the mask and gloves as I entered the greenhouse.

Every licensed dragonsbane farmer is issued a greenhouse made of diamond glass. It's just like normal glass in a greenhouse; the difference is simply that diamond glass is impenetrable. The only way to get in and out is through the one door. The structures we made for the farmers also had a floor of diamond glass, so no one could dig underneath either.

Inside, it was humid, and I breathed in the beautiful moisture as I gave each plant a tracking enchantment. "I'll put tracking spells on these plants now, so if they're moved outside this greenhouse, we'll be alerted. If you need to move them, please send word directly to Prince Xerus."

Nixon nodded. "I appreciate the extra security, Your Highness. Never can be too careful with such deadly plants." He nodded again and backed away.

I remembered from the list that Nixon had a license for twenty dragonsbane plants. And as I looked upon their faint purple leaves and dark-green flowers, I counted the twenty and nothing else. Often, farmers would get a license to grow dragonsbane just so they could have a coveted greenhouse. Twenty plants took up only a small portion of the greenhouse, and it became a safe storage place and comfortable growing environment for other exotic flowers and plants. Most farmers with licenses also grew tropical plants to sell to flower shops and nonregistered plants for apothecaries alongside the dragonsbane.

I didn't close my eyes as I worked my magic this time because Nixon was busy tidying up the rest of the shed. As I sent out my light enchantments for alerting and tracking, I kept tabs on the ends of each beam so I could connect them to something concrete when I got back to the palace.

I looked around then and saw a beautiful yellow lily with a purple center and thought of Brixelle.

"Would you like it, Your Highness? The yellow lily?" Nixon asked as he looked over and followed my gaze.

"Yes, I think I would. How much, Nixon?" I reached for a pouch of coins in my pocket.

"Nothing for Your Highness. I appreciate the extra enchantments and the work your family does for this realm."

"Thank you," I replied. I picked up the flower and left the greenhouse, removing my mask and gloves. After gently storing it in my bag, I flew into the air with Xerus, who'd been waiting outside the greenhouse to move on to the next farm.

# CHAPTER SIX
## XERUS

A S SOON AS I'D seen Alexius carrying that flower, I knew he'd want to stop before we arrived at our next farm. His destination was only a little out of our way, but I have to admit I was glad I didn't see anyone at the main house. We had a long list to get through, and I don't like to be waylaid while on task.

I watched from above as Alexius flew down to the stone hut and gently placed the flower on their doorstep. While I was there, I took a quick glance at the magical system he'd installed yesterday. I had to admit I was impressed with how he'd laid his enchantments in sections, just barely overlapping. To me, his magic was made of red light, faintly detectable and only because I was so familiar with him. I'd trained him after all. I smiled thinking of the time he'd turned Aexie's hair bright red and then bright purple. Her hair had kept flashing red and then purple and back to red until my father finally fixed it because it was giving him a headache.

When Alexius finally flew up to meet me, I raised my eyebrows to ask if he was ready and he nodded. We flew out to the next farm to do the same as we'd done at the last two. I had Alexius do every other farm for practice.

We stopped overnight at one farm and slept in their barn. I set up wards and charms for the night just in case. You couldn't be too careful as a royal. We ate silently and fell asleep promptly. Using magic in such a careful and precise way took a toll, especially on Alexius, and he fell fast asleep as soon as he'd finished his portion of dried meat.

I was a little more restless and stayed up longer. At first, I just watched Alexius sleep. He was still so young. I often forgot he was seven centuries my junior. He'd been forced to learn to change into his human form so young, and he'd learned everything else at a very young age too. He had been one of the youngest dragons ever to learn to control his magic and fly. Especially after Danxing passed, he seemed to always be trying to catch up to us, and now it seemed as if he had. I wondered whether he'd grown up a little too quickly, if maybe we should have treated him like a dragonling for longer.

*Helloooo,* Xenon said in my head.

*Hi, Xe.*

*Where are you? It stinks.*

*In a barn. Alexius and I are checking the dragonsbane farms in the realm, and we stopped overnight before we finish the rest tomorrow.*

*How many are you checking that it's taking you so long?*

*I'm letting Alexius do half. He needs the practice.*

*Ah, a little dragonling training.*

*I was just thinking about whether he was still a dragonling or not.*

*Sweetheart, I'm old. You're all little dragonlings.*

I laughed at that and covered my snout to not wake Alexius. *How are you? Have you finished your mission already?*

*Yes, I'm done. It was pretty easy. I'll be heading to you tomorrow.*

*I'll be glad to see you.*

*I'll be glad to hold you in my arms again, my darling. Have you told your parents I'm visiting?*

*And how am I supposed to explain how I know?*

*You still haven't told them of our blood oath?*

*It's been exactly two days since you last spoke to me, so no.*

*Xerus, you need to tell them. They're going to figure it out when they see us together. It's better if you tell them first. Knowing Rixen, he might already know.*

*I'll tell them tomorrow when I get back. When do you expect to arrive?*

*Late afternoon. You should sleep now though. I can feel how tired you are.*

*Yes, I suppose. Good night then.*

*Sweetest of dreams, my little dragonling.*

Xenon must have sent a wave of sleepiness through our connection because it was all I could do to lay my head down before falling asleep.

The next morning, I woke to Alexius nudging me awake. He looked excited and couldn't help but lick his lips as he marched outside the barn.

"Your Highnesses should be eating properly. And my sheep are some of the best." The farmer was roasting a sheep for each of us in his firepit.

"That's very kind of you, sir," Alexius said as he drooled.

I rolled my eyes at my brother. "That is indeed very kind. Thank you."

"It's my absolute pleasure." With that, the farmer tossed the three sheep from the spit up into the air, and I caught one, Alexius caught another, and the farmer caught the third. We ate in quiet contemplation for a time.

"It's not every day I get to eat with royalty," the farmer finally said. "Thank you for your services, Your Highnesses. Its my honor to share my sheep with you."

"You honor us with your hard work. Thank you," I said as Alexius licked his lips again to clean whatever juices might have remained on his maw.

I raised my eyebrow at him, and he coughed and straightened, remembering his manners.

"Thank you, sir. You've honored us, and now we'll be off to continue our work," Alexius said, and he shook claws with the farmer before checking with me. I nodded and leaped up into the sky ready to move on to our next farm.

Alexius was right behind me. We finished with the rest of the farms on the list and returned to the palace just before lunch that day. He was tired from using his magic, so I sent him to get some rest as I was sure Jax would want him to train after lunch.

"Thank you, brother. I enjoyed learning from you," Alexius said as he nodded and left me to go bathe and nap in his own chambers.

I decided I would go bathe too before telling my parents of my blood oath with Xenon. I shifted back to human form, entered through a side door, and nodded to the guards there. Ducking into my rooms, I snapped my fingers for water to fill the pool and then let magic seep into the water to heat it so that as I stepped down into the bath, it would be exactly the temperature I preferred. I sank into the water, letting my human form soak in the heat, and hung my hair over the edge of the pool. I would clean it later. Closing my eyes, I thought about last year's summer solstice when Xenon had made his oath to me. Then I let my mind drift to the day I'd met Xenon. I'd been just a dragonling. I'd just learned to fly, and Xenon had come to visit my parents to bestow a gift on me as their firstborn.

I remembered seeing him later in his human form, tall and slender with bright-silver hair, not white, but pure shiny argent. That day, he greeted my parents as we stood in line to receive him. I had just learned to change to human form and was struggling to keep hold of it. His gaze turned to me, and I remembered the warmth of his golden eyes. It was such a strange combination, that silver and gold, that I couldn't stop staring at his eyes. And he in turn seemed to take a liking to me. He smiled warmly, and I remembered thinking how intriguing it was that this powerful dragon was paying so much attention to me.

He turned to talk with my parents, and I was excused to go off and play as I hadn't had enough practice with my human form to keep it for long.

I'd found out later that he'd given me one of the greatest gifts a dragon could: a favor.

The next time I'd seen him, I'd been what you might consider a teenage dragon, almost full-grown. We were at the annual winter celebration, and Xenon had come to celebrate with our family. The moment I caught sight of him, I recognized him as the silver-and-gold dragon. That night, we were all in dragon form, and Xenon was the most beautiful dragon I'd ever seen. He was long and thin, the embodiment of an ancient dragon, his body mostly a dark silver that reflected the flash of the flames from the bonfire. His claws and scales were accented with a silver so dark it was black. And his eyes were the same dark gold as when I'd first met him. He came over to say hello, and we eventually started dancing in the crowd of dragons.

Xenon told me later that he had tried to stay away. He'd known I was his mate when he met me as a child. He'd just had to wait. I'd been too young, too immature for it to be appropriate, but because he'd waited centuries to meet his bonded mate, he'd known he could wait a few more centuries. He'd traveled around all the worlds after that night to try and occupy himself.

It wasn't until Alexius's first solstice that he finally approached me. On that summer solstice, he came to visit my family a week before the celebrations started. He told my parents he'd come to see if they wanted to collect on the favor he'd gifted me, but they deferred to me since I was old enough then to know what it meant and understand its significance.

*I'm here.* Xenon's voice suddenly interrupted my thoughts, and I leapt up, sloshing water everywhere.

*You're early,* was all I could manage through the connection.

A guard knocked at the door to my chambers, and I grabbed a cloth to wrap around my bottom half as I answered my chamber door.

"Your Highness, Lord Xenon has just arrived at the palace entrance. Your parents request your presence as quickly as is convenient." He bowed and I nodded in return.

I threw on my usual pants, shirt, and long-tailed jacket—the one Xenon had said was his favorite the last time he'd seen me in it—and ran out the door of my chambers. I ran into Jaxon carrying an armload of weapons out the door of his own chambers right beside mine.

"Xer, calm down. Lover boy will wait for you," Jax said. He grinned and picked up the swords I'd made him drop. "I'll be outside all afternoon, just so you know," he added. I ignored him as I adjusted my pace and strode as calmly as I could, straightening my jacket.

I entered the receiving room and was a little surprised not to see my parents there given they'd requested my presence. Xenon stood by the fireplace, and when he saw me, his grin matched mine. I couldn't help but enjoy the rush of heat that flowed through my body, making me glow like a teenager, I was sure.

Xenon had a little more control over his own flush, but we took two rushed steps before our lips crashed into each other and we gripped each other tightly. Our bond had snapped back into place like an elastic, and I wanted to be in this moment forever.

A knock on the door interrupted us.

Xenon pulled away first, not letting me go completely, rather snaking his arm around my back as I managed to say, "Come in," trying not to squeak as I said it.

My father and mother swept into the room after a beat, probably because they knew we needed a second to compose ourselves.

"Xenon," my father said as he approached us.

"Rixen. It's a pleasure to see you both again." He hugged my mother and father.

My mother looked a little perplexed. "I wish we'd known you were coming. We'd have been better prepared to receive you," she said, ever the hostess.

Xenon turned to me. "You haven't told them yet?"

"You were early." I felt like it was a childish retort, but I couldn't help myself.

"Told us what?" Father's face was calm, but my mother glanced from me to Xenon.

Xenon sighed, sitting down. "Please, sit. We have something to tell you."

My father and mother sat down, my mother's anxiety clearly mounting.

I sat next to Xenon and gave him a traitorous glare. I was going to tell them—I'd promised him—but now it felt like he was forcing me. Part of me wanted to rebel. Our mental connection was silent for once, and my guess was that it would remain silent until my parents knew the truth.

"Rixen, Elenex. You know by now that Xerus is my bonded mate," Xenon said, giving me an opening.

My mother and father nodded.

I took a deep breath and then spat it out. "Last summer solstice, Xenon swore a blood oath to me."

My father's eyebrows only moved an inch. He'd suspected it then. And my mother's eyebrows also went up, her mouth popping open in a bit of an "O." She was faking her surprise then. I'd seen her do that before when one of her children threw something at her they thought would be a surprise. Somehow, not much got past my mother, or my father for that matter.

"You knew," I said flatly.

"I felt the shift at solstice. And I'd be lying if I said I didn't know when Xenon was near. Through your familial bond, I can feel Xenon. So yes. We knew," my mother said.

Xenon let out a breath, though he also looked a little anxious. I could now tell he was going through all the things he'd said to me through our connection and wondering whether my mother had sensed any of it.

My mother leaned forward and smiled. "I only know when you're approaching. It feels like a slight alert. I don't get much more through the familial bond," my mother said to put Xenon at ease.

I thought it was funny that an ancient and powerful being like Xenon could be nervous around my mother.

"Xerus, did you know all the implications of the blood oath Xenon made before he did it?" my father finally asked. He'd been quiet all this time, and the seriousness of the question startled me.

"Yes. I made sure he knew all the implications, and I want you to know that I made my oath first so he could understand. He has not made his oath yet," Xenon said, becoming as serious as my father.

My father ignored him, looking to me.

"Yes, Father," I said as I nodded. "I did—and do—understand the blood oath. I realize that if I reciprocate, we will be forever tied together in life and in death, that we will know each other's feelings and thoughts, though Xenon taught me to shield against him even along the ties of the oath. And I know that if one of us dies, the other typically dies within a year, such is the strength of the bond."

He nodded.

My mother looked at my father skeptically, and they seemed to confer with one another silently. Then she finally turned back to us. "Welcome to the family, Xenon. Would you two object to a celebration of your union?"

"It would be an honor," Xenon said before I could say anything.

"How long will you be staying, Xenon? Nex can probably plan one while you're here if you're staying for a few weeks." My father sat back in his chair.

"I'll stay for at least a year if Xerus will have me." Xenon looked at me.

I nodded.

"Xenon, you must be weary from your travels, so please, let us not keep you from resting. We'll tell the rest of the family at dinner and start our planning afterward?" my mother asked.

Xenon took the hint. He bowed to my mother and father, kissed my hand, and left the room. He knew the way to my rooms and whispered only, "Good luck," through our connection before he closed the door behind him.

"Why didn't you tell us earlier?" My mother's voice was soft and held a tinge of hurt.

"I didn't know how you might react."

"Have we ever given you any indication we wouldn't welcome your relationship?"

"No. It's just, well, I know Xenon is a lot older than I am, and that could raise a few eyebrows. And, well, I suppose I'm just used to keeping it quiet," I said.

"Son, I wish you'd have told us sooner, preferably before it happened. We could have helped. And we would have liked to have been part of it, made it more ceremonial."

"I'm sorry," I said, glancing down at my hands.

"No matter. What's done is done," my father said. He was silent for a moment before asking, "Do you know the hierarchy of bonds?"

"I know that the blood oath is the highest."

"It stands equal with the familial one. Depending on the strength and desire for the familial one, both the familial bond and blood oath can stand together in a single dragon. However, the blood oath's rules are unbreakable, which could at times supersede the other," my mother explained. Then she jumped up and switched gears. "Come. Let us celebrate. My firstborn has taken his first step toward starting his own family. I can't wait to have granddragons!" my mother squealed as she pulled me up, hugged my shoulders, and led me out of the room, leaving my father to trail behind us.

# CHAPTER SEVEN
## JAXON

I STAYED OUTSIDE AS long as I could. First I trained with Alexius, then Aexie. I worked them both until I saw their muscles shaking. Then I worked them in their human forms. As dragons, we had to master combat in both forms in case the time came when we could only use one. Human forms were so much more vulnerable.

"Jaxon, why are you working us so hard? I'm exhausted!" Aexie complained.

"Xenon's back," was all I said before I turned on my brother and sister and took them both on at once. They didn't work together—as was usual these days—so it made my job easier.

We only used wooden weapons when we were in human form. Human skin is so easily broken, and my parents would be furious if I sliced my siblings open or they sliced themselves open by accident.

"Your Highnesses," A guard stood at the edge of the outdoor training field. "I'm sorry to interrupt your training, but I have a guest here to see Prince Alexius."

I motioned for Alexius to go. "Be quick. I want you to fit in one more sparring match before we go in for supper."

He nodded and left with the guard. My suspicion was that it was that farmer, Brixelle. When dragons fell in love, it was strong and deep and quick. That was one reason I'd wanted to get out of the palace so quickly: Xenon and Xerus were deep into their relationship right now, and though they weren't as bad as they had been at the beginning, their public displays of affection twisted a knife in my heart.

I was only two centuries younger than Xerus, but I had yet to find my mate. And as much as Aexie loves to read those romantic stories of princes and princesses, it had been me who had introduced her to them. I'd stopped reading them two centuries ago. It hurt too much. I shook my head, turning back to Aexie.

"It'll happen," she said, reading my thoughts.

I swung my wooden broadsword at her head in response. I was heavier-handed than I should have been, but I didn't want to talk, so I kept Aexie on her toes and too strained to comment more.

Alexius returned after a couple hours, and Aexie used his appearance to leave. "I have to go get ready for supper. It feels like an important one," was all she said before she threw her wooden sword at Alexius and practically ran back into the palace.

Alexius only raised an eyebrow as he tossed the wooden sword back and forth in his hands to test the weight of it.

"How's Brixelle?" I asked.

He glowed, matching the sky as the sun started its descent behind the palace.

"She's good. She came to thank me."

"Did something set off your enchantments?" I asked, both curious and anxious for something exciting to happen.

"No. I ... I brought her a lily that reminded me of her today. She wasn't home, so I left it on her doorstep. She came by to thank me."

"And you set up another time to see her?"

Alexius glowed even more now. "Tomorrow morning, after breakfast."

I nodded, then proceeded to pound him with my wooden sword. He took it well, bracing himself and learning from his mistakes.

"Your Highnesses, Her Majesty asked me to come and remind you that supper will be in an hour, and she expects you to be dressed for a party. Take your human form." The same guard was back but barely visible in the darkness.

"Thank you," I said and stopped railing on Alexius. I flicked my wrist and tossed his sword in the air with my own, catching it in my other hand. Then I turned around to gather the other weapons and take them back to the Jade Room.

When my arms were full, I turned and saw that Alexius had gathered the rest of the weapons, so I nodded my appreciation before heading back into the palace and the Jade Room.

"I just wish you would have told us." My father's voice drifted toward us as we approached the Jade Room, which was adjacent to the receiving room.

"I'm sorry," came Xerus's voice. Xerus was perfect. What could he have screwed up that he had to apologize for?

"What's done is done," was the last I heard as Alexius and I pushed open the doors to the Jade Room and saw the extravagant setup for the dinner party.

It would only be family apparently as the table was quite small, but on the table, silver and gold plates were stacked atop each other. The decor was all silver and gold, so it must be in honor of Xenon's arrival. Alexius and I looked at each other and put the weapons away as delicately and quietly as we could. Neither of us wanted to disturb whatever was happening next door. As we worked, we watched as staff brought out our fancy chairs and started to decorate the rest of the Jade Room.

"If we're eating in here, they must be making a big announcement," Alexius said.

"Must be THE announcement. For Xerus and Xenon," I said. Alexius kept his expression neutral as we snuck out the side door of the Jade Room so we could go bathe and dress.

We went our separate ways, and I slipped into my chambers. I looked around at the weapons my family had given me as gifts over the years which I proudly displayed on the walls. Then, stripping down, I walked to my bathing chambers, where I filled the tub with water. With a snap of my fingers, the bath filled with ice water and I eased into it, enjoying the cooling of the muscles I'd worked hard all day.

As I soaked, I reviewed what I'd seen that morning at the dragonsbane farm and went over the report I'd sent to Father's office. There probably wasn't much that Xerus hadn't already seen, just the footprint of a medium-sized male dragon and a bit of pegasi fur I'd found under a counter the plants had sat on. The farmer had no contact with pegasi, so that might help narrow our search a bit. At the thought of the dragonsbane, I floated my daily dose over and drank it from the bottle. As my body froze in the ice water, I snapped my fingers again to first warm the water. Once my body was warm, I let the water get as hot as I could possibly stand.

I washed my hair, glad that it was short, then got out of the bath and went back to my chambers. I stood in front of my closet for a few minutes wondering what I could get away with wearing tonight. From the way that table had looked, it would be formal for sure. So, I decided to play it safe and went with Xerus-style elegance, choosing a midnight-blue jacket with tails over a cream shirt and a navy-and-yellow kilt with silver trim. The kilt was a couple shades darker than the jacket, so I pulled on cream socks and wore navy shoes. I chose a bow tie to match the kilt and ran my fingers through my hair, relieved that it was already dry.

I walked down to Aexie's room then, registering the silence within Xerus's chambers as I passed, and knocked on the door.

"Come in." Her voice was light and musical. That was a surprising change.

I walked in to see Aexie still half naked and painting her face. "You look handsome tonight," was all she said to my reflection in the mirror, opening her mouth wide while she painted around her eyes.

"You should really only let me in when you're fully dressed," I said, plunking myself on her couch.

She just rolled her eyes. "What do you need help with?"

I pointed to my undone bow tie.

"Just a sec," she said before leaning away from the mirror to look at one side of her face, then the other. I couldn't see a difference, but apparently she could because she applied more paint to the right side.

I looked around Aexie's room while I waited. The bright, sunny-yellow decor was mostly unchanged, but a glint of silver underneath her pillow caught my eye. Her bed was messy as usual, but I was surprised that she was now keeping a dagger under her pillow. Whom didn't she trust? A couple books sat on the low table in front of her couch, and I picked one up. I flipped through it, not really reading it, until Aexie finally turned her attention back to me.

She now wore a loose shirt and had come to sit on the low table before me, so I sat up so she could do up my bow tie for me.

"It belonged to Danx. It was the first dagger she got from Mom and Dad," Aexie said as she focused on tying the bow.

I smiled to think of the little dagger Mom and Dad had given our youngest sister when she was a dragonette. It was blunt, but she'd always thought there were monsters under her bed, so Father had given it to her as a present so she could slay her own monsters. She had worn it at her side for two centuries before finally switching it out for a real one. "I miss her too," I said.

Aexie's eyes started to fill with tears. She blinked and a fat tear dropped from her eye onto her shirt. She finished tying my bow tie and patted the little knot at its center, straightening the edges before leaning back. "I know," she whispered. Rising then, she said, "You're going to make me ruin my face," and went back to her dressing table to dab at her eye with a soft cloth. She blinked the rest of the tears away. "I'm almost ready. Will you wait for me?"

I nodded. I hadn't seen this softer side of my sister in a long time. She'd been so prickly lately that I'd do anything to see more of it. It was more her, or the her I used to know.

She disappeared into her closet, and I took another careful look around her room. It looked as it always did, but I noticed the pages of the journal she kept were in disarray as if she'd torn some out and stuffed them back in.

I also noted that her bed was more ruffled than usual. Both sides were turned down like two dragons had gotten out if it, not just one. I wondered who had been sharing my sister's bed. The protective brother in me snarled a little on the inside, and I vowed to figure out who it was. Aexie had always controlled her own life, but I knew whomever she was taking to bed was a distraction, likely to make herself feel better or forget her grief.

"Well, what do you think?" the softer version of my sister asked.

I turned my head to see my sister in a cream-colored, drapey dress. "Beautiful as always," I said as I stood, my body stiff from sitting.

Aexie saw me cringe. "I'm glad I'm not the only one who's sore." She laughed, making my heart happy.

I offered her my arm and we left her room to join the rest of my family in the Jade Room.

# CHAPTER EIGHT

## AEXIE

I WAS SURPRISED WHEN Jax led me to the Jade Room instead of the dining room. We only dined in there if it was a very special occasion. It was fortuitous that Jax had come into my room looking for help with his bow tie. It'd given me something else to think about and someone to share my good mood with. Getting dressed up always made me feel good.

Jax has always been the observant one, and I'd been a little nervous that he'd know that I'd been taking Drax, the guard posted in our hallway, to bed. Thankfully, Jax hadn't said anything.

The Jade Room, in all its green-and-white glory, was absolutely glowing tonight. Mother had had them decorate with gold and silver; they were Xenon's colors, so it was probably to honor him. And given how carefully and elegantly the dinner table was decorated, Xenon and Xerus must finally be getting married. They were obviously bonded mates. They were bonded mates before I was even born, and them being together was as normal to me as my mother and father being together.

"Aexie." Xenon approached me and gave me a hug and a kiss on each cheek. I noticed his hands shaking, and that surprised me. Xenon was one of the most powerful dragons in the world. It was strange to see him nervous.

Mother had really outdone herself. The chairs were draped in cream with gold and silver shimmering down their backs in thin waterfalls, so you'd only see them if the light caught them right. The tablecloth was a silver so light it was practically white. The utensils were all golden, and the plates were a tinted glass that when stacked together, created the same argent color as Xenon's hair with hints of gold. The centerpiece was a tall bouquet of blue flowers, dark and light, none matching Xerus's blue exactly, but representing every other shade of the color.

"Mother." I approached my mother and hugged her. She was just about to burst with happiness, confirming what the occasion must be. "It looks beautiful," I said, sitting next to her.

Alexius was the last to arrive, and he did a fine job of keeping his eyeballs in his head as he took in the opulence of the room and dinner table. I almost laughed as he approached me and gave me a kiss on the cheek as was custom. He sat down next to me as Xerus took his spot to my father's right and Xenon next to Xerus.

"A toast," my father said. We all raised the glass of bubbly golden liquid that had appeared in front of us.

"To Xenon's blood oath to my eldest son," Father said. Mother hiccuped as she tried to hold her tears in, and I turned to look at Jax and Alexius as they looked at me. A blood oath?!

My mother and father had not even taken a blood oath. We'd been taught that a blood oath was not something to play around with and needed to be considered for centuries before taking it. It had been pounded into our brains that among dragons, blood oaths had to eventually be reciprocal, but with other beings, only a dragon had to take one for it to affect both parties. It tied you to the other creature like a slave. They would have access to all your thoughts and emotions. It even tied your lives together. If one died, the other would not live past another year.

I elbowed Alexius, whose mouth hung open, as I blinked. From the stern look on Jax's face, he was thinking the same thing as me. And Xerus hadn't told us. I suddenly felt a wave of sadness as I realized that Xerus hadn't told any of his siblings about it. He'd performed a blood oath and hadn't asked even one of us to witness it. He hadn't even asked our opinion. Danxing had held us all together. She had a big mouth and would blab anything you told her, but it was impossible not to confide in her. She was perceptive and would bother you until you spit out whatever you were hiding. Then she'd run to the other siblings or call a siblings-only meeting to discuss it.

I glowed as I thought of the first time I'd taken someone to bed and Danx had found out. She'd called a siblings-only meeting, and my brothers had sat, awkwardly furious, as my sister had told them what she'd discovered. No one could be mad at her, as usual, and I'd played it off as my own choice and none of their business. But I'd felt a strange kind of family pride when my first lover had been reassigned to another post far away from the palace thanks to Xerus, sported a black eye thanks to Jax, and worn clothes full of itching powder thanks to Alexius. We hadn't been as close since, and I choked back a sob.

Alexius reached over and squeezed my hand. I swallowed the lump that had risen in my throat and struggled with my emotions until I couldn't handle it anymore. Danx had done it all the time, and I was about to continue it. *Soxkendi, sibling meeting, right now!* I shouted through my familial line. Then I got up and fled the room, headed for the library. I practically pulled Alexius with me, and Jaxon rose, looking a little startled but nodding. Only Xerus was left at the table to explain to Xenon what had just happened.

I marched into the library and Jaxon manned the door, making sure only Xerus and not Xenon came in.

Alexius sat down on the couch, crossing one leg over the other, and it struck me that his legs were so long now. Xerus finally came in then, and Jax closed the door.

"That was rude, Aexie," Xerus said.

That's when I lost it on him. "Rude? You ..." I started to pace as Xerus sat down opposite Jax and Alexius. "You want to talk about rude? How could you not tell us? How could you let Father just say that, like it was any old normal thing? A blood oath?! Are you insane, Xer? We need to talk about this. You should have talked to us about it already or at least given us a heads up. Or how about asking us to be there? To witness your entire world shift? Do you even know how old Xenon is?" I finally stopped, panting as I tried to catch my breath in my very tight dress.

"You better sit down before you faint in that dress, Aexie," Xerus said. "I don't owe you anything. I haven't even—"

"Uh uh. Nope, you can't say that." Jaxon stood up. "You were the one to set the rules for soxkendi. You made sure we had a safe place to talk, for our siblings to be one, cohesive unit. You said we all come first, that we don't hide anything from each other. That doesn't just apply to us. It applies to you too."

I sat down, stunned that Jaxon had been the one to speak up.

"He's right. We always call sibling meetings to talk about important things, and you had plenty of opportunity to do so, but you didn't. We deserve an apology and an explanation," Alexius piped in.

That was brave for him.

Xerus sat down with a sigh. "Fine. You're right. It's been tougher since Danx. But all right, you win. It's late, but let's have it out now."

# CHAPTER NINE
## XERUS

I TOOK A DEEP breath in and out as I perched on the edge of the couch, my hands grasping my knees, my thumbs rubbing the sides of my knees. I looked up at the patiently waiting faces of my siblings, then glanced back at my knees because I could barely stand the various degrees of frustration on their faces. They were right of course. I'd spent so much time making sure they were all right, that they had a safe place to talk. I'd vowed that we were all in it together, so we could call soxkendi, a sibling meeting, for any reason at any time. Nothing was unimportant. We were to always talk to each other. So now I had no choice but to face the uncomfortable. I needed to make sure we stayed close and that I didn't play by my own rules.

I raised my hands, thinking I was ready to begin, then exhaled and dropped them back onto my knees a second time. No one said anything. They were letting me go at my own pace, just as I would have done for them. "I'm sorry," I forced out as I looked up. Staring back at me were no longer angry faces but compassionate ones. That had been a lot easier than I'd thought it would be. "You all know Xenon and I have been together for a while, a long while."

Aexie rolled her eyes and Alexius nodded, but Jaxon just sat waiting for more.

"Well, last year, we only got to see each other three times. And that's difficult when you love someone. His position makes him travel a lot, and he can't exactly send letters regularly, so I started questioning whether our relationship was worth it."

My siblings had become very still.

"Why didn't you share this with us?" Jax said. "This is the kind of stuff you're supposed to tell us. We would have tried to help."

I exhaled, letting my shoulder slump. The human form was truly very expressive. "I ... I didn't want to bother you. It seemed silly. Here I'd found my bonded mate, something that some dragons wait centuries for, and I was thinking about throwing it away."

Jax moved closer and put a hand on my shoulder.

"At summer solstice, I told Xenon what I was thinking. And he was so still. I expected anger or for him to be upset to some degree, but he just froze and watched me carefully like he was too busy thinking to move. I felt the separation in our age more than ever then. You know, when the older dragons forget to move for a while and stay frozen like they're statues?"

They all nodded.

"So I finished what I had to say, and I waited for him to respond. I didn't know what I wanted or what I wanted from him or why I'd even told him that. I didn't want to part from him, but at the same time, I didn't know how to handle the long silence between our visits. Then I waited for him to say or do something for so long that I was about to get up and leave when he finally said, 'Is the only problem our separation?'"

I looked at my siblings pleadingly. I needed them to understand. "I didn't think it quite boiled down to any one thing, but I supposed that most of what I felt stemmed from not being able to at least talk to him regularly."

Alexius nodded, making me wonder if somehow, now that he'd met Brixelle, he had at least an inkling of how that felt.

""Do you know what a blood oath is?' Xenon finally asked me. And I nodded, of course. But I must have looked surprised or shocked or something because he said, 'I know you've doubted my true feelings for you, especially with the gap in our ages. And I know no better way to show you how much you mean to me than by committing myself by blood oath to you. I don't want you to bond yourself to me just yet though, not until you're older and surer about us. But even one sided, it would solve our communication problem. We could communicate with each other through the blood oath no matter where we are.'"

I stopped here to try and judge how the others were taking this. Aexie's eyes hardened but didn't shutter, Jax leaned forward with surprise in his eyes, and Alexius eased farther back against the couch and nodded. They hadn't forgiven me yet, but they didn't hate me either, so I continued the story. "I wasn't sure what to say. I only knew how often Father had stressed that blood oaths were to be taken seriously, and we were not to commit ourselves to one unless we'd truly thought about it for at least a century. So, I hesitated.

"But he didn't. Xenon said, 'Xerus, I'm not asking you to take a blood oath to me. I'm telling you I'd like to bond myself to you, not that you must do the same. I can be patient. I'll wait for when you're ready. But I know my mind and heart, and they both belong to you. My every thought returns to you, and my every action is for you. I've lived a long life, but I feel like it didn't even start until I met you. Even when you were a child, I knew. But I also knew it wasn't appropriate, so I stayed away so you could grow up in peace, grow up to become the dragon I'd glimpsed when I'd first met you. And now I've waited centuries for you. I can see how it seems ... strange, half a blood oath, but I am yours and a blood oath to you would be my honor.'"

Aexie sighed and relaxed, the muscles in her jaw visibly shifting.

"He told me to think about it and meet him the next day if I wanted to accept it." I tried to continue, but Jax interrupted.

"I remember that day, that one when you walked around in a haze with the wrinkles in your forehead scrunched together. You were in a whole other place and didn't talk to anyone," Jaxon said, smiling.

I chuckled. "Yeah, well, by the end of that day, I decided that if Xenon was willing to vow a blood oath to me, and I didn't have to do the same, it was worth a try. Like I said, I really didn't want him out of my life, I actually needed to be closer to him somehow. And I think part of me wondered if he'd really do it. I still have a hard time believing that a dragon like Xenon would want a dragon like me." I raised my hand to quiet their defensive comments on my behalf.

When they'd silenced mid-comment, I continued. "The next day we met, and he had this giant galinka root with him. I could barely speak so I nodded, and he bit into his own arm and let the blood drip down his claws onto the galinka. He walked over to me and told me to open my mouth. I did as he said, and he dripped some of the blood from his arm to the galinka to my mouth. I was surprised at how sweet it tasted.

"'Light the root with your fire,' he said then. So I gently blew fire onto the bottom of the galinka, and we watched it burn. As we did, he said ..." I felt my cheeks warm as I thought about what he'd said and decided to leave that part out. "...he recited the oath. When he was done, I noticed his arm had healed. He placed the burnt end of the galinka in my mouth and told me to chew and eat it. Suddenly, I heard him in my head.

"I felt his joy and happiness through a beam of light in my mind, and I strangely felt content and whole. He spent the next few days teaching me how to shield my mind against him in case there was something I didn't want him to know or feel. It's a lot like how we shield ourselves from each other in here." I tapped my temple with my index finger. "I guess a small part of me had always doubted his feelings for me. But after the oath, I could feel what he felt, and it was reassuring. He might be able to hear my thoughts now, but the blood oath somehow offsets the imbalance our age difference creates."

Now that I'd finished my story, I took a deep breath and searched my siblings' faces for judgment. Alexius looked curious. Aexie looked like she was enjoying the story too much; she had that dreamy look on her face that she usually had when she was reading one of her romantic novels. And Jaxon looked ... well, happy and sad at the same time.

"So, do you plan to oath yourself to him?" Alexius asked.

"Yes. I think I'll do it while he's here. Mom wants to make it cere-monial," I replied.

"Wait a minute, did she say something about a wedding?" Aexie squealed.

"She may have mentioned that," I said with a relieved chuckle. It dawned on me that a royal dragon wedding would be a spectacle. My eyes widened as I thought about the fanfare and the decorations and the grandness of it all.

Jax, as usual, read my mind. "Did you really just realize that Mom is going to make this the wedding of the century?"

I could only nod.

"We should probably get back to dinner," Alexius said.

"Wait," I said. "Would you stand with me? All of you? My bond with Xenon changes nothing for us. You are my siblings, and we will always have each other and our meetings."

Alexius looked terrified, but Jaxon laughed and nodded. Aexie only squealed again and said, "I'm not wearing silver." She smiled and walked out of the library.

Jax followed her and Alexius held the door open for me, muttering only, "It would be my honor, brother," as I strode by him.

We walked back into the Jade Room, and my stomach growled its impatience at our detour. I wondered what Xenon thought about our meeting.

*How'd it go?* he asked in my head.

*Well. I think. Did we say yes to my mother planning a ceremony? I think so. You're worried about the fanfare?*

I didn't answer. Instead, we all sat down, and I looked to my mother and father to see if they were wondering why we'd all left so suddenly.

"Better?" my mother asked. My father just looked hungrily at the supper he'd been forced to stare at for the last hour. I nodded and she signaled for more food to be brought. We dove in. Everyone must have been as hungry as I because no one spoke. Even I cleared my mind and started to eat. Xenon left me alone, so I figured I'd talk to him later that night. But I looked around the table and was pleased to see my siblings looking less tense as they ate. Aexie was practically glowing at either my story or the prospect of a grand wedding.

I looked at Jaxon and wondered if he'd be fool enough to challenge Xenon in some strange kind of family welcome. I cocked my head, wondering for a moment if Jaxon would stand a chance against Xenon. I knew Alexius wasn't quite sure what to think just yet, and he'd probably be in the library tonight looking up blood oaths. Alexius soaked up knowledge like a sponge soaked up water.

My mother watched me carefully, and I wondered whether she was imagining what outfit she could convince me to wear. But while that thought made me cringe, I did notice the smiles Aexie and my mother both wore. It had been a long time since they'd smiled, and I realized that if it made them happy, planning a big ceremony for Xenon and I would be well worth my own discomfort.

Later that night, when Xenon and I were finally alone, he finally asked, "What was that all about? Your mother only explained that you were not to be interrupted, and you'd be back when you were ready." He sat on my couch and twirled his fingers. A steaming cup of clear liquid appeared in his hand.

I removed my formal coat and put it gently on the back of a chair before sitting beside him. A steaming cup appeared in my hand too. I smelled the steam and smiled at the mint tea. "That was a sibling meeting. Danxing started it when she was little. She'd call a sibling meeting and then track each of us down and drag us into the library. When she was little, it was to announce things like, 'I ate my first sheep,' or 'I flew today,' before she regaled us each with the story that would follow the proclamation. Then one day, she called a sibling meeting, and instead of announcing something and regaling us with a tale of her accomplishment, she pushed Alexius into the middle of the room. 'Tell them,' was all she said as she held his hand.

"Her little face was so serious, and his face was so somber, I remember exchanging worried glances with Jax and Aexie. Then they stared at our youngest siblings with the same curiosity I felt.

"'Tell them like you told me,' Danx said gently, taking Alexius's free hand in her own.

"Alexius struggled to speak. 'The guard, he ... he hit me for leaving the library so late. He said it was my fault that he'd missed supper, and he was going to teach me a lesson in being considerate. I ... I just wanted to read my book.' Alexius was so young then, and his little eyes filled with tears. Danxing hugged him and said, 'You're safe. These are our siblings. You can always count on them. We will always be able to count on each other.'

"Aexie went to hug them, and Jaxon stopped me as I was about to charge out of the room to send the guard to the dungeons for laying a hand on my little brother just for reading. Jaxon kneeled and put both hands on Alexius's shoulders. 'Thank you for telling us, Alexius. I know it was tough. You're very brave. You can always tell us if you feel like something's wrong, all right?'

"I went to join them and decided right then that if one of us ever said 'soxkendi' or 'sibling meeting,' it would be a sacred word. We would drop everything and immediately meet." I looked up at Xenon. "So, I'm sorry if it was sudden and rude, but it's become official protocol now." I searched Xenon's face for mockery.

"I think it's beautiful," he said. "I'm not here to come between you and your siblings. You're going to need to be strong to take over the realm when your time comes. As powerful and old as I am, I won't be able to make up for the three of them."

"Four," I said. Even though Danxing was gone, she was still the glue that held us together.

Xenon nodded. "Four."

After a moment's silence, I asked, "You really don't mind?"

"Not at all. I still get you all to myself often enough. And I'm not fool enough to think that you and I alone can rule this world. It takes a team. Your siblings are smart and powerful and skilled warriors. You might not realize it, but tomorrow when Jaxon challenges me in the training ring, I'm going to have my work cut out for me. You lot are more skilled than you've been led to believe."

"When did he challenge you?" I thought I'd been careful to make sure he never had the chance.

"He hasn't yet, but I read it in his face. He'll challenge me tomorrow."

"I'm sorry," I said, shrugging my shoulders and drinking the mint tea.

"You're worth all of it, and more," Xenon said. He finished his own drink, kissed me on the forehead, and yawned. "Speaking of which, I'm going to need my beauty sleep if I plan to take on your ridiculously well-trained brother."

I snorted at that. Then I finished my own tea and headed to bed.

# Chapter Ten

## Jaxon

I STARED AT THE ceiling. I should be asleep. I'd trained so hard that my body should have been tired enough to whisk me away to sleep no matter my mental state. But my body was practically buzzing with energy. My mind kept racing through all my memories of Xenon and Xerus together. I knew Xerus had meant me when he had said he counted himself lucky, that there were dragons who had waited centuries and still hadn't found their mate. Actually, he'd meant both me and Aexie, though Aexie seemed happy enough for the couple.

I thought back to when I'd been almost fully grown. I had been practicing archery in the garden in my human form when Xenon had come out of the palace. Instead of giving me some tips like most other adults, he complimented me.

"You're a very good archer, especially as young as you are," he said.

"Thanks," I mumbled. I wasn't especially comfortable talking to people yet, particularly those who weren't family. I noted the mud on Xenon's boots, as if he'd been trekking through the forest, and his coat, which was finer than the rest of his outfit, like he'd just thrown it on top of a more casual outfit. So he'd been hiking that morning in the woods. I wondered then whether he'd had a specific purpose or if he just enjoyed hiking.

I could practically feel him wanting to ask if I had seen Xerus but not wanting to be rude. Instead, he asked, "What do you want to do?"

I was so surprised by the question all I could manage was a shrug as I notched another arrow and aimed.

"If you'd ever like to travel, I have some distant family on the eastern continent. They'd appreciate a warrior like you. They'd probably also challenge you to test your skills, mind you. But you might enjoy learning a different style."

"Trying to send me away?" I asked.

"No, not at all. But with how quickly you're mastering all the combat arts here, you'll probably get bored soon enough. And if it's combat you like, then the world has different styles for you to seek out," he'd explained.

"Xerus is in the pit," I said, trying to get rid of him.

He looked surprised at first, then glowed a touch as he clearly realized how transparent his efforts had been. "Thank you," was all he managed before heading in that direction.

Now I shook my head, bringing me back to the present as I tossed and turned, trying to get my mind to shut off. But Xenon hadn't been wrong. I did want to travel and learn. But I couldn't leave until after the wedding. My mother would chain me to the palace if she had to.

Finally giving up and throwing off my blankets, I pushed myself out of bed and let my feet slap on the floor as I made my way to my chamber door. I opened it and almost ran into Alexius in the hallway.

I was momentarily surprised until Alexius just said, "Library," and kept walking down the hall.

I should have known. I shook my head and headed to the kitchens. Perhaps a warm drink would help calm me. If I was going to challenge Xenon tomorrow, I should at least be at my best.

In the kitchens, I heated some water in two cups, poked a teabag in one with a spoon, and swirled it around trying to get the flavor out faster. The kitchens were relatively quiet, the bakers not yet awake to make bread. I did the same to the second cup and put some honey in both cups before taking them to the library. If I was going to be awake, I could at least help Alexius pull books about blood oaths.

The library had always been his haven. Once, our palace had been infiltrated by a winged lion who had gone mad. Our guards had been ushering us all into the underground bunker when we realized Alexius was missing. I'd found him on top of a bookshelf in the library, reading. He hadn't even realized anything was happening. His guards had been punished for not keeping track of him, but he'd been in there the whole time. Of the whole family, it was between him and Aexie as to who was the most well-read.

I pushed the door open gently, and sure enough, Alexius had a couple dozen books spread out in front of him on the table. He was flipping from one to another, reading whatever he could about oaths in general and blood oaths in particular.

"Tea?" I asked.

He jumped, startled at the interruption. "Thank you, Jax," he said, taking it in his hands and using magic to flip pages as he breathed into the mug.

"Can I help you in any way?" I asked. I didn't know if he'd need more books or maybe some help finding something specific in his books.

"No. I'm just doing a little light research. I couldn't sleep."

"Me either," I said.

Suddenly, Alexius turned to me. "Do you think Xenon will join our familial bond once Xerus joins him in the blood oath?"

"I'm not sure," I said. It was an interesting thought. What if Xenon had access to Xerus's bond to the rest of us? Would he be able to communicate with us through Xerus? Would Xenon have access to our thoughts and feelings through Xerus? Would we have access to Xenon through Xerus? This was not going to help me sleep.

I sat on the chaise and put my feet up, cradling my mug of tea and thinking about whether I'd ever read anything about how different oaths interacted. I closed my eyes, then woke up to the first rays of light streaming through the window. I looked down to find my half-cup of tea missing from my hands and a blanket over me. I guess I'd been wrong. I turned to where Alexius had been sitting last night to find him still bent over a book, reading carefully. He'd placed my cup of tea on the table so I wouldn't spill it.

"I drank the rest of it," he said as he shrugged.

"That's fine," I said as I stretched.

"You snore."

"I was tired." I stretched my legs, feeling a lot more refreshed than I would have thought. "Find what you're looking for?"

"Some. If Xenon really taught Xerus to block him out, then Xerus should be able to keep the familial and blood oaths separate. But if he chose to link them—and that would take a lot of effort—we'd be privy to whatever the blood oath gives Xerus," he said.

I shook my head, not sure if that made sense yet.

"There's coffee over there," Alexius said then, not looking up from his book but pointing beside the door.

"Thanks." I wondered when and who had brought it, then went over and poured myself a cup. Afterward, I chose to go stand by the window to watch the sun rise over the hills as I let the coffee do its work.

"Will you challenge him today?" Alexius asked.

"Yes."

It was tradition for one family member to challenge a new member to a sparring match until first blood was drawn. In the past, it was probably to establish one's place in the hierarchy, but now it was tradition. I thought of it as a test of my skills. If I could beat Xenon, even barely, I would travel without a doubt. It was like the final test for me.

"I think I might challenge him too," Alexius said.

"Oh?" Alexius was a good warrior, but he still had miles to go before he'd be a worthy opponent for Xenon.

"A match of wits. I know I'm not nearly good enough to challenge him in combat," Alexius explained.

"Go for it," I said. Alexius knew a lot about a lot. It wouldn't surprise me in the least if he knew a little more than Xenon, despite the older dragon's age.

I finished my coffee and felt the buzz as it started in my lower limbs and worked its way up. "Did you get any sleep, Alexius?"

"No. This stuff was too interesting," he said.

"Maybe take a nap before you go challenging him?"

"Will do," he said briskly.

I could tell he was getting tired of my questions. "I'm going for a run," I said.

"Have a good one."

I put the cup back on the tray and eased the door open. Life was starting to waken in the halls as light poured in through the windows. Popping out through a side door, I breathed in the cold morning air. I started with a brisk walk before breaking into a run, joining a team of guards as they ran the perimeter of the palace.

I noticed more guards—probably as extra precautions for Xenon's presence—out than usual. There were usually a dozen running in the morning before work, or after finishing their shift, but today there were easily two dozen.

After my run, I transitioned into warming up with the guards, using low strokes and easy movements and stretching in between. Aexie had showed up earlier than normal, probably to get her training out of the way, and I sparred with her until Alexius finally showed up. The number of off-duty guards milling about and sharpening and cleaning weapons around the training ring easily made a crowd. I blocked them all out as I focused on the job I still had to do.

A cough interrupted me as I watched Aexie toss Alexius to the ground again. I looked up to find Xenon standing there in pants and a loose shirt.

"I'm here to accept your challenge," he said.

"One usually waits for a challenge to be issued before replying to it," I said.

"You were planning on challenging me, yes?" he said.

I nodded.

"Then here I am. Let's do this," Xenon said.

Aexie helped Alexius up, and they moved out of the way.

"As the challenger, you get the first pick of weapon," I said.

Xenon nodded. He picked up a staff and I replicated his choice, picking my own staff and testing its weight.

The ring cleared out, and everyone gathered on the edges. I stood patiently, waiting for Xenon to make the first move. He swung from the side, and our staffs created a quick *clack clack clack* as we met every stroke. Then he tried to surprise me by swinging the end of his staff up between my legs, but I leaped away, swinging my own staff around to sweep his legs. He jumped up then and swept his own staff downward. I met his staff crossways above my head and had to slide to the right half an inch when he almost hit my fingers. But taking the opportunity, I grabbed his staff where it crossed mine and brought it down quickly, shoving it toward him. He hollowed out his stomach, tightened his grip on the staff, and somersaulted in the air, forcing my staff down as his hit the ground and came back up, bringing his staff up behind him. But instead of bringing it straight down on me, he moved to jab me with the end of it and rolled away. I rotated, both hands still holding my staff.

"Switch," Xenon said, and he tossed the staff to the side before taking up a sword and dagger instead.

Alexius tossed me my favorite dagger and sword, and I recognized that Xenon had switched to get a second to catch his breath. We circled each other. This was the main event. The first to draw blood would win. I felt an eerie calm as my mind thought of the various scenarios that could play out.

These swords weren't particularly sharp. Only the ends were sharp, just sharp enough to draw blood but not kill anyone. That was the last thought I had the luxury of as he jumped to attack. I met his every stroke with my own, and our *clack clack clack* became the heavier *clang clang clang* of metal on metal as we danced around each other. He was trying to make me rush, to keep me on my toes, but I often sparred with those faster or stronger or heavier handed. I quickly settled into the rhythm he established. I could tell he hadn't had as much practice keeping up his stamina when each counterstroke became minutely slower than the previous one. So I waited patiently, matching every stroke until I saw the opportunity to set up a motion where he'd have to go high to meet me. Then I threw my dagger along his arm as it moved to meet my sword, grazing his skin at the perfect moment.

It was just a small scratch, but he stopped immediately.

"I yield," he said, sinking to one knee. I wiped the sweat off my brow and offered him a hand.

"Welcome to the family," I said.

The crowd started to disperse into smaller groups, already rehashing what they'd seen. I was surprised to see my mother and father watching from a palace window as I turned.

"You're a real credit to your family," Xenon said, taking my hand and rising.

I clapped him on the shoulder. "As a member of the family, your training is now under my supervision. You'll report at the same time as Xerus for training."

"But ..." Xenon started.

"No buts. If you're here, you train. No exceptions. Even Mother and Father train in the Jade Room every day."

Xenon looked a little surprised but smiled. "I take it I can't ask for a rematch?"

"Nope," I said. I went to put away the weapons, grabbing a towel to wipe my brow with on the way.

"Are we good here then?" Xenon asked.

I nodded. "I think Alexius has something he wants to ask you though," I said, glancing at my brother at the edge of the ring. He nodded at me, and I left the training ring to check on my parents' training. I couldn't help puffing my chest out in pride as I strode down the hallway.

"Did you have to cut him?" Xerus asked as he caught up to me in the hallway.

"It's first blood, brother," I said. He wasn't going to take this moment away from me.

"You didn't have to. You would have won."

"And drawn out the match a lot longer. It's not smart to draw it out if you don't have to, not for him or me. I didn't sleep much and I'm tired, so unless you want to join Mother and Father's training, you should probably go check on Xenon. Alexius mentioned a challenge earlier." I couldn't help but smirk.

Xerus's eyes went wide, and he hurried off in the direction I had just come from.

I felt on top of the world as I walked in to run my parents' drills.

# CHAPTER ELEVEN

## ALEXIUS

"Xenon, may I have a word with you?" I asked as he turned and came over to me.

"Of course," he said, and we strolled toward the edge of the forest.

"Would you like to touch it?" he asked.

I startled a bit, glowing in embarrassment as I realized I'd been staring at his argent hair. It was such a strange color, even among dragons.

"I apologize. That was rude."

"It's not every day you see someone with hair my color. I have to say its uniqueness is both a curse and a blessing." He pulled his low ponytail loose and offered the curtain of hair to me.

I couldn't help myself. I reached out and touched the shimmery dark-silver strands. They felt the way I imagined liquid silver would.

"Before you apologize again, please don't. You are as much a little brother to me as you are to Xerus. He talks about his family a lot. I feel like I've watched you grow up, little dragonling," he said as he ruffled my hair. He swiftly tied his own hair back, and I started losing the nerve to challenge him.

Xenon was not just any adult dragon. He was an original. One of the first dragons, as old as the world of Etciel itself. It would be foolish of me to challenge his knowledge when he was probably the one who'd discovered much of it. My thoughts drifted to Brixelle, and I couldn't stop myself before the words came out of my mouth.

"How did you know Xerus was your true bonded mate?" I asked, belatedly clamping my traitorous mouth shut.

"Ahh." He breathed out a sigh. "I thought you were going to challenge me. Though I don't know if this answer is any easier."

"This morning, I thought to challenge you, but I don't know what I was thinking. There is no way you'd have less knowledge than I do. You wrote half the books I've studied."

"While that is true, trying to be accepted still makes me nervous. You are Xerus's family, his trusted siblings. You are all important to him, therefore, just as important to me."

"Is that what being bonded is like?" I asked. The secret was out already, so I figured I might as well try to get an answer.

"I have been on this world for a very long time. I've met many a bonded dragon, and from the outside, I can tell you that position, status, money, none of that matters. I've seen opposites attract, I've seen two peas in a pod—whatever the saying is—and it's all possible."

"I think that makes it more confusing," I said.

"Did you know I have a bit of foresight?" When I shook my head he said, "My grandfather could see into the possible futures of others, and I think in some way I have a touch of that ability. The moment I met your brother, even though he was very young, I saw flashes of his future. I saw us together. I saw him as an adult, and I saw how happy we were together. And I felt how happy I was, so I knew."

"You never doubted?"

"When you're as old as I am, you learn to trust those instincts or those strange feelings you get."

"Is that advice?"

"I'm not sure you'd let me offer you advice yet." He looked at me with a raised eyebrow.

I shrugged. I wasn't sure either. "You can offer advice, but I'm not sure if I'd take it."

"That's why they call it 'advice.' I think I'm glad you didn't challenge me. You're an intellectual. I'd have my work cut out for me."

"I'm not so sure you answered my question," I said.

"Dragons as beings are special. Many other creatures look up to us, not only because of how much power we can wield but because of the strength of our bonds. There is nothing more sacred than a bonded dragon pair. I'm glad for it, really. Xerus—please don't be offended—but he's not who I would have pictured as my perfect mate. But the moment I'm with him, there's a ... a ringing in my core. It's like two bells that have been struck at different times that still find a way to resonate together."

I scrunched my forehead.

"So how do I know if she feels the same way?" I asked.

"You ask. You'll be like magnets, impossible to separate for very long," he said.

"Then how do you leave Xerus all the time?" I ask.

"With great difficulty. Sometimes it's like straining the end of an elastic. The longer I'm away from him, the more hollowness I feel inside, like an abyss has opened inside me."

"The blood oath. Did you really offer to do it as a way to ease your separation?"

Xenon's face showed his surprise for a moment. "He really told you everything?"

I nodded. "Those are the rules of soxkendi."

"Your family is truly wonderful," he said. "And yes. If there is one thing I'm sure of, it's that Xerus and I are a bonded pair. My life is nothing without him in it. And I've lived a long time without him."

I nodded. I wasn't sure what I could say in reply to what he'd just admitted. I'd always known he loved my brother. Their relationship was very much like my mother and father's. They were better together. Xerus was calmer, more settled, more confident with Xenon around. I wondered if Brixelle and I would work well together. She was different from anyone I'd met before, and I could feel it in my core, some fundamental connection. It was a little early yet to feel what Xenon had just described, but I understood what he meant. My whole center had shifted as if Brixelle was a new part of my identity.

Following the treeline, we walked back to the palace. As we neared it, I saw Xerus trying not to run up to us. Before he even had a chance to say anything, Xenon swept him up in a hug. "My love, thank you for joining us. Alexius and I were just having a nice brotherly chat."

"Was that all?" Xerus asked, trying to give me the stink eye over Xenon's shoulder.

"Nothing I can't handle," Xenon said as he let Xerus go and turned to wink at me. "You won't begrudge me time with your siblings, will you?"

"No." Xerus looked defeated.

I smiled. I always enjoyed Xenon handling Xerus. My brother was always so in control and almost arrogant about it that it tickled me to see him give in to Xenon so easily. They were definitely better together.

"Alexius, I'm here for you anytime you want to chat," Xenon said. "I believe, however, that it's time for Xerus and I to go warm up for our training session. Jaxon will be finishing up with your parents' training shortly, and I don't want to be late for my first class."

Xerus grumbled something in return, though it was clear his grumbling was only halfhearted as he let Xenon drag him by the hand toward the training ring.

"You can come out now," I said to the trees above me.

"When did you know?" Aexie asked, popping back into existence. She'd mastered invisibility so well she could do it in her human form.

"I saw your shadow when we turned the corner. How long have you been listening?" I was a little self-conscious about the conversation I'd just had.

"Long enough to know he didn't threaten you," Aexie said.

"I can handle myself, Aexie, though I appreciate your caring."

"Who said I cared?" She pretended to look at her fingernails.

I started getting angry with my sister again. "Whatever." I turned and popped into dragon form before flying up over the castle.

"Tell Brixelle I said hi!" she shouted up at me.

I hadn't known where I was flying to, but at Aexie's shout, I decided that's where I was headed. I flew to Brixelle's farm and just enjoyed the midmorning flight.

As I conjured up a couple drafts in the air to help me along my way, my heart thumped a little louder and quicker the closer I got to her farm. Finally, her yellow and purple scales caught the sunlight, and I flew down to where she was working in a field, moving hay bales into a shed.

"Hi!" I squeaked. I swallowed quickly, willing myself not to glow as I tried to get a handle on my voice. Since she was in her dragon form, it was only polite to stay in mine.

"Your Highness!" she exclaimed. She was covered in bits of hay, but she smiled, and my heart skipped a beat. Brushing herself off, she tried to get the hay off her scales. "I wasn't expecting you!" she said as she tried to pull a piece of hay from her head.

I reached over and picked out a couple pieces from behind her ear. "I was in the neighborhood and thought I'd pop by. Would you like help?" I knew she must be busy, and I didn't want to create more work for her by spending time with her.

"Oh ... umm ... have you ever stacked hay?"

I tried not to let my heart run away with me as she glowed. "No. But I'm a quick learner."

"Alright. Sure. I'm not going to say no to some extra help. I'll check the hay, and you can just stack it as neatly as possible. The neater the stacks, the easier it is to store and get to later without creating a hay avalanche," she said. She led me to the hay shed, then stuck a claw in the middle of each bale strewn on the ground outside the shed. Then she inspected each thoroughly and handed it to me.

I stacked each one carefully, wanting to impress her with my precision. "Why do you check them?" I asked.

"To check the heat or they'll catch fire," she said.

"Really?" I almost lost a bale from the stack I currently had in my arms.

"Did you know human farmers also do this by the bale?" she asked.

"How? They're so small. They must be stronger than I'd read."

"Strong, yes, hardworking too."

"How do you know so much about humans?"

"My mother tells me stories. When she was little, she was obsessed with them."

"How is your mother doing?" I asked.

"She's much better! Thank you! She'll be thrilled to see you if you'll come in for supper?"

I smiled and nodded, happy to think she'd like to spend more time with me and excited to spend more time with her.

The sun started to set, and I put myself to work in earnest to get all the hay stacked. If there was one thing I hated, it was not finishing a job. We found a rhythm as we worked together, and by the end we were moving so quickly that my hand brushed hers as I grabbed the last stack of hay from her. The warmth of her hand traveled up my arm and snaked into my body, striking a chord in my core. It was like I'd immersed my arm in warm water.

She looked up as I looked up, and we glowed. Then she yanked her gaze away from mine and bent to pick up the loose twine bits in the waning light.

I cleared my throat and readjusted the already perfectly stacked hay bales.

"Ready to go?" She came up next to me, readjusting the same perfectly stacked hay bales I'd just readjusted. Her hands wandered close to mine, and I couldn't control myself as my hand wandered over to hers. I took her hand and brought it to my lips. She glowed, and in the growing darkness, it was as beautiful as a sunset. She smiled and held my gaze. When I made to drop her hand, she wove her claws within mine and led me out of the storage shed. With a couple flaps, we were in the air heading back to her home and supper, still hand in hand. Despite the beauty of the landscape at sunset, my attention was focused only on our joined hands and the warmth that blossomed from them in a direct line to my core.

We landed lightly in front of her house, and she opened the door. "After you," she said, finally letting go of my hand.

"Finally! Did you get half the hay stacked, darling?" The older lavender dragon had transformed from the bedridden one I'd met a few days earlier. She was busy mixing food in different pots and didn't turn around. "Go get yourself washed up. I've worked hard to make this meal, and I will not have it seasoned with hay!"

I coughed and she whirled. "Oh my goodness, Your Highness!" She dropped into a curtsy, and the sauce-covered spoon, still in her hand, landed in the lap of her apron.

"Madam." I bowed my head. "Brixelle was kind enough to invite me for supper. I hope it's not too much of an imposition."

The lavender dragon looked stunned for a moment as she rose. She blinked a few times before coming back to herself. "Of course, Your Highness, I'd be delighted if you honored us with your presence tonight. I just wish my daughter had given me warning." She looked pointedly at Brixelle, who was hiding behind me.

"I'm the one to blame for that, madam. I was in the neighborhood and dropped in to visit Brixelle. I had a free afternoon, so I helped her stack the hay and she was kind enough to invite me to supper in return."

"Of course, of course." The older lavender dragon looked flustered as she motioned with her sauce-covered spoon and sauce flew up to hit the ceiling.

Wanting to give them a moment together, I asked, "Could you point me to your facilities? I'd like to wash up if I could."

"Yes, of course, Your Highness. The door down the hall to the right," the older dragon said, her eyes going wide for a moment before she recovered once again.

I heard a quick exchange of murmurs as I made my way to the facilities to wash up. I loved the beautiful home they'd made. Purple flowers had been painted on the stone walls, and the bathroom door looked like a trellis among the purple flowers and green vines, as if the outside had been brought in.

Everything in the house had a double or triple purpose, such as the string over the bathtub that pieces of fleece hung from. They must have been recently shorn and washed, and they dripped water into the tub, where plants sat absorbing the water. I smiled at how one thing was used to feed another.

I took my time washing up. When I emerged, Brixelle had gotten all the hay off herself and was setting the table.

"How many sheep do you have?" I asked as I came back.

"Eight thousand, nine hundred, and fifteen," Brixelle said. "Why?"

"There were only a few hundred fleece clips in the bathroom drying. Where are the rest?" I asked honestly.

"We only have the space to do a few hundred at a time," Brixelle explained. "It's also easier on us if we do it in cycles."

"That's a lot of sheep to sheer."

"We have to do it in human form too. Dragons are too big to handle sheep."

"Makes sense," I said. I sat down opposite Brixelle. "It smells wonderful in here."

"Mama's making her famous meatballs." She smiled as she watched her mother flit from pot to pot.

"It's but a humble dish, Your Highness. If I'd known you were coming, I would have made a feast more worthy of your status." The lavender dragon bustled over with a plate laden with a stack of meatballs the size of my head.

"They look delicious. I'm excited to enjoy some home cooking." I smiled, trying to put Brixelle's mother at ease.

I tried to politely grasp one meatball from the top of the pile, but it fell and rolled unceremoniously onto my plate. I looked up at Brixelle and saw she was trying to hold in a laugh.

At my sheepish look, she gave up. "We're pretty casual here," she got out between laughs as she used her claw to spear a meatball.

# CHAPTER TWELVE

## AEXIE

I STOOD OVER A magical map of our kingdom I'd made when I was younger and watched as a little red dot glowed as it moved back toward the palace. I sighed, watching it cross a field drawn in crayon and marker. I glanced at the other dots, seeing Xerus in his room, Jaxon sliding to the library, and my parents both in their sitting rooms for the night. I gently touched each little light, feeling comforted to know where my family was and that they were safe.

I watched the only little red light still moving as it continued to near the castle. I could practically see him flying across the various farms as he approached. The guards would have spotted and identified him by now I knew, but I held my breath until he arrived at the palace and entered his room. I let out a sigh. Alexius was home and he was safe. I knew I was overthinking it, but still I strained to hear into the corridor for any sign of trouble.

A knock on my door made me jump. I quickly folded the tabletop back over my hidden map and placed my vase of flowers on the center of the table, then moved a few books from the chairs to the table. I took one quick look at it before going to the door. Opening it, I blinked a few times. Xenon stood in the doorway with a tray of tea.

"Do you have some time, Aexie? I was hoping to share my tea with you." Xenon lifted the tray.

"All right," I said, feeling my defenses slide into place. I'd grown up knowing Xenon as Xerus's partner, but I'd never really developed much of a relationship with him myself.

Xenon strode in and gently settled the tray on the low table by the couches. He was dressed nicely but comfortably. No jacket, just fine soft pants and a button shirt, both with silver and gold thread embroidered throughout. It looked more like Xerus's clothing than his own.

"I know. Xerus had them made for me, and while they're not very subtle, he was excited for me to wear them." Xenon shrugged, looking down at the elaborate swirls of silver on the left side of his shirt.

I didn't say anything. What was Xenon doing here? "What do you want?" I asked. It came out more acidly than I had planned.

Xenon raised an eyebrow as if he was surprised at my vehemence. "Have I done something to offend you, Aexie?" he asked calmly.

I clenched my teeth. Humans had such a range of ways to express themselves, and I was using all of them. So I forced myself to yawn, relaxing my jaw muscles for a moment.

"No," was all I said.

"The blood oath then?"

I shook my head. Even though I wasn't pleased that Xerus had allowed a blood oath and hadn't discussed his feelings or consulted with any of us, I had watched how Xenon treated him and was glad for my brother. I knew Xerus was more confident and self-assured, bolder even, when Xenon was around. Xerus didn't get as lost in his thoughts, so Xenon was good for him. And I wouldn't begrudge him his love, his mate.

Xenon remained silent for a minute, turning his attention instead to the tea service he'd brought. He carefully placed two cups on saucers and poured the tea. Then he added a decent spoonful of honey to my cup. He must have asked Xerus how I liked it because he made it exactly as I would have. When he finished preparing my cup, he took his own, strode over to the nearest plush purple couch, and sat back, taking a sip. Looking like he was content to sit quietly in my rooms just drinking tea, he glanced around the room politely, not forcing me to speak.

After a few deep breaths, I felt calm return to my body, so I went and grabbed my tea, then sauntered over to the couch across from him. I crossed one knee over the other and watched Xenon taking careful sips from his cup.

"The loss of a loved one is significant," he suddenly said, his voice whisper soft. "I've known individuals who became shadows of their former selves, who went mad with grief and isolated themselves completely, never to be seen again. I'm not going to say that I understand your grief because I don't think anyone can claim that. I feel your family's suffering acutely though. Xerus calls out for her in the middle of night, reliving those last moments at least once a week." He still hadn't turned his attention back to me but seemed intent on examining the intricate wallpaper in my room. "I do understand that you might not be able to explain all your feelings. But if you ever want to talk about them with someone outside your family, I can be that for you. Just don't push everyone away. You may think they don't need your negative feelings, but they do," Xenon murmured as he stared into his cup of tea. "They need you in whatever form you can offer, and you will need them."

I could only nod gently, distracting myself from crying by taking another sip of tea. To my amazement, my cup refilled itself. I glanced over at Xenon and couldn't help but smile. His finger barely moved as his own cup refilled.

"Xerus said your parents aren't fond of using magic to do things you could physically do yourselves. But I believe in enjoying the luxuries as much as anyone." He smiled into his cup.

I looked into my own cup, catching the swirl of honey that magically appeared. I took a cautious sip and realized it tasted like the one he'd made physically.

"Could you teach me?" I asked.

"Absolutely. It's tougher than it looks, but I know you'll have no problem learning. You see magic like your brother does? Like light?"

I nodded.

For the next couple hours, we played around with filling cups with tea and adding honey to them. At one point, I added honey to one of the decorative bowls on the table by accident, but Xenon wasn't one to scold. He only laughed and smiled and told me to try again, snapping his fingers to fix the mistake.

A knock finally interrupted us as I practiced filling Xenon's cup for him. "Come in," I said. I saw Xenon's smile and knew Xerus was at the door.

"Here you are," Xerus said, walking in and making himself comfortable on the couch.

"You know where I am at all times, darling," Xenon replied, but as he brought his cup to his lips, he wiggled his eyebrows at me.

I rose and went over to the tray to grab a teacup. Then I came back and placed it on the table in front of Xerus, filling it with tea and adding almost as much honey as there was tea for my brother.

"Thanks, hun," he said as he took the cup and glanced at Xenon, obviously assuming he had done it, before bringing the cup to his lips. Xenon winked at me. "My pleasure," he said. I wasn't supposed to do that kind of magic, so I was glad Xenon had taken the credit. I smiled as I sat and took another sip of tea.

"Xe, you're going to have to come with me to talk to Mother. Maybe she'll actually listen to you because she sure doesn't listen to me. This thing is already being blown out of proportion. She's planning to invite everyone, like I mean *everyone*. Between all your extended family and mine, it'll be like *all* the dragons in all the worlds are invited."

"You say that like it's a bad thing." Xenon smiled, throwing me a quick glance as if to say, "Just watch."

"What?! You want a big party?" A breath before he unloaded on Xenon, he caught himself, the knowing look in his eyes telling me he knew Xenon was trying to goad him. "Well, I think the diamond-studded outfits my mother plans for us to wear are beautiful ... especially with the gold hats," he said, taking a small sip.

Xenon just smiled, his smile saying he knew full well that Xerus was trying to rile him. Rather than taking the bait, Xenon rested his arm on the top of the couch and said, "I think your mother has lovely taste. I fully trust her opinions and yours. She is a queen after all. Her taste in decorum has always impressed me," Xenon said, tipping his cup a bit my way to show me it was empty.

I concentrated and filled it, but I must have given something away because Xerus was the next to speak. "Xe, you didn't. You taught Aexie your cup-filling magic?" he asked bluntly.

Before I could say anything, Xenon was quick to defend us both. "Whatever I've said to Aexie is between us, darling. You wouldn't want me to betray her trust so early in our relationship." He winked at me with one eye, tapping a finger on his cup and pointing at the tray on the table.

I glanced over and saw that the teapot was filled with yet more tea.

"Now, shall we get going to bed? I think we've talked Aexie's ear off," Xenon said, and he emptied his cup before rising and returning it to the tray.

"Aexie, don't let Mother and Father know Xe taught you. Actually, don't even let them see you do it," Xerus said. He turned to Xenon. "As for you, don't think I'm just going to let this slide. You can't be a bad influence on my siblings. I won't allow it," he said to Xenon's now retreating back.

"So bossy," Xenon muttered as he turned at the door and smiled and winked at me once more. Then he followed Xerus out and clicked the door shut behind him.

I practiced filling and emptying cups for a little while longer until I finished the pot of tea Xenon had refilled. I got up and realized I was more tired than I'd thought. Focusing on my magic and directing it so finely was more costly than I had realized. I went over to my table, carefully took the books and vase off, opened the map, and checked on everyone before I went to bed. Now, faintly glowing, a little silver dot had appeared next to Xerus's blue one.

Scanning everyone's whereabouts a final time, I closed the table, put everything back on top of it, and tucked myself into bed. I used a little magic to heat the bed as I lay in it. One of my mother's ladies-in-waiting had taught me how, and I enjoyed nothing more than a warm bed to fall asleep in.

# CHAPTER THIRTEEN
## JAXON

I WOKE UP SUDDENLY before the first rays of sunlight touched the sky, just as I always did. Jumping out of bed, I tested my body for any new sore spots, thinking of how I'd worked it yesterday. It was easy to determine which muscles hadn't been worked in a while, which muscles I had overextended, and which muscles I had worked yesterday. I made a mental list of the exercises I needed to go through today to balance out my body.

After glancing out the window, I grabbed a sweater, left my rooms, and walked as softly as I could out the palace's side exit. The guards nodded at me, and I nodded back in greeting.

Once outside, I started a slow jog around the palace. Strengthening and increasing stamina was so much easier to the human body than the dragon one, but the results of whatever we did in our human bodies showed in our dragon selves too. It was just much easier to lap the palace's perimeter in human form a few times than to have to fly to one edge of the realm and back.

"Your Highness, the king requests your presence in his office immediately," a guard in the front courtyard said, stepping out of his position to give me the message.

"Of course. Thank you," I said, stopping and following the guard inside. Then I made my way directly to my father's office, wondering if I'd forgotten to fill out some paperwork. I went through my to-do list in my head as I hurried down the halls.

I greeted the guards posted at my father's door, and they immediately opened it for me. I stepped inside, looking fondly at the familiarity of books strewn across every surface and stacks of papers piled high. "Father, you asked to see me?"

"Yes. I need you to get ready to fly out with me this morning."
My father stepped to the side of his desk, and I saw that he had
donned his battle armor.

I knit my brows together. "What's going on?"

"There was an attack on the western wall. The griffins have fled
to safety. I'm not sure if they've contained the attack or if they've
surrendered the area, so you need to gather your regiment. We'll
head out as soon as we can."

"Shall I go wake Xerus?"

"No, I'm leaving him here in case anything else happens. Between him, Xenon, and your mother, they'll be able to hold the
palace should there be an attack," he said.

I nodded and turned, then left to gather my soldiers. The military
arm of the realm had always appealed to me, and I'd worked my
way up to captain on my own accord. Many of my soldiers were
friends I'd grown up with.

I marched down to the barracks, where Gabol, my second in
command, had said he'd be staying for a while. "Gather the regiment," I ordered as I strode in and approached him. "We're leaving
after breakfast." I could tell that the soldiers already had some idea
that something was going on.

"Who's going?" he asked.

"Our regiment and my father's," I said.

Gabol nodded, his lion's mane bobbing.

"You're looking ... um, extra fluffy today?" I said, taking in the
unusual puffiness of his golden coat.

"My mother and nieces. I went to visit them yesterday, and my
mother insisted I bathe the moment I crossed the threshold. Then
my nieces begged me to have a tea party, so they made me pretty
for the party," Gabol explained, clearly bracing himself for the
expected abuse.

I smirked. Gabol was a griffin, but in his current state he didn't
look nearly as menacing as usual. Then my smile disappeared as I
remembered where we were going. "Gabol, you should prepare yourself. The griffin lands were attacked. That's where we're going. Most
fled to safety, but I'm not sure what we'll find when we get there." I
hoped he would pass the knowledge on to the other griffins in the

regiment. It would be better if the news came from him. The squad was professional, but that was their home.

He nodded and I couldn't help but press my lips together to contain a chuckle as his coat moved in waves with the motion. "You think he'll scare them off with his fluffiness?" Frinder came over and purposely patted Gabol on the hindquarters, sinking his hand into the puffy fur.

"Be ready," was all I said in response to Frinder's smirk as Gabol rolled his eyes. At that, I returned to the palace and dressed for battle. Then I looked at my walls and all the weapons adorning them, trying to choose which I would bring.

I started strapping knives and daggers on everywhere I could. You never knew when an extra knife might save your life. Though I was sure we'd be fighting as dragons, I wanted to equip my human form as well as possible. The little bit of magic that kept my human adornments with my human form and my dragon ones with my dragon form was the most useful bit of magic I had.

A knock on my chamber doors sounded. "Come in," I said as I continued doing up all the buckles and straps.

Xenon stuck his head in and bowed at the neck. "Prince Jaxon, Xerus told me you'll be going to the western wall this morning, that there was an attack on griffin lands?"

I nodded, wondering what Xenon was doing here.

"In my travels of late, I've noticed more animosity between griffins and centaurs. The centaurs have been increasingly arrogant."

"And that's your guess as to who attacked the griffins?"

Xenon nodded. "It would be a bold, brash move, but I thought you might want to know."

"Thank you," I said. "And Xenon?"

He paused in his retreat.

"Keep my family safe. Understand?"

He nodded and disappeared as I finally clasped the last buckles. I hurried outside to meet my father.

In the courtyard, my siblings had gathered, and I hugged each of them in turn.

"I'll save you a pie for when you return," Aexie said. She was grim-faced but less harsh than usual.

"And I'll bring you the claw or paw or hoof of our enemy to eat it with," I said in return. We grinned at each other. It was our usual exchange that had become as much superstition as tradition.

"Be safe, brother," Alexius said.

I nodded.

"Don't do anything stupid," Xerus said, looking from Xenon to me.

I nodded in reply.

Finally, I hugged my mother, who added, "Don't be too brave, Jaxon. Do you understand? I'd rather you be observant." She hugged me an extra second longer than normal. I turned away from them and nodded to my father, who then bent and whispered something to my mother.

I called on my magic to secure the extra weapons and armor I'd strapped to my human form before popping into dragon form. My father was next, and we took off, flying out of the courtyard and over the barracks, where we both cried out, calling our regiments to us.

The pegasi and other dragons would join us in the air. The griffins were airborne already, circling to warm up and gather the rest of the group. Gabol was waiting for me on the far western edge of the sky. My father and I flew up to meet our seconds, and together, we flew to the western wall.

It felt like a lot longer than it probably was before we reached the last hill and could see the griffin's lands. I stopped short when I saw the flames and dark, scorched gashes that had been scratched in the wattle-and daub-houses. We'd lived in peace for so long, it was startling to see such an act of violence. And I couldn't see anything moving—griffin or otherwise.

"Sweep the perimeter to check for traps and ambushes," my father ordered his regiment. "Use magic. Once we see your all-clear signal, we'll search for survivors and take the injured to that field there." My father nodded to an open field free of gashes, then turned to me. "Afterward, take your team and establish the extent of the damage." His face was grim.

The signal came quickly, and I whistled my orders to my regiment in various tones. My team took off in two lines along the outer edge of the damage. I flew directly up the center with my father, his second, and Gabol. Each flap of our wings brought only more scorched and burned buildings into sight. They looked like cardboard houses that had been knocked over and set aflame.

The only thing I was glad for was the lack of bodies. There weren't any bodies—dead or alive—that we could see. I hoped that meant the griffins had been able to reach safety quickly.

"Go check the path." My father nodded at me and Gabol, so I took a sharp right toward the tallest tree on the edge of the forest away from the village.

We flew as fast as we could, and I was happy to see the trampled grasses along the hill leading into the forest. Many paws had traveled here. We arrived at the large tree, and I turned my back so Gabol could reveal the tree's secret. The tree's most immense root suddenly moved, rising to reveal a wide cave mouth beneath it.

I nodded to Gabol, and he proceeded into the cave as I kept watch. I extended my magic to see if anything felt out of place but couldn't detect anything. It was as if these lands had been abandoned.

Gabol emerged a minute later. "They're safe," he said, the relief evident on his face. He closed the secret door, and we took to the skies again, looking for trouble. I clasped my claws into fists and released them.

My regiment had set up a perimeter around the scorched and destroyed area. Scouts circled in the air, waiting for anything to show up. I flew over the area, looking carefully at the ground. If whatever had attacked wasn't still here, then it must have made a quick escape. Had it taken to the sky? Or was it possible it had gone underground? I simply couldn't find any evidence of a creature leaving.

I flew higher and higher until each attacked village was just a dark shape. A shimmer of a magical trail led into the river from each scorched blob that was a village. I zoomed back down and headed straight for the river.

I used magic to scan within it, looking for anything unusual, and found a gaping hole in the middle of the river floor. Somehow, it wasn't pulling water in like a hole ought to. The water seemed to be skating right across the hole as if it didn't exist.

I whistled for a few of my soldiers to keep watch and went to find my father. "There's a hole in the riverbed, but the water doesn't flow into it. From above, it looks as if the attacks on the villages originated from that hole."

My father's body tensed. It didn't make sense. This village had been destroyed by fire and something powerful. A water-based creature wouldn't have used fire and was not that powerful. We should have found flooded houses or houses crushed by water pressure.

I led my father to the river, and as we approached it, a huge flame licked the skies further down the river. If it hadn't been for the break in the trees the river offered, we would have missed it.

I took off into the air immediately, Gabol right behind me. I whistled for my regiment to break their perimeter and follow except for those guarding the hole in the riverbed.

We flew off in search of the fire. My eyes narrowed when I saw a sea serpent blowing purple fire at the houses at the edge of another village. It was the strangest sight I'd ever seen, sea serpents this far inland. On top of that, it was unnatural for a sea serpent to have anything to do with fire.

I whistled another order, and we created a shield, blocking the other half of the village from the sea serpent still flailing about.

"By order of the king of this realm, you will cease further action! If you do, you will not be harmed!" I shouted to the serpent.

The serpent didn't respond, but instead started to flail even more as if it didn't know what it was doing or was having a seizure of some kind. It flailed back and forth, smashing more and more houses and spraying more fire. The creature was easily ten times my size, but I called the strongest in my regiment to me. I wanted to see if I could grab its tail and pull it out of the village to an open field.

The serpent flopped around as if it had no control of its body, occasionally blowing fire from its mouth and smashing houses seemingly by accident.

Frinder and I and two other dragons flew behind the serpent, who didn't seem to notice us at all. I picked up one side of its tail, carefully avoiding its flailing head and side fins, while Frinder grabbed the other side, and we flew upward. The other two dragons met us in the air, and together, we grasped the tail and pulled, hauling the serpent into the open field. I whistled for the others to let go. We all shot up into the air to get out of harm's way.

The serpent continued to thrash back and forth, probably doing more damage to itself than to the grasses around us. My soldiers cleared the perimeter of the open field in case anyone was lingering within reach.

The serpent continued to randomly blow fire and thrash around as if it were a fish out of water. However, as we stood watching nearby, I saw that the substance coming out of its mouth looked a lot less like a gas and more like a liquid, even if it did behave like fire. That didn't make any sense.

# Chapter Fourteen
## Xerus

I WAS PACING THE length of the Jade Room. "They should have sent word by now."

"They just left. They would have just arrived and checked the perimeter. They won't send a message until they have something to report," Xenon reasoned.

"What would attack the griffins? Why now? Is there some tension or conflict I don't know about?" I asked, looking at Alexius. "Are there creatures with ancient grudges against griffins?"

"No. None. Griffins live quietly and privately so nothing sets off their angrier instincts," Alexius replied. He was training with Aexie, but they were only half-heartedly circling each other.

"So why? Why would something disrupt the peace?" I asked.

"Honey, you should sit down before you give me a headache from all your pacing," my mother said from the couch, where she sat knitting as she raised her eyebrows at me.

"I second that," Xenon said.

I quit pacing and went over to sit beside Xenon. But moments later, my leg started to bounce up and down as I continued to think of the possibilities.

A soldier knocked and announced himself as he walked into the Jade Room. I leaped up to meet him at the table we'd set up in case we needed to strategize.

"All is well on the palace grounds and in the nearby villages. So far, reports have come in from half the other lands. Nothing out of the ordinary," the soldier said.

"Good. That's good," I said. "Thank you. Let me know when the rest of the lands have reported in. Please send out auxiliary soldiers to the bases."

An auxiliary group always trained at the palace. They were a team of ten magical creatures trained to handle a variety of situations as a single team, though two creatures were always assigned to one base. That way, they could cover all the bases: water, air, earth, fire, and essence. A single auxiliary team could generally command a couple hundred soldiers with nonmagical abilities.

"See, nothing to worry about. It was an anomaly, not the start of something. Your father and brother will be back soon to regale us with the tale of a griffin that went crazy," Xenon said.

Another soldier knocked on the door before entering and strangely approached my mother instead of me.

She looked serious as he whispered something in her ear. She nodded and sent him off. She put away her knitting needles and stood. "The griffins have started to arrive from the escape tunnel," my mother announced. "Alexius, Aexie, come with me and we'll figure out suitable arrangements for them. And Xerus, you and Xenon will remain here to wait for the rest of the reports."

I nodded. My mother, when she had become queen, had created an initiative that called for all the lands of our realm to put together an evacuation plan from their lands to the main palace. At the same time, it had also offered the palace multiple evacuation routes to the other lands in every direction, so my father had been all for it. Considering the possibility of so many new inhabitants at the palace, my mother had also commissioned a multiroom, multilevel building be built on palace grounds. It hadn't been used yet, but we'd always kept it clean and had started using it for storage. Now my mother and siblings would have to move what was in storage and welcome our new guests.

"I wonder if we'll have enough space," I said.

"Does anyone have enough space for an entire population?" Xenon asked.

I filled him in on the building my mother had commissioned. "Wow, you really are ready for anything. She's a smart lady."

"However, if the entire griffin population shows up, we'll have to set up a tent city. I don't think that building will be enough to house everyone. And that means a tent city will likely take up all the flat land behind the palace." I groaned at not having the necessary space to take our dragon form within palace walls for a while.

"It's rather exciting here. I always thought palace life would be so boring," Xenon said.

"I'm going to ignore that insult," I said.

"Not you. I meant I was kind of looking forward to some quiet R&R, getting to know your family. But this, well, it's ... unexpected."

"Just wait until Mother asks you to help with the griffins. You'll be put to work then," I said, pacing again.

"It'll be fine, I promise, Xerus. Whatever this is, your family is one of the strongest in all the worlds. And if I may be so bold, I'm here too. I'm pretty capable. So I doubt anyone would be fool enough to cause meaningful trouble, especially if they didn't want to face the wrath of the queen if they ruined her son's union ceremony." Xenon raised an eyebrow.

I laughed at the image of my mother chasing after someone.

"You know, I've never seen my mother in battle, in full form," I said.

"And I hope you never will," Xenon shook his head. "I've seen her, just once, in full battle glory as a Wild One. It's a formidable sight. An entire regiment of nonmagicals turned and fled just at the sight of her."

"Really?" I had only heard whispered stories. My mother never let my father talk of it. And besides her annual return to the wild, I knew nothing of her family.

"It's like when a dragon glows. I know that seems counterintuitive, but think of a glowing dragon, except instead of embarrassment, it's like radiation causing it. It's inner power that radiates outward. And there's so much power in her, it's not like just an army is behind her, energizing her, but more like the whole world is there to power her."

Another soldier knocked and entered. "All lands have reported back, and nothing appears out of the ordinary. They've all been notified about the attack on the griffins. Wagons from the first lands to report in are nearing the palace."

"Wagons? What for?" Xenon stood.

"For supplies, sir," the soldier said.

"Supplies?" Xenon asked.

I was writing up a report for my father, so I nodded at the soldier to explain to Xenon.

"The supplies for the griffins, sir. The other lands know they've had to flee, so they've sent extra supplies for them," the soldier replied.

"Arrange them in the front lawn," I said. "I'll send Alexius out to organize everything." The soldier nodded and left.

"Wait, you're not surprised by this?" Xenon asked.

"Surprised by what?"

"You mean to tell me the pegasi, even the harpies, have sent supplies—at no cost—for the griffins? They've just donated it all?"

"Yes." I really didn't see what he was so astounded by.

"Of their own free will."

"Yes. It's not required. But it was part of the protocol my mother created when she built the evacuation system."

"So the other lands send wagons full of supplies," he repeated.

"Yes." I clenched my jaw, biting back my annoyance.

"Do you realize how incredible that is? This is the most amazing realm I've ever seen." Xenon sat down, taking a little notebook out of his breast pocket and writing something down.

"What's that for anyway?" I asked, looking at the notebook.

"I'm taking notes. If I'm going to be part of this realm, I want to be knowledgeable, especially about the family protocols."

*Oh*, I thought. That was sweet of him. I supposed that if one hadn't grown up in this family, it would be a tough one to join. We had rules and expectations. I had even been surprised that Xenon wasn't used to training on a regular schedule.

Our family played to our strengths, but we also worked together. That's just how it had always been. I suppose we were rather extraordinary with the way we did things.

*Alexius*, I thought along the sibling bond.

*Please say you have another job for me. Mother has me folding linens.*

*I do. But it might involve more linens. Wagons have started to arrive from the other lands. You are to organize the wagons and supplies.*

I felt a groan along the line. *Yes, brother*, he said before closing the door of our connection.

I was tempted to send Jaxon a message. He might get it if he wasn't too busy, but I didn't want to distract him. He would send a message when he could. I'd have to be patient until then.

*Brother.* Jaxon's thoughts popped into my head.

It was like I'd anticipated his message. *I'm here.* Jaxon's particular beam of light shone through, and I saw what he was seeing: a great sea serpent thrashing about in a field.

*Have you ever seen anything like it?* Jaxon asked.

*The sea serpent, yes. The thrashing and fire pouring out of her mouth, no.*

*Will you ask Xenon? And Alexius. We aren't sure how to proceed. It's out of harm's way for now, but I'm reluctant to attempt any of our usual restraint tactics. I'm not sure it's safe.*

*Yes, I'll ask them,* I said. I sent the images to Alexius and Aexie, then Xenon, so they could see the image from Jaxon's eyes.

*That's a sea serpent from the northern oceans. It's come awfully far south,* came Alexius's reply.

"The whole thing is inconceivable," Xenon said. "Alexius is right. It shouldn't be down here, but that's not fire. It's acid. Aerosolized acid. Make sure no one gets sprayed. If they even get just a little bit on them, even a bit of a mist, it could peel their scales off."

I passed the message along to Jaxon.

*Thank you. Our plan for now is to let it tire itself out,* Jaxon said.

*Ok. Let me know if that doesn't work. Oh, the griffins have started arriving. Mother is seeing to them.* I knew Gabol would want to know, and Father too.

*Good, thanks,* he said. He closed our connection, and I made sure I relayed the message to Aexie.

"No wonder you were so good at talking along the blood-oath line so quickly," Xenon said aloud.

"What do you mean?" I asked, turning my focus away from a thought drifting along the edge of my mind.

"You have practice with a familial bond. Wait, don't tell me. You didn't know that's also very rare. I suppose the wild magic from your mother would have helped," Xenon said. He crossed his long legs, leaning back on the couch, and I couldn't help my heart's extra leap as he sprawled out.

"When we were little, we'd go for days without physically speaking. I think when Alexius was old enough, we even went a couple years without physically speaking to each other," I said.

"Well, let me be the first to tell you that your family is the first I've seen where all the siblings can speak to each other at the same time," he said.

"Maybe you just haven't seen it in other families. If I hadn't opened that particular door, you wouldn't have heard them. So, maybe you just haven't had the opportunity to see it in another family."

"No, you're probably right, but still, you get this look on your face ... It's awfully cute." Xenon grinned wickedly.

I rolled my eyes, turning my attention back to my report.

# CHAPTER FIFTEEN

## ALEXIUS

I TOO NOW HAD my regiment, having just earned it on my last hatching day, so I called them to me as I headed for the front lawn. I would need the extra hands to help me organize all those wagons. But first, I had my regiment set up massive tents to hold everything: linens in one, tents and building supplies in a second, food for the next few days in a third, and food that could keep in a fourth. The pegasi had been generous, even sending a few wagons of wine for the griffins with a note saying, "To ease your pains now and to a better tomorrow."

I stood in the middle of the lane, directing the incoming wagons. They could circle the courtyard, dropping off their supplies in the various tents as they went, and exit through the gate.

"Captain, we have two wagons of wheat approaching," one of my soldiers, a pegasus, trotted up to tell me.

"Direct them to the grain silo around the side of the castle," I ordered, and he took off into the air to lead the wagons in the right direction. Then I turned my attention to the dozen soldiers I'd posted along the lane up to the palace as they searched each incoming wagon.

I wasn't about to take any risks. Queen Elenex's protocols, as they were called, were well-known. Whoever attacked the griffins would know they would come here, and I wasn't about to throw caution to the wind and allow an opportunity for a second attack.

*It looks like all the griffins evacuated. We're going to need more tents,* Aexie's voice emerged in my head.

*I'll send some more your way,* I replied. I called one of my sergeants over and sent her to grab some tents from the new supplies and take them to Aexie. My mother's protocol was proving itself quite useful. That said, I was also impressed with how many wagons lined the lane now, highlighting the generosity of the other lands in Etciel.

As I took in the sight, I noticed a wagon slowly making its way up, and I recognized the familiar purple paint and the symbol on the side. I nodded to one of my soldiers and pointed at the wagon. They strode over to it and pulled it out of the line. Then they examined it inside and out, bottom and top, before sending it my way.

"Foxall," I said, extending my hand to the driver as he hopped off the driver's seat.

"Your Highness," he said.

"Foxall, it's very kind of you to offer your services."

The village apothecary nodded and said, "It's kind of your family to offer the griffins shelter."

"It's all my mother's doing. Her protocols and all," I said. "If you want to head around back to meet Aexie, just follow Knox." I motioned to a smaller brown dragon, my third, and Foxall climbed back into his wagon and followed him behind the palace.

*Sister, Foxall just arrived. I'm sending him your way,* I told Aexie.

*Thank you. We've mostly got sprained ankles and cuts and bruises, but he'll bring comfort with his presence.*

I turned my attention back to the approaching wagons. Suddenly, two wagons and their drivers caught my eyes. I couldn't help but smile as my heart started to thud a little faster.

I watched as my soldiers searched her wagon. She looked nervous. Then she watched carefully as they searched her mother's wagon behind her. Once done, they sent her up the line, and my grin widened as she caught sight of me. She glowed and smiled back, waving at me. I couldn't help but walk over to meet her partway. "Hi," was all I managed to say.

"Hi! We heard you might need some help. I've got a wagon of sheep and a wagon of hay to feed said sheep," she said.

"That's very thoughtful of you," I said, leaping up onto her wagon and sitting next to her before showing her where to go. We made our way behind the palace as my second took up my previous post directing the incoming wagons.

"Do you need help with the griffins? My mother and I, we're pretty handy at wrapping bandages," she said.

"That would be wonderful!" I said, and before I could say more, my mother suddenly appeared next to the wagon.

"Your Majesty!" Brixelle exclaimed, trying awkwardly to dip into a curtsy while seated on the wagon. She almost fell off the seat as a result, and I grabbed her leg to make sure she didn't.

"Brixelle? It's nice to see you again," my mother said, extending a hand to Brixelle, who instead of shaking it, dropped to the floor of the wagon to kiss it.

I hopped off the wagon, then turned to help Brixelle as she leaped lightly down. We'd pulled out of the line and pulled around behind the tents to let the sheep out. Two soldiers were already setting up a penned area for the animals being donated and were glad to receive the hay to feed them. I left them to unload the wagons, wondering for only a moment how my mother knew Brixelle had arrived.

"And may I introduce my mother, Roxana." Brixelle's mother had also leaped off the wagon with ease and come up beside her daughter.

"Your Majesty, it is an honor to meet you. And I must compliment you on your son. He was gracious enough to heal me, and not only has that saved our farm, but it has saved my daughter the heartache of watching her mother deteriorate," she said.

I couldn't help but glow a bit.

"That's very kind of you. I'm glad my son could be of service to you. Now, if I heard right, you and your daughter are willing to help us wrap bandages?" my mother asked. She steered Brixelle and her mother away from me. "Don't you have wagons to see to, son?" she asked over her shoulder before diving into conversation with Brixelle.

*I can't believe you told her she was here, Aexie,* I said down the line.

*It's not my fault. You projected your feelings to the rest of us like a torch light. You should know better.*

I rolled my eyes and turned my attention back to the wagons, which had started to pile up from my neglect. My second could only do the job alone for so long. I rushed over to help untangle and direct wagons, hoping Brixelle wouldn't be angry with me for leaving her alone with my mother.

# CHAPTER SIXTEEN

## AEXIE

I WAS CURIOUS ABOUT the dragonette that elicited such feelings in Alexius. He'd forgotten to close our sibling door when he'd seen Brixelle arrive, so we'd all been walloped with our little brother's feelings for her. Did love really make you that careless? I wasn't sure I wanted to feel that way.

My mother, for one, was excited to get to know Brixelle and her mother. Winking at me knowingly, my mother had said she recognized the signs that Alexius had found his dragon mate. For good or ill, it had happened much quicker for Xerus. "Xenon knew when he met Xerus as just a dragonling. He stayed away though, for which I'm forever grateful. It must have been difficult waiting until Xerus was older. But the moment they met as adults, Xerus flew through the stages of bonding given Xenon already knew of and accepted the bond."

It seemed strange to me that someone could refuse the bond. Why would you?

My mother came around the corner again and I busied myself folding more linens.

"Aexie, this is Brixelle and her mother, Roxana. They're going to help with the bandages," my mother said.

I took a good look at Brixelle. She was a plump purple dragon with deep-yellow spines. Her accents were all the same yellow shade, which was rare. Usually dragons had one accent color, but it would vary in shade. "It's a pleasure to meet you." I smiled and curtsied. My mother would skin me alive if I didn't at least use proper manners.

"It's an honor to meet you, Your Highness. Alexius is very fond of you," Brixelle said as she curtsied deeply in return. I wondered briefly if Alexius had told her to flatter me.

Brixelle's mother—Roxana was it?—was a beautiful and elegant dragonette with light-purple scales along her body the color of lavender and milk. Her accents were a pale yellow, much like Brixelle's, but so many shades paler. They both had yellow eyes, which was common enough among dragons.

At that moment, Foxall rolled up in his wagon. He'd gone the long way around the palace to better maneuver his supplies. "Your Majesty, Your Highness, I've come to help any way I can," he said. He jumped out of the wagon and bowed to my mother and me, then nodded to Brixelle and Roxana. So they knew each other. Interesting.

"We've tried to make the injured griffins comfortable in the tent nearest us. We were just about to triage them," my mother said as she set her chin. Foxall nodded.

Foxall had long been a family visitor. He was our apothecary whenever we needed one, and we were grateful for his help today. Now, he strode over to me.

"Well, Princess Aexie, shall we start? You have enough healing knowledge now. Let's make two lines and send them all where they need to go. Her Majesty and Roxana can handle the bandages. Brixelle will assist me, and you will triage the griffins. Does that work?" he asked, raising his eyebrows.

I was very fond of Foxall and was surprised he'd picked Brixelle as his assistant. That just confirmed what I'd thought. They definitely knew each other. I nodded as Foxall pointed at a row of griffins taking up beds. I recognized one of the griffins I'd spoken to earlier who only needed a tincture that she'd forgotten when she'd fled and directed her to Foxall first. That would be a quick and easy fix.

Foxall set himself up with a rolling cart, and Brixelle started searching through to find the ingredients he needed to mix the tincture for the griffin I had just sent to him. Cuts and scrapes were unavoidable when stumbling through tunnels in the dark, so those griffins I sent to my mother and Roxana. They were a quick and efficient team, and I continued to send griffins to either to my mother or Foxall based on their needs. I'd always been Foxall's assistant whenever he visited the palace, and it had rubbed me the wrong way a little when he'd appointed Brixelle instead of me. I knew in my head that my current position was proof of his trust in my abilities, but I still missed his kind words and the responsibility of handling the different liquids, pastes, and plants in his cart. Even when I was a child, he'd send me to run to the wagon to fetch a specific herb or plant stored there. The myriad of tiny drawers was always confusing to Danx and Alexius, but it was a masterpiece to me. So many different possibilities all organized in neat little boxes.

"Your Highness, please, my baby. She won't settle. I'm at my wits end." One griffin held a baby in her arms, and as I looked, the baby screwed its face into a knot to wail some more. There was a line of five griffins waiting to see Foxall, so I told the woman to stay in line as I took the baby from her so she could have a few minutes of relief. As I held the baby in my arms, the little griffin seemed enthralled with my skin as she petted me, feeling the soft texture of human skin. I continued directing griffins with one arm; most only needed bandages for this or that scrape, so my job was rather easy. I queued the line of griffins waiting to see Foxall behind me so as to not crowd the apothecary. The rocking motion of my directing must have soothed the griffin baby because when Foxall came over, I was surprised to realize I was still holding the baby, who was fast asleep in my arms.

"It's quite a talent to be able to soothe a griffin baby, princess," he said.

I grinned at the compliment and gently put the baby back in her mother's arms. She nodded her thanks.

He waved his fingers over the baby to check her health, then directed Brixelle to make a concoction of ginger root to help the baby's indigestion.

I was sad to see the baby go but kept busy enough when I saw a new influx of griffins. As I continued my job, I turned to see Brixelle hard at work. She was careful to put things back where she had taken them from, and she took her time measuring out the various doses. "Foxall, how do you know Brixelle?" I asked.

"Her mother was quite ill for a long time. I saw them almost twice a week for the last decade until she reached a point where there was nothing else I could do for them. I told her she might go to the palace and seek magical assistance, but she was too proud to do such a thing for the longest time. I'm glad she finally went. It was fortunate Alexius paid them a visit. Your brother did a wonderful job healing Roxana. I haven't seen Roxana out of bed in five years."

"What's Brixelle like?" I asked him.

Foxall's eyebrows rose a millimeter, but he answered anyway. "She's a good daughter, a good farmer too, kind and gentle with her sheep. Why?"

I looked at Foxall, not sure how much I should say to someone outside the family, though anyone who saw Alexius and Brixelle together would know.

"Alexius and her—" was all I needed to say before Foxall interrupted. "Ahh, so the rumors are true then."

"What rumors?" I quirked an eyebrow.

"The rumors that the youngest prince has found his dragon mate at the same time the oldest prince will be marrying." Foxall popped a plug into a bottle and shook the contents.

"It's early. But you should see them together. I think it's more obvious to the rest of us than to them," I said.

"Time will tell and unfold as it is meant to unfold," he said and with that, turned his attention to the line that had formed.

Foxall approved of her, and that earned Brixelle a point in her favor.

I finished sorting the lines and said, "That's it for my job, so I'll grab some water and go help with the bandages."

Foxall replied over his shoulder. "Actually, princess, if you would, four hands are better than two when making tinctures."

I nodded as I left. I'd have to thank Foxall later. He was giving me the opportunity to get to know Brixelle for myself. I took the next recipe and started to assemble it opposite Brixelle.

"I need to heat this one. Do you know where the burner is?" she turned to ask me. She looked a little frazzled but determined.

"Here." I took the bottle she was holding and held it away from the griffins and the wagon, calling up my own flame and blowing on the bottom gently.

"You have amazing control," she said, her face filled with admiration as she took the bottle back from me.

I nodded my thanks. It was rare for dragons to be able to use their flame when they were in human form, but I'd spent so much time switching back and forth, it was barely a thought to me now.

I started to assemble the ingredients for the next recipe, watching how gently Brixelle handled each ingredient, and was suddenly struck with how she moved so much like Danx. Danxing had been true to her name, always dancing and elegant in every movement. And I realized that was how Brixelle moved. Her movements too reminded me of the gentle flow of a creek.

The next griffin stumbled up to us, practically falling over as he came up to our table, a recipe for a needed tincture in hand. Brixelle was there in a flash, supporting the griffin so he could stand with dignity. *So she is quick and strong. Makes sense for a farmer,* I thought.

We ended up working surprisingly well together. She read the list of ingredients before she assembled them, and it gave me the chance to hand her whatever ingredients were closer to me as I worked. She was slower than I, so that made me feel good, but it was probably unfair since I'd been doing this for Foxall every chance I could get since I was born.

We had just finished with the last tincture and were putting everything away in the covered wagon when Brixelle put the last bottle back and rocked back on her feet, hands on her hips, and stared straight at me.

"So, how'd I do?" Brixelle asked.

I was a little taken aback by her directness. "You did fine. The tinctures looked right, and if they met Foxall's approval, then I'd be proud if I were you."

"No, not as Foxall's assistant. How'd I measure up for you? Will I do for your brother?"

Again, shocked at Brixelle's bravery, I finished putting the herbs and plants away before I answered. "Some of your movements remind me of my sister," I said softly.

Her face fell. "I'm so sorry." She was quiet for a time, then offered, "Alexius hasn't said much about her, but I can tell it really affected him."

"He was closest to her," I said.

Brixelle nodded.

"So do you feel the same for my brother as he obviously feels for you?" I asked. Since we were being bold, I wanted to take advantage of it.

"I do. I've often wondered whether I would find my bonded mate, but the moment I saw him in the throne room, I knew. I didn't think he'd think the same of me though. I'm just a farmer after all."

"The bond doesn't care about status or wealth, or age for that matter," I said, thinking of Xerus and Xenon.

"I know. I just want to go slowly. I don't think Alexius is ready to accept our bond," she admitted softly, glowing a bit in the dark wagon.

"He will. Just—he'll kill me for telling you this—but the life of a princess isn't all pretty things and good manners. This family is a team. You need to know that before you accept your bond," I warned.

"Thank you," she said. "I'll put much thought into it, and if I accept a bond with Alexius, know that I'll be prepared to give your family my all."

I nodded, but before I could respond, Foxall appeared at the end of the wagon. I wondered if he'd been listening the whole time. He had this uncanny knack for manufacturing moments like this.

"Ready to call it a day?" he asked.

I hopped down from the wagon, noticing how easily Brixelle did as well.

"I'll see you at supper, Foxall." I gave him a quick hug and turned to walk back into the palace. I wanted nothing more than a hot, steaming bath, so I trudged to my rooms and threw off my clothes.

As I prepped the bathwater, I thought if my brother were to bond with someone, Brixelle wasn't a bad choice. She wasn't silly or stupid. I laughed to think of my knowledge-loving brother bonded to someone stupid. They'd probably kill each other.

I chuckled and slid into the bathwater, moving on to wondering whether Jaxon was back from his battle and what he and Xerus would think of Brixelle.

# CHAPTER SEVENTEEN
## JAXON

I'D SEEN HER EYES. Her soul was missing. So now I couldn't decide whether the sea serpent was flailing out of fear or if she was under a spell of some kind. Either way, the serpent wasn't consciously thrashing.

She continued to thrash, letting acid—*Thank you, Xenon*—spew in generally just one direction, though the sprays came less frequently and with less volume now, and we easily avoided them. It had become mostly an aerial situation though since most of the ground was covered in the spewed acid, burning and sizzling as we flew above.

We weren't sure how to proceed. It was no longer as clear-cut as something evil attacking the griffins' lands anymore. This creature hadn't been aware of her actions—and still wasn't. Therefore, we could not kill it unless it had conscious, malicious intent, that it had meant to do harm.

Her thrashing developed a rhythmic pattern, so I decided to fly in and investigate more closely. My father had forbidden us to infiltrate her mind to be safe. We too would be vulnerable to whatever disease had infiltrated her mind, if in fact that was what had happened to her. I wondered if someone had simply let her loose in this particular area, expecting general destruction and chaos, or if some creature had more nefarious intentions.

My mind was whirling, trying to figure out why and how someone would do such a thing. I'd sent my suspicions to Xerus earlier, and he was on the lookout for trouble elsewhere in case this was supposed to be a distraction.

We'd had skirmishes before, but this was the first time that it wasn't clear who the enemy was or what their motivations were.

Frinder came over to me. "You know, if it's thrashing like a simple, nonmagical animal, we could treat it like one, cover its eyes, see if that would calm it down."

"And then what?"

"I'm not sure. I didn't think that far. It must be exhausted." Sympathy shone in Frinder's eyes as he thought. "Maybe if we can calm it, it would realize it's tired enough to at least stop thrashing. You know, like how sometimes my kids are beyond excited before supper, and when they sit down for supper, they fall asleep in it."

"Remind me not to eat supper at your house," I said, winking before flying over to my father to share Frinder's plan. He agreed because at least it was something, and we could likely achieve it without injury to the sea serpent or us. I used my magic to weave nearby leaves into a blanket big enough to cover the sea serpent's head and, with Gabol and Frinder's help, draped the blanket over its back then up the creature's neck until finally we dropped it over her eyes, using wind to tuck it under its head.

The serpent thrashed more intensely for the next few seconds before finally slowing and falling asleep in its own pool of acid. I waited for it to move, to breathe, but it didn't. I narrowed my eyes to watch more carefully. The horizon that was its body was so still. I looked carefully for any small movement, even inches. "Frinder."

"Yes, sir." He had seen what I had, so he flew over to the sea serpent's body. He was the quickest flier in my regiment. If the serpent moved suddenly, Frinder would be in the air before he could be injured. He flew close to the body and carefully touched her with a hoof. Then he furrowed his brow.

My father flew over to me, and we watched as Frinder looked up and shook his head.

"It's dead?" I asked out loud.

"She must have spent her life energy thrashing," my father said.

"But how? Why?" I asked. We'd spent so long trying to figure out a way to save her, and here she was, dead.

My father whistled his orders, and I released my magic, the leaves falling from the serpant's face to reveal eyes white with death. The two regiments gently curled the body up before my father flew over to set fire to it. I stationed water creatures along the perimeter to control the fire in case it was tempted to leap to the forest. But the pool of acid she lay in contained the flames, and we watched her body shrivel and disappear within minutes of my father setting it aflame.

I flew numbly home. Frinder flew next to me, gently guiding our direction and my regiment behind me. How and why and what had happened today? It was so strange. I was saddened by the serpent's death. Surely it hadn't wanted that. I felt like we had been too late to the battle.

As I flew closer to the palace, I felt Alexius's core glow with love. His mate was near him, and he'd forgotten to close the rest of us off. Despite my concerns, I closed my mind off from my siblings as the familiar ache of loneliness rung in my core.

# CHAPTER EIGHTEEN
## ALEXIUS

*M*OM'S INVITED *BRIXELLE AND Roxana to supper.* Aexie's thoughts brushed my mind as I finished directing the last wagons back out of the palace grounds.

*Thank the Ancients! I'll get a break from flowers and color palettes.* Xerus's voice broke into my head.

I was surprised that Jax hadn't put his two cents in. I had seen them fly back and he'd looked lost and tired. He must be filling out his paperwork now before going to bathe and rest before supper. Maybe he'd have something sarcastic to say about Brixelle and me later.

"Hi," a soft voice behind me said. I whirled around to see Brixelle glowing faintly and smiling as she tucked a strand of purple hair behind her ear.

"Hi," I managed to say. "How was it?"

"It was tough work, but I like tough work," she said.

"Are you done now?"

"Yes. All the griffins are settling in for the night, so Foxall sent us on our way."

"I'm pretty much finished here. Would you like a tour of the palace?"

She nodded. "That would be lovely. You'll have to excuse my overalls though."

"I think you look beautiful in your overalls," I said. Then I suddenly realized how stupid that sounded and clamped my mouth shut.

Brixelle giggled. I didn't think there could be a lovelier sound.

*Close your damn door,* came Jax's voice as he slammed the door to our familial bonds.

*Sorry,* I said and sealed the door to the others.

"What were you just doing?" Brixelle asked.

I looked at her as we walked into the gardens and considered whether it would be harmful to tell her about soxkendi. It wasn't exactly a secret, so I supposed it wouldn't matter too much.

"Did you know that my siblings and I are bonded? We call it soxkendi."

"Oh! I think I remember hearing about that somewhere. You and your siblings can speak to each other without physically speaking?"

"Yes. It's like we share a room in our minds that we all have access to. We can share pictures, words, thoughts, feelings."

"What's that like?"

"It's nice to have access to my siblings so easily and quickly. Though I have the least control, so sometimes my siblings get annoyed at me for leaving the door open so to speak."

"Do you have to continually ... um, hold the door closed?"

I nodded. "It gets easier with time and practice. I have the least practice. So much of the time, my siblings close it for me or just keep theirs closed. I'm learning though. I can hold it without much effort. I just have to remember to open or close it."

"Do you ever meet together in the same room physically?" she asked as we passed my mother's prize roses.

"Yes. We have soxkendi in the physical world too. If one of us says 'soxkendi,' we immediately get together, usually in the library. It's a safe place for us to speak, share concerns, or share ideas and thoughts." I couldn't help but think of the first time we called soxkendi, and Danx had made me tell the others what had happened.

"That must be nice," Brixelle said.

"It is. But it can get a little crowded sometimes," I said.

"I've never had a sibling or a close friend," Brixelle said.

"Really?" I tried to think of my life without my siblings. It was impossible.

"I was my mother's only child. We were always too busy working for me to play with friends."

"Do you at least like the work?" I asked.

"I do. I love it. There's nothing that beats working in the quiet dark of the morning and watching the sun rise. It's so peaceful and quiet. Those are my favorite hours of the day."

"Sounds ... cold," I said and cringed. I liked early mornings, but they were for cozy fires and books. I couldn't imagine having to be out in the cold working then.

Her hand brushed mine and suddenly all I could think about was how her hand might feel in mine. My hand was burning, itching to grasp hers. *Would it be unwelcome? Is it too early?* I wondered as we strolled through the hedge maze my siblings and I had often played in as children. Even now I could hear children, probably griffins. Suddenly, two came barreling around a corner. I grabbed Brixelle's hand and pulled her out of the way.

The two little griffins stopped dead in their tracks as they stumbled past us. "We're sorry, Your Highness." Their eyes were wide.

"It's all right. Just be more careful around the corners," I said.

They nodded and ran off, and I realized I still had hold of Brixelle's hand. She hadn't pulled away yet either, so I brought it to my lips and kissed the back of it. "This hand and everything attached to it is precious to me. I'd hate to see harm come to it," I said.

Brixelle glowed. "I bet you use that line on all the dragonettes." She grinned, teasing me.

"There are no other dragonettes. You are my one and only," I said, looking into her beautiful golden eyes. I was never one to play games or to play coy.

She glowed a little brighter and broke eye contact by looking down at our joined hands. "I've never felt like this before either," she whispered.

My heart felt like it would burst. I knew exactly where we were and led her along a couple quick left turns into a little courtyard with a fountain and a bench where we could sit.

She raised her other hand slowly to cup the side of my face, and I leaned into the touch, closing my eyes, wanting to focus only on the feel of her callused hands on my skin. Humans could feel things so much more deeply.

"You're so beautiful. How could you fall for a dragonette like me?" she whispered.

My eyes flew open. "How?" I let go of her hand and held her face with both hands. "You are the most beautiful creature I've ever laid eyes on. You're strong and smart. You're so caring and kind, any dragon would be lucky to make your acquaintance. I'd be lucky just to know you. But to ... to call you mine—if I can? It would be my life's greatest honor." The words spilled out of my mouth.

Her glow brightened and she smiled as she said, "I'm the luckiest dragon in all the—"

I couldn't help but press my lips to hers before she could finish. The moment our lips touched, something warm in my core expanded until it exploded, and I felt Brixelle's soul join with mine like we were two pieces of a puzzle that finally clicked together.

"Ahem." A cough sounded to our right, and we jumped apart, startled. The guard glowed out of pure embarrassment. "My apologies, Your Highness, but your mother requests your presence for supper." He quickly melted back into the bushes.

"Guess we better go," she said.

"Wait." I stood up, grabbed her hand, and turned her back toward me. Holding her as softly as I could, I kissed her again and let the warmth flood my body. I could get addicted to this feeling. I wanted to get lost in it completely.

She gently pushed me away. "I know she's your mother, but she's my queen. Plus, I've also abandoned my mother among royalty."

I laughed. "But wait, just one more." And I pulled her in again, kissing her only briefly before she pushed a little less gently this time.

"We'll have time for that later. I'm not planning on going anywhere." She grinned and let go of my hand. "Maybe you'll just have to catch me." And she ran back into the maze. I thought for sure she would get lost, but as I chased her, I was amazed when she completely reversed our walk in and was out of the maze in a few short minutes.

"You have a knack for mazes," I said.

She giggled, taking my hand at last and dragging me toward the castle. "Hurry up. I need to at least bathe before supper. My mother will kill me if I show up at a royal supper in my overalls."

I let her drag me. I would let her drag me anywhere.

# CHAPTER NINETEEN
## XERUS

W E'D ALL FELT IT. I had been in the library with Xenon and Aexie when we'd felt Alexius's stream of light brighten and reverberate. I'd looked up and met Aexie's gaze. She'd quickly returned to the book she'd been reading, concentrating as hard as she could on words that likely weren't registering just then.

Alexius might not realize it, but I knew that watching him and Brixelle together would torture Jaxon. As tough as he looked on the outside, Jaxon missed nothing. And growing up with the mother and father we had, Jaxon wanted nothing more than to find his mate and start a family. Xenon had told me enough about how some dragons went crazy trying to find their mate. Some obsessed over it, or about traveling, in hopes of meeting their mate somewhere else.

I kept an eye on Aexie too. Because Alexius was the youngest, the general assumption was that he would always be the last to do everything: the last to learn to fly, the last to master each weapon, the last to meet his mate. And here he was, meeting his mate just as he was becoming an adult. So, I watched my sister carefully. We all knew Aexie had started taking partners to bed a few years ago, but we also knew none were her mate. I was sure Jaxon would soon have a fit over how many soldiers he kept having to send to the realm's boundaries to keep them away from her.

*Young Alexius has just accepted his bond, and so has Brixelle,* Xenon said in my mind.

*How did you know?* I asked.

*I saw a bright glow in the maze over there. And I can feel the change in you, the worry.*

*Am I really so terrible at keeping my feelings to myself?*

*I love that about you. You're always so worried about everyone else, like a mother hen.* I saw Xenon grin, even though he was pretending to read his own book.

"We better get ready for supper," I said out loud. Aexie was already dressed, her dress hiked up to her hips as she sat scrunched up in her usual spot by the window.

Xenon rose and put his book under his arm. "Shall we?" he asked, offering me his arm. I sneaked another glance at Aexie before leaving. I wondered whether I should call soxkendi later tonight or tomorrow.

"They'll be all right," Xenon said as we walked down the hall.

"How can you know that?"

"Because they have you for a brother. Because your family is one of the strongest and tightly bonded I've ever met," he said.

I pushed open the doors to my chambers. I had already bathed earlier, so I let Xenon bathe as I went to pick out our clothes. I set his out before picking something for me that only matched a little bit. I was thoroughly enjoying matching with someone else, even if Xenon insisted he could only tolerate a touch of matching.

My thoughts drifted again to Jaxon. He'd said he wanted to travel. I wondered if it really was because he wanted to learn more of combat or if he wanted to go in search of his mate.

"Gold brocade. Really, Xer?" Xenon came out of the bathing room in a towel, and I stared openly at the clear-cut muscles of his chest.

"What's wrong with gold brocade?"

"It's a little showy, isn't it?"

"Says the dragon made of silver and gold," I said, rolling my eyes as I turned.

"You better put a shirt on before I make us late for supper." He'd come up right behind me and whispered in my ear. I fully enjoyed the shivers that tingled from my ear down my body.

I pulled a shirt on, wanting to check on Jaxon and Aexie. And Alexius. He was so young. I still saw him as a little dragonling, trying to make sure he was walking like us and schooling his facial expressions to match ours.

*Hey, Xer, can you look at my report tonight? The serpent today, it's giving me a strange feeling.* Jaxon's voice entered my head.

*Sure thing. I think we should call soxkendi tomorrow morning.*

*Probably a good idea. Something about today is giving me a bad feeling.*

I nodded and Xenon looked at me like I was insane. "You need to get a better handle on that. You looked like a crazy dragon."

I stuck my tongue out. We finished dressing and headed for the dining room, hoping the attention would be off us and on Alexius now, or even on Jaxon and the sea serpent.

"Foxall!" I smiled as I entered and saw our old family friend. I went to greet him.

"Prince Xerus, congratulations on your upcoming ceremony. Your mother is very excited," he said.

"I hope she didn't bother you too much. We've barely had any say in the ceremony, but I think it's already organized," I said.

"It's been lovely to see her enthusiasm," he smiled. "Xenon. It's good to see you again. Congratulations to you as well."

Xenon nodded, shaking Foxall's hand but keeping his smile tight and thin.

I was about to ask him through our bond what that was about when Alexius and Brixelle slid to a halt just inside the doors. My brother wore the biggest smile I'd ever seen. I looked at him and raised my eyebrows.

"We thought we were late," he explained, not letting go of the pretty girl next to him. She was definitely attractive with her dark-purple hair and golden-yellow eyes.

She pulled at her dress, pulling the front up again and again. It was one of Aexie's dresses, but she didn't quite fit Aexie's reed-thin frame. Her chest threatened to spill out the top.

Alexius pulled her forward. "Brixelle, this is my brother, Xerus, and his partner, Xenon," he said, beaming at her the whole while.

"It's a pleasure," Xenon said, bending low over her hand so she wouldn't have to move.

I wiggled my fingers a bit and altered the bodice so it provided a bit more coverage.

She looked down as it happened and then caught my wiggling fingers. "I'm forever grateful, Your Highness," she said as she curtsied, obviously relaxing a bit more as she didn't have to make sure she was spilling out somewhere.

"Grateful for what?" Alexius asked.

Brixelle leaned in and whispered in Alexius's ear.

"Oh. If it was bothering you, I could have done that too." He pouted.

I rolled my eyes. My brother still had so much to learn.

I caught Xenon shortening the hem of the dress so it wouldn't drag on the floor, and I grinned at him. Suddenly, the dress that Brixelle had crammed herself into fit beautifully.

"We outsiders have to stick together," Xenon leaned forward to whisper loudly to Brixelle.

She smiled at him. "You honor me, sir. Thank you."

Brixelle couldn't see everything Xenon had changed, but the dress definitely was more flattering.

Jaxon stomped into the room. When I caught his eye, he stopped, took a deep breath in and out, and came over, schooling his face into a friendlier version of his previous scowl.

"Jax! This is Brixelle. Brix, this is my other brother, Jaxon."

She curtsied and it looked very elegant in her newly altered dress. "It's an honor to meet our land's most famed defender, Your Highness," she said.

Jax actually smiled at the compliment. "It's an equal honor to meet the dragonette who captured my brother's heart." He bowed low over her hand and kissed it.

She glowed a little and I grinned. Jaxon was a true charmer when he wanted to be. Alexius glanced from Jax to Brixelle and tucked her hand into the crook of his arm. "Shall we sit?" he asked, pulling her away from Jax. I pressed my lips together in my attempt to hold in a laugh. I hoped I'd never been that obvious.

*You were,* Xenon said in my head.

I swatted his arm before we took our seats.

# CHAPTER TWENTY
## AEXIE

I ROLLED MY EYES at Xerus and Xenon. They were such an adorable couple, it raised bile in my throat. Xerus was still a control freak, but somehow, Xenon softened him. We all knew he was the only one who wouldn't suffer the repercussions if he teased Xerus.

Xerus had mentioned soxkendi tomorrow morning, and I wasn't surprised by it. My guess was Alexius's new romance was the subject. Alexius had wandered around looking stunned at first. Then, after they'd taken their places, he held Brixelle's hand under the table as if trying to keep it a secret. I wanted to roll my eyes again. But I knew my mother was watching us and wanted us to be on our best behavior. If I did it a second time, I'd get in trouble.

Part of me wanted to ask Alexius how he had found his mate, how he could be so sure. Part of me also wondered whether Brixelle was authentic. I watched her carefully, though she'd be wary of all the eyes here. Who wouldn't want to be bonded to a prince? Alexius was inexperienced with courtship and seeing the games people could play, games I liked to play. He'd have been an easy target.

A guard standing by the door behind Alexius caught my eye. He stared straight at me, a lascivious grin on his face. I winked at him. Maybe I would have some entertainment tonight after all.

I looked away and set my sights on Jax. He was in a mood. He sat there, brows furrowed and not looking at anyone, just staring into space as if searching through his own memories to find one particular thing. Then again, he was always a little short-tempered when Xenon was here, and I supposed if Alexius had really found his mate, Jax would be even more jealous.

*It really is too bad*, I thought as I sat back, making sure my bodice fell lower for the guard I knew was watching as I bit my lower lip in contemplation. I glanced quickly at the guard from the corner of my eye and saw his Adam's apple bob. I crossed my legs, wondering whether my parents would interfere with Alexius's wishes. We hadn't known anything of Brixelle before the other day.

Suddenly, a side door burst open and a guard hurried over to my parents. He leaned over between my mother and father, while the rest of us snapped to attention. My siblings and I stared at the griffin's lips, carefully lip-reading.

A baku? They hadn't been seen in a very long time.

*What's a baku?* Alexius suddenly asked in our soxkendi mind room.

*It's a creature with the paws of a tiger, body of a horse, head of a lion, trunk and tusks of an elephant, and the tail of a snake. Here, I'll show you.* Xerus created a picture in his mind, and it looked like a very strange creature indeed.

*They are holy creatures. Almost as pure as unicorns but not as showy. They tend to keep to themselves but usually bring warnings and ward off evil. It's said that their presence alone has warded off wars,* Jaxon explained.

*And what would it be doing here?* I asked.

*Looks like there's going to be a meeting as soon as dinner's finished,* Alexius said. He had the best view of the griffin's lips.

The guard straightened and my parents did as well, the rest of us trying to look innocent as we continued with dinner. I looked over at the guard who'd been giving me the eye only to see that he now wore a serious expression and was no longer paying me any attention. Shame. Those biceps would have been fun to play with again.

My mother smiled, careful not to show her concern as she continued honoring the dinner guests she'd invited from across the kingdom to introduce Xerus and Xenon. Even Alexius seemed distracted as he whispered with Brixelle. I listened in but he didn't mention anything of the baku. They spoke mostly about the rest of us. Brixelle was asking questions about us in what I assumed was the hope of gaining our favor. If she wasn't an idiot, she'd have realized how close we are as a family and known that we would stand in her way if we thought we needed to.

The rest of dinner felt like it passed excruciatingly slowly, but it finally came to an end. My mother and Alexius walked our guests out, and the rest of us rose as one. Xenon hadn't been filled in, and he sat in his chair, momentarily puzzled as to why we would all move in synchronicity. "You need to work on your subtlety. I don't know what's going on, but it wasn't subtle," he said.

I shot him a pointed look as Jaxon did the same.

"All right, I get it now. I'm going to go look for a book in the library if anyone needs me," he said as he raised his palms in the air in surrender and made his own exit.

When he was gone, my father spoke up. "I suppose you know what's going on?"

"Going on, no. But we know there's a baku in the palace, and you and Mother are planning to meet with them," I said.

My father let out a breath and his shoulders slumped. "I suppose it's time you met Katsuro. I think I've taught you too well, children." He shook his head as if defeated. Then he led the way out of the dining room, and we followed him to one of the sitting rooms off the main hallway. It was already brightly lit, but I was surprised to see the pink-and-gold room devoid of guests. For the most part, we usually used this room for small concerts or greeting our most honored guests. The fact that no one had been in here when we'd arrived meant that my parents held Katsuro in such high esteem that they would be the last to enter.

I sat on the couch, on the end nearest the window. I'd have my siblings at my back that way, and I'd be able to see our guest from head to toe when he entered. Jaxon stood by the window, hands behind his back like a guard, and Xerus stood by the piano forte. Knowing him, he'd sit on the stool just at the edge of the conversation.

The door creaked and I jumped. Mother and Alexius entered, and my mother threw her hands up. "Of course you're all here," she said.

"I think we taught them to pay attention to details a little too well, darling." My father took my mother's hand and led her to the other end of my couch. Alexius sat between us, and Father sat down in the chair adjacent to Mother, leaving the chair across from her empty.

Interesting. So the baku was here to see my mother.

We sat in silence for a few minutes before there was a knock on the door and a guard opened it. We all rose, and I was surprised to see a man enter, a man with dark-blue skin. He wore long silver robes, intricately embroidered with dark-silver images, and his hair was a little wild, reminiscent of a lion's mane, but light blue like the sky on a bright and sunny day. I was surprised to see his eyelashes and eyebrows matched his hair, and while his pupils were black, the irises were light silver like a star twinkling in the sky. He was stunning. I continued to examine the small nose set in his wide face and the sharp chin contrasting his tall, slender body. His entire profile shouldn't have been pleasing to the eye, but it was.

"Katsuro." My mother smiled. She sounded truly happy to see him. Faster than my eyes could follow, he was before my mother and holding her hands. "Ellie." He embraced my mother, and I saw my father's jaw clench. This was getting very interesting very quickly.

He pulled away and turned to my father. "Rixen." When my father stuck out his hand, Katsuro moved instead to hug him as well.

"Katsuro, it has been a long time. Allow me to introduce our children." My mother turned and Katsuro rose, releasing my father. "My eldest, Xerus."

Katsuro enveloped him in a hug as soon as my mother gestured in his direction. Xerus looked stunned at the affection and physical contact. "I remember meeting you as a little dragon. Couldn't change into human form or anything yet." Katsuro smiled and laughed. "Ahh ... you are finally with Xenon. I will have to say hello to him a little later."

"And Jaxon," my father continued. Katsuro whipped over to Jax so suddenly I don't think any of us actually saw him do it. He pulled Jax too into a long hug. My brother looked incredibly uncomfortable but didn't move, probably because he was too polite.

"My daughter, Aexie," my mother continued. And then Katsuro was suddenly in front of me. He took both my hands and bowed low to kiss them. His eyes twinkled with mirth as he smiled at me as if he and I shared a private a joke.

"And our youngest, Alexius," my mother said. Katsuro popped over to Alexius and wrapped him up in a hug too. *Wait*, I thought, *I'm the only one who doesn't merit a hug?* Not that I wanted one, of course.

Then suddenly, he was at his own chair, tossing his coat tails out behind him as he sat down. "You'll have to excuse my rapid movements. It's been a while since I've taken my human form. It takes some getting used to."

*That was weird*, Jaxon said through our sibling bond. Katsuro turned to Jaxon, still smiling. Could he hear our thoughts?

"How were your travels, Kat?" my mother asked. For them to be using their first names, especially shortened versions, meant they were close. I'd never known my mother to use an abbreviated name outside of family. She must have known him a long time.

"Oh, Ellie." The odd man giggled as he bounced his feet on the ground. "They were marvelous. I saw so many interesting beings, so many interesting things."

"That's wonderful!" my mother said.

Had the man called my mother Ellie? Twice now? No one had ever been that casual with my mother—ever.

"Your children are beautiful, Ellie. They are important too. I wish I could say one more than the others, but ... well, just wait 'til you see all their adventures!" He looked at Alexius.

My mother looked surprised as she too turned to Alexius.

Katsuro suddenly sat still. "You should trust her," he told Alexius.

"Who?" Alexius said.

"Not her," he said as we all thought of Brixelle. "When your head doubts your heart, go with your heart." He sat incredibly still as he looked at Alexius. Then, shaking his head, Katsuro bounced up and down in his seat again.

My mother looked a little taken aback. She blinked to recover.

Suddenly, Katsuro was sitting on the low table in front of the couch, holding my mother's hands again. "I'm so very sorry about Danxing." I watched as a tear slid down his cheek.

My mother swallowed and I knew she was trying to keep it together.

"She is in a much happier place. And she dances around all of you. She hopes you'll forgive her for leaving early, and she asks her siblings to be nicer to Lexi."

I inhaled a sharp breath. Only Danx had called Alexius "Lexi."

"Thank you, Kat," my mother finally managed, taking a deep breath in and out.

"I should like to stay for a while, if that's all right with you," he said.

"Of course. As long as you like," my mother replied.

"Something strange is happening. Serpents are out of place, not in their right minds," he said as looked at Jax. "A shift in the royal family." He looked at Xerus.

Xerus and Jaxon suddenly looked both serious and confused.

"Ellie, may I bless your children?" Katsuro asked.

My mother nodded. "It would be an honor, Kat."

Again, he popped over to each of us and with his thumb, drew a cloud on our foreheads. He whispered something to each of my siblings, and when he got to me, he said, "Choose to be sweet, my dear one. No one likes a sour apple." He said it so quietly, I wondered if I'd misheard him.

When he finished, he zipped over to my mother again. He drew a cloud with his thumb on her forehead too. "Rest, my dear, Ellie. I will be here as long as you need me."

He jumped up. Everything was so sharp and sudden with him. "I shall bid you all a good night. I will see you tomorrow." He left, making the guard scramble to open the door for him.

The moment he was out of the room, I felt incredibly sleepy. I looked at my brothers and saw they were feeling what I felt.

"Get to your beds, children. We'll see you in the morning. And don't stop walking until you get to your bed," my father instructed. Mother had fallen asleep on the couch, and he went to scoop her up. I watched as he kissed my mother's forehead and gently carried her to their chambers. He stopped at the door and said something to the guards.

Before I knew it, there was a guard at each of our sides, gently guiding us to our rooms and our beds. Every step felt like I was trudging through mud. The guard at my side held my elbow, guiding me along. Eventually, it felt as if he was dragging me forward until finally, he ducked down impossibly fast and scooped me up as my father had done with my mother. I closed my eyes.

And I saw Danxing twirling on a cloud. I smiled and called out to her. She turned and smiled back, waving, then continued to dance to some imaginary song.

# CHAPTER TWENTY-ONE

## ALEXIUS

**M**Y MOTHER HAD SEEMED giddy after we'd seen our guests out of the palace that night. She had offered them all a ride home in one of our carriages, but they'd all politely refused. As she had bid the other guests farewell, Brixelle and I had made plans to see each other the next day. But as my mother and I had walked back into the palace, she had rushed ahead with unusual eagerness, clearly anticipating our meeting with the baku.

It had been a surreal experience to see someone move so quickly. I'd seen only a blur as the baku had moved from person to person. He'd said, "Learn as much as you can, little one," as he'd drawn a cloud on my forehead. Then I'd heard my father mumble something about trying to get us all to bed, but my eyelids had felt so heavy, I couldn't be sure I'd heard correctly.

I woke this morning feeling more refreshed than I had in years and went straight to the library to find what I could about baku. I wondered if they were all like Katsuro or if Katsuro was particularly strange.

I pulled out two books from the shelves as they appeared and brought them to the table. By the sounds of it, everyone was still asleep. I loved the quiet of an early morning in the library, so I sat and opened the books, learning what I could about baku.

"I'd be happy to answer your questions." A voice behind me made me jump.

I darted up. "I'm sorry. I didn't ... I didn't mean any offense. I've never even heard of your kind." Why was I being more honest than I had intended?

Katsuro went and sat on the couch, elegantly resting his legs on the chaise and reclining like he'd be fed grapes any moment. At least this time he hadn't just appeared there.

"No offense taken. You won't find much in those books about my kind anyway. We're pretty secretive. But for Ellie's little dragon, I'll answer any question," he said, pretending to eat grapes he plucked from the air beside him.

"Do you all look alike?" I asked.

"Baku come in six different colors, depending on your family line: blue, violet, green, yellow, orange, and red. We are creatures of the sky. Starlight lights our eyes. It would be difficult for you to look upon an orange, yellow, or red baku as they are modeled after the sun and therefore very bright."

"Do all baku have your gifts?" I asked.

He smiled at that, halting his fake grape feast. "And what gifts do you think I possess?"

"Foretelling the future? Some kind of sleep inducement, swiftness." I stopped there. I needed more time to think of the others.

"Baku were made to bring good dreams to others. I blessed your family so you may always sleep well and soundly with good dreams. You'll find you can accomplish a lot more after a good night's sleep. As for seeing the future, that is specific to blue bakus only. I see all the possibilities of the future. They interweave among each other like the fine threads of a fabric. I never know which will be the real future until it happens. But by then, it's not the future anymore." He giggled.

"And the swiftness?" I asked.

"Baku do not usually take human form. We usually travel in the sky, so the much smaller movements take some getting used to. They're so slow too. Humans move so slowly. Baku don't understand why dragons choose this form. I'd prefer a bird if I could choose, but I take human form for Ellie. For your family."

"How do you know my mother?"

Katsuro suddenly sat up and put his hands together in his lap, which was a very somber pose for him. "I am young for a baku. I knew your mother when she was a Wild One. We played together, we grew up together, and we became good friends ..." He drifted off into his thoughts. "Kat and Ellie were inseparable ... until they were separated," he said softly. I wondered what the extent of their relationship was—or had been.

"Baku, when they are a certain age, must take on their responsibilities to all creatures. We eat bad dreams. We bring good fortune.

We bring good luck. We eat bad. There are many creatures in all the worlds. Many bad dreams to eat. Many to bring good fortune to." He lay back down on the long chaise and stared at the ceiling, randomly plucking a piece of air in front of him and eating it.

If that was the explanation for how he knew my mother, then I supposed I ought to be grateful it made any sense to me since nothing else seemed to make sense about him. "What did you mean about what you told me yesterday?" I asked.

"It was clear, no? You're going to meet someone very important. She who will save us all. She will need your guidance. You will be her friend and teacher, so you need to learn everything you can now to help her help save us."

"Who? And what do we need saving from?" I asked.

"That is not for me to tell. I cannot set you on the strand of your destiny. Only you can choose which path to take. But on all paths, she is absolute," he said in a near whisper.

The library door opened then, and Xenon came in. "Oh, my apologies. Am I interrupting anything?" He looked at me, and I shook my head. He turned to the baku. "The great and honorable Katsuro. It is my deepest honor to see you again," Xenon said as he approached him.

Kat jumped up and met Xenon halfway before hugging him, making me wonder whether all baku were as big on physical contact as Katsuro. "It is my honor, Xenon. I am glad you have found your mate," he said.

"As am I."

"Come. Let us take a corner and catch up on all life's happenings." Katsuro led Xenon to a corner of the library, and they conversed in hushed whispers.

I was glad to have the knowledge that Katsuro had so openly shared with me, but I wasn't about to trust it completely. I opened my books, scanning for information on the baku.

A few hours later, I had not found much more on baku except to confirm they existed in different colors. I wondered whether I ought to record the information Katsuro had given me for future knowledge seekers, but then my brothers and Aexie came in and Xenon and Katsuro rose to greet them.

Xenon raised a hand. "Don't even start. We'll leave." Then he turned to the baku. "Come on, Katsuro. They're having a special sibling meeting," Xenon said, then asked, "Are you hungry? They have the best porridge here."

"Ohh ... soxkendi!" Katsuro exclaimed, giggling and clapping his hands together. "What a pleasure to see it in real life!" He leapt up in excitement, somehow clapping his hands and feet together before landing.

The old dragon and the baku crossed the room then and left with a nod, closing the door behind them.

The rest of us sat down around the ring of cushions in the middle, the bookshelf in the middle disappearing for now.

"Jax, why don't you start?" Xerus asked.

"Have you all read the report?" Jax looked around. We all nodded. "What I couldn't say in the report was what it felt like. Things don't add up. All the griffins got out safely, which means they had enough time to evacuate. And I saw that thing spew acid. Death would have been instantaneous. So, they must have had some kind of early warning. And then there's the serpent itself. Why was it so far away from the ocean? The poor thing clearly wasn't in its right mind either. We couldn't risk entering its consciousness, but it didn't act like a sentient being. It was as if it couldn't control its own movements, like it just thrashed for no reason. It just thrashed and thrashed without stopping, without even pausing to catch its breath. It used up its entire life force. Why didn't it siphon magic from the environment around it instead of acting as though it was being controlled?"

"What are you saying, Jax?" Aexie asked.

"There's something else going on. It's like that was just a demonstration. Or a distraction. I was sure I'd get a report from one of you saying the palace was under attack or something. It just felt odd," he said.

"Do you think the serpent could have gone crazy?" I asked. I had read books about potions that drove creatures mad.

"Yes and no? The hole in the river was very precise. The serpent came out of it and approached the village, then thrashed around spewing acid without reason. The goal was obviously destruction, but the serpent didn't destroy anything outside the village. It just destroyed the village, then stopped and moved on to the next one. And it did so several times. Seven griffin villages were reduced to rubble."

I looked at Xerus's serious expression. Jax's forehead crinkled and Aexie stared out the window.

"You think it will happen again," Aexie said.

"Maybe not the same way or with the same creature. But yes. I think it was a test. I think it was meant to get our attention or test something. I'm just not sure what or why," Jax said.

"I'll alert the auxiliary groups. Maybe we should put a magical detection barrier up around the villages. Or should we focus on those closest to the river?" Xerus asked.

"My gut is telling me it might not be a sea serpent next time," Jax said.

"All the villages it is then." Xerus nodded and wrote himself a note. "Now. Our next order of business," Xerus said, looking at me.

*Uh oh*, I thought. *What now?*

"Alexius, we all felt what you felt with Brixelle. Besides the fact you need to work on maintaining your shielding," He paused to let that sink in. "How much do you really know about her?"

I suddenly felt defensive and pressed my lips together to prevent myself from saying something I would regret. "I know she's a farmer. She cares for sheep and grows hay to feed them. Her mother was sick with a black sludge that coated her lungs, I removed it, and it made her better," I finally said.

Jaxon chimed in. "We're not trying to attack you, Alexius. We just want to know what you feel for her, besides your emotional flare-ups."

I took a deep breath, looking at my hands as I answered my brothers. "I'm not sure. I think I love her. I think she's my bonded mate. But I recognize I don't have any experience in this, so I hesitate to do anything drastic."

"Good," Xerus said.

"How about you, Xerus? How do you feel about the upcoming ceremony?" Aexie asked, turning the attention thankfully away from me.

Xerus sat up, surprised, but then paused to think about the question seriously. "I'm not sure how I feel about the grandness Mother's turning it into. But Xenon is flashy at even his most subtle, so I suppose it makes sense.

"Have you spoken to him about what role he'll play in the monarchy?" Jax asked.

Xerus nodded. "He said it's up to me. But he'd prefer to stay out of most royal affairs and leave it to me. He'd prefer to be prince."

I nodded. I had been ready to accept Xenon taking on royal duties. I mean, he'd been a part of our lives for so long, it just seemed natural.

"Is that what you want?" Aexie asked.

"Yes. I think so. I would have welcomed someone else to take most of the attention away from me, but I'll have all of you to help me. And it'll make decisions less complicated if we don't add another person."

I was quiet. I understood what Xerus was saying. Everything was all his responsibility, and a small part of him wanted someone else to help carry the load. I'd never envied his position, knowing that in the wake of grief over our parents, he would have to take on the responsibilities of the crown. We served our people, and Xerus had always been learning as much as he could to be able to do it well. But still, it was a lot to give up your life for the sake of the realm.

"Of course we'll be here to help you," Jaxon said.

Xerus nodded.

"I—" I started to say. All my siblings turned their attention to me. "Xerus, Xenon told me that he knew the moment he'd met you, even as a dragonling, that you were his mate. But when did you know he was yours?" I asked.

Xerus smiled. "I'm told it's different for everyone. But for me, I feel a glowing warmth when he's near. And when he's away, I feel a seeping cold darkness, like my insides are wrapped in darkness and it squeezes. But when he's near, it's like ... well, comfort and hearth warmth and wind under your wings when you're flying, that same heart-expanding feeling."

"You didn't answer his question," Jaxon interrupted. "When did you know?"

"The summer celebration after Alexius was hatched. I was testing my fire breathing with Jax by the rock faces, and Xenon walked by with one of The Four. And it was like my whole world shifted in his direction. I kept trying not to look at him. Which, of course, was partly because he is literally gold and silver, but also partly because Xenon is a lot older than me. I knew even then that our age difference could be construed as wrong when I was still so young, and all the friends he was with that day were a good deal older than me too.

"But it was like I always knew where he was. He continued walking the perimeter of the festivities with this creature or that, and I always knew where he was without looking. It was like an inner beacon had awakened in me. That night, we found ourselves on the edge of the crowd, and he grasped my hand and pulled me into the forest. I knew I shouldn't go—as the heir to the throne, to be alone with a much older dragon who could kill me off in an instant was not wise, especially in my newly practiced human form—but it was like I didn't have a say. My feet just followed. In the woods, he kissed me, and it was like an elastic band snapped into place."

I swallowed. That's exactly how I'd felt when I kissed Brixelle the other day. I wondered if that was love or if that was truly the drag-on-mating bond being cemented.

"Like an elastic?" Aexie asked, sounding surprised.

Xerus nodded. "Yes, as if it had been there all along and suddenly I just realized it."

Jaxon sighed and a faraway look crossed his face. I tried not to look at him because he'd probably beat me to a pulp in our next training session if I added my thoughts now that I'd experienced it.

"It's exciting when you're in love, but I can't say I've ever felt an elastic snapping into place," Aexie said.

Well, that answered my question. What I felt for Brixelle was real. It *was* the bond.

Xerus looked pointedly at me. "We waited a few centuries before he took the blood oath."

"I get it, don't take the blood oath anytime soon," I said as I thought about Brixelle.

"Or ever," Aexie added. "Mother and Father are bonded, but they haven't done that."

"Just remember, you can't take it back," Xerus said, turning his head to look wistfully out the window.

"I know. I'll let you all know when and if I ever think of doing that," I said.

"Promise?" Aexie asked as she looked at Xerus and then back at me.

"Yes. I promise." I don't know if I could ever oath myself to someone. To tie your life with theirs was a deep commitment to someone who might not be as skilled or careful as you are with your own life—no matter how much you love them.

"Now, since we have a little time, you should practice shielding," Jaxon said, finally snapping out of his reverie.

I nodded and closed my eyes. I felt someone poke my eyes and jerked back.

"Never with your eyes closed," Aexie said. "How will you see anything coming?"

So I kept my eyes open this time and brought up my shield in my mind. I envisioned the light of my magic filling the spaces around the door of the room my siblings and I shared in our minds.

Next, I felt Aexie's green light shining at my door. She looked at me with her eyebrow quirked and her head tilted. The green light was looking for a crack in my own light, any spot I hadn't filled. I felt Xerus's blue light shining like a laser, trying to penetrate the wall I had erected with my magic.

Suddenly, I felt Jax's orange light hammer at my light as it thumped on the edge of my magic, trying to gain access. Though it felt like I was being ganged up on, Xerus was calmly reading a book as he continued to poke my mind with his sharpened magic, Jaxon was doing push-ups on the floor as he tapped the edges of my magic, and Aexie was reclined, examining her nails as she mentally blasted me with her green light.

"Better," Xerus said as he flipped a page.

I tried to set up a channel to indefinitely feed magic into my door, then picked up a book like Xerus had. Orange and red reached into a crack momentarily as I tried to focus on the book's text. Then it began to weaken at the top. Xerus's blue light needled in during that millisecond, and I slammed the wall back up, using my own light to blast his out.

"That's probably good for now," Xerus said. "I'm going to start testing you throughout the day though. You need to be able to hold those barriers up for lengthy periods."

I nodded.

"Good. Let's go train," Jaxon ordered. "Everyone to the training area. Xenon showed me a few new things, and I want to test them out on you."

"Which one of us?" Aexie asked, cringing a bit.

"All three of you at the same time," Jaxon said.

My groan matched Aexie's as we trudged out of the library and toward the training area.

# CHAPTER TWENTY-TWO

## AEXIE

I WAS QUICK TO shower after training. Alexius had mentioned that Brixelle was meeting him later in the afternoon, so I wanted to catch her by surprise this morning.

I flew the long way around to her farm, flying by the closest tavern and taking note of its location. If Brixelle was going to see my brother this afternoon, then I would go to the tavern and listen to the latest gossip. At best, I'd learn some secrets about Brixelle after my surprise visit. At worse, I'd eat some tavern food, have a glass or two of wine, and head home. That led me to wonder whether my handsome guard would be on duty tonight and if I'd be back at the palace in time to summon him to my chambers.

I shook off that delightful thought and focused on the business at hand. I wanted to surprise Brixelle to see how she handled it and the interruption of her work in hopes of learning more about her personality. However, being the sparkling emerald-green dragon that I am, I was afforded only so much subtlety. I was only a farm or two into the countryside when farmers began to look up at my glittering green form. At least I could fly faster than word could spread.

I landed in the grass next to a simple stone hut, dragon-sized but on the small side. It was no larger than half the size of our stable. The hut's entrance was packed dirt, so some was still muddy from the previous night's rain.

"Princess Aexie, how may I be of assistance?" The older lavender dragon curtsied low as she came out of the stone hut, then wiped her claws on her massive apron. It wasn't common for dragons to wear clothing while in dragon form, so it was a strange sight to see a giant pink apron covering the bottom half of a dragon. "Strange, I know. But I'm making pies today, and its nice to have a towel on me to wipe my claws on. I'm a messy cook." She leaned in and lowered her voice like it was a secret as she said the last bit.

I couldn't think of anything nice to say, so I just smiled and nodded. "I assume you're here to see Brixelle? She's the only one who attracts royalty lately."

I decided to change tactics. "Actually, would you like a spare pair of claws? I wouldn't mind learning how to make pie." I swallowed my discomfort at thinking about how dirty I might get, how dirty my nails would get.

"Oh? Well, absolutely. Come on in," Roxana said.

I followed the older dragon into the stone hut, noticing the worn rug, the edges patched and frayed. In place of a front door, the inner walls were situated to create two turns, one to the left and one to the right, to protect the hut from the elements. Once in the main room, I took in the sparse furnishings: a great stone table in the middle with long stone benches along each side tucked under the table's edge and a fireplace to the left with an overhanging hook. A pot of what smelled like stew swung from the hook over the fire. Roxana tossed another log onto it as I turned my attention to three stone ovens beside the fire. The oven doors were no more than flat rocks balancing on ledges.

Everything was simple but well-used and well-worn. I wondered whether Alexius had even taken note of these things when he had been here. If he had, he probably would have insisted on helping them with some improvements instead of leaving them to live in squalor.

"You can put yourself to use by kneading that dough on the table for me," Roxana instructed. She turned her back to pull out and stir the pot of stew. She tasted it, then thought a minute with her claw on her hip before taking something out of a jar on the shelf and sprinkling it in.

I walked up to the dough. I had kneaded dough in the palace kitchens before, and I actually found it relaxing. The kitchen staff weren't very talkative, so I often went there to be left alone and let my body work as I thought.

So I jumped in and started kneading the dough without hesitation before looking up to see Roxana's surprised face. "You'll forgive me for saying that I'm impressed," she said. She grabbed some apples and used her claws to peel and dice them. They looked tiny in her claws, and I wondered whether she would get anything out of them.

"What are you making?" I asked.

"Apple pie."

"A pie with just apples?" I asked.

"Yes, with sugar and sour berry juice."

"Why would you want that? Is there also sheep in it?" I asked.

"I learned this recipe for apple pie long ago. It's sweet tasting and good for after a sheep stew or sheep pie."

To eat something sweet after the sheep? That seemed strange, but I was taught not to be rude, so I just nodded.

"You'll see. We're making some to bring to your family."

I quirked an eyebrow. "Oh?"

"Brixelle's idea. She's very fond of your family and was hoping they would like it," she said, turning her attention to the pile of apples she was peeling and chopping in practically one motion. She'd done this many times before apparently.

"What was Brixelle like as a child?" I asked, hopefully sneaking in my true goal.

Roxana smiled. "She was a serious child. She'd always follow her father around the farm, trying to lift things that were too heavy. One time, when she was a youngling, she even dragged a bag of feed halfway across the field before her father got there. She learned to feed all the sheep on her own by the time she was just three decades old."

"What happened to her father?" I knew it was bold and perhaps a little rude, but there were no signs of a male dragon in the hut, and he would have been at our dinner last night if he were still part of this family.

"'Bout a century ago, he died in his sleep. Farming ain't an easy job, and it took its toll on Brix's daddy. He'd been feeling extra tired around then, and Brixelle was running most of the farm already. But we went to bed one night, and when I woke up the next morning, her daddy was gone." Her claws stilled over the pile of apples. "Brixelle was always daddy's little dragonette, and she was devastated. It took a few decades before she could even look at a picture of him again without bursting into tears."

"I'm sorry," I said. I couldn't help but think of Danxing. I still cried when I stared at her picture too long, and I was surprised Roxana wasn't shedding a few tears still for her husband. But then I looked up to see her looking at the corner of the hut. I followed her gaze and saw a tiny painting of a handsome dark-blue dragon on a tiny shelf.

"Brixelle painted that one when she was about a century old, back when she had time to do such things," she said, turning back to the apples.

I kneaded the dough one last time and felt its gluten pronounce its readiness. "I think the dough is done," I said.

She came over, sticking a claw into the dough. "You've quite a feel for dough," she said before gently taking hold of the dough and separating it into several balls. "You know how to roll a crust?"

I nodded. She returned to the apples again and I began rolling out each ball of dough into flat disks. "Has Brixelle had many ... um ... suitors?" I asked, not sure what the right word was.

"There were a couple dragons that had a way of always being around, but I don't think she returned their sentiment. She's been focused on this farm her whole life. Well, that is until your brother came by."

"Mama, who are you talking to in here?" The dragonette herself came around the bend in the wall.

"Oh my! I'm so sorry, Your Highness. I didn't know. Mama, you should have told me." Brixelle glowed from embarrassment.

"Don't worry about it, Brixelle. I was happy to come help. I find working with dough ... well, relaxing." I did my best to put her at ease so she wouldn't put her defenses up.

She smiled at that.

I had noticed that Brixelle always wore her emotions on her face. She was quick to feel things, and it always showed, seemingly whether she wanted it to or not.

"You better stay for supper, missy. This one," Roxana pointed at Brixelle with a claw. "is leaving me for that brother of yours. Keep an old dragon company, would you?"

"Mama, I'm sure Princess Aexie is busy," Brixelle said.

"That's fine. It'd be my pleasure," I said. This old purple dragon's presence was strangely comforting.

"Are you sure? You don't have to. She's really good at guilting others into doing what she wants them to. I won't be here and that's my fault, not yours," Brixelle said.

"Still, it would be my honor," I insisted.

"Your mother sure taught you well. Both you and Alexius have the most outstanding manners," Roxana said.

"My mother would be pleased to hear it," I said.

Brixelle strode down a hallway and disappeared into a bedroom then, presumably to bathe and change, and I continued rolling out crusts. My whole body was covered in flour, and I supposed it was better that I didn't go back to the palace for supper. I'd just have to bathe again, and my scales had been feeling dry of late already.

*I'll be out for supper. Be back before bed,* I sent to my brothers.

A knock on the wall startled both me and Roxana as we'd been focused on the rhythm of our work.

"Come on in, Your Highness!" Roxana called out.

I had to think quickly. Alexius would wonder what I was doing here.

Alexius turned the corner, and I was surprised at how clean and shiny he looked. I wondered if he'd borrowed some of Xerus's special oil to shine his scales. I contained my smirk as he recovered from his surprise at finding me here.

"Aexie. What are you doing here? I thought you were with your ... friends," he said. He clearly didn't want to offend Roxana with the word "lovers."

"I'm making pie. Can't you see that?" I asked as I rolled another crust out.

His eyes narrowed, but he couldn't say what he really wanted to out loud. *What are you doing here, Aexie?* he said in our minds instead.

*Making pie. I already said that. Getting to know Roxana and Brixelle.*

*I can take care of myself you know.* But out loud he said, "Is Brixelle around?"

"She's just getting ready. She'll be out any time now. I'd get you to roll crust out too, but I don't want you to get covered in flour. Besides, your sister is doing a marvelous job."

*Don't ruin this for me,* he warned me.

*I don't intend to ruin anything for anyone,* I retorted, straightening my shoulders.

Brixelle came out then, just in time I thought. She looked beautiful and radiant, even glowing a bit.

"You sure it's okay?" she asked me again.

I nodded, smiling a friendly smile to reassure her.

"It's okay to what?" Alexius asked.

"None of your business," Brixelle said.

Okay, I liked her a little more now.

"Mama, I'll see you later tonight," she said, taking Alexius by the claw and leading him out. "See ya later, Princess Aexie," she said.

I liked her more and more as I got to know her. She could hold her own against royalty. That was something. And she bossed Alexius around. Even better.

"Yes, she's always been that bossy," Roxana said.

After a dinner of sheep's stew and after finishing the apple pies, which Roxana wouldn't let me sample because she wanted to present them to the royal family and have us share the experience of eating the pies for the first time together, I said my goodbyes and flew to the tavern I'd seen nearby. As I flew, I thought, *Huh. Roxana and Brixelle seemed to be a down-to-earth family. Strong dragonettes. Not what I'd expected.*

When I landed, I changed into my human form but went invisible to better observe without being observed. I waited by the door until someone opened it, then slid in as it was closing again. This tavern was clearly for smaller shapes only. Everything was human-sized, and besides a few strange faces and oddly shaped creatures, it looked similar to many taverns I'd visited before. I slowly made my way to an open window in case I needed a quick escape and sat still, invisible to the tavern's patrons.

I couldn't help but tap my foot on the floor as I waited. This tavern was far more boring than the ones I'd visited in the past. It was full of old farmers discussing the weather and their crops. The most exciting thing they mentioned was whether they could risk squeezing in another crop before the end of the season. I wanted to scrape my ear drums with my nails just for variety.

I was tempted to leave, maybe go back to the palace to see whether my guard was finally off duty, when I heard someone mention dragonsbane. That perked me up. A group of human-looking creatures at a table two over from me sat crouched together.

"Did you hear Dex's place was robbed?"

"Why didn't he report the robbery?"

"He was growing dragonsbane on the side. Didn't want them to slap him with penalties."

"How much did he have?" I was glad the curious farmer was asking my questions for me.

"Forty plants. They took 'em *all*." The man was definitely enjoying the attention.

Forty plants was double what had been taken from the farms we knew of. I continued to listen carefully, hoping to learn what stage the plants had been in when they had been stolen, but the men moved on to another topic. This was quickly becoming my favorite group of farmers, especially when their next topic was my real reason for being there.

"Did you hear Brix snared a princeling?" the curious farmer asked.

The dragonsbane storyteller scoffed, clearly not pleased to have the attention taken away from him. "I heard something like that. Didn't think it was true. Brix giving up farming and becoming a princess? No way. She's a farmer through and through. I give it a year and she's back to her sheep."

"I dunno. I saw them together when I was helping Len in his fields. They looked like the real deal."

"What's a prince want with a farmer anyway?" a younger farmer said, looking grumpy.

"Just because she turned you down, don't mean she'll turn a prince down. He's a prince after all."

"She wouldn't have to lift a finger again. No more manure piles, burning under the sun, working until it's dark and waking before it's light. I'd marry a prince for that," an older, wrinkled farmer quipped.

They knocked their mugs of ale together and guffawed. Then they moved on to the horrific topic of squeezing in another round of hay this year. I rolled my eyes and snuck out the window. I stayed invisible and made my way to an open space so I could take dragon form again and fly back to the palace. As I flew, I focused on staying invisible while in dragon form. It was particularly difficult because I was so much bigger, but I wanted to master invisibility. It was too useful not to.

I needed to tell my brothers about the dragonsbane plants, but I also wondered what to make of what I'd heard about Brixelle. She could be using my brother to live an easier life, though she'd be sorely mistaken. I too woke up while it was dark and went to bed after night fell, all the while entertaining and smiling and talking politics on top of the training we endured. Others thought we lived a life of luxury, and though I liked pretty things, there were strings attached to each and every gem. Maybe I'd ask Xerus or Xenon about what they thought of all I'd heard.

Landing at the palace, I went looking for Xerus and found him with Xenon and Jax in the library. Xenon was drinking copious amounts of a brown liquid, his book abandoned on the table, but Jax was putting in his reading time. Xerus was doing research of some kind.

"I have news," I said as I walked in in human shape.

"Where have you been? You're filthy," Xerus said.

I forgot that was I completely covered in flour and bits of apples. "Never mind that. I was at a tavern. Forty more dragonsbane plants are missing from an illegal operation."

Xerus and Jax looked stunned. Xenon made to get up.

"It's not like you won't hear it from Xerus. You might as well stay," I told him. I had thought to ask him to leave, but there was no way Xerus wouldn't tell him.

Xenon sat back down, settling back into his comfortable position.

"You're sure?" Xerus said.

I rolled my eyes but nodded. I eased into our shared mental space, closing Alexius's door, and showed them what I'd heard—including the part about Brixelle. Xerus's frown deepened.

"Should we tell Alexius? And Father?" Jaxon said. "About the dragonsbane obviously. But the part about Brixelle?"

"Ohh, now it's interesting. What did you hear about Brixelle?" Xenon asked as he propped his chin on his hand, his elbow on his knee.

It was clear Xerus was sharing the information with him since he froze for a second.

Was Xenon pouting? Whatever that look had been about, he came back to himself and said, "That's not terrible. Farmers gossip worst of all. Just show her what it's really like to be one of you. She'll be bored out of her mind in no time," Xenon said.

Xerus gave him a look that said, 'Like you are now?' making Xenon glance down.

"Trouble in paradise?" I asked as I pranced further into the room.

"Mother's been doing research, and she wants to mirror a human ceremony because she thinks it will be good for the public to see," Xerus said.

"What's wrong with the dragon one?" I asked.

Xenon answered before Xerus could. "She said it'd be too frightening for some folks."

"But we *are* dragons."

"Well, you should see the guest list. Maybe she's worried about space if everyone takes dragon form," Jaxon said. He was bouncing a ball from floor to ceiling and catching it as he read his book.

"Mom will kill you if you break something with that," I said.

"Then I won't break anything, will I?" Jaxon said, bouncing it again. He was in a mood still.

"Well, should we tell Alexius?" I asked.

"I think Xenon's right. If we show her what it's really like to be a royal, it would dissuade her from that path if her motive is a life of luxury," Xerus said, looking pointedly at me.

"Why are you looking at me like that?" Dread settled in my gut as he continued.

"You're a princess. You're the best one to show her what it's like," Xerus said.

"Xenon is the new addition. Why can't he show her?" I whined.

Xerus just raised his eyebrows, not willing to succumb to my childish whining.

"What's more important is the dragonsbane. We need to get to the bottom of this." Jax caught his ball then.

Xenon suddenly jumped to his feet, sweeping his coat to the side rather formally.

The door opened and my mother and Katsuro entered the library. "Children! Look at you reading. It warms my heart. Aexie, why are you so filthy?" she asked as she strode over to me.

Katsuro tilted his head to the side as he looked in my direction. He jumped up and down, letting go of my mother's arm. "Oh, I'm so excited for tomorrow. It will be soo yummy!" He clapped his hands together and looked out the window as if searching for something beyond.

"Would you like us to leave, Mother?" Xerus asked.

"No, no, we can join you, can't we?" she said. "Kat here was going to add to our library."

We all froze and stared at her. Mother's library was more precious to her than probably all of us put together. Only family was allowed in here, and I expected Xenon wouldn't have been if he weren't an old one and bound to Xerus. We knew it was magically maintained, but my mother had collected books from all parts of the world. Guests often strove to bring her an original she'd never read before, but for someone else to be allowed to magically access her library was new. It was frightening to realize just how much our mother trusted this baku.

Xenon got over the shock first. "Oh, that's interesting. What is he adding?"

"I'm not sure. I've left it to him to find the gaps," my mother replied.

I had to make sure my jaw hadn't dropped to the floor. To be given free rein to add whatever he liked to the library was ludicrous. Was my mother feeling all right?

Glancing at my brothers, I saw they were just as shocked. Xerus probably hid it best.

"Oh, I almost forgot!" Katsuro suddenly broke the tension in the room and ran out of the library.

"Mother, how well do you know Katsuro?" Jaxon asked.

Was my mother glowing? She didn't have a chance to answer as Katsuro burst back into the library with an armful of books.

"I brought these for you, Ellie," he said.

I didn't even need to look through our own collection to see whether we had them. I'd never even seen books like this. One was translucent like water, with a rainbow sparkle to it. Another looked like it was bound in gold plating. The rest looked as if they were bound by elements you might see in the sky.

"I had to improvise the binding at home. Sorry they're not like the others, Ellie," he said, carefully placing them on the table Xerus sat at.

My mother's eyes widened when she saw them. "Not at all, Kat. They're beautiful!" she exclaimed, gently taking each book and opening it, glancing at the content. "You honor us, Kat," she said.

"Save the blue one for Alexius. He'll want to read it," Kat said. I looked at the blue one, and it shifted colors like a sky. How was that even possible? I squinted to see if I could read the title. *History of Bakus.* I thought I'd like to read it too. Baku seemed like interesting creatures, though I wondered if Katsuro was the same as the others of his kind.

Katsuro then gently took the books, except for the blue one, and put them on the lone bookshelf in the middle of the room. After he stepped away, the bookshelf shone brightly, and the books disappeared. Katsuro put both his hands on the bookshelf and creased his brow. His eyes darted back and forth as if he was reading something incredibly fast.

My mother coughed. My brothers and I had all been staring at this fascinating man. Jaxon pretended to return to his book but glanced up between lines. Xerus went back to his research, but I could tell he was keeping an eye on Katsuro from his periphery. And I sat down. I hadn't gotten a book before Katsuro started doing his thing with the shelves, so I didn't have a book to read. I thought about grabbing that blue one that was supposed to be for Alexius, but Xerus was eyeing it already, so I knew better.

"Aexie, why don't you go clean up?" Mother suggested. She was probably worried I'd get flour on one of the couches.

I nodded, then curtsied in Katsuro's direction and my brothers', and Xenon nodded at me as I left the library. I went to my rooms, passing Alexius's and hearing giggling. I rolled my eyes. Did love make you stupid? Brixelle didn't strike me as a silly giggler.

But my attention was diverted as I neared my rooms. One of the guards at my door was my special guard. Maybe I *could* have some fun tonight. "I should like a guard inside my chambers. I will be opening the windows," I ordered, looking only at the handsome male guard and ignoring the female one. His jaw was chiseled like marble, and his wide shoulders stretched his uniform so I could see all the muscles of his chest.

He opened the door, nodded to his partner, and slipped in behind me. He stood at attention inside, then searched the rooms before returning to stand at the door. No guard would be stupid enough to shrug their duty, but it didn't mean I couldn't have a little fun of my own.

I went to my closet and sighed at all the pretty clothes. I slipped out of what I was wearing, leaving it on the floor, and pulled on a white silk robe—a short one that only went to mid-thigh. Tying it loosely, I exited the closet, passing my bed. I opened the window by my sitting area, bending over the table to push the windows open and letting the robe slide up in direct view of my guard. We may have had fun other times, but teasing him was one of my favorite parts.

I turned around to catch his Adam's apple bob again as he quickly averted his gaze.

"Darox, I shall be taking a bath," I said. He gulped. I walked past my sitting area to the bathing room. Everyone in my family was lucky enough to have a sunken tub. And I enjoyed mine way too much. There was already water in it, and I snapped my fingers to heat it to the temperature I preferred. I untied my silk robe and tossed it into the sitting room. Oops!

I slipped into the bath, watching as flour slipped off my body into the water. I floated there, letting my hair soak and the water take all the flour and butter and everything else off me. Then I decided I'd like to have longer hair and directed my magic to growing long, luscious, wavy emerald green hair.

Letting everything else slip away from my mind, I focused on the warmth in the water and my breathing. I enjoyed the heat so much, I barely noticed the time. Then I figured I had tempted Darox long enough, so I got out and wrapped a towel around me. I shimmered with the oils I'd added to the water. Longer hair was heavy, so I had to take extra time to comb it out before I left the bathing chambers. I used magic to dry it even though I wasn't supposed to because I was anxious to continue my fun. Besides, there was no way Xerus kept his hair as smooth and flat as it was naturally.

I popped into the sitting room and saw my guard still standing at the door. His eyes immediately went to my towel and then to my dripping feet. "Did I throw my robe over here?" I asked, playing stupid.

He coughed and dipped his head to indicate where the robe currently was.

"Thank you, Darox," I said as I tiptoed over to the robe, draping it over my shoulders and slipping my arms slowly into the sleeves one at a time. I turned my back to him and dropped the towel, stepping daintily out of the little circle it made. Then I tied the robe barely closed and bent over again to pick the towel up.

"Darox?" I asked, returning the towel to the bathing room.

"Yes, Your Highness," he said as he stared a hole through the window.

"Do you like my new hair?" I swung it from side to side, getting used to how it moved.

"It's very nice, Your Highness," he said, still staring at the window.

"Darox, when is your shift over?" I asked.

"In another hour, Your Highness," he said.

I pouted. "Hmm, what should I do for another hour then?" I asked out loud, taking a strand of my hair and twisting it around my fingers. His Adam's apple bobbed again. I sashayed up to him, keeping eye contact until I got to the door. I opened the other door and stuck my head out.

"When the guard changes, I won't need a guard stationed inside. I've closed the window," I told Trixie, the guard standing outside.

She winked at me and I winked back. "Have a good night, Your Highness," she said.

I closed the door, twisted the bolt, and eased slowly around Darox. I looked at the clock. Fifty-five minutes to go.

I sashayed back to the couch, picked up a book, and lay down in full view of Darox, my robe draped scandalously as I started to read to kill time.

# Chapter Twenty-Three

## Jaxon

I CLENCHED MY JAWS together as Darox squeezed out of Aexie's rooms and snuck down the hall toward the barracks. I smiled thinking of the torture I could inflict on him. Aexie could do what pleased her, but I liked to discourage the dragons who called on her. Or rather, the creatures that responded to her calls.

Ducking out the side door for my run, I nodded at the guards posted there. I'd never been interested in casual dalliances like Aexie. I just didn't understand. If they didn't mean anything, why have them at all?

I ran the last lap pushing myself harder than usual, anxious to get to the training ring. When I rounded the corner, I almost jumped back at the sight of a great blue snake hissing at me.

A *pop* sounded and after I blinked my shock away, Katsuro stood there in dark-blue track pants with the fanciest silver embroidery I'd ever seen on such casual pants.

"My deepest apologies, Prince Jaxon. I was hoping to stretch my legs in another form," he said, bowing.

"There's no need to apologize. It was just startling as I've never seen a baku in baku form before. You're welcome to take your true form here. This training space was made for big and small ones. But if you'd like to stretch your legs undisturbed, behind that rock wall over there is a large open area, if it pleases you," I said. I sounded strangely formal to my own ears, but the baku who commanded so much of my mother's respect intimidated me.

"Thank you. Perhaps I could come and train with you later this morning?"

"I would be honored," I said, bowing deeply.

Katsuro skipped in place. "We will have much fun! I will be back shortly," he said as he skipped off. After a soft *pop!* the enormous blue creature sailed through the sky past the rock face I had mentioned.

I blinked once and headed for the training ring. Most of the guards were just arriving and starting their laps, and they had all turned toward where the baku had flown off. "Back to it!" I shouted out. They all turned back to their tasks with an extra burst of energy.

I spotted Darox in the back of the pack, lagging behind. *I'll task him with training the newest recruits on top of his regular duties*, I thought. Then he'd be too tired to do anything but sleep for the next few months.

"Prince Jaxon, would you like to start now?" Katsuro said from behind me.

I jumped again. He was quieter than a mouse. "Of course," I said, remembering now how quickly he had moved the other night. I wondered whether the rest of us seemed to move slowly for him.

"Today, we shall fight in our human form, yes?" he asked. Katsuro was very still, like he wasn't even breathing. Then he rotated his head to take in the surroundings.

"Whatever you think would be best," I said.

"Good." He looked around at the practice weapons, squinting as he looked at the long oaken bo staffs.

"What do you think we should use?" I asked heading toward the bo staffs.

"Nothing for now," he said. "Is this where you want to practice?" He indicated the sandy ring we stood in.

"Yes," I said.

"I will add a layer of softness to this. You will need it," he said.

I had to admit that bruised my ego a little. I was the best fighter in the realm. I didn't think I'd be bested all that quickly or often. I shook my head. But then, if he had a lot to teach me, I should be grateful for it.

Katsuro snapped his fingers and suddenly I found myself wearing an orange gi, a heavy canvas jacket with thick trim that crossed my naked chest, canvas trousers, and a simple silver belt knotted neatly around my waist. I'd heard of gis but had never seen one in real life.

"I have folded your clothes and left them in a pile over there." He pointed. "This is the uniform that we will practice in." He himself wore a dark-blue gi with silver stitching.

I wasn't sure what to do, so I readied my stance, standing tall with my legs apart and knees bent, hands up so I was ready to block whatever came my way.

"I will move slowly so you can see what I do," he said.

I nodded.

Instead of aiming a fist at me, he swung an open hand in my direction to grab the collar of my gi with one hand and my sleeve with his other hand. Then he spun around, and before I knew it, I was staring at the sky. That landing had definitely been softer than it would have been on sand, and I was now appreciative.

I stood up. "Again, please."

This time, I paid closer attention as he came at me. As he'd thrown the one hand toward me, I had moved to block, but he'd used my own momentum against me and simply twisted and guided my body to the ground. Genius.

"The style I will teach you first uses momentum against you. You are a strong opponent, but you will, in your lifetime, encounter someone stronger, or you will be tired. This uses minimum effort for maximum effect. The goal is to get your opponent on the ground on their back or pin them so they must submit or you can easily deliver killing blows."

I got up and realized that the guards had all stopped what they were doing and were circling the ring, watching carefully. Some looked stunned. I noted that Alexius, Aexie, and Xenon hovered along the perimeter too.

Alexius stepped forward. "May I also join you? That way, Prince Jaxon can see what it looks like from the outside," he said.

"Yes, of course." Katsuro nodded and Alexius was suddenly wearing a gi in his own colors: red with green stitching.

I watched as Katsuro moved to grab Alexius's collar and opposite sleeve. As he moved to counter, Katsuro twisted to the side, sending Alexius over his hip to the ground.

"That feels a lot faster than it looks," Alexius said as he stood up.

Katsuro motioned for me to join him again, while Alexius stood off to the side. "Move to strike me, up here." He motioned his torso.

I sent a halfhearted punch to his face, but he eased out of the way and stepped past me. Suddenly, I was on the ground again.

I jumped up. This time, I paid attention to what my body was feeling, trying to keep better track of Katsuro. As I moved my arm toward him, he slipped sideways and stepped behind me. Then, just as I turned, he stuck his leg out behind my leg so that when I moved to step backward, I tripped on his leg and fell on my back.

I jumped up again and switched places with Alexius. I watched as Katsuro eased past Alexius's punch and planted his leg between Alexius's from behind. The baku even reached up and pushed Alexius's shoulder as he stepped back and fell over his leg, landing hard on the ground. I had a newfound appreciation for whatever layer of softness Katsuro had magically placed on the ground.

"You. Come," Katsuro suddenly said as he pointed to Darox. Alexius joined me on the sidelines as Darox came through the crowd looking a little nervous.

"I should like to give our princes a break," Katsuro said. "This move is best learned by observation first."

*Did Katsuro just wink at me?* I must have imagined it.

He turned back to Darox and said, "I want you to try to punch me right here." He indicated his stomach.

Darox nodded, looking more than a little nervous now. Alexius might be young, but he was a stronger fighter than most of the guards. But Darox moved to punch Katsuro in the stomach as bid, and Katsuro grabbed his sleeve, ducked between his arm and body, then pulled his sleeve downward as he thrust his backend out into Darox. He flipped the muscular guard over his body like a rag doll so the guard landed on his back, his sleeve still in Katsuro's hands.

"Come, come. Again." Katsuro patted the guard's cheek with his hand, smiling sweetly.

Darox stood. Looking dazed and using the other hand, he punched low this time. Katsuro again spun in toward Darox, pulling down on his sleeve and bumping a hip outward into Darox's body, throwing him off balance and forcing his body to bend. Again the baku threw Darox over his shoulder. The guard landed on his back, his face scrunched in pain.

"Oh, my apologies, Master Darox. I got a little carried away. It's been so long since I've trained in human form."

Darox got up and clenched his jaw. He'd landed on his back twice, so he'd be sore for days. I smiled. Maybe Katsuro did know where Darox had been last night.

"Anyone who would like to learn is welcome," Katsuro said. "But first, you must warm up. The body needs to be limber and twisty so you do not hurt yourself."

Half the guards tentatively edged closer, and Alexius, Aexie, and I made up the first row as Katsuro led us through some of the warm-ups and basic movements we would need to master. I was excited at this new technique. It was a perfect tool in my close-combat arsenal. I hoped Katsuro would stay a while so I could learn as much as I could from him.

He turned to smile at me as if knowing what I'd just thought. I shook it off as he turned back around and proceeded to show us how to twist safely without injuring ourselves.

A few hours later, I walked back to my rooms, very much looking forward to a hot bath as Katsuro had ended our session by giving us free rein to toss each other around on ground that was not magically softened.

Unfortunately, I was thwarted. I rounded the corner to see a very angry Aexie standing outside her door, arms crossed. "How dare you let that happen! Why would you tell Katsuro about him—us? He's your own guard and he's going to be sore for weeks!"

"You were there, Aexie," I sighed. "I didn't tell Katsuro. He picked Darox at random."

"I saw him wink at you," she said, whispers of smoke coming out of her ears.

"I promise you, Aexie. I told him nothing. I said nothing, I thought nothing, and I didn't even indicate him or look at him," I protested.

"Baku, especially blue ones, can tell the future," Alexius added. I hadn't even noticed him there, quietly curled on a bench reading a book.

Aexie stuck her tongue out at Alexius. "You need to shower. You stink."

"I will," he said. "And while Katsuro can't tell the past, the past *is* yesterday's future."

"What does that even mean? And why would the baku care what I do?" Aexie asked.

"Maybe because he's Mother's best friend and he cares about your well-being? Or maybe because you also look a little like Mother did when she was a youngling?" Alexius offered.

"It's none of his business!" Aexie yelled as she turned on her heel and slammed the door to her rooms.

"Thanks," I said to Alexius. He nodded, turning back to his book.

"You really do need to bathe. I can smell you from here," I said, entering my own rooms. He just shrugged without looking up from his book.

Alexius amazed me with how quickly he could relax and read. I was too high on adrenaline to read, but the bath would soothe and calm my nerves.

After my bath, I went to visit Mother for our daily discussion. I knocked on the door after the guard had creaked it open and stepped aside.

"Come on in, Jax," she said. She was talking with one of her maidens and motioned for me to come in. "I should like a walk in the gardens. What do you think?"

I nodded and offered her my arm as we left the palace and walked among the gardens. As guests arrived for the ceremony, the grounds became more populated than usual. She put a magical bubble around us to ensure our words were secret, and I filled her in on all the things I'd observed, down to the color of the threads in our gis and how Darox hadn't gotten one when he'd accepted Katsuro's challenge.

She nodded as she patiently listened, testing my knowledge here and there as she asked me about this detail or that. Finally, when I was done, we decided to continue strolling through the maze we had all long ago figured out.

"Mother, how do you know Katsuro?" I asked.

"Tell me what you have observed."

"You two are very close. I've never known anyone to call you by a shortened name, and I don't think many dare do the same with a baku's name."

She nodded.

"He seems to revere you, like you're his muse. Or perhaps ..." I couldn't bring myself to accuse my mother of having a lover.

"Before I ever met your father, when I was a little wild dragonling, there weren't many dragonlings my age in my family. So, I often played alone. Then one day, this little lion with a big, long nose came out of the woods. He was as young as I was, and we quickly got to playing. He'd meet me every time I was lonely and wanted someone to play with." She smiled. "I know now that he'd seen into the future and knew when I'd wanted a playmate. And you well know not many can play with a dragonling. You saw your brother and sister when they were little. You don't have a lot of control over your fire or any of your magical abilities. But the little blue lion controlled his magic well and could tell if I was about to do something I shouldn't. He would contain my fire or tell me to calm myself so I could better control the magic around me."

"So you were friends?" I asked.

"We were best friends, like siblings even. Except, when you're not actually siblings, as you grow up, you run the risk of looking at each other in a new light."

"You became ..." I still couldn't bring myself to cause my mother offense.

"Yes. We became lovers and intendeds." She smiled, obviously thinking back on those times.

"What happened? You said this was before you met Father?" I asked.

"We were young. Not even five centuries old. But baku do not grow up like we do. When Kat turned five centuries, he was sent out into the world, to learn, to help. By that age, they can no longer survive on simple food but must eat bad dreams to survive. And when they do, they go through a dramatic change. Gone was the small blue lion with a big nose, and in his place was a full-grown baku."

"What happened then?" I asked.

"When they go through that change, they are banished from landing on earth for many centuries, until they learn what it means to be a true adult baku. Katsuro didn't want me to wait for him. He said he could feel the change coming and that he would be a different being when it was done. Baku lose a large part of themselves in the transition." She looked at me wryly. "As you can imagine, witnessing all the evil in the world and eating it so it doesn't happen would take a toll on anyone."

I was quiet as my mother and I sat on a bench by her favorite fountain.

"I waited. It was silly, I know now. But I did. I was a wild dragonling after all. So even as the few children I knew grew up and found mates, I refused. I thought I'd already found my mate. But when he returned, he wasn't quite the same Kat I'd come to know. He had a faraway look to him then, as if he could see the entire world at once. Baku are famed for being solitary beings. They do not often enjoy the company of other creatures. And when you see the world's pain, how could you?"

I only nodded when she looked at me. I had no answer, no words.

My mother gazed at the hedges across from us, a faraway look in her eyes. "He'd been present enough to know that the plans we'd made in the past could never come to be. In fact, Kat saw your father and I together and knew that he would have to bow out. He even put me in your father's path so we could meet, you know. One day, he asked me to meet him in town as a human and wait for him, but your father flew over to me to see if I needed aid as I stood there waiting. And well, you know the rest." She patted my hands.

"Katsuro must be lonely," I said.

"I don't think the baku feel loneliness like we do. The fact that Kat is here at all makes my heart warm. I've met other baku before. They are bitter and mean and solitary. Kat, at least, has not let go of his inner joy."

"And how does Father feel about it?" I asked.

"Like anyone might feel when an old rival is near. He's a little grumpier than normal. But he knows I am bonded to him and Kat is no more than an old friend, though one I trust completely," she said.

She rose, and I followed. I took her arm and led her back out of the maze.

As we neared the exit, Alexius's voice popped suddenly into my head. *Jax, are you with Mother? She needs to come quickly. Katsuro is in a panic, and I don't know how to calm him down. We're at the quarry.*

I looked at my mother and relayed the message. She nodded.

"We need to fly," I said and popped into dragon form as my mother did the same. I had to catch up to her as we took to the sky to get to the quarry. As we flew, I couldn't help but admire her form once again. She was as ancient as Xenon, and the older a dragon, the larger yet more refined, graceful, and controlled they became. As we neared the quarry, a blue cloud diverted my attention.

# CHAPTER TWENTY-FOUR
## ALEXIUS

I T WAS LUCKY THAT I'd been walking in the woods with Katsuro when it had happened. The palace was filling with guests, and I'd wanted some time away. One minute, I'd been asking him questions about his daily life and skills, about how he'd come to learn all the things he had, and the next, he'd suddenly stopped and stared northward. I'd had the sense that he wasn't staring at the tree before him, but beyond it, at something far beyond it. A heartbeat later, he'd begun to change, so I'd popped into dragon form. Knowing we were close to the quarry, I'd led him there as gently as I could. I hadn't known what was happening, but it hadn't felt good. No sooner had we cleared the trees when he'd popped into his baku form.

If dragons were big, baku were even bigger. I was probably the size of his head—and I was in dragon form. He stood still, his massive body frozen except for his tail. The snake head at the tip of his tail looked around at the surroundings as if to keep lookout behind Katsuro as he continued to stare northward.

Then he started to pace, and even in the quarry he didn't have much space. I backed off, flying out of range, and wove a protective wall of light around the quarry's perimeter. Katsuro paced faster and faster until he was a blur of blue streaking from one side of the quarry to the other, dust flying and taking on a blueish hue as he wore a path in the ground.

I called for Jax to bring Mother immediately. Whatever their relationship, she seemed to know how to calm him. Moments later, I saw two dragons flying near, and for a moment I marveled at my mother's flying form. She elegantly dropped from the sky in front of me, and Jax nodded his head.

"Good thinking with the quarry," he said.

My mother watched Katsuro for a full minute, trying to spot him in the blue dust cloud that he'd become. Then we rose and flew above the quarry a little ways away so as not to be enveloped in the dust cloud.

Eventually, Xenon joined us in all his golden glory. Even I was a little surprised at how brightly he glowed gold.

"Can you turn it down?" Jaxon asked.

"Nope," Xenon said. "You have no idea how hard I've tried." He nodded at the blue dust cloud. "What's got his tail in a knot?"

"I don't know. We were just walking in the forest, and then he started to change, so I guided him to the quarry thinking whatever was happening, he'd have the space to deal with it here without injuring himself or anything else," I said.

Xenon exchanged a look with my mother.

"I'll hold the wall," my mother said. "Alexius, Jaxon, go get your siblings and father and meet us all in the Jade Room. The rest of us will be there shortly."

Jaxon and I exchanged a glance.

"Go now," my mother commanded.

We flew off, compelled by her orders as our mother and queen.

Jaxon and I flew toward the palace even as we sent the message to our siblings in our minds. I showed them what had happened through my own memories, and Jaxon relayed Mother's instructions.

*I'll get Father,* Xerus said.

We ran to the Jade Room the moment our feet hit the ground. The Jade Room had its own magic, and even as we stayed in dragon form, it expanded to meet our needs. It grew in height and space to accommodate all five dragons. This room was also magically protected, so it was our most secure place; it kept us safe from prying ears and eyes.

Jaxon started to pace the length of the room, and it was on his third trip back toward me that Xenon finally entered, still in dragon form. I watched, fascinated, as the room expanded to comfortably accommodate him. The magic required to create a self-adjusting magical room was complex, and I still wondered at it.

My mother came next, and the room expanded some more. Finally, Katsuro entered, in full baku form but smaller, dragon-sized now I supposed. Now that we were all here, we settled ourselves on the stone benches along the sides of the room and waited.

Katsuro looked at me. "Prince Alexius, I'm terribly sorry to have startled you, and I'm grateful for your quick thinking, leading me to such a large area so quickly. I am in your debt." Even Jaxon's eyebrows shot up in surprise. For a baku to owe you a favor was a big deal. "However, you should all know that if there is ever need, you may all call on me," Katsuro added, turning to my siblings.

Now Xenon's eyebrows shot up in surprise.

"Why don't you tell them what happened?" Mother gently prodded.

"Yes, yes, of course," Katsuro said. "When I was out walking with young Alexius," He nodded at me. "something to the north caught my attention. I could not see it clearly, but the threads of the future suddenly changed when I looked in that direction. When I started to pace," again he looked at me as if trying to explain, "I was trying to see where the change had happened and what had changed."

"What do you mean?" Xerus asked.

"Baku see future possibilities, but we also store past futures. I was going through my memory to look at past futures." At this, his cheeks turned a bit purple—was he blushing?—as he glanced at my mother. "The future for the North hasn't changed much for a long time. It is strange for it to experience such a sudden change," Katsuro said. His brow creased and I felt fear. I'd never seen Katsuro so serious, and I knew whatever he had seen would concern us all. "I can't say much, however. I will keep an eye on it though, and I will stay here. Some baku are already heading north. There are many bad dreams there," Katsuro continued. He turned to Xerus and Xenon then. "Do not let this ruin your happy nuptials tomorrow!" Suddenly, his expression went from fearful to joyful, and he clapped before dancing from paw to paw. "I'm very excited for tomorrow! Ellie always plans the best parties!" And with that, he popped back into human form and we all followed suit.

While the rest of my family exchanged glances, I kept my gaze on Katsuro, who then looked at my mother, his expression turning serious and sad for just a moment before he turned to dance around Xerus and Xenon.

Xerus looked a little shocked, and Xenon tried to smile as he held Xerus's hand. I left the room, turning invisible and waiting by my mother's rooms. While Aexie had mastered invisibility, she wasn't the only one capable of it. It just took me more effort. I had a feeling

Katsuro would want to speak to my mother alone and waited for them to approach.

Through our bond, I felt my siblings obey my mother's direction to go wash up for supper, for it would be a grand one with all the guests now starting to fill the palace.

I saw my mother stride up the hallway then and Katsuro hurrying to catch up. "Ellie, may I have a word with you?"

"Always." My mother opened her door, and I snuck in after them before the doors closed.

She sat in her favorite chair, but the baku paced in front of her. Then he glanced up at me as if he saw me standing to the side. He nodded at me and then kneeled in front of my mother. "Would you accept me as your personal protector, Ellie?"

My mother was taken aback. "Kat, you couldn't. Not as a baku. Your family!"

"Ellie, you are more family than mine ever was, you and your family. They are all so beautiful and so important. Let me protect you and your family."

"Does that include me?" My father strode out of the adjoining chambers, and I wondered how he'd gotten there so quickly—and ahead of me.

"Of course, Rixen. You are Ellie's mate. I am like her brother. You cannot begrudge me this," he said.

"Rix," my mother said, tilting her head and giving him a pointed look.

"No, Elle, Katsuro is welcome as a guest and teacher." He glanced harshly down at the baku. "But we are not so weak as to need your protection."

My mother rose and went to my father. They shared a few whispered words, and Katsuro glanced at me again. Then, in a low voice, he said, "I pledge to protect you and your family, Elenex." He glanced at me one last time and stood. "I will leave you two alone to discuss." He trod softly to the door and opened it, holding it and stilling momentarily.

I took the hint and left the room. He then bowed and exited right behind me. I started walking toward my own rooms, but he followed me. When I turned another corner, I lifted the invisibility and continued walking toward my rooms. I opened the door when I arrived and left it open. Katsuro followed me in.

"You saw me that whole time?" I turned to ask.

Katsuro nodded. "Though I think of all your siblings, you need to be the most informed."

I nodded, still wondering why. "Would you like a drink?" I asked. Tea had been placed in the sitting room, and I went to pour him a cup of mint tea.

"Thank you," he said.

I handed him his cup and sat down to make my own. "You pledged yourself to my mother and family even though she hadn't accepted it?" I asked.

Katsuro blushed, his face glowing purple, and nodded as he took a sip of tea. "I did not want to speak of it to Xerus and Xenon as they should not have a cloud hang over their union."

"Speak of what?"

"There will be a battle in six month's time. Two days from now, I will tell the rest of your family so they may prepare. There will be a fight for this very palace, and along one of the threads of the future ..." he shook his head.

I guessed he had seen some kind of unfortunate event for my mother. I swallowed hard and said hopefully, "But it's not always set in stone. There are many future threads."

He nodded, closing his eyes. A tear escaped, and strangely, it was light blue like the sky. "It is only a possibility."

I nodded. "Well, then I'm glad you did that, and I will accept being witness to your pledge." If he could save my mother or my family, I was all for it. For that matter, if there was a battle coming, I wasn't stupid enough to think we wouldn't need all the help we could get.

"You'll tell them in two days' time?" I asked.

He nodded.

"Can I tell Aexie and Jaxon?" I asked.

He shook his head. "They have a party planned tonight for Xerus and Xenon, some human tradition they read about. It will be filled with fun. You should not darken the experience for them. The battle is half a year away. Two more days will not make much of a difference."

I suddenly thought of all the secrets that Katsuro must have to keep, how he must be careful of what he says to whom. No wonder the baku were solitary. It would be difficult to be around creatures whose fates he could constantly see swimming in his mind and not try to influence their choices. It made me grateful for who and what I had, even if it was difficult sometimes.

# CHAPTER TWENTY-FIVE
## XERUS

I HAD ALMOST FORGOTTEN that the ceremony was tomorrow. There had been so much planning, so much discussion and preparation, it was difficult to believe that the time for the fanfare my mother had planned was finally here. Even as my family had spoken in the Jade Room, still more relatives and creatures had been arriving. I was starting to feel nervous, not about joining with Xenon, but about standing in front of all those guests, about being the center of attention.

As our discussion with Katsuro had come to a close, I had noticed a shared look between Jaxon and Aexie and wondered what my siblings had planned for me. Then Alexius had left the room quickly, making me doubly curious about what they were up to.

I'd find out eventually, I decided, so I steered Xenon back to our rooms so we could rest ahead of our big day. I picked up a stack of documents to go through, noticing a letter from my cousin, Thaxton, but my thoughts continued to whirl. Katsuro had behaved so strangely. But if he wasn't concerned, then we shouldn't be, right? He seemed so devoted to my family, I couldn't imagine he wouldn't warn us if there was something we needed to know.

"Getting cold feet?" Xenon asked. He took the mail and opened my hand, palm up. A cup of hot chocolate appeared in it.

"No. I know I want to do this. It's just ... Katsuro. He acted so oddly," I said.

"All baku are strange," Xenon said. "They don't ever spend time with other creatures, so in truth, it's weird that Katsuro has friends at all."

"Oh?" I asked.

"Absolutely. I've seen baku of almost every color but only ever in passing. They avoid other creatures at all costs. I've only ever seen them fly across the sky because I was at the right place at the right time. The fact that Katsuro is here, and is still here, is a big deal."

"So that would be why Mother has asked him to perform the ceremony?" I asked.

Xenon's eyes went wide. "Wow. Now *that* is an honor."

A thought suddenly occurred to me. "Are you getting cold feet?"

Xenon shook his head delicately as he tipped his cup all the way up, affording me a view of the bottom as he polished off the last of his beverage.

"Are you sure? Spending this much time around my family? Being pinned down in one location? It's not too much for you?" I asked. This was probably the longest Xenon had ever stayed in one location.

Xenon looked into his cup, and I guessed there was more than tea or hot chocolate in it. He thought a moment before continuing. "I thought I'd be a little caged in here. But it's not so bad, really. Your family is interesting. But if it's all right with you, after our ceremonies, I might go up north to check out what's going on."

"You're asking me?"

"Yes. That's what partners are supposed to do: consider the other's opinions and thoughts," he said. His cup refilled and he drained it again. Then he put it down on the table, stood up, and came over to put his arms around me.

"So ... what do you think?" he whispered in my ear. Shivers bloomed into warmth, and it made it hard to think.

"I think you drink too much." My nose crinkled. "But as for checking out what's north, that might be a good idea."

He squeezed me around the middle. I relaxed into the warmth of his body behind mine.

"Did you tell your parents about my upcoming princehood?" he asked.

"Yes. And I'd be lying if I said they're not grateful," I replied, remembering the relief on my father's face.

Xenon laughed, and I enjoyed the rumble in his chest. "I bet. Your father has been setting up this realm for your siblings and you to rule from day one. I'm sure when he saw who you were going to attach yourself to, he was a little worried his plans were going out the window."

"And your plans? Attaching yourself to someone who can't go anywhere?" I shuffled some books around on the desk in front of me.

"I welcome changes to my plans. I welcome the stability. And I think I'm going to like settling down, seeing the same beings every day. It's comforting. That guard, Darox, is quite good at dice, by the way."

"Oh?" I asked as I craned my neck around to see his expression.

"He'd taken half the guards to the cleaners. That is, until I joined them." He smiled in my neck, and a shiver ran down my spine.

"Jaxon mentioned sending Darox to the patrols."

"Do you send all of Aexie's lovers to the patrols?" Xenon asked.

"Yes," I said. My sister was welcome to do what she wanted with her body, but I couldn't help the protective big-brother feelings that reared their head when I smelled her on them.

"You won't have any guards left eventually," he pointed out.

I turned around, pulling out of his grip. "It's my sister."

Xenon threw his hands up. "I'm sorry. But she likes to have fun. I respect a female dragon who takes control of her own ... fun."

I let my shoulders drop. "Maybe we should talk to the guards themselves." I rubbed my temples, not looking forward to that task.

"Hey, where's my outfit for tomorrow? I should probably take a look at what I'm wearing," Xenon said, obviously changing the topic.

I rolled my eyes but led him to the closet, where everything had been laid out for us.

"I'm going to look stunning," he said, looking over the gold-and-silver suit.

"We both will." I looked at the blue—both light and dark—-and silver suit I would wear.

"So tell me again, how is this ceremony your mother wants supposed to go?"

"Apparently, you'll stand by Katsuro at the front of the crowd, and my parents will walk me down the middle of our guests. Then Katsuro will say a bunch of fancy words and we'll take the oath. My siblings will stand with me. Do you have anyone you want to stand with you?"

"Should I?" Xenon asked.

"Well, I think Mother wants things to be even. So maybe you could have The Three stand with you?" I asked.

"I'll ask. That reminds me, my guests should be here by now. Maybe I'll go say hi," Xenon said as he started to pull away.

I groaned, thinking of the long list of guests I should probably go visit. It was yet another thing to add to my ever-growing list of things to do.

"Forget the list for today. Just go say hi to your friends. The rest can wait until after tomorrow," Xenon said.

I sighed. I supposed he was right. I put my jacket back on, and Xenon tidied his own appearance. But the moment I stepped out of my chambers, I almost stumbled on a messenger looking excited to find me.

"Divide and conquer?" Xenon asked at the messenger's appearance.

I nodded and waved Xenon off. I hoped the messenger had only routine reports and nothing urgent.

# CHAPTER TWENTY-SIX

## JAXON

D ESPITE THE STRANGE OCCURRENCES with Katsuro and the attack on the griffins, Aexie and I had done some research on the human union ceremony and found that there was always a big party the night before. It was supposed to be a last chance to party before being forever joined to another person. While it seemed strange, Aexie and I had thought it a good idea to throw Xerus and Xenon a party with their close friends the night before. I thought Aexie was just looking for any excuse to party though.

To begin the festivities, we'd planned a fun kidnapping of sorts; apparently that's how humans did it. But we would have to kidnap Xerus to get him away from work anyway. Of course, we'd run it past our parents first. Then we waited until after supper when we knew Xerus would be in the offices, working. Aexie was to get Xenon, and Xerus my responsibility. I wondered briefly how she was going to get Xenon to the banquet room but then decided to focus on my own prey.

I waited at the end of the hall, where I could see the office. My father left the office right on time, glancing at me and giving me a thumbs up. I had invited my parents to join us, but he had said he would be busy helping my mother with the decorations.

I walked into the office where my brother sat hunched over papers. He looked up when he heard me enter. "Put the papers down," I said.

"Why? What's happened?" he asked, suddenly worried.

"We have to get to the banquet room," I said. This would be a lot easier than I had thought. I schooled my own expression to one of seriousness.

"What happened?" He stood up, scraping the chair on the floor, and dropped the papers he was holding. He came around the table and I held the door open for him.

"You'll have to see for yourself," I said, hurrying to the banquet room and maintaining my serious expression.

Xerus raced along beside me, continuing to ask what had happened. I opened the banquet-room door and motioned for him to enter. He walked in ready to face anything.

I entered and closed the door behind me as a chorus of "Surprise!" filled the room. "It's human tradition to have a party with friends the night before a union," I explained.

He took a deep breath and recovered. Then he smiled. "This is what you and Aexie have been planning?"

I nodded. I saw Aexie off to the side with Xenon, who grabbed a couple drinks. She did the same, and they came over to join us.

"So what do you do at one of these human parties?" Xenon asked.

"Well ..." Aexie said before clapping twice. Two chairs appeared in the middle of the crowd. Aexie and I pushed Xenon and Xerus toward and right down into them. Then I watched as a group of males with perfect physique sashayed into the room in very little clothing.

Xenon grinned and Xerus glowed. I smiled to see Xerus glow from the embarrassment. He'd never been one to handle sexuality well. Aexie whooped and clapped from behind them as the men started their show.

I left to find Alexius then because I had asked him to get part two ready. I walked to the palace's back gardens, where the open training fields were now covered in high walls of straw bales. Alexius and Brixelle were giggling as they stacked the bales. The maze in the front gardens had been built for Xerus when he had been little, and he had always loved it. He'd finished it many times, even blindfolded. He'd been the one to take us through it and teach us how to solve it, so I had asked Alexius to create a difficult maze and build it with Brixelle. She had been only too happy to find the straw bales that we needed and help build the maze.

"Almost done!" Alexius shouted when he saw me. He and Brixelle were in dragon form, so moving the bales was easier. I walked in as a human to make sure it was tall enough. Xerus was a little taller than I, but the two had stacked the bales a good few feet above my head.

I didn't know what Xenon thought of mazes, but we knew our brother more than we knew Xenon, so he'd just have to deal with it if he didn't like it.

I nodded, satisfied, then went back to the banquet hall, where a couple dozen creatures still remained in their smaller, human forms.

Xerus was giddily laughing as he held Xenon's hand. I nodded to Aexie, and she jumped in front of them.

"Now, it's time for part two. If you'll follow Jaxon," she instructed, motioning to where I stood. Xerus and Xenon rose and came over.

"Thank you, brother," Xerus said, smiling.

It had been quite a long time since I'd seen him smiling and relaxed. That made me even more excited to show him our surprise. So, I led them out to the back gardens, and when he saw the straw bales stacked taller than he stood, he gasped.

"Xenon, I'm not sure if you know this about my brother, but he loves mazes," I said.

"I can tell," he replied.

Like a little dragonling, Xerus hauled Xenon to the maze entrance where Alexius and Brixelle stood, straw all over themselves.

"Have fun!" Alexius said, motioning for him to enter. Minutes later, Alexius and Brixelle started letting small groups of creatures into the maze every few minutes to stagger them. Each group was told to send sparks up should they require aide.

I spotted Katsuro standing off to the side as a human. "Katsuro, would you like to join us in the maze?" I asked as I looked at Aexie.

"Ohh, yes please!" He clapped his hands together, suddenly looking excited. He, Aexie, and I walked up to the maze and Alexius waved us in.

"Want to join us?" I asked him.

"I'd spoil it for you," he said as he waved us in. Following his glance to a grinning Brixelle, I nodded and continued. Katsuro started down one path and then stopped suddenly to turn the other way.

"No fair, Katsuro, you're using your gifts," Aexie said, pretending to pout.

Katsuro grinned and clapped his hands together excitedly as he continued. I happily followed him, noticing this was a tough maze. I'd never been great at mazes, so I was glad to have Katsuro guide us through.

Earlier, my mother had shown Alexius, me, and Aexie our outfits for tomorrow and had gone through what she wanted us to do and where we needed to be when. It struck me as strange to have so much standing and waiting in a celebration. But I was curious to see what the oath ceremony would be like. As I continued to follow Katsuro, who was now arm in arm with Aexie, I wondered whether Alexius would perform the oath with Brixelle. They were obviously a bonded dragon pair to anyone who watched them together.

It had been drilled into us our whole lives not to perform a blood oath. Even Mother and Father hadn't bonded in blood, and Mother had later explained she was glad for it because if one of them died, it would not only leave the throne vulnerable, but it would also mean no one would be left to take care of us. Their mate bond was so strong anyway, I couldn't imagine how much stronger a blood oath would have made their relationship.

"Jax, come on you slow slug." Aexie giggled ahead of us as she followed Katsuro.

When we finished and exited the maze, we saw Xerus and Xenon arm in arm, talking with various guests.

*How long did it take you?* I sent to Xerus.

*Seven minutes,* he replied.

*Shoot. It took us eight.*

*That's pretty fast. It's taken most everyone about twelve.*

*We went in with Katsuro.*

*So you cheated,* he teased, his smile tugging at his lips as he nodded in response to the griffins he was speaking to.

*Sure. Or we were gracious hosts.*

*I still beat you though. But thank you for all of this.*

*Anytime, brother,* I said, turning away from him. Aexie had started to introduce Katsuro to some of our closer friends, those she knew would be kind to a baku despite his oddness and rarity.

A messenger poked his head out the back doors of the palace, and after looking around, walked casually up to me.

"Your father requests your presence and Princess Aexie's and Prince Alexius's help when you've finished here," he said, leaning in.

"We'll be there in a couple hours," I said.

"Very good, Your Highness," he said, looking frazzled.

"Is it bad?" I asked him.

"It is ... a lot," he said.

*What did that mean?* But I nodded and he slipped back into the palace.

*Father has requested our assistance when we're done here,* I sent to Alexius and Aexie. Aexie and Alexius looked over and nodded before returning to sending groups through the maze. It must be a hit because our guests were going through it multiple times. I decided I may as well help them out, so I went around to the exit. That way, I could let my siblings know when each group was done. That occupied my mind for a while until the guests had petered out and I went and sent Xerus and Xenon to bed on Mother's orders. Then, between the four of us, we stacked the straw bales quickly back on Brixelle's wagons. She would take the bales back to the various farmers tomorrow afternoon after the ceremonies, so for now, we tucked the wagons in the forest so they would be hidden from view tomorrow.

Finally done, we flew around to the front of the palace and stopped short. The entire front lawn sparkled with silver moss. Long gold benches with dark-blue velvet upholstery were arranged in dozens of rows in four columns. Before all those benches stood a raised stage completely covered in silver moss as bright as starlight. The wire frames of giant square arches lined the middle aisle, where Mother and Father were busy directing a few dozen staff.

"Great! You're finally here," Mother said as we walked up, popping back into human form.

"This is incredible, Mother," Alexius said breathlessly. He looked around in awe.

"Thank you, dear. How was the party?" she asked.

"I think they both enjoyed it," he replied.

"Good. Aexie, darling, could you put some big, twisty vines on those arches? Fill in the frame and use silver vine with gold leaves. Make sure the vine twirls around the frame."

Aexie nodded and went to do as bid.

"Jax, darling, can you go check the flowers on the back wall and make sure all the holes are filled in?" She nodded at the back wall, which was actually the palace wall covered in white flowers. "And Alexius, can you go change the moss within the arches along the aisle to gold? Almost a tarnished gold."

Alexius nodded and we each headed our separate ways. Father nodded at us as he helped someone hang a strand of flowers in the nearby trees.

Even though my mother had hundreds of helpers already, I knew we'd be here until morning getting everything just right. At the same time, I'd had no idea so much gold and silver could still look so beautiful, but my mother was talented at so many things.

# CHAPTER TWENTY-SEVEN

## XERUS

I OPENED MY BEDROOM doors to find a breakfast buffet in my sitting room. I was nervous about saying my vows accurately today though, so the sight of food turned my stomach.

That didn't, however, mean I didn't desperately need that coffee in the middle of the table. I made a beeline for it and poured myself a large mug full of it. Then I went to sit in the windowsill, gazing out. I held the mug close to my chest; its hot contents to me were holy and a representation of all things good in life.

"Are you worshipping the coffee?" Xenon came out wearing only pants. Even though he was as ancient as a dragon could get, he still looked like he was in his early forties when he was in human form. Then again, I supposed he could make himself look however he wished.

I didn't answer his question. Nothing good ever came out of my mouth before I was caffeinated. I watched as some of our guests joined Jaxon on his run, and I smiled to think of how he must be frowning. His morning run was like my coffee: he liked to do it alone and he didn't like to speak until afterward. Chances were he was running extra hard or fast to try and shake the group that had joined him. Then I spotted some family from other realms. Uncle and Aunt Owyxko in particular caught my eye. They looked well, and that made me happy. It was good that they were taking care of themselves. Their son had died centuries ago. I thought of my sister, Danxing, and a wave of sadness swept over me. She would have loved today. I knew Aexie was excited for today, but Danx would have been beyond excited, beyond thrilled. She loved pretty things and family coming together.

Xenon cocked his head at my non-answer and came over, carefully grabbing the coffee carafe on the way. He reached out tentatively as if I might explode and refilled my cup, mocking me as he backed up carefully, one hand in the air. I rolled my eyes. At that, he chuckled and turned to the buffet. He dove in, munching on one pastry after another.

I turned my attention back to the window and wondered how my bond with my siblings would change after today. Right now, I could choose when to let Xenon in. Would that still be the case after I'd taken the blood oath? Even now, even with my walls up, I could feel his excitement. He looked much calmer than he really was, likely appeasing my slow morning start.

I watched as he moved on to a plate of fruit, having polished off all but one pastry. Part of me noted it was my favorite pastry, and I slowly dimmed the thin mental wall I usually kept between us. He froze for a moment, probably receiving my feelings, then continued to ignore me as he devoured the fruit—all but the grapes. He knew me so well.

I turned my attention back outside. My window looked out on the forest and the training grounds. Guards were still training regardless of the special day, and I noted the extra bodies there as our guests had also brought guards. Even the griffins who had joined us had joined the sunrise training session. The grounds were nearly full.

The griffins' camp was far enough away from the palace that we hadn't been tripping over each other though. We let them run their own affairs, but they were welcome at our public events. Some of the elder griffins had even been invited to the ceremony this afternoon. I continued sipping my coffee, letting the warm liquid slide down my throat as I imagined it filling my veins with energy. The bottom of the cup came too soon, even after Xenon's refill.

"Ready to join the world again?" Xenon said, finally turning to face me.

I nodded. I wasn't quite ready to talk yet. He brought me a plate with all my favorites on it, then leaned down, kissed my forehead, and said, "You need to eat something. It's going to be a long day. I'm actually surprised no one has come through those doors yet." He pointed to the golden double doors.

I took the plate, looking at the various options. I picked at a few of the grapes and ate a pastry but put the plate down when Xenon turned and headed back into the bedroom. He emerged a minute later with a shirt on. As he pulled down the hem, a knock on the door to the rest of the world sounded. "Guess I jinxed it," he mumbled, hurrying to the door. He opened it and stuck his head out. I thought it was sweet that he was protecting me from the world for another moment. I took a couple deep breaths and then put the coffee mug down on the table.

Xenon opened the door, swinging it wide.

*I'm glad I put a shirt on*, he thought in my head. I sensed surprise from him.

The door opened and a griffin elder walked in. I instantly felt underdressed. From the items tied in his mane, I realized he was an important and high-ranking member of the griffins.

"Your Royal Highness, I apologize for the intrusion at such a personal time," he said.

I bowed low to him. If he wasn't the highest-ranking griffin, he would be pretty close to it from what I could tell. "I apologize for our appearance. If we'd known you were coming, we'd have better prepared to receive such an honorable guest."

"You flatter me, Your Highness. It is my own fault for having given you no warning. Please accept my apologies for barging in here," he said.

"Apology accepted," I said.

"The griffins, in thanks for the aid and graciousness your family has shown us in our time of need, would like to bestow upon you a griffin honor in light of this afternoon's ceremony."

I immediately wondered if they had ulterior motives. Perhaps they intended to put on some kind of "See, we've gained their favor" show for the other creatures of our world.

"It will not leave any visible marks, so only griffins will be able to tell that you have been given this honor," he said as if reading my mind.

*If you refuse, they'll be very insulted*, Xenon added in my mind.

"That is very kind. I could not refuse such an honor. Thank you," I replied, hoping it wouldn't take long. It was rather an inconvenient time for me to go off gallivanting with griffins.

Xenon pressed his lips together, holding back a laugh.

"If I may approach you?" the elder griffin asked.

I bowed my head and strode to meet him in the middle. "May I ask what this ceremony will entail?" I asked.

"You need only sit. I will draw a symbol in your aura, blessing you with bravery and wisdom, two traits held dear among griffins. Then I will ask you both to sit so I can bless your bond with good fortune."

At that, I went and sat on the couch. Xenon moved the table so the griffin would have an easier time maneuvering around the furniture. Griffins didn't often take another form, so a lion walking around the room was a little more awkward than people.

"Oh. Can you wait a moment?" I asked. My siblings had been angry at me for not telling them what was happening before, so I reached out to them now, summing up what had just happened. Moments later, Aexie slipped, invisibly, into the room, but I could feel her close by. Alexius came in next. Jax was busy outside but took a moment to observe through my mind.

At my nod, the griffin came over and started waving his paws around me, drawing some strange symbols about three inches away from my face. He then stopped and motioned for Xenon to sit next to me. He ran his paws back and forth over us, again inches away, before muttering something. Suddenly he roared, and had it not been for Alexius slipping out to calm the guards, they would have rushed in expecting danger. I was startled but sensed Xenon's calm.

*I've seen it done before*, was all he replied.

The griffin bowed and said, "Thank you. I will see you this afternoon at the ceremony. May you continue to honor your family," he said.

Once the door closed, Aexie popped back into sight next to Alexius.

"That was a griffin goodbye," Alexius said.

"So, are you one of them now?" Aexie asked.

"I guess so? Maybe?" I replied, noticing my siblings were in their training gear. Jaxon must have given me and Xenon the morning off if he hadn't bothered us yet.

*You're welcome. Happy ceremony day*, came his reply in our heads. He closed the mental door, returning to supervising the morning's training.

"Where's Jaxon?" Xenon asked.

"Still training," the rest of us said together.

Xenon only raised his eyebrows. Then he nodded. "Don't worry, Xer had his coffee."

Aexie and Alexius smiled knowingly.

"Do you two need anything?" Aexie asked.

I looked at Xenon. "No, nothing really. We've had a pretty easy morning," I said.

"Wait until you see the decorations for the ceremony," Aexie said, her eyes shining.

That anxious knot returned to my stomach.

The rest of the morning passed quickly as I was sent from place to place to bathe in water, soak in oil, and be buffed until my human skin shone as brightly as dragon scales. There was so much to do that lunch went ignored. So when we had a quiet moment, I asked Aexie to get Xenon and me some food for lunch. Otherwise, Xenon would become as angry as the bear people very quickly. She came to the rescue with a plate full of meat and fruit as we started to dress. She had even nabbed a pile of leftover pastries from earlier in the morning.

I shoved one in my mouth and passed the plate to Xenon, who scarfed down the rest like he hadn't eaten in days. "Don't even say anything. The food hasn't made it down yet," Xenon said as I was about to comment on how fast he was eating.

Aexie helped us dress, the intricate knots strangling our necks. It was all a bit flashy, but our coats were definitely masterpieces. The long-tailed coats had small collars, Xenon's silver with gold embroidery. I looked closely at his coattails and realized the embroidery told his life story in swirls and images. Red jewels were encrusted in the images too, red being Xenon's family color. My own coat was dark blue with silver embroidery. I looked closely at my tails, realizing my story too was embroidered on them, right from when I was a child. The design included all my accomplishments, my siblings, my interests, everything. The jewels in my coat were green though, my family's color.

The coats were simply magnificent, and I couldn't imagine what would happen when the light shone on them. While they were heavy, I was proud to wear mine. Lots of work, planning, and careful thought had gone into each coat. It was the most stunning work I'd ever seen.

"You two look ... incredible," Aexie said.

Alexius nodded before leaving to get dressed himself. He'd helped Aexie hold this or that as she made sure every detail was perfect.

Aexie took one last look and nodded, apparently satisfied. "Good luck, Xerus." She reached over and hugged me, then scurried to her own room to get ready.

I turned to look at Xenon, and he outshone anything I'd ever seen. My heart expanded in my chest; I was so proud that I had the opportunity to let the world know that this dragon would be mine and I would be his. His own pride and love oozed through our bond, making me realize I couldn't wait for him to finally feel the same thing from me later today.

"Ready?" he asked, holding his hand out to me.

I nodded. "I'm excited."

He smiled even wider.

We took a deep breath together. The double doors to my chambers opened, and we stepped through them together. Always together. Forever, together.

# CHAPTER TWENTY-EIGHT

## AEXIE

I LEFT THE BOYS to canoodle one last time before their big ceremony and shrugged into my own silver dress emblazoned with emerald embroidery. It was heavy from all the beading and sequins and crystals but otherwise hugged my body. There was a rather long train on it, and knowing how cumbersome that could be, I'd made sure to add a hidden hook and loop to the dress so I could pull it up later. Then I used magic to do my hair since I was short on time. The boys were all hopeless without my help, which took time away from my own preparations, but I took pride in the bows I tied for them, or the cufflinks I pinned at certain angles, or the lapels I finessed on their coats.

Jaxon had already been by earlier as I was fussing over the happy couple, asking for help with his outfit. He'd promised me he wouldn't crease or winkle anything. It was very like him to consider that.

Alexius hadn't yet been by, but that was also like him. He would probably read in the library until the last minute. It didn't seem to matter that he hadn't slept last night since he'd been busy helping us decorate. His magic seemed stronger than it had been not long ago, and he'd wielded it with more precision and lasted the whole night without tiring even once.

A knock sounded on my door. "Come in," I said. Alexius popped in, surprising me. "I was about to come and get you, except I wondered if maybe Brixelle had helped you," I said.

"I know this means a lot to you, Aexie. I wouldn't take that away from you. We are your brothers after all," he said with a wink.

I stuck my tongue out at him, then opted to forgo sarcasm and just smiled, putting my finishing touches on his outfit. Then I backed away to have a proper look.

Alexius's suit was like Jaxon's. His long-tailed, deep-green coat with silver embroidery along its edges was adorned with a swirly version of our crest on the back. Since I'd be standing between Alexius and Jaxon, we'd all look stunning in our silver and green. I wondered what Mother had made Xenon's friends wear.

A knock on the door while I tried to battle with Alexius's bow tie one last time told us it was probably time to go. "Come in," I said.

A guard poked his head in. "Your Highnesses, they're ready for you."

I nodded distractedly, finally getting Alexius's bow to sit as I wanted it to. "There. Now we're ready to go," I said.

"Shall we?" Alexius offered me his arm as I slipped into my spiky shoes. How did humans wear these infernal things? Then we marched proudly to join the rest of my family in the Jade Room.

"Good. You're all here," my father said as he beamed.

"You all look splendid," my mother added. She wore a dress like mine, except emeralds shimmered from every angle. Her dress wasn't quite as flashy as the suits Xenon and Xerus wore, but she was certainly eye-catching.

"I know I tell you kids never to do this, but today's a special occasion," my father said. He snapped his fingers, and we were suddenly all in a tent. I heard the murmurs of the guests, and I looked down to see grass. We were on the front lawn of the palace.

"Ah, there you are. We're ready to start then." A little yellow dragon acting as usher waddled his way up to us as my siblings and I, then my parents, got in line. "Xenon, you will pop into place outside, and if you could, direct your friends to do the same please."

"We are perfectly capable of directing ourselves," a deep voice behind us said. We spun around to see the new arrivals. They were splendid in lush velvet, silver coats with black trim. Gold embroidery shone faintly on the plush fabric. It caught the light, but it wasn't too obvious. I gulped when I realized who they were.

"May I introduce Vadentia, Talmaro, and Yagaron," Xenon said. He moved to embrace each of them in turn and exchange jovial greetings.

I had almost forgotten that Xenon was one of The Four. The Four were a deadly band of warriors, so dangerous and so famous, that the number four in some languages was synonymous with death. Every youngling had heard stories of The Four: Xenon, the dragon; Vadentia, the female minotaur; Talmaro, the cockatrice; and Yagaron, the manticore. Stories of their battles were renowned throughout the entire world, even in other worlds, I'd heard. To see them in the flesh was extraordinary, breathtaking even. I looked over at Jaxon, who must have been in shock since his jaw was hanging open. As a dragonling, he'd pretended he was part of The Four, re-enacting various battles.

"It is an honor, Your Majesties, Your Highnesses." The three spoke in unison as they sank to one knee.

"To see you all together is quite an occasion!" my father said.

"We wouldn't miss Xenon uniting with his bonded mate for the world," Yagaron said.

"We grow tired of his pining. So we owe you a great debt, Your Highness, for finally relenting," Talmaro said as he bowed his head so low to Xerus, he exposed the back of his neck.

Xerus grinned. He looked surprised but not as shocked as the rest of us. I wondered if he'd met them before. I saw Xenon roll his eyes at his friends. He seemed more relaxed around them, younger even.

My mother coughed to get us to hurry up. "Shall we?"

"Your beauty is highly understated throughout the lands, Your Majesty," Yagaron said, taking my mother's hand and kissing the back of it, lingering awhile.

My father coughed and raised an eyebrow.

Xenon shot my father an apologetic look and reined in his friends. "Let's go." Before we could blink, The Four *poofed* out, and a sudden hush went over the crowd gathered outside. We assumed that meant Xenon and his friends were now standing at the end of the aisle.

"They take orders well," my mother commented, peeking her head out. "Ready?" She turned back to the rest of us. "You all really do look splendid," she said.

We nodded but looked at Xerus. He nodded too, taking my mother's and father's arms.

The flaps opened—apparently today was the day for magic to be used for impractical things—and the basilisk musicians began their re-sounding throat singing. Notes of all kinds filled the space, resonating so deeply I felt it in my chest, yet so delicately I imagined a field of sparkling flowers. This ceremony was oozing with magic.

Jaxon stepped out first, and then it was my turn. I walked out and blinked. Even though we'd seen the setup last night, it was a whole new experience seeing it in the daylight. I was surrounded on both sides with bright colors and shapes as creatures of all kinds were among the hundreds of guests. The main aisle was on a bit of an incline, so I walked uphill along a brassy golden carpet. Every twelve feet, I walked through an archway covered in flowering vines, the flowers so silvery and golden they caught the light at every angle. The raised platform where Xenon and his companions stood was itself the purest of whites. Beside Xenon was Katsuro, splendid in a silver brocade robe with a scarf in all the colors of the baku draped over his shoulders. I smiled with every step as I realized how long this aisle really was and felt a boost of admiration from the guests as they *oohed* and *aahed*.

I fought the temptation to look behind me to see where Alexius was. He wouldn't like this kind of attention, and I wouldn't be surprised if he turned and fled back into the tent. I knocked on the door of our soxkendi room in our minds. He opened it, and I saw that he was anxious but smiling through it. I sent him a little of what I was feeling, hoping to bolster his confidence so he could enjoy the moment a bit more. And it did ease some of his anxiety.

*Thanks.*

*Anytime, little brother.* I caught a glimpse of him holding a picture of Brixelle in his mind before I retreated back to my own side of the door and wondered whether this experience would deter him from uniting and taking a blood oath with her.

Finally, the end of the aisle met the platform, and I went to stand beside my brother in a "V" shape so we could all be seen. The tent flaps had closed behind Alexius, but as Alexius tucked himself beside me, they opened again. Xerus and my parents filled the opening, and I sucked my tongue to the roof of my mouth as I tried not to let my emotions spill through my eyes. Xerus glowed, and the light bouncing off the silver and gold wreathed him, boosting his own glow. My mother had planned the most spectacular visual moment.

The crowd hushed in reverence as Xerus's gaze found Xenon. Then Xenon looked up. He returned the smile and held himself a little taller, a little more proudly. Xerus hugged our father and mother and took the last few steps on his own, taking Xenon's offered hands.

Xerus and Xenon ducked their heads and murmured to each other. I caught Talmaro and Vadentia looking me over and raised my chin a bit. Then as soon as Xerus and Xenon stood tall, Katsuro began reciting the words my mother had written for this ceremony.

He told the story of how Xenon and Xerus had met and fallen in love. Every guest was riveted; they would spread this story far and wide across the worlds. I looked out at the guests and saw many familiar faces, my cousin Thaxton. I hadn't seen Thaxton in some centuries, but he seemed healthier than his sickly dragonling self. It felt like everyone I had ever met in my life was here: the dune dragons, the oceanic dragons, even the aerial dragons. Griffons—including the elder I'd seen this morning—smiled and nodded as they beamed with pride as if it was their own son uniting. I saw more manticores, cockatrices, and minotaurs, even pegasi. Every creature in this world was here and watching closely. This was the first ceremony of its kind in our world, and these creatures would bear witness to the future monarch uniting with his mate in this fashion.

"And now, the blood oath," Katsuro said. I was surprised at how serious he'd been this entire time. I'd half expected him to giggle and clap his hands together partway through.

Jaxon stepped forward, presenting the dagger strapped to his side to his brother. Xerus took the dagger, and I heard a knock on my soxkendi door. I opened it.

*I want you all to bear witness to this,* Xerus said. We all gathered in the soxkendi room, our mental space, wondering what would happen when the blood oath took place. We weren't sure if the familial bond would hold or if we'd be shoved out of Xerus's mind.

I swallowed and watched as Xerus took the dagger and sliced his hand. Then he took the giant root that Katsuro presented him with. Xenon sank to his knees on the platform, opening his mouth as the blood dripped down the root. Before the first drop entered his mouth, Katsuro snapped his fingers and lit the end of the root on fire.

We could sense Xerus's anxiety. He too was nervous about what would happen next, so nervous, he also let us see Xenon's unfailing confidence in and love for him. He likely hadn't meant to. Xerus was intensely private.

After nine drops of blood had entered Xenon's mouth, Xerus started to whisper. I risked a glance at Xenon's companions. They had turned their attention to the guests, watching for threats while their companion was vulnerable.

Looking through my brother's eyes, I saw the root burning and felt the magic Katsuro used to shield Xerus's hand from the fire. It traveled down the length of the root, and as it reached the end and Xenon returned to a standing position, I felt a shift in our soxkendi room. Since all the doors were open, we all saw in our minds the ancient magic that was Xenon as if it was a mist filling the space near us but not directly in us. We felt Xerus's elation that we were still there along with the love he could now share more directly with Xenon. Alexius, Jaxon, and I politely closed our mental doors then and returned fully to ourselves to allow the new couple their privacy.

I watched them physically and looked away from the unabashed love and pride they shared. It really was just like the stories said. I wondered if I'd ever experience sharing that look and those feelings with someone.

Suddenly, the hollowness of my fun escapades hit me, and I swallowed to maintain my composure in front of all these creatures. Feeling the bond Xerus and Xenon shared had changed something deep within me. But now was not the time to examine it, so I forced myself to look at the happy couple and smile.

# CHAPTER TWENTY-NINE
## JAXON

I WAS HAPPY FOR my brother, truly. But I couldn't bear to watch them. It made my stomach turn and my heart twist, so instead, I watched the guests. There was a large crowd, and my brother was vulnerable, so I scanned the area, looking for anything that might signal danger. My parents, Uncle Owyxko, and some of our extended family had tears in their eyes. Even Thaxton, our strange cousin, was present. He normally never attended public events. And despite how outlandishly my extended family was dressed, our guests' attention all seemed to be caught in the beauty of the moment rather than the spectacle of my family's wardrobe. Through our bond, I saw that Aexie felt like the guests were all trying to memorize every detail, and she wasn't wrong. I had even seen some guests writing notes as I had walked up the aisle.

If I was being honest with myself, I had to admit this was the occasion of the century. We were indeed making history. And seeing The Four together in my own home had been a bit of a shock for me. I had always known that Xenon was part of The Four. But to know it and see it were two different things. As much as this moment belonged to my brother, I was excited to hopefully have the opportunity to test my skills against The Four later.

A cheer went up, and I snapped my attention back to the couple at the center of it all. They had joined hands and now turned to the crowd. They walked back up the aisle hand in hand, stopping every once in a while to shake hands with this guest or that. When they finally made it to the end, Father snapped his fingers and we all—the entire wedding party—were back in the tent.

"My apologies if I imposed on you, but I wanted to make a quick exit before everyone tried to seek us out," my father explained, looking at Xenon's companions.

"No apologies needed. I felt the same change in the crowd. And we are family now!" Yagaron clearly spoke on behalf of the minotaur and cockatrice because they nodded and smiled.

"If you'll follow us this way, the couple of the day will need our support as they greet all their guests," my mother said, gesturing for Xerus, Xenon, and Xenon's three friends to follow her and my father. Before leaving the tent, she turned back to me, Alexius, and Aexie. "You remember what you're to do now?"

We nodded and left through a side flap, trudging to the other side of the front lawn, where an outdoor feast was set up in honor of the festivities. My parents had also arranged for food to be sent out throughout all the lands to celebrate the day. I guessed it would become a holiday of sorts for everyone. Aexie was to double-check the decorations, Alexius was to give the kitchens notice so the food would be out the moment guests arrived, and I would just do whatever Aexie asked me to. My mother knew me too well. Had I had the kitchen task, I probably would have eaten a few of the sheep and chickens on their way out. I was already starving.

We added sparkle and shine to anything we could while we waited, and as the first guests started to arrive along the longer, prettier path, Alexius joined us, and we greeted and escorted each guest to their table.

My foot tapped in impatience as I waited to ferry the next guest to their table, and it took much of my energy to remain politely smiling. All I wanted was to jump into the training ring right then. I wasn't sure how long I could stand this celebration of a love I still hadn't found. Unfortunately for me, I was stuck entertaining guests and pretending to be happy. I did get to eat though, and the rest of the night was a happy celebration without any real incident at least.

# CHAPTER THIRTY

## ALEXIUS

I STRAINED MY NECK looking through the crowds to try to find Brixelle. I'd spotted her and her mother among the guests in the back earlier. Her smile had been the only thing that had made me step out of the tent at all, so walking further down the aisle away from her had been difficult. During the ceremony, I'd imagined how it might look if Brixelle and I took Xerus and Xenon's place. It was terrifying to stand in front of so many creatures, but I'd do it for her. I wondered whether she'd want that much attention, but my guess was she wouldn't. I'd ask anyway though.

After the ceremony, we had all gathered behind the palace for the evening feast. I had helped my family escort all the guests to their tables. Then I finally found myself with a brief moment before I would have to take my place at the table with my family. I wanted to find Brixelle before I lost the chance. Thankfully, I caught a flash of purple hair many tables away from mine, so I waded through the tables full of guests.

Right before I was about to tap her on her shoulder, she looked over at me, and the smile on her face made my insides feel melty. I stepped back, right into my cousin, Thaxton. "My apologies, Thaxton." I reached out to help right him and nodded, turning back to Brixelle until I felt his bony hand grip my shoulder and pull me back around.

"Cousin, if I could have a moment of your time," Thaxton had placed himself directly in front of me.

I glanced at my table, and my mother gave me a look; I needed to hurry.

"Xerus will gladly take an audience with you, Thaxton, tomorrow. If you'll excuse me." I patted his shoulder and ducked around him to the waiting Brixelle, barely registering his frustrated grunt.

"Finally," Brixelle said. "I was wondering if I would get to see you at all." She smiled.

"I don't have much time because I'm supposed to be at the main table with my family soon, but I wanted to see how you were." I felt stupid as soon as it came out of my mouth.

"I'm wonderful. I met many interesting people, and the ceremony was beautiful. I don't think I've ever seen anything quite so spectacular." She rose and turned to me. "You looked incredibly handsome, my prince." She tipped her head to the side as if wondering if she should have said that. I, for my part, wondered if she had meant her words possessively—they had made my skin tingle—or if she had just been trying to be formal. I hoped it was the former.

"I am yours," I said before thinking about it, then took her hand and kissed it. I pulled her toward me, away from the crowd and behind a stately ancient tree. Her dark-purple dress flared out at her hips, making her look a bit like a bell, and the edges were trimmed in her family's lavender purple. With her purple hair and a golden belt cinched around her middle, she was the most beautiful dragonette I'd ever seen. "You are beautiful," I whispered on a breath. I didn't seem to have much control over my own mouth lately.

"Thank you." She dipped her head, her cheeks glowing a bit as she stared at the ground.

"Hey, Alexius, let's go," Jaxon said as he came around the tree and motioned toward the head table with his head.

"One second," I said.

Jaxon rolled his eyes. "Why don't you just bring her with you?"

I turned to Brixelle and raised my eyebrow questioningly. There was nothing I'd like more than to show our friends and family who I'd bonded with, but I didn't want to pressure Brixelle into anything. "Do you want to come with me?" I asked.

"What does that mean?" she asked, sounding hesitant.

"It would be an announcement of sorts to our friends and family that we're together, that we're a bonded pair." I swallowed hard. I knew Brixelle was my dragon mate. I knew it in my core. This was the first time it had occurred to me that she might not feel the same way.

She pulled away to better look in my eyes. "I'm ... I mean, are you sure?"

I brought my other hand up to squeeze hers. I didn't want to force her into anything. "It's completely up to you. I would love for you to join me and my family at that table. But if you're not ready, I'm okay with that too."

"Will Xerus mind? Or ... The Four?" she asked.

"Xerus won't mind. And I think The Four would love someone else around to liven up the conversation." The second part was just a guess.

She glanced at her mother, who had settled at their table and was deeply in conversation with the griffin beside her. Despite her obvious interest in the conversation, her mother glanced over her shoulder at Brixelle and winked before returning her whole attention to the griffin. Brixelle looked back at me then, searching my face as I held my breath. "Okay."

I put my arm around her shoulders when what I really wanted to do was whoop and holler and shout my love for her to the world. But I settled for bringing her hand to my lips to kiss as she giggled.

We turned and approached the head table, and I nodded at the guards. Mother saw us coming and leaned over to whisper to a server, who nodded and waved a hand in the air. In a blink, three servers rushed over, scrambling to add another place setting next to mine. Xenon looked over at me and raised a glass to us, nodding at Brixelle. Xerus looked over too as I approached and smiled widely as I helped Brixelle into her chair. I made sure to seat Brixelle between me and Aexie so she would feel included and have two of us to help her.

I shared a look with Aexie, and she nodded, understanding my request to help Brixelle without a word.

Jaxon had followed us back to the table, so once I had taken my seat beside Brixelle, he leaned in behind us and said, "Finally. Congratulations, you two," before taking his own seat.

My mother nodded in our direction, and the looks and stares began. Most of the attention was on Xerus and Xenon thank goodness; they still sparkled brighter than a treasure chest. But I saw a few guests dart quick glances our way, and I felt Brixelle shift uncomfortably in her seat.

After my parents had welcomed everyone and called for the first course to be served, I leaned over to Brixelle. "How are you doing?"

"I'm all right, I guess. At least fewer creatures are staring than I thought would. I'm a little rusty with dining in my human form though," she whispered.

"You look beautiful." I continually found excuses to look at her.

She grinned. "You're not terribly ugly."

Aexie choked on her drink and started laughing. Jaxon managed to swallow before his deep rumbling laughter made its way to us.

I couldn't help but grin. My heart warmed at the acceptance I felt and at having Brixelle by my side. I didn't have as much time to talk to her as I would have liked because of all the speeches, but I could feel her there and that was enough. Xenon and Xerus each spoke, Yagaron said a few words, and Jaxon gave a short speech, all in the pauses between each course. Even a representative from each population stood and offered blessings of good fortune and words of congratulations. I didn't pay much attention because not only were none of the speeches truly interesting, but they were all so formal they sounded very much the same. We all toasted each speech, but while mead and ale flowed into our guests' cups, the head table did not have the luxury of mead or ale. My parents weren't ones to risk a scandal, so we all had berry juice, much to Aexie's and Xenon's dismay.

Everyone ate and drank and conversed until long after the sun had set, and as the evening wound down, Xerus, Xenon, and my family gathered to say goodbye to each of our guests, thanking them for sharing our special day with us. On their way out, each guest adorned Xerus and Xenon with necklaces of all kinds: wooden beads, jewels, even popped corn. The necklaces were symbolic of the blessings each creature had bestowed on the newly united couple. Two hundred strings of anything was bulky, and I doubted a smaller dragon could have shouldered so many necklaces with as much ease.

After the last guests had gone, I found Brixelle helping the palace staff put everything away. Part of me wanted to go to bed, but the chance to spend more time with her led me to join in. To spend even a few more minutes with Brixelle, I'd do anything.

"We can handle the rest from here, miss." The little yellow dragon usher bustled over and shooed Brixelle off. I nodded my thanks, as did Brixelle. My family had already retired to their rooms, probably crawling into bed, leaving only the two of us here with the staff.

"Why don't you sleep in the palace tonight?" I asked. As soon as I said it, I realized how that might sound, so I hastily added, "In a guest room." I couldn't stop my cheeks from warming; surely I was glowing in the dark.

"That would be wonderful, actually. I sent my mother home with one of the neighbors," Brixelle replied. "And I'm supposed to spend tomorrow with Aexie anyway."

"Oh?" I was surprised that Aexie hadn't mentioned it to me. "What are you two doing?"

"I'm not sure. But I thought it would be good to get a female perspective of palace life and to spend time with your sister," she said.

I nodded and extended my hand. She took it, wrapping her fingers around mine. We walked back to the palace from the lower back lawn, and I couldn't help but move around to hug her from behind, making it awkward to walk as I waddled around her but wanting to hold her close to me for forever. She giggled as we tried to make our way the last few feet to the stairs of the main entrance. There, I reluctantly parted from her but kept hold of her hand.

"Did you mean it?" Brixelle stopped just inside the main doors after I opened them for her. I nodded at the guards posted at the entrance.

"Mean what?"

"Tonight. Sitting at that table with your family. It was ... well, nothing I ever expected to do in my life," she said.

"Is that good or bad?" I asked.

She stopped walking and took both of my hands. "It's exciting. But you ... oh, I don't know." She shrugged and smiled, then let go of my hands and skipped around the abandoned front hall. I jogged to keep up.

She stopped suddenly at an intersection of hallways, so I pointed in our intended direction. Even though all the guest wings were full, my parents always kept a couple extra rooms in our familial wing in case they hatched more children. They were kept pretty bare though, and I hoped Brixelle wouldn't mind.

"That's your room, right?" She pointed at the red-trimmed doors near the end of the hall. I nodded, and as we continued down the hall to my room, I pointed out my siblings' rooms too: Aexie's next to me, Danx's across from me, Jaxon's across from Aexie, and Xerus's—and now Xenon's—next to Jaxon. A hallway separated Jax's and Danx's room, but when Danx was little, she'd built a little overhead tunnel she could crawl through to get to Jax.

I took Brixelle to the last room, the one next to mine specifically, and opened the door. "It's pretty bare in here. I hope you don't mind," I said. Brixelle walked in and looked around, taking in every detail. "It's beautiful. Besides, I could sleep on a hay bale at this point."

"You should find some extra clothes in the dresser. I'll let the guards know you'll be spending the night here. Oh, the bathing room is just through those arches there. Did you want me to warm the water for a bath?" I asked. I coughed to erase the image of Brixelle bathing.

"Yes, please. I'm exhausted, but I don't think I could sleep in this beautiful room if I didn't freshen up," she said as she spun around, her arms wide open. I grinned. She looked so excited—by a room.

I strode through the arch to the bathing room and snapped my fingers; the water warmed to the temperature I assumed she liked. Then I realized I'd better not assume. "Do you like your baths hot or warm?" I asked over my shoulder.

"Hot, please," she replied.

I took off my jacket—Mother would kill if me I got it dirty—and folded it over a nearby chair. I rolled my sleeve up and dipped my hand in the water. Probably warmer. I snapped my fingers again and steam rose from the water. That was probably good. I looked around the bathing room and saw little jars of oils tucked into an alcove. I took them out and set them on the little table beside the bathtub. "It's ready," I said, turning around to leave.

And stopped short. A very naked Brixelle stood in the archway. My heart started to pound out of my chest. I pushed it down as my gaze took in every curve of her body. She looked up at me through her lashes, her cheeks and upper body glowing as she blinked coyly at me.

"Would you like to join me?" she asked as she walked toward me.

With every step, I thought for sure my heart might explode out of my chest. "I ... I ..." was all I could manage as I dropped my gaze to the floor. I shouldn't stare. Or should I? My insides were all hot and jumbled up, and I didn't know what to do. Suddenly, I saw her toes. And then I was staring at her naked human form.

She gently took my chin and raised it so I was looking into her eyes. "Why do you do that?"

I had no words.

"You do or say something that lets me know you love me, but then the next second, you back away like you're startled." Brixelle cocked her head, clearly confused.

"I—" I didn't have time to speak as her lips met mine. Her hands slid to the sides of my face as our lips explored each other. Then her tongue joined the dance, coaxing my tongue to join in too. I kept my hands at my sides, keeping a tight rein on my desires.

One hand left my face to run down my arm and take my hand. She put it on her waist, then did the same with my other hand. I held her waist, barely resisting the urge to let my hands explore her body. Her hands returned to my face, then circled the back of my neck and up through the back of my hair. I could feel my grip on myself unraveling quickly, so I pulled away, holding Brixelle away from me.

We both panted as I tried to catch my breath and let my heart calm itself. "Wait," I managed between pants.

"Do you not want to ...?" she started, and I saw hurt flit across her eyes.

"No. I do. I really, really do." I continued to pant, trying to gain control over my breath and my racing heart.

"Then what?" she asked, her hands lingering on my arms.

"I'm not ready," I said, looking down. I saw her adorable toes wriggle. "I know you're my bonded mate. I do. I just need to go slowly. I've never ... I need time to ... oh, I want to enjoy this and do this properly. I want to know everything about you. I want to worship you. I want to adore you."

Those adorable toes disappeared from my view and her waist left my hands. I thought I'd surely said something wrong. My hands were now on my knees instead, and I was flying through what just happened and what I had done wrong. But then the toes were back. And they came closer. And closer. My heart started speeding up again. This time, a pink silk robe filled my gaze.

Again, Brixelle's soft hand found its way under my chin. She tipped my head up to look into my eyes, then led me to a built-in bench and guided me to sit down before sitting on my lap. She moved my hands to circle her hips. "Well, my prince. I didn't think I could love you more. But I think I do now," she said, smiling wide.

"You're not mad?" I asked.

She pursed her lips. "Hmm … frustrated, yes," she said with a laugh. I smiled. "But not mad. I guess I assumed you'd have a lot of experience in this area. You're a prince after all."

"What does being a prince have to do with it?"

She raised her eyebrows. "Really? You're a royal prince. Doesn't every dragonette throw themselves at you?"

"No. They throw themselves at Jaxon. Sometimes Xerus," I said.

"Well, lucky me then." She moved to kiss my lips, then darted to the side and kissed my cheek before sliding over to my ear. She nibbled my earlobe and I swallowed again.

"You've … you've done this before?" I asked.

She nodded into my neck. "Do you care that I'm not …" she whispered into my neck, resting her head on my shoulder now.

"No. I don't. Was it … gentle?" I asked. I knew enough to know that many male dragons were quite rough when it came to mating.

She nodded into my shoulder. "We thought we were a bonded pair. We'd grown up together and did everything together. Goodness, we were only about a century old, young dragonlings, really. He'd caught his older brothers doing it with various dragonettes in the hay barn. So he explained it to me, and I thought it would cement our bond. He did too. He even let me control all of it."

"Was it painful? That first time?" I asked. It was easier to talk to her when we weren't facing each other, but I enjoyed feeling her voice on the skin of my throat, her fingers trailing up and down my arm.

"Yes. It was. But after we'd tried a few times, we had to face the fact that we were not a bonded pair. That was more painful."

"I'm sorry," I said. She shivered and I wrapped my arms tighter around her, planting a kiss on her forehead.

"It's not your fault." The tub of water must have caught her eye then because she uncurled herself from my lap, undid her robe, and slid into the bath.

She turned and leaned her head on the edge of the tub. She crinkled her nose and pouted. "It's cold again."

I raised an eyebrow and snapped my fingers.

"That is handy," she said, sinking back into the tub of water. I walked over, flipped a bucket over, and sat down at the end of the tub, gently unfolding her purple hair from the tub and draping it over the edge. "Will you tell me about him?" I asked.

"Mmhmm," she said, purring like a griffin as I brushed out her hair, rubbing soap into it before bringing a full bucket of water to it to rinse it out.

I sorted through her tangles gently, enjoying the relaxed cadence of her voice as she told me all about her years as a dragonling, her best friend, and her father. I was surprised not to feel jealous of this other dragon but rather happy that he'd been there for her. It even brought me a sort of peace to listen to her joyful memories.

# CHAPTER THIRTY-ONE

## JAXON

I WOKE WHEN I always did: with the first rays of the morning sun. Perhaps with a bit of a headache from the last two days' activities, however. As I pulled a loose shirt on, I wondered if I would have time to take a nap later, maybe in the library by the window where the sun shone through in the afternoon.

The moment I walked out of my room, two messengers passed my door, shattering my peace and reminding me how many guests were still in the palace. I exited through the side door, grabbing a cloak hanging next to it. I muttered an apology to whomever I'd borrowed the cloak from, but I hoped it would give me some anonymity. It was a cool morning, and the staff were still cleaning up from last night's festivities.

I decided to go for a run around the quarry. I would be less likely to run into someone there. As I made it to the massive wall, I thought to myself how much taller and imposing it looked from a human perspective. Since I was here, I chose to scale the wall, grabbing a handful of the rubble from the ground and rubbing it between my hands before shoving my fingers in the cracks and beginning my ascent. I'd long since learned the exact way up the rock wall, so to add to the challenge, I let my legs hang, using only my fingertips. I knew it had been a while since I'd last scaled it with only my fingers, but that was the point of exercise: to conquer something difficult. I grunted with the effort and threw my arm up to catch the top edge of the wall when I finally made it to the top. I swung my leg over the wide wall and took a moment to breathe. Looking down, I was surprised to see two more humans scaling the wall as I had. I squinted to get a better look. I hadn't met them before, but they looked familiar. After I'd sniffed the air, I realized I had met them only yesterday.

I moved aside as the first person swung himself over the wall. His appearance was deceptive in that he looked like an old man as a human, so it was disconcerting to watch him scale a rock wall when he looked like he had difficulty just standing up.

"You make that look pretty easy," he said as he worked to catch his breath. "Xenon said you were a good warrior, but I have to admit, that was tougher than I thought," he said.

A woman swung herself up next to him and wiped her forehead. She'd morphed her bull head into the features of a plain woman with dark-brown hair and brown eyes the color of evergreen-tree bark in winter. "That was fun," she said, looking at Yagaron, flushed from the exercise but all smiles. "What's next?" she asked, turning to me.

"What do you mean?" I asked.

She shrugged. "Your morning workout today is fun so far, so what's next?"

"If you don't mind us tagging along, Your Highness," Yagaron added.

"Please, Jaxon is fine," I said. I hadn't wanted company, but to spend time with two members of The Four, I'd make an exception. I leaned over the edge. "We climb back down."

They both gripped the edge of the wall and leaned over.

"How, exactly, do you do that in this form?" Yagaron asked, a crease forming in his brow as he probably wondered if it had been foolish to climb up in the first place.

"Like this." I pulled my boots and socks off one at a time, stuffed my socks in my boots, and dropped them down the wall. They sent up a dust cloud when they hit the bottom. Then I rubbed my hands along the edges of the stone, grabbing any dust and dirt I could. I slipped over the edge of the wall, holding on by my fingertips alone, and swung around Yagaron's and Vadentia's legs like a human gymnast back to the same craggy ledge we'd scaled up. Then, still gripping the top of the wall, my toes searched for the same holds that my fingers had found on the way up. When my toes had found solid purchase, I slid my hands off the top ledge and down the wall, flat against the surface.

"Are you part monkey?" Yagaron asked as he watched me step with my toes and slide with my hands.

"I can't believe I signed up for this," Vadentia said, dropping her boots before swinging around to do as I had.

My toes knew the way, though they tired more quickly than they should have, so I depended more heavily on my arms. It was good to know what was weak so I could work on it. I landed softly on the ground and found my boots, using my socks to brush off the bottoms of my feet before putting them back on.

They both did the same and then looked at me expectantly. Fine. If it was a workout they were looking for, then that's what we would do. So I started running back toward the palace, but instead of aiming for the main building, I ran along the perimeter of the palace grounds, around the griffin's temporary encampment, and back toward the guard tower. Masons were repairing some of the eroded stone walls on the far eastern side of the palace grounds, and there were often large stones laying about that needed transporting to the wall.

A burly man with gray hair the same color as the stone and eyes a shade darker waited for us to approach when he saw us. "Morning, Your Highness." Dixon nodded at my companions and indicated a pile of large round stones. "More than usual. Good day to bring friends."

I nodded and proceeded to the boulders. I picked one up with a grunt and trudged toward the wall undergoing repairs. As dragons, even in Dixon's smaller dragon form, these would be easy to move from one place to another. But as humans, it proved a challenge and a good workout. I heard Yagaron grunt behind me as Vadentia's steps quickened.

"Slow down up here. Ground's tricky," I warned.

I heard her slow behind me, and I too was careful about where I placed my foot before putting all my weight on it. The masons were already hard at work, and those who'd taken their larger dragon shape moved aside as we placed the boulders in the wall. The masons swiftly poured the wet mixture on top of and around them, packing it all in to hold the boulders in place. Before Yagaron or Vadentia had a chance to speak, I ran back to the pile of boulders. We'd have three trips each before I went to hit the training ring. We worked quietly, and I suspected the other two didn't normally train this way. After we had moved the last set of boulders, I took off again at a run but this time to the training ring.

"Finally, something I recognize," Yagaron said. He seemed to almost sag as we arrived at the training yard.

"You can take that ring over there if you wish to spar," I said, directing them to one of the other many training rings that made up our training grounds so they wouldn't garner too much attention while I attended to my own duties. I wanted so badly to join them, but that would have to wait.

Vadentia and Yagaron turned to the ring and nodded. "Come join us when you can."

I nodded and turned away as my captain strode up to me. "Is that who I think it is?" Gabol asked.

"If you mean two of The Four, then yes," I replied, jumping in between a couple of guards to fix their stances and arm placements as we passed some training soldiers.

Suddenly, my attention was drawn to one corner of the training area. Raised voices and angry words filled the air. Then one guard spat in another one's face. I immediately threw up a bubble of magic before they could get to each other and strode over, furious with their behavior. I had warned all the guards to be on their best behavior while we had guests. For them to show such disrespect greatly disappointed me, so I would make sure they never forgot.

"What is going on here?" I growled, my voice low and cold. I dropped the magic that held them frozen, staring at each other. "A stupid disagreement, sir," one said, though his stance didn't relax.

"Well, I hope it was worth the punishment," I said. "For the next two weeks, you are to remain in your human forms. You will help the masons in the afternoon, and you will report for inventory duty in the evenings. Is that understood?" They both deflated at that and looked down at their feet. They were obviously not happy, but they nodded. Gabol scribbled down my orders and sent messengers with notes to the kitchen and the masons. Then once the two guards had assumed their human forms, I put magical tags on them; if they changed forms, I would know.

"That was harsh," Gabol said.

"I warned them to be on their best behavior. There are eyes watching us very closely, Gabol," I said.

He nodded. "There are reports of wagons filled with straw and wood being lit on fire on the northern edges of our lands."

"What do you think?" I asked him.

"Probably just younglings being stupid," Gabol shrugged. "I wouldn't normally bring it to your attention, but you said to bring everything to you while there are guests at the palace."

I nodded. Gabol took the dismissal and continued about his duties. I watched more of my guards training, correcting postures and angles as I went. It was almost lunch time when they finally filed out and I turned to see Yagaron and Vadentia still training. Talmaro had joined them now. I was more than a little excited that I could still catch some of their training.

"They tell me I missed a grueling workout this morning, Your Highness," Talmaro said as I strode over. He was scrawny in his human form, scrawnier than any dragon in human form.

I shrugged. "I've been getting sloppy lately. They caught me on a motivated day."

"Well, I'm glad I missed it this particular morning; however, I look forward to catching it another time," he said, watching his two friends. "Denty, hand first, then elbow. You'll get your face cut into ribbons like that."

She growled but engaged Yagaron again.

"Are you too tired to spar?" Talmaro asked me. He eyed me up and down, probably trying to judge for himself whether I was truly fatigued.

"No, I'm not tired. I'd never pass up a chance to learn something new, especially from one of The Four," I said.

"Don't start with the flattery, Jaxon," Yagaron shouted. "If you blow Talmaro's head too big, it'll never deflate."

Talmaro rolled his eyes at his friend, and we moved to an empty ring.

He raised his hands, and I felt a thrill of excitement at the possibility of learning more of what Katsuro had taught me. Talmaro stood further away than Katsuro had though, and I wondered if I was about to learn a whole new style of fighting. I aimed a punch at his jaw, but before I could move, the air whooshed out of me. Talmaro had kicked me smack in my middle, not with his foot, but with his ankle.

An "Oof!" escaped me before I could help myself as I landed hard on the ground. It had been a long time since that had happened to me—except for when facing Katsuro.

"Please, Tal, remember we're guests of the royal family," Vadentia said. I bounced back up, not wanting to get caught by surprise again. I mentally reviewed what Katsuro had taught me, then moved to punch the other side of Talmaro's face. This time, I was ready for the ankle kick, so as his ankle neared my middle again, I brought my right arm down and leaned over, clamping his leg to my body. I slammed his opposite shoulder with my free hand, and he fell with a loud thump onto the ground.

Vadentia and Yagaron stopped sparring and glanced over at us. "Serves you right," Vadentia said.

I offered Talmaro my hand, hoping he wasn't too offended I'd just sent him flying onto his back.

Thankfully, he was smiling as he took my hand and stood up. "Who taught you that?" he asked, blinking in surprise.

"Katsuro," I replied.

"Well, you're not as one-sided as I thought then."

"Why did you kick me with the top of your foot, not your bottom?"

"There's more strength in the blow if you use that part of your foot than the toes or sole." He pointed at his own foot as he explained. "You have to train though. You could break these little bones very easily," he added, indicating his ankle.

I nodded.

He continued his instruction. "This is the ultimate range for this kind of combat, leg-striking distance." To illustrate, he pivoted on one foot, brought the other leg up, then outstretched his leg at the knee.

"But how do you punch someone from that distance?" I asked.

"You throw your whole body into it," Yagaron said. He shooed Vadentia into the ring with Talmaro and they demonstrated. I had never before seen a fighting style so committed. Every movement used their whole body.

"Doesn't a kick from so far away leave you more vulnerable?" I asked Yagaron.

"Yes. In this particular style, you need to be quick, but you also need to be flexible, adaptable, and committed. Tal, grab her leg this time," Yagaron said.

Talmaro grabbed Vadentia's leg at her next kick, which she'd aimed at his face. When Talmaro grasped her leg, she swung her other leg around and hooked it behind Talmaro's neck, essentially hanging off

Talmaro's neck with her legs. The moment her hands hit the floor, she swung Talmaro headfirst to the floor. He ducked his head, tucking to roll, and landed flat on his back. They stayed on the ground for a minute, catching their breath.

"That was incredible," I said.

"Would you like to learn? Xenon has mentioned your interest in diversifying your styles," Yagaron said.

I nodded vigorously, then stopped as I probably looked like an overeager child.

"Tomorrow morning after your workout, join us," Yagaron said.

Talmaro groaned as he stood up. "I'm done. Hot bath time." He threw his hands up, then extended a hand to help Vadentia up.

*Jaxon, Katsuro has something to tell us. Father's office, as quickly as you can,* Xerus suddenly said.

"I would really appreciate it, thank you. But if you'll excuse me for now," I said, bowing. At Yagaron's nod, I turned and ran toward the office. I too had been looking forward to a bath, but that would have to wait.

# CHAPTER THIRTY-TWO
## XERUS

I WOKE IN XENON'S arms. He held me close and as I blinked, he groaned softly and tightened his grip on me. It took a lot of coaxing to untangle myself from him, but I slipped a pillow in my place so he could encircle that instead of my middle. I had already slept in by my standards, and I wasn't about to let my work pile up.

It was cooler than I was used to on this morning, and I pulled a warmer shirt on before padding silently to my common rooms—our common rooms now I supposed—happy to see my coffee waiting for me on a tray with a few selections of fruit. I poured my coffee carefully, bringing it to my adjoining office and enjoying a few sips before starting on my paperwork. I was glad my assistant had at least stayed on top of the paperwork during the chaos of the last few days. Things were piled into "Need to sign," "Check on," and "Opinion" stacks, but the dragonsbane paperwork had its own pile.

I got to work signing everything in the pile that just needed my signature. I glanced over them and found nothing unusual or suspect. It was a simple task I could fly through. At least one stack would be gone then. When I finished signing the last document, I moved the whole stack to the table I'd designated for "Completed" papers so they could be taken away. Then I turned to the next stack and sighed before sitting down with the pile of papers that I needed to sort through and read. I was about halfway through when my coffee ran out.

A cough at the door made me look up. My eyes widened. "Xe! This is public space. You need to put clothes on!"

Xenon stood stark naked in the doorway, but he didn't even flinch. "I don't have anything to be ashamed of."

"No, you don't. But you might give the staff a heart attack if they walk in. Or my siblings. Or my parents," I said, trying to get him to put something on before my staff started flowing in at any moment.

I sensed his mischievousness then, that he wanted to rile me up, so I turned back to my paperwork and ignored him. He walked closer to my desk until he stood within my peripheral vision, trying to elicit a reaction.

I clenched my jaw, holding in my words. If Xenon wanted to expose himself to my staff, then that's what he would have to experience. I kind of hoped my father might walk in. That might teach him to cover up in public areas.

Xenon started to twist from side to side, and I couldn't help myself. I put my papers down and shot him a look.

*Really?* I asked him through our bond.

Xenon shrugged. *You're being too serious. I endured that ceremony, so I should get you all to myself for at least one day.* He pursed his lips.

He looked ridiculous when he pouted. "You're how many millennia old, and you're pouting like a dragonling," I said out loud.

"So what?" he said, continuing with his side-to-side dance.

A knock on the door made us both jump. "Come in," I said. If Xenon wanted to play chicken, then I wouldn't fold first.

"Your Highness, Katsuro is here to see you." One of my clerics marched in and grabbed the stack of papers on the outgoing table. I looked over at Xenon and saw he was now clothed in loose pants and a loose shirt.

I rolled my eyes. Of course he had used magic to instantly dress. Suddenly, I sniffed something much like the lingering smell of a candle being blown out.

*That's the smell of my magic. Now that you've also taken the blood oath, you'll smell that whenever I use magic,* Xenon said.

*Do you smell it too?* I asked.

*No, but I can smell it through you. To me it smells more like ashes.*

"Please let Katsuro in," I said out loud as I rose.

"Your Highness, Xenon, I'm so sorry to intrude this morning. I wanted to wait until later, but your clerics insisted you'd be awake and working at this hour." Katsuro walked in and was before me in the next blink of an eye, taking my hands in his.

I stood and smiled at Katsuro. "Please, have a seat. And don't worry about the hour. I'm always up early."

"Shall I excuse myself?" Xenon asked Katsuro.

The baku glanced at Xenon. "Oh, no. I think you'll want to hear this too." Then he turned back to me. "But I was hoping you'd bring your siblings to this meeting too?" Katsuro tapped his head with a finger.

"Of course," I said and mentally knocked on our soxkendi doors. When they let me in, I asked them to join us in Father's office.

"Shall we gather in my father's office then? It's a little more spacious," I said as I opened a door at the back of my office that was enchanted to take one to the other side of the palace to my father's office.

We stepped through the door one after the other and into my father's more spacious office.

"Xerus. You're up early today," my father said, looking up from his own paperwork stack.

"Katsuro has asked to speak to us all." I motioned behind me to Katsuro as he entered. Xenon brought up the rear, looking back through the doorway with curiosity.

Alexius knocked on the main door and entered, Aexie close behind. Jaxon was probably out in the training field, so he'd take a little longer to get here.

Alexius sat down, looking at the map that covered the table. He looked to the north and his brow creased, making me wonder what he was thinking about. One of the gifts my parents had received when they had united as a mated pair was this very table, and on its surface was a model map of our realm, our lands, and the topography.

Jax finally knocked and entered, looking dirtier and sweatier than usual.

Katsuro motioned for us to sit. My mother arrived at that moment and sat next to Alexius. Without preamble, Katsuro began. "There will be a battle. Someone, or something, is coming from the north, and they wish to take your lands for their own."

I was glad I was sitting down. Xenon put a hand on my shoulder as Katsuro turned to us. "I'm sorry to have to bring you this news so close to your union. But they will be here in six months. I wanted to give you ample time to prepare," he said.

My mother rose and we all watched as she approached Katsuro and took his hands. "Kat, thank you for this invaluable information. Please let us know how we can repay you," she said. She was so gentle with him.

"Ellie, I wish to stay to help. To fight. To protect you all," Katsuro said.

"Can you share with us what you've seen in the fabric of futures?" my father asked.

Katsuro turned and smiled at us all. "There is so much, so many options. I see only that your family is at risk. I do not think it will be a war though. It will be a single battle, and they mean to take you by surprise. I cannot yet see who it is, but they built their army in the north and are preparing to travel here."

"Who would do that? For that matter, how do you bring an army so quietly it's a surprise? We'd see them for miles, wouldn't we?" Aexie asked.

"We should be able to. But what if they're invisible?" Jaxon asked. He turned to Katsuro then. "Can you tell if it will be an assault from the air or the land?"

"It will come from all directions, from within the earth, the air, and the land," he said.

"From the earth? What does that even mean?" Aexie asked.

"Like the sea serpent," I explained. "The attack on the griffins must have been a practice run."

"We had a terrible time containing only one of those creatures. If there were ten, or even three of them ..." Jaxon shook his head. "We'll have to call all our patrols back to help."

"And leave the borders unprotected and unable to call a warning?" Alexius asked.

I took a deep breath. This would be a long day. "Katsuro, do you know why the enemy wants our kingdom?" I asked, turning to him.

"I can not yet see it. But there is no logical or reasonable explanation," Katsuro said, now sitting with my mother.

"We need more information," Xenon said just as I thought it. I put my head in my hands knowing what that would mean. "We will go and get more," Xenon said. I knew the "we" he referred to was The Four. My father turned to me. It would be my decision since Xenon was my mate.

Reluctantly, I nodded.

Xenon said, "I will go get ready." He nodded at us and left through the main door, squeezing my hand before leaving the room.

"He was planning to head up north anyway," I said to no one in particular. I rested my elbows on the table and put my head back in my hands as I took a deep breath.

Aexie came over and poured me a cup of coffee. I took it gratefully and looked over at Jax. He was deep in thought, probably thinking of who to pull from where and how to call the troops to arms quietly.

Finally, I looked at Alexius. He was studying the map of the realm, clearly already thinking about strategies.

"The first thing you need to do is fortify the ground," Aexie said. "Surprise is bad. And those serpents popping out of the ground like spring flowers is most definitely a surprise."

We all nodded in agreement. "What if we created a warning system like Alexius did for Brixelle's farm? But in the ground rather than the air." Jax asked.

I nodded. "That's a good idea. It wouldn't take much energy, and we could set the alarms covertly. We'd need to tie the system to multiple sources of magic though." I didn't add "in case one of us dies." I didn't want to think of it.

"We'll tie it to all of us. Then we'll all know if something is coming from beneath the ground," Alexius said before turning to Jax. "How far underground should we go?"

"Depends on how much warning you want. That sea serpent moved awfully fast on land, but I don't know how fast they'd travel through the dirt," Jaxon said.

"What if we made the alarm system like a reverse dome under the palace and the surrounding area?" Alexius asked.

"But how far out?" Aexie asked.

"To there?" Jaxon suggested as he pointed to the mountain range in the far distance.

I nodded. "That would give us plenty of warning."

"Okay, you're all talking about warning, which is great, but is there anything those serpents can't get through? Shouldn't we put that in the ground to protect us?" Aexie asked.

We all agreed on that, but we hadn't gotten to what that could be before a knock on the door diverted our attention. Xenon stuck his head in. "We're on our way out," he said.

That felt terribly fast. "Let me walk you to the courtyard," I said, leaving my siblings to discuss logistics and best options.

My mother had risen and spoken softly to Xenon before holding the door open for me. "I'm sorry to throw your first days together into chaos," she said.

"It's not your fault. And we'll have time together when he returns," I replied as I slipped out. I already felt like I was tearing myself in two, half of me wanting to stay in the meeting and the other half wanting to go with Xenon.

Thankfully, Jaxon let me in on the conversation in our minds. I made eye contact with him as I turned to shut the door and nodded my thanks.

Xenon took my hand as we walked down the hallway to the courtyard, a hallway that suddenly seemed too short. Xenon chuckled. "This is the first time I almost don't want to go on an adventure." He grinned wryly.

We stopped just inside the doors, the guards moving further away to give us some semblance of privacy.

"Be safe," I said. There were no other words that I could think to say as I sent the love of my life, the other half of my beating heart, into danger.

"We will," he said. He suddenly grabbed my face and kissed me hard. Then he softened the kiss as I wrapped my own arms around him. Running out of air, we finally broke apart, and he turned to walk away from me.

I could feel that this was difficult for Xe too, so I let him choose how to say goodbye.

"Not goodbye. Just ... see you later," he said out loud.

I nodded. "Check in as often as you can," I said, tapping my temple. I felt him confirm it in that little room in my head that was all his.

He trudged through the doors, and as they closed, I couldn't help myself. I burst through the closing doors, watching as The Four popped into their original forms and took off.

"Don't worry! We'll have him back in no time!" Talmaro shouted as he caught up to the others. He was the last to leave because he had the largest wingspan and needed to give the others space to catch the wind.

I raised a hand in the air and nodded, gulping back a sob as I watched Xenon become smaller and smaller in the distance.

# CHAPTER THIRTY-THREE
## COUSIN THAXTON

"**H**OW WAS THE CEREMONY, master?" The gray cockatrice asked as he bowed to me then took my coat.

"Beyond beautiful. My aunt really outdid herself. And my cousins looked perfect, as always," I snarled.

"Very good, sir." The cockatrice started to back out of the room.

"Wait. The wagons, have they left yet?" I asked.

He squirmed away from me, and I growled. I was in a foul mood after having to fly back without so much as an audience with my own family.

"Your Majesty, the wagons have been delayed. The dragonsbane is still growing, sir." He cringed in anticipation of the blow I did indeed deal him. Then I kicked him out the door, not fully satisfied with just one blow as he'd moved faster than I expected. Damn cockatrice.

I supposed I was being impatient. These stupid underlings couldn't know my plan. It'd been in the works for years. They would all see my army soon enough, and the wagons of gifts I was sending the happy couple. The bile rose in my throat. It was all so disgustingly happy.

All I'd wanted was an audience with my uncle, the king, and my aunt, maybe even one of my cousins, but I kept being told they were too busy, that they would get to me. Get to me?! They were probably "too busy" tending to their new pet griffins. Well, they'd regret ignoring me—again. They'd brought this on themselves. The destruction and chaos and citizens dying in the streets, it would all be their fault. Then I would rule. The kingdom needed a strong hand, not a cute, lovey-dovey one.

# Chapter Thirty-Four

## Aexie

I knocked on Brixelle's door. Alexius had said that Brixelle had stayed the night in the spare room next to his. I was a little surprised she hadn't just stayed in his room, which led to my wondering if they'd had any bedroom fun before I shook my head. Maybe I didn't want to know.

"Morning!" Brixelle's door flew open as she answered.

"You're certainly chipper in the morning," I remarked.

"I'm a farmer. I'd have had most of my chores done by now."

I peeked into the guest room and saw that barely anything had been disturbed. "You could have come out of your room if you wanted," I said.

"I wasn't sure what I was allowed and not allowed to do. So I just stayed in bed." Brixelle seemed pretty happy about that. I supposed I might have been too.

I nodded as Brixelle swished out the door and closed it behind her. I might need a cup of Xer's coffee to keep up with this kind of morning cheer. "You didn't want to stay in Alexius's room?" I asked, glancing at her sidelong.

Brixelle glowed brighter than I thought she would have. So something did happen.

"He didn't really give me the option if I'm being honest. I ..." She looked at me, a question in her eyes.

I nodded at her to continue as we headed for the seamstress wing.

"I ... I wanted to, but he said he wasn't ready," she said, then glowed some more.

She must be looking for someone to talk to if she was sharing this much information. I tilted my head from side to side, pursing my lips. "You're the first dragonette he's ever cared to spend any time with." I made a mental note to leave a few specific books in Alexius's rooms, or maybe have Jax talk to him. Would Xer be able to guide him through this? I shook my head. All I really knew was that Alexius would be mortified if I tried to talk to him.

But I was saved from my thoughts as we arrived at the doors I'd been leading us to. "How do you feel about clothes?" I asked.

Brixelle looked at me blankly, glancing down at her own loose dress she must have borrowed from the closet. "I can't say I know much about them besides how to put them on."

"Well, when you become part of this family, you'll have to have a lot of outfits, for all sorts of occasions. The boys have it easy: the same few outfits, different tie or bow tie, maybe a different shirt. The tailors usually just check their measurements and then their outfits show up in their closets. I come here at least once every few days to be fitted and poked and to choose what to wear for what occasion," I said.

"Oh." Brixelle's face fell. I pushed the doors open and watched her face closely as she took in the chaos that was the seamstresses' room.

The "O" of her mouth got bigger and wider, and I pressed my lips together and tried not to laugh at her expression. It was probably one of the biggest rooms in the palace, and there were people everywhere sewing and organizing textiles and walls of thread and fabric bolts.

"Ah! Your Highness! How are you today?" Annoir, the head seamstress, came up to us. "This is Alexius's mate, yes?" she asked. I nodded.

"Come, come." She took our hands and led us into the world of fabric.

"Your Highness, I have some things for you to try over there." She squeezed my hand and tilted her head to the left. "And if you would take a look at some of the designs. I want to take a close look at this pretty little dragon." She turned to Brixelle, whose eyes were still as large as saucers. Annoir led her to the pedestal in front of the wall of mirrors, gently guiding her to step up. Then she left Brixelle to stand there as she looked at the young farmer dragon from all angles. Sometimes, I wished I could see what Annoir could; somehow, she could size anyone up in a flash.

"That dress you wore yesterday was perfect for you," Annoir said. "Your mother made it?" Brixelle nodded. "And in dragon form, you are purple and yellow, yes? Like these?" The seamstress asked, pulling two bolts out.

"A richer yellow," I interrupted, giving Brixelle a bit of a break. "Like the inside of a daisy in the shade."

"Yes, yes, I see it now," Annoir said.

Brixelle finally shook her head and blinked, coming back to reality. "This place in amazing," she said.

Annoir beamed at that and started pulling fabrics out. "This one, or this one? Don't think, just say which you instinctively like more," Annoir said.

Brixelle pointed to one, and I ducked into a room off to the side to change into some of the dresses that Annoir had prepped for me.

"But when will I ever wear something so beautiful?" I heard Brixelle ask. I grinned from my side of the partition. She and Annoir would get along just fine.

"You'll need it if you're going to stay at Alexius's side," I shouted.

"She's right. Now this one or this one?" Annoir continued.

After working up a sweat in the seamstresses' wing, I led Brixelle out of the palace to the griffin camp.

"That was a whirlwind. Have you always drawn your own designs?" Brixelle asked, jogging to keep up with me.

"I do a few, but most are Annoir's design," I said.

"You're very talented. I have no idea how I'd even start imagining those things," she said. "Where are we going now?"

"To the griffin camp," I replied as we neared the camp. The griffins had organized themselves much better recently. Those whose villages had been unaffected by the attack had even gone home. That meant the camp was thankfully much smaller now, and I led Brixelle down the main path to a slightly bigger tent we'd erected near the forest.

"After you," I said. She ducked into the tent, and I followed, smiling as I heard the giggles of little griffins. This was where all the children learned and played together while their parents were busy taking care of their camp and rebuilding their homes.

"Princess!" they shouted. Tiny beaks rubbed against my legs and soft paws tried to climb up them.

I laughed and waded through them, shuffling so as to not step on any tails, then stopped in the middle of the room. "What kind of story would you like to hear today?" I asked the dozens of eyes that had all turned to me. The older griffins in charge of taking care of the little ones sighed and sat down at the back. They would get a break while I entertained the little ones for a spell.

"A dragon one!"

"A griffin one!"

"A serpent one!"

I smiled as they shouted different ideas before I began one of my favorite tales about a dragon prince who had to go into hiding because an evil sorcerer had stolen his throne until the dragon met a griffin, fell in love with her, and took back the kingdom with her. When I finished, the adults were leaning in, and all the little griffins were sighing at their daydreams.

When I finished, I looked over and saw that Brixelle had become a couch. A group of tiny griffins had piled themselves on top of her and looked content to stay.

"One more! One more!" they shouted.

"I think I know one," Brixelle said.

All eyes turned to her beneath the pile of little griffins. She told an old farming legend, spinning it into a story with pegasi, dragons, and griffins. I was surprised by how well she kept their attention and the details she wove into the story.

We snuck out of the tent after that, and the older griffins thanked us for our time.

"Where did you learn that story?" I asked her as we headed back to the palace.

"My father used to tell me a story every night when I was a dragonette," she said. "He was a true storyteller like you. He could make them up as he spoke."

I glowed a bit at her compliment as we continued our walk. As we reached my rooms, Xerus's voice popped into my mind. *Katsuro's asked to see us all right away in Father's office.*

"I have to go. There's a family meeting. But do you want to borrow one of my books before I go?"

"Sure." Brixelle grabbed the nearest one, and I found myself hoping she liked the same kind of books I did. She accompanied me to my father's offices, and we parted ways: she to the courtyard and me to the family meeting. I can't say I wasn't more than a little bit jealous that she'd get to spend time reading outside today.

# CHAPTER THIRTY-FIVE
## ALEXIUS

I FINALLY FOUND A moment to sneak out of my father's office. We had been discussing strategy most of the morning. Fortifying our security and preparing to evacuate the citizens was to be our starting point.

I had to hurry, though, because I'd told Brixelle to meet me in the courtyard after lunch so we could spend time together, and it was getting late. I was worried she would think me too young and inexperienced any minute, or maybe too preoccupied—especially with the way this morning had gone—and decide I wasn't worth it.

As I jogged through the halls and out the doors, I wondered what she'd decided to do when Aexie had left her to attend our family meeting. I burst into the courtyard and saw Brixelle sitting on a bench beside a rose bush. My heart warmed as I drank in the sight of her reading in the sunlight. Her face was turned up to catch the sun as she held her book out awkwardly. I wondered what she liked to read.

"Hi," I said as I neared.

"Hi! Was that *The* Four I saw launch into the sky a few hours ago?" she asked.

I nodded. "Have you been here a while then?"

She nodded, smiling. "Aexie said she had a family meeting, so she offered to lend me a book. I just grabbed the closest one and came out here to read."

"Did you have anything to eat yet?" I asked.

She shook her head. I loved her human form as much as her dragon form, maybe more even. The curves of her human body made my hands itch to hold her.

I offered her my hand, and she snapped her book shut and took it. Putting my other arm around her, I guided her to a smaller dining room so we could find some lunch, or in her case, brunch. "So what did you get to read?"

"A story about a prince meeting a princess—"

"Ahh. Aexie's preferred reading material," I said.

"There's nothing wrong with that. Maybe one day, someone will write a book about our love story. You are a prince after all." Her eyes sparkled with an unspoken challenge.

"Maybe," I said, not rising to the bait and opening the door for her instead.

"Afternoon, Brix!" Jaxon said. He sat at a table laden with food, helping himself. Aexie sat in a chair beside him eating mostly fruit, and Mother sat at the head of the table, a generous selection of food on her own plate too.

"Come, join us!" Mother said, grabbing two more plates from the side table and placing them before the two seats to her right, opposite Jax and Aexie.

"Are you coming to train with these two this afternoon?" Jaxon asked.

"Umm ..." Brixelle said. Her eyes were wide as she looked from my mother to Jaxon to Aexie, then back to me.

"If you're joining the family, you're training. Even Xenon does, though I haven't seen him in the training rings yet ..." Jaxon continued.

I only raised my eyebrows and threw my hands up, shrugging as she turned to me. If Jaxon had set his sights on seeing Brixelle trained in combat, there was no stopping him. I had to admit, I'd appreciate it if there really was a battle coming our way. "Don't worry," I said. "I'll be there if you need me."

"Sure. I don't have much experience—any, really—in combat, but I'd love to learn," Brixelle said. With those words, she opened the floodgates, but she also won Jaxon over.

Jaxon nodded, happily continuing to devour the leg of lamb he'd grabbed, its juices running down his fingers. My mother coughed and looked pointedly at him, so he gently put the leg of lamb back down and used his knife and fork.

"I believe that's one of the sheep you generously gifted us," my mother said.

"It's delicious," Jaxon mumbled, still chewing, as he cut a piece off the leg.

Brixelle glowed. "Thank you," she said as she studied the hearty bounty before her. She had definitely just won Jaxon over, or he wouldn't have said another word to her. That made me wonder how her morning with Aexie had gone.

As if reading my thoughts despite my mental door still being closed, Aexie said, "Annoir sent a message. Your new clothes will be in your room by the end of the day."

"Oh! That was fast!" she said.

"Do I get to see these masterpieces?" I asked.

Brixelle shrugged. "Depends on the occasion I suppose." She returned her focus back to the food.

I glanced up to see my mother looking at me. She nodded, so I helped Brixelle with her food first, holding the platters for her before serving myself. After looking over to see if that had appeased my mother, I silently focused on eating. I had hoped the room would be empty, but I should have known better. Jaxon was as often eating as he was training.

Brixelle and I ate as quickly as was polite. Then I made our excuses, promising to meet Jaxon for training shortly. After we left, I took her hand as we walked through the palace.

"Your Highness." A messenger came up to me, and I groaned on the inside.

We stopped and I nodded to the messenger to continue.

"The education council would like me to impress upon you the importance of your attendance at today's meeting."

"You can tell them that, as I told them the other day, I am indisposed today."

"Very good." The messenger left, glowing with embarrassment.

"I'm keeping you from your work," Brixelle said, looking sad.

"As I keep you from yours," I replied, thinking of her farm and her mother.

She looked up and smiled at me. "Touché."

I led her out of the palace then and into the maze. I wanted to show her the pool deep within the maze. As we strolled, still hand in hand, I couldn't help thinking that Brixelle still had a farm to run. Part of me wondered what she was thinking. I couldn't ask her to give up her farm, but I couldn't live on a farm either. I had my family and so many council meetings and responsibilities. And she too had family to think of.

"How is this going to work, Alexius?" she asked as we entered the maze.

"I was just thinking the same thing," I replied. We continued walking in silence for a little while, her hand in mine warming me. I could walk the world with her hand in mine. I wanted to. "I could commute from your farm."

Brixelle turned. "That's not safe or practical."

"I can't ask you to give up your farm," I said.

"Do you have land near here? Something closer to you, where I could raise my sheep?" she asked.

I thought about it. That sounded like a feasible option. "There is a pasture in the back, a little ways into the forest, that could probably keep sheep if we built fences."

"I could sell the farm and move my sheep," she said.

"Really?" I asked. I already felt guilty for making Brixelle give up something that had held a place in her heart for so long. "Are you sure you'd be okay with giving up your family home?"

"It's just land. My father's father bought it, but I don't feel particularly attached to it. Mama has already started talking about selling it and moving closer to the village now that she's getting older. That land could be someone's livelihood." She thought for a moment and nodded. "Do you think there's enough pasture to build a small home for me and my mother there?"

"I'm sure there is, but maybe your mother would like living in the palace? You could both move in here," I said.

Brixelle smiled at that. "My mother would probably love living in the palace." Her smile reached her eyes as she thought, likely about how happy her mother would be.

"What about the farming life?" I asked. I didn't want to make her feel like she had to completely change her life.

"Alexius. I love you. I also love my sheep. But the hay, the fields, I was never a big fan of that. I did it because I had to. But if I could bring my sheep ... well, I could still raise them and be productive. I get up earlier than most of you anyway, and they wouldn't take that much time from me on a day-to-day basis. Besides, my mother's active enough for now. She'll help with the sheep too. It'll make her feel useful, like she has a purpose," she said.

I was shocked. "You'd give up your life for me?"

"I'm not giving up anything." She ducked into one of the maze's miniature gardens and sat me down on a bench. "I've waited my whole life to find my mate. And now that I have, it's like I'm finally alive. You are my world now. And your world just happens to be a little more important and a little busier than mine. Anyone can be a farmer. But you, there's only one you. You might not see it, but I do. Your family needs you, depends on you. I can't take that away from them. It's just me and my mother. We can move. You can't. Besides, my mother should enjoy life instead of working so hard, and she'll be able to do that here."

"And the sheep?" I asked, still stunned.

"I love my sheep. If I can keep that one thing, then that's what I'd like to do. And I think my mother might go crazy if she didn't have a little bit of something to do."

"It's yours," I blurted as I sat on a bench.

"Sorry?" Brixelle looked confused.

"The land, it's yours. We can build a fence tonight and get started on a cottage right away if that's what your mother wants. But she can also live in the palace too. Whatever she prefers."

"My mother would love that. But don't you have to ask someone? Like run it by your siblings at least?" she said.

*The field behind and to the west of the castle, just within the forest, can I gift that to Brixelle and build a cottage there for her mother if she doesn't want to live in the palace?* I sent the message immediately to my siblings, making extra sure Xerus heard me.

*Fine by me. Good to get some use of it,* Xerus said.

*Go for it, little bro.* Jaxon said.

*Should I have Brixelle's things sent to your room instead then?* Aexie said. I could practically see her smirk.

*Not yet,* I replied. *Thank you.*

"I just asked them. It's yours," I said. I was thrilled I could do this for her.

"You are incredible," she said. She moved to sit in my lap and grasped the sides of my face. She kissed me and we sat there, lips locked, until we came back up for air.

"Wait," I said, standing up and scooping her up with me. "I want to show you something."

"I can walk," she said, clearly not impressed by my carrying her.

I put her gently back on the ground, but she held my hand as I led her further into the maze. A few turns later, I said, "Close your eyes." She raised an eyebrow at me but then closed her eyes. I led her around one last turn and then placed her right in the best spot to appreciate the view. "All right. Open them."

When she did just that, watching her take in all the beauty of the pool made my insides feel all warm and soft.

"It's beautiful. How is this even here?"

I turned to look at the pool with anew, to see it with fresh eyes like she did.

On one side of the pool was a beach, the white sand sloping down toward the shimmering silver of the water. The water had a pearlescent sheen to it instead of the normal blue that most bodies of water took on. On the other side was a huge, bright-yellow tree with blue leaves that we'd long ago tied a rope to, on one of the highest branches, to swing from. We hadn't been here in a long while, but along the edge of the pool, yellow wildflowers with pink or white middles had sprung up, giving the space an even softer look.

"Want to go for a swim?" I asked, stripping to my undershorts.

Brixelle flashed me a lopsided grin and began to take all her clothes off. My eyes widened, and I looked away out of respect and politeness.

I heard a splash and looked back to see that Brixelle had jumped into the pool. I jumped in after her and took a moment just to enjoy swimming in these silky waters again.

I felt a hand on my back and turned my head. Brixelle was snaking her arms over my shoulders. Before I realized her nakedness, her legs encircled my middle, and she hugged my back.

I swallowed hard, trying not to focus on the body parts pressing on my back.

"Is this all right?" she whispered in my ear.

I nodded. I just continued swimming, carrying her along the edges to show her some of the hidden spaces we used to hide things in. "This used to be Jaxon's hidey hole. He always kept a dagger or something in there." I showed her a hole he'd made in the side of the pool, just above the water line.

"Did you each have one?" she asked.

I nodded, hoping her legs wouldn't slip further down.

We swam over to my hiding spot. I reached in and pulled out a smooth round rock. I showed it to her. "I can't believe this is still here."

"A rock?"

"Not just any rock. A perfectly round rock. It's a perfect circle." I looked at it and thought of how old I'd been when I'd put it in there almost a century ago.

"So you collect rocks?" she asked.

"No. Just this one," I said, putting it back. "My sister, Danxing, gave it to me. The night before we left for my aunt's. She said it was perfect like me, and when I forgot that, I was to look at it and remember."

"I wish I could have met her," Brixelle said.

"Me too. She would have really liked you, though she might have made you wear more sparkly, princessy things." I grinned, thinking of all the frilly, shimmery, extravagant outfits she'd preferred.

Brixelle ran her hand down the front of my chest, and I closed my eyes, just enjoying the feel of her touch. We stood in the water for endless minutes enjoying each other, the water lapping at us, and the quiet afternoon.

"You tell me when you're ready," she whispered. Then she suddenly reached around my head to kiss my cheek before sinking back to once again hug my back, pressing her cheek to my shoulder blade. I felt cherished. I wanted this moment to last forever.

# Chapter Thirty-Six
## Xerus

I OPENED THE DOORS to my rooms, and sadness dripped into my heart. I had half expected to see Xenon lounging on the couch with a drink in his hand. But my rooms were empty. So, I changed out of my day clothes and into the loose pants and shirt I often slept in. My family and I, and our officers, had spent the day speaking at length about the steps we needed to take to defend the palace. Tomorrow we'd start implementing our plan. Step one was redoubling our efforts to rebuild the griffin villages the sea serpent had destroyed. We needed to get the griffins home before we put them in danger. At the same time, rebuilding would serve to bring most of the patrols in closer to the palace without raising suspicion. We'd start fortifying our physical and magical protections tomorrow too. This would likely be my last quiet night for the next six months. Even now, I half expected a messenger to knock on the door. Or maybe I hoped a messenger would knock and pull me from my loneliness. I shook my head and searched for a book to read in bed.

*You free?* Xenon asked.

Joyfully, I plopped down on the bed, crossing my legs and putting my book beside me. *Yes. Are you all right? Are you safe?* I pulled a fluffy blue throw blanket over me.

*Yes. We're safe. And we're fine. We're just scouting, remember?*

*Have you found anything?*

*No. We're only about halfway through. We'll finish tomorrow around midmorning and then we hope to be on our way back.*

*I miss you,* I said.

*I miss you too. You have no idea how much. I forgot how loudly Tal snores.*

I laughed.

*How was your day? I expect full of lots of organizing and tactical planning?* he asked.

*Mostly. We're fortifying the magical barriers and adding alert systems in the ground. We're also calling in soldiers to help rebuild the griffin villages, so they can return to their homes earlier. They'll be safer there if a battle is coming, and our soldiers will be closer.*

*Good. I hope we find some useful information here. How's Alexius?*

*Alexius? He's fine as far as I know,* I replied.

*I only ask because I saw his lady dragon in the courtyard before we left.*

*Was she doing something questionable?*

*No. She was just reading a book. But take it easy on her. It's tough to face your entire family, never mind trying to get one of you alone for any length of time.*

I rolled my eyes.

*It's true, Xer. I knew your family long before I courted you. Even then it wasn't easy to gain an audience, and that's coming from me.*

*I suppose. You'll be glad to know then that I was nice today. Alexius is giving Brixelle a field in the forest for her sheep, plus building her mother a cottage. The dragonette is moving into the palace.*

*Nice. That will be good for Alexius—wait. Is that the field where we ...?*

*Yes. Now don't mention it again.*

I felt Xenon laugh. It brought a warmth to my insides. I wondered whether he enjoyed feeling what I felt as much as I enjoyed feeling what he felt.

*Hey, Xer, does Alexius ...well, has anyone ever taught Alexius dragon-mating logistics?*

*What do you mean?*

*I mean, does he know what he's doing with a dragonette, physically?*

*I think so? Maybe?*

*Well, you might want to check in with him.*

*I'm not exactly the right sibling to teach him the logistics of male-female coupling.*

I felt Xenon roll his eyes. *I had to teach you from the start. So obviously your parents didn't teach you. And Alexius would be horrified if Aexie tried. So that leaves you and Jaxon. You could get Jaxon to talk logistics, but you could speak to the mating bond itself. You know enough about that.*

*Fine,* I said with a sigh.

*Just looking out for family.*

I smiled at that, loving how Xenon now considered my siblings his. *I better go get this over with then,* I said reluctantly.

*Good night. I love you.*

*I love you too.*

I threw the blanket off then, leaving the warm coziness of my bed.

*Jaxon, Alexius, do you have some time for a chat?* I asked in our shared mental room. Before she could take offense, I privately told Aexie, *Xenon's asked me to talk about the logistics of coupling. We thought it might make Alexius less embarrassed if it were just his brothers.*

*All right, though I think I have the most experience of all of you. Let him know if he has any questions, I can answer them. Wait, why are you going?* she asked.

*Xenon said I could speak to the dragon-bond part,* I replied.

*Ah. Have fun.* I felt Aexie grin as she likely dove back into her book.

Then I spoke with just Jaxon. *We need to talk to Alexius about coupling.*

*Really?* he asked. *Maybe you should just leave it to me?*

*I can help him with the dragon bond,* I said.

*I suppose. Where are we meeting then? Alexius's rooms? What if Brixelle is there?*

I physically ran into Jaxon in the hallway right in front of Alexius's rooms.

We nodded in agreement, then turned to Alexius's door and knocked.

"Come in," Alexius said. We opened the door and found him alone in his rooms.

"Where's Brixelle?" I asked.

"Home. She's going to start packing up. Can you guys help me build her mother a cottage tomorrow? She said they wouldn't mind living in the palace, but I wanted to give them their own space too," Alexius said.

"Sure," Jaxon replied.

Still sitting in his chair with his book, Alexius asked, "So?"

"Put the book down," I said as I sat down on the couch across from him. Jaxon sat on the other end of the same couch.

"Wait, can I see that book?" Jaxon asked. Alexius glowed a bit as he handed it over.

*You're welcome,* came Aexie's voice. *I too thought he might not know, so I left a few strategic books in his room.*

*Thanks,* I said.

"We're here to answer questions you might have about coupling with a dragonette." The words rushed out of me, and I clamped my mouth shut.

Alexius looked at me and raised an eyebrow.

"Don't worry," I hurriedly added. "I'm only here to answer any questions you might have about the mating bond."

"Oh," Alexius said. "Is it different with your dragon mate?"

"I don't think so. Have you felt it snap into place?" I asked.

He nodded. "When we were kissing in the garden." He started to glow and averted his eyes, but I could tell he was trying really hard to stay objective.

I nodded. "So ... well, do you know where she is all the time? What direction she's in relative to you?"

Alexius nodded. "It's like I'm tethered to her. I know the moment she's in the building and before she comes through the door."

"Have you felt anything since then, on this tether?" I asked.

"It ... um, glows? When I'm in contact with her. Like my magic does, but less controlled by me and more controlled by our proximity," he said.

I sighed. "We all interpret magic in our own way. Our family sees it as light, but I also feel it like a glow between Xenon and I. The more the two of you that touches physically, the more ... consistently the bond will glow. And after ...um, physical connection, you'll be able to sense what she's feeling."

"But we're not—"

I shook my head. "You'll still feel what the other feels even without it. The blood oath just magnifies it for me. But we could feel each other before then, Xenon more than I because he knew what to look for and was more attuned to it."

Alexius nodded, looking thoughtful. "Thank you, Xer."

I was often surprised by how thoughtful Alexius was despite being the youngest.

He turned to Jaxon then. "I have a few questions now that I've read these books."

I started feeling queasy as he described female body parts, so I strode out of earshot.

"Xer, if this is uncomfortable for you, I can handle it," Jaxon offered.

Alexius nodded. "I think I only have technical questions now. I'll ask if I have more about the bonding."

I nodded, feeling relieved. "I'm also supposed to tell you that Aexie welcomes your questions too, but we thought it would be awkward if she were here too."

Alexius nodded again, glowing as he turned back to Jaxon and whispered his questions.

I made a quick exit then. I loved my sister and I certainly appreciated dragonettes' beauty and strength, but hearing about their body parts grossed me out.

Finally, I returned to my own chambers, excited to have time to dive into my book and read in bed, hoping to forget all I'd heard about female parts. So, I settled under the covers, tucked my sheet in around me, and used all the pillows to prop myself up. I grabbed the orb of light that Uncle Maddox had gifted to me from my bedside table. He'd given me a white stone orb enchanted with light when I was just a young dragonling. Depending on how many times I tapped it, it could fill a room with daylight. Tonight, I kept it at a low glow. It was incredibly useful for reading at night.

Settled in then, I opened my book and started to read. After initially glancing at my doors at the end of every page, I finally sighed and dove fully into my book, getting lost in a fantasy world about human creatures ruled by greed and power and lacking bonded mates. They didn't even have any magic. Instead, they captured other creatures, thinking themselves superior, and enslaved them for their own evil purposes.

I shook my head. Perhaps this was too dark a read before I fell into the land of dreams.

*I'll tell you a story*, Xenon suddenly said.

*You're still awake?*

*I was listening to the story you were reading. You're right, it's too dark for bed. Let me tell you a better one.*

I put the book down, spread out the pillows again, and put my hands behind my head, looking up at the ceiling and settling in to listen to Xenon's story.

*There was once a very, very old dragon, who was an incredibly skilled warrior and extraordinarily wise.*

I grinned. Xenon was never humble.

He continued after a chuckle.

*He had lived a long time and had lived well. He'd witnessed the lives and passing of many other creatures. One day, his family told him they would be leaving to visit the king and queen of all land creatures because the royal couple had been blessed with a baby. The dragon wasn't too keen on going, but baby dragons were rare, so he at least looked forward to seeing a baby dragon, especially his friends' baby dragon.*

*So he and his family flew, dressed in their best and most imposing outfits given the warriors they were. The king and queen greeted them heartily, and when the new parents presented their little dragonling, the old dragon's world changed completely.*

*He was awestruck for a moment as he saw into the dragonling's future. He saw what the dragonling would look like as a young dragon and as an adult dragon. Then he saw the baby together with him, the old dragon, not just as friends, but bonded mates. How could that be, he wondered. He blinked and saw once again a little dragonling, just a baby dragon.*

*Confused and shaken, the old dragon gifted the king and queen a favor and made his excuses, trying to leave. His family followed, bewildered. Long moments later, they settled in one of their nearby homes, and his family ripped into him about how rude he had been and how it could have terrible consequences for them in the future. So the old dragon told them what he'd seen. He told them that the little dragonling was as precious to him as any of them, more maybe because he was so young. But he would have to stay away until the dragonling was an adult, old enough to be a dragon's mate. Thankfully, his family understood.*

*It was difficult though, staying away. The old dragon's whole world had shifted to focus on this one little dragonling, and all he wanted to do was watch him grow up. The old dragon wanted nothing more than to be there to protect him, to see if this young dragon would be attached to him even as a youngling. But his family knew that could be dangerous, so they kept the ancient dragon busy with missions far away. So, he spent centuries fighting and planning and helping others as far away as possible until the prince was old enough for a bonded mate.*

*His family often debated how old a dragon would have to be to be ready for a bonded mate. So they kept their ears open, listening to other dragons, learning how young they had been when they'd discovered their mates and asking when they'd been old enough to not completely turn away from their own lives. The old dragon and his family had heard many stories of dragon mates meeting too young and going crazy with obsession, losing themselves in the relationship. He wanted to do it properly, not just for himself, but for the dragonling. And this dragonling wasn't just any dragonling, but a prince and heir to one of the greatest realms in this world ...*

# Chapter Thirty-Seven

## Jaxon

OVER THE NEXT FEW weeks, I was lucky enough to squeeze in some training sessions with Katsuro. The Four had been gone for a few weeks now, and Xerus had mentioned something about following leads.

Katsuro had so much new and foreign knowledge, and it had been fascinating to learn something so novel and incorporate it into my regular training. I had started teaching my siblings some of the new moves too, and Katsuro had been kind enough to train them whenever he had some spare time. But every day, he spent some time with my mother. They usually went for a walk together in the garden or played a game on the lawns behind the palace.

Unfortunately, Katsuro seemed to become more and more on edge as the days passed. He was less patient with me and my siblings when we made mistakes in training, giving me an eerie feeling that he was training us with great specificity. I wondered whether he'd seen the fights we'd face and was training us specifically against them.

"Your Highness, the griffins wish to speak with you." A messenger poked his head in the door.

"Please show them in," I said. I was sitting in my small office in the guards' barracks reviewing our progress. We'd rebuilt the griffin villages in just a couple of weeks thanks to the soldiers we'd sent there to help, and the griffins had started moving back.

Three griffins squeezed through the door, and I quickly realized that my tiny office would not fit three full-sized griffins, even though I was in human form. "Gentle griffins, I did not realize you were coming. Please, let me honor you and move our meeting to a more comfortable room," I said.

They nodded and backed out of my office. I bit my tongue to keep from laughing as they squeezed back out.

I shot the messenger a look as I exited and signaled one of my staff to bring proper refreshments as we moved to the more spacious receiving room. It had been Xerus's idea to make sure I had a large, lavishly decorated space in case I needed to receive more important guests in the barracks. The jig was up though. The griffins had seen my messy office, strewn with papers and maps of all kinds.

"Your Highness, thank you for the honor." The eldest griffin spoke as I bowed.

Running through griffin decorum in my head, I remained mute. I wanted to ensure that I didn't insult them by accident.

"Most of our population is currently returning to their homes. The griffins owe a great debt of gratitude for your family's efforts in defending our lands, sheltering us, and providing for us during our displacement." He bowed. I noticed the gray in his mane and thought it looked quite regal. Suddenly, I realized this was a conversation for Xerus or my father, the king, not the leader of the militia.

"You'll forgive my confusion, but should I invite my brother and father?" I asked. The refreshments arrived, and I was glad of the formality my right-hand man served our guests with. After he had excused himself, the griffins continued.

"We will be sending the same message to your father and brother; however, there are a few things we'd like to discuss with you."

I wondered what they could be.

"We would like to leave a contingent of griffins behind. They would like to join your army," the older, graying griffin said.

"Oh," I said, quickly recovering. I could imagine who, as I'd seen them join our morning training sessions. They hadn't missed a single training session since, and I'd seen them chatting with some of the guards and soldiers near the barracks.

"We'd be honored to have more griffins join our militia," I said.

"We would also like to add two griffins to the royal guard, specifically, His Highness Xerus's personal guard," he added.

I blinked. Then I remembered that this elder griffin had performed some kind of ritual that had made Xerus one of their own. I supposed I should have seen this coming. "Your offer is generous, and I would gladly accept your warriors into the royal guard. But they must fulfill their training and pass the required challenges before being accepted into Xerus's personal guard."

The griffin looked a little offended, and I held my breath, wondering if I'd just caused an incident. "You have to understand that I speak not to your warriors' skills but to the teamwork required. Your griffins will be new to the royal guard. The royal guard eats, sleeps, and trains together. Therefore, they are deeply bonded so they can work as a team when it comes to the safety of the royal family."

The tension in the griffin's shoulders released. "Of course. You have another griffin in your ranks—I believe he's grown up with you—Gabol?"

I nodded my head slowly.

"Would it suffice to have him join your brother's personal guard temporarily while our own warriors bond with them?" he asked, pausing noticeably around the word "bond."

He was testing me. I wondered what would happen to Xerus if I pushed it. "Gabol is his own being. I will ask him if he will join the guard temporarily, but I will not force it upon him."

The elder nodded. "Can you summon him now? I wish to speak with him."

I nodded. Poor Gabol. I rose and moved to the door, opening it and sticking my head out. "Would you please find Captain Gabol and ask him to come to the stone room right away?" I hoped the guard would understand my message and the formality of it.

After retaking my seat, I asked, "How is the return to your lands going? Can we offer more assistance?" I knew Aexie had taken care of all that, but it was a place to start.

The griffins shook their heads, but again, the old one spoke. "I do have a personal question for you though, Your Highness."

I froze momentarily, then nodded, hoping I could answer without increasing the tension in the room.

"I've heard a rumor that the royal family can speak to each other mind to mind, no matter where they are."

I nodded. I saw no reason to deny it, so I waited patiently.

"Is it true?" he pushed.

I weighed the consequences of telling him the whole truth. Most of the kingdom had guessed it already. We were secretive about it, but enough staff and soldiers and guards had witnessed it over the years that it really was more of an open secret. "My siblings and I can speak to each other within our minds, yes," I replied. I didn't want to give away more information than needed though, so I chose my words carefully.

"How convenient ... and interesting," he said. I wondered if I'd have to add griffins to my watch list.

A knock on the door saved me. Gabol entered, clean and tidy and formally dressed.

"General." He bowed his head to me. Then he turned to the griffins and said, "Elders, it is an honor to be in your presence." He bowed low.

"Young Gabol. Are you aware that we have inducted His Royal Highness Prince Xerus into our ranks as an honorary griffin elder?"

Gabol nodded.

"As such, we will be leaving behind two warriors to join his personal guard; however, His Highness, Prince Jaxon, has informed us they must spend time bonding with the other royal guards before reporting for duty. Therefore, he has agreed—if you accept—to temporarily post you in the elder prince's personal guard as a representative of the griffins' protection."

Gabol nodded. "If my general wishes it, and my elders wish it, then I will gladly serve."

"Good. The matter is settled then." The elders rose, and I bowed deeply as they left.

Gabol turned to me when the door had closed, relaxing his posture. "Should I tell Xerus or should you?"

I ran my hand through my short hair, rubbing the ends back and forth. I sighed. "Let me. You're stuck by his side for a few months."

Gabol nodded, then looked at the door. "Funny. I was orphaned by those very same elders, and now that I'm useful, I'm given a position of honor."

"Honor?" I asked. Had I missed something?

"Yup. As an official griffin representative, I now have the right to land and a home in griffin territory." He cocked an eyebrow and grinned at me.

I grinned back. If that was the case, I was happy for my friend. "Congratulations then."

"What should I do with my newly gained land? Because I am surely claiming it," he said.

"Build a castle?" I suggested.

"Dig a mote?" he said.

"And take over the world," we said together. When we were younglings, we'd always said that when we'd played in the palace grounds, smacking each other with wooden swords and running around the maze and gardens like we were spies.

Still chuckling, we left the barracks and walked back to the palace. As we neared, I said, "I'm going to go tell Xerus. You can join the next rotation."

Gabol suddenly stopped dead.

"What's the matter?" I asked.

He groaned. "I'm going to have to tell Felix." His face twisted in fear.

I laughed. Felix was my third in command and handled the schedules for guards and militia. "Good luck. You're going to need more of it than I will," I said as I turned to leave him. I only heard grumbling behind me as Gabol went to find Felix.

In my momentary solitude, I realized the weather was quite nice for the season. But then I slipped into my work and noted the specific patrols going by and how much attention they paid to their surroundings as they walked. As I entered the palace, I glanced at the posted guards and made a mental note to check their faces against the names on the postings roster.

When I reached the conference room, where we often met with our staff and soldiers and hashed out strategies, I only briefly knocked on the door before entering. I already knew Xerus was here and that he was alone. At the moment, he was standing among a couple dozen books open to various pages. Glancing over at them, I saw they were about magical defenses. "I thought we already did that," I said.

"We did. But I'm checking to make sure there isn't more we can do or there isn't something we missed," Xerus said.

"In your spare time?" I scoffed.

"I know. But I don't want to overlook anything," he said. He blinked and squeezed his eyes shut. So he'd been at this awhile.

"Why don't you ask Alexius? He loves this kind of stuff."

"You mean reading books?" He grinned at me.

I rolled my eyes. "I read books," I huffed and sent for Alexius.

"I don't want to bother him. He's getting Brixelle settled," Xerus said.

"That's too bad because he's on his way."

Xerus sighed and sat down, closing some of the books. "I assume you're here for a reason," he said, rubbing his eyes. Xerus only did that if he'd been up all night reading.

"The griffins came by my barracks' office on their way out," I said.

Xerus raised an eyebrow even as he continued rubbing his eyes.

"They'll be coming by to thank Father, and likely you. But they've given us a dozen new recruits for the army. Oh, and you'll have two new personal guards at their request."

"What?"

"I already negotiated, so there's no way out of it. I told them their two recruits needed to be trained in our system so they could develop the necessary bonds to work as a team."

"And do *I* get a say about *my* personal guards?" he asked.

"They insisted. You're an elder or something of theirs I hear, so now you need their protection. I wasn't going to fight them on that. *You* accepted that one. I bought you some time, though, before you have griffin guards watching your every move."

"So, am I free until you assure the training of the warriors they send is adequate?"

"Nope."

"Sorry?"

"You'll have Gabol by your side. They bought Gabol. Kind of. Gabol is joining your personal guard until the other two are trained."

I could see him ping-pong that in his head, whether he should fight them on this or save it for another battle.

"Fine," he finally said.

"Really?" I asked.

"Yeah. You're right. I got myself into this, and you did me a favor by putting Gabol in. I'll have to thank him for his boredom as he follows me around for the next few months."

"Good," I said, now at a loss for what to do. Thankfully, a knock sounded and Alexius entered. I turned to him. "Alexius, Xer needs some help doing some research. He wants to make sure we didn't miss anything with the magical wards we set up or if we can't add to them in some way, or even if there isn't something else we could also do. You know, he needs you to do your researching thing," I said before Xerus had a chance to send him away.

Xer looked at me like I was stupid. "But first, how are you, Alexius? How is Brixelle settling in? Does her mother like the cottage?"

Alexius looked from me to Xer, wondering what was going on. "I'm fine. Brix is in love with her new wardrobe but mumbled something about there being way too many clothes. I let Aexie handle it. And her mother loves the cottage. Mother and Father are there visiting with Roxana now."

"Well, that's wonderful news. So if you're too busy to do the research, it's fine. I can—" Xerus started.

"It's no problem. I look forward to it actually. Brixelle is ... well, very excited to be here. I'd like the excuse to dive into the library for a few quiet moments alone," he said softly, looking back at the door just in case.

"Good. It's settled," I said.

"You three have to stop having these secret meetings without me." Aexie appeared out of thin air.

"That was impressive, Aexie," Alexius said.

"Thank you," she replied, beaming at the compliment.

"I agree. I didn't even know you were here," Xerus added.

Aexie shrugged a shoulder, and I caught her up on what she'd missed. "Sounds good. So, Xer, what's the latest from Xenon?" she asked. I wished she'd softened the question a bit. I would bet Xerus's exhaustion was partly because of Xenon's extended scouting mission.

Xerus put his elbows on the table and his head in his hands. "I haven't heard much from him in the last day," he paused, staring at nothing. "Actually, I haven't heard from him at all in two days." He stared at the table then, and I felt the worry in him now.

"Is he all right?" Aexie asked.

Xerus nodded slowly. "I'd know if he was in serious trouble. But I'm not sure if I'd know if he was injured. All I know is he warned me he'd go silent if he discovered anything or if things got tough." Xerus started to rub his neck with one hand.

Alexius looked at him knowingly. "I'm sorry, brother. I'm sure he's safe and you'll hear from him soon."

"I, for one, can't just keep sitting here doing nothing," I said. "We need to prepare more."

"We can't do much until we know who we're up against," Xerus said.

"The army will soon get restless now that we've called them back. That'll just cause trouble. They need something to do, something to focus on." I stopped there as I realized I too was rubbing my neck, trying to release some of the tension there. But I couldn't help smiling when I looked over and saw Aexie—and Alexius, nose deep in a book—doing the same thing.

"It's like we're related or something," Aexie said, noticing the same thing I had.

"Huh?" Alexius looked up from the book he'd been reading.

I shook my head. "Any ideas about what the army could do for now?"

"How about that wall we're rebuilding?" Xerus asked.

"Almost done. They might be able to use half a dozen soldiers, but no more, and not for long," I replied.

"You should send them out to patrol nearby," Alexius said.

"Why? We'd just worry the citizens," Aexie said.

"Not if they're also running safety drills," Alexius said, sticking his tongue out at Aexie.

Sometimes I forgot they were still dragonlings really.

"Send the soldiers out to knock on doors, run safety drills, meet the citizens. It'll give the folks someone familiar to turn to if something does happen," Alexius suggested.

"You also might get more recruits that way too," Xerus said.

I exhaled a deep breath. The army wouldn't be pleased. Gabol would think he dodged an arrow though. With the army going door to door and being on their best manners, despite the odd drills, they'd be chomping at the bit. I was going to have to double their physical training just to keep them in line—and in shape. "Fine. I don't know if it will really solve their restlessness, but it can't hurt," I said.

"Do you think this attack will involve dragonsbane?" Alexius asked suddenly.

"I don't think so. Dragonsbane went missing locally. Katsuro said this was a threat from the North," Xerus replied.

"How long does it take for dragonsbane to grow?" I asked Alexius.

"Four months under the right circumstances," he replied.

"We're immune to it, so they wouldn't gain much of an advantage," Aexie pointed out.

"They might not know that," I said. "And what of the other uses for dragonsbane?"

"Good point, Jaxon. Maybe you could look into that again, maybe go around asking the farmers again if they've heard anything more since?" Xerus asked.

I nodded.

"Oh, before I forget again, Mother was asking for you, Alexius," Aexie said.

Alexius's head shot up from the book he was reading. "Did she say why?"

"My guess is that it has something to do with Brixelle." Aexie stood and frowned at her nails, then turned to leave. "We done here?" she asked over her shoulder.

Xerus nodded, and we all took that as our cue to leave.

# Chapter Thirty-Eight

## Alexius

I HEADED FOR MY mother's chambers, but the guards directed me to the Jade Room instead. As I made my way there, Jaxon caught up with me in the hallway. "Sorry, I should have told you. Mother and Father usually train in the Jade Room these days with all their additional responsibilities thanks to this looming attack."

I shrugged. I just hoped their meeting with Brixelle and her mother had gone well. "How's Brix doing with her training?" I asked.

"She's a quick learner. Strong as an ox too. She can outlift half the newest recruits." Jaxon grinned.

I nodded. Jaxon had assessed Brixelle's combat capability a couple weeks ago and decided to include her with the army's newest recruits, though he usually spent time at the end of the session teaching her privately. As much as I would have liked to teach Brix myself, she'd asked for Jaxon.

She wanted to get to know my siblings on her own, and I respected her choice. In return, I made a point to spend time every day helping her mother with things in her new cottage so I could get to know her too. She was still thrilled that my siblings and I had built the cottage in a day. I'd leveled the land one night before dark, clearing out a large area because I knew Brixelle and her mother preferred their dragon form. In the morning, Jax and Xerus had raised two walls by the time my father had come to help.

I was sure if Xenon had been here, he would have just used magic, but my father was a firm believer in doing what you could physically, especially if you were capable. But with his help, we had the walls up by noon, the roof an hour later, and the interior done by that evening. In one more day, we'd flown all their things from the farm to the new cottage.

"If we tie the sheep together, we could probably take a dozen each and move them all in one more trip," I'd said, landing as Brixelle had taken one last look at her farm.

"No. I think I'll herd them back myself. Mother wants to walk with me."

"Are you sure? It would be much quicker if we flew. My siblings don't mind."

"I think my sheep might die of fear if they fly through the air."

"Do you want me to come with you?" I'd asked then.

"No. Your family's taken plenty of time to help mine. I'm sure you have things to do at the palace. We'll be there by sundown," she'd said, then reached over to kiss my cheek.

"Can I leave a guard with you?"

"If you must, as long as he doesn't get in the way." She'd raised an eyebrow in challenge.

"I'll leave Aster. He was a farmer. He might even be useful." I'd smiled, then kissed the top of her head before adding, "See you tonight." I'd leaped up then, popping back into dragon form and taking to the skies.

She'd moved into the palace a week ago, and her mother was thrilled with her new cottage. She usually joined us for suppers in the palace, and Brixelle was getting used to the chaos that was palace life. I breathed a sigh of relief as she seemed quite happy to join the ups and downs of my life.

As I shook off the memory, Jaxon and I opened the doors to the Jade Room to find my mother and father sparring. Most would think my father would be the better fighter, but my mother was a Wild One, and this was where her ferocity really shone. Katsuro sat at the edge of the room, and he cheered for my mother each time she landed a hit on my father. Jaxon joined right in, striding up to them and fixing my father's posture and the angle of his staff.

"Oh, Alexius, honey, come here." She tossed her staff to Jaxon, who caught it without looking back and stepped in to spar with my father slowly, showing him the steps that he wanted him to practice and the delicate angles to pay attention to. My poor father looked like he'd rather be buried in paperwork.

My mother was barely sweating. She took off her gloves and put them on the table. "Will you walk with me? I'd love to cool down outside." She led me to the balcony and opened the doors to a vast balcony big enough for a full-sized dragon to land on.

"Is everything well, Mother?" I asked.

"Oh yes. You needn't worry, Alexius. So, your father and I went to visit Roxana."

"I know."

"Well, your father and I are wondering if you and Brixelle would like a formal ceremony to acknowledge your bond?" She sat on one of the stone benches. It was made for a dragon, so with my mother's slight human figure sitting on the edge, the back of it dwarfed her.

My chest constricted at the thought of Xerus and Xenon's ceremony. "Not like Xenon and Xerus's," I said, then added, "I mean, it was stunning, but we aren't really ready for all that ... attention." I wondered if I'd just insulted my mother or my brother.

"Oh, it doesn't have to be that grand. It can be small if you like, even just family. Maybe even out here? A quiet little ceremony to acknowledge your partnership?" My mother looked into my eyes like she was searching for an answer to a question she wasn't about to ask.

"We aren't planning blood oaths if that's what you're wondering," I volunteered, sitting down next to her.

"Oh?" the relief on her face said that had indeed been the question on her mind.

"I can respect Xerus's decision to do so, and while I suppose it would be easier at times to know exactly how Brixelle was feeling, if we were to ever have children, I couldn't have them orphaned if something happened to one of us. Besides, having my three siblings in my head is sometimes a lot. I can't imagine having yet another voice in it," I explained.

My mother nodded, obviously holding words back.

"I'm happy to explore the mating bond though, and Brixelle is too. I don't think she'd want to blood oath herself to me either. She's more independent than that. Plus I don't think I could control it as well as Xerus and Xenon do," I said.

My mother nodded again. "Truth be told, I'm relieved that their blood oath doesn't affect them nearly as much as I've seen it affect others, and I give Xenon the credit for that. He's maintained strict control over his own blood oath and taught Xerus how to control it too instead of letting the oath take control of them and their lives."

I looked out over the balcony to Roxana's cottage and her little white clouds of sheep. "I think Brixelle would love a ceremony here."

Seeing what I was looking at, she said wistfully, "She really loves those sheep."

I smiled. "I don't really understand it, but I love her, and the sheep love her. So I don't mind sharing her with them."

My mother smiled at that. "Have you met her sheep?"

"Only from afar. They don't seem to especially like males."

"I'm sure you'll win them over eventually," my mother said. "How about we have the ceremony when Xenon returns?"

I nodded. "I'll ask Brixelle."

As the youngest in the royal line, I was of the least concern when it came to the bonds I made, not that anyone could control who you bonded with. But still, it made me happy that my parents had thought of me.

That night after supper, I walked with Brixelle through the halls. Because she was trying to learn how to get around the palace, we would often wander for a while. Then I'd pick a room for her to try navigating to by herself.

Finally, I screwed up my nerve. "My mother was wondering if you'd like to have a small—and she defined small as immediate family only—ceremony on the balcony of the Jade Room. It overlooks the rear forest so you can see your sheep and the cottage," I said.

She turned to me, her eyes shining. "That would be lovely. And I even have a dress for it now." Brixelle smiled.

I could feel my scales glowing at her happiness. "Do we do it in human form?"

"I think so. It's much easier to decorate this form." She looked down at her clothes. I was impressed that she'd really settled into wearing many outfits a day quite easily.

"Just family? Is there anyone else you might want to invite?" I asked.

"No. Family's fine. Just Mother for me," she said.

"Are you sure you don't want to invite some of the other farmers nearby?"

"Hmm ... you mean all those farmers who thought I'd never be able to keep my sheep alive for more than a few months? No, I'm good, thanks."

"How about that one dragon, the one you grew up with?" I asked.

"Would you be all right with that?" she asked hesitantly.

I pursed my lips. "Yes, I think so. I'm glad he was there for you. You didn't even know me then. I don't think I have anything to be jealous of."

She grinned at me. "Then, yes, maybe him. Did your mother say when?"

"When Xenon returns. The Four will probably want to be there now that we're kind of family, I think."

"Wow. The Four. I can't believe the company I keep nowadays," she said.

"All right," I said as I looked around at the hallway we were in. "Jade Room." We'd wandered down to the armory, and I was making her cross half the palace to get to the Jade Room in our family's private wing.

Brixelle stopped to think for a minute before she started to stride down the hall like she knew where she was going. I followed a step behind her. She'd been angry with me the first time I'd tried to assist, so I pressed my lips together this time and followed.

Finding the Jade Room was relatively easy. There were about five different ways to get there. Brixelle had a keen sense of direction outside; she always knew north and south. But when you put her inside a building, suddenly, she could barely figure out where the front doors were.

She stopped at an intersection, and I had just opened my mouth when she said, "Shh. I don't want your help."

I promptly closed my mouth again. She took a wrong turn, but when we came to a window, she looked outside for a minute before turning back around. Finally, on her second attempt, we arrived at the doors of the Jade Room.

"I did it!" she exclaimed and did a little dance. I grinned and she threw her arms around me, so I twirled her around.

"Want to see the balcony?" I asked. It would be dark, but she'd be able to see the light from her mother's cottage. She nodded and I led her through the echoey room.

"Wow. I forgot how beautiful this room is," Brixelle said as she looked around her. I stopped to let her take it all in. I had grown up here, so the novelty had worn off long ago.

Her gaze flew around the softly lit room to take in all the details: the green jade, the white stone, and how they intermingled to create a formidable, breathtaking room.

"It's magic too. It changes size to house whatever dimensions its inhabitants need," I whispered in her ear, wrapping her in my arms.

"It's incredible," she whispered back.

I slowly started to guide her to the balcony, where I pushed the door open and led her through, even though she pulled at me to stay in the Jade Room.

But then she looked out into the dark expanse of forest and took a deep breath. She went to the railing and leaned over, inhaling deeply.

"The forest smells so different from the farm. But this is now my favorite spot in the whole palace."

"Why's that?"

"I like being able to see my mother's cottage, and the sheep." She looked at the little group of white spots that reflected the moonlight. "When I was farming in the fields at night, it was dark. And I don't just mean dark like here in the palace where there's always a strip of light from under a door or lanterns giving off a little glow. I mean in the forest, it's a lot like the fields back home: pitch-black dark."

I came up behind her again, snaking my arms around her. "Most creatures are afraid of the dark."

She shook her head. "Not me. It's quiet and peaceful. And if it's truly dark, you have only your thoughts for company. There's no noise, no distractions," she said.

"And some people can't stand to be left alone with their own thoughts either."

"That was my favorite part of being a farmer, the quiet hours where all I had was my own thoughts and nothing else," Brixelle whispered.

I started to sway with her in my arms and she turned around, tucking her head into my neck and wrapping her arms around my middle. We held each other tightly as we danced gently around the balcony in the dark, with only the light of the moon and stars illuminating our dance floor.

# Chapter Thirty-Nine

## Aexie

F EELING ESPECIALLY RESTLESS, I'D concocted an excuse to visit Jaxon in his office and glanced at the duty rosters posted on the wall. So I knew Darox would be done his shift on the roof late at night, and I waited for him in an alcove, not visible to the other guards but still out in the fresh air.

"Hey, stranger," I said as he passed me on his last rotation. Then I pounced, not giving him a chance to reply. I had worn a dress that I would call irresistible with its low-cut bodice and slit up the side. Others would probably call it barely a dress, maybe more of a sparkly slip.

I was fully enjoying exploring Darox's mouth with my own and his hands running along my body, and I wondered whether we'd be able to make it to my room or if this little alcove would be space enough for our fun. But after I kept bumping into a stone ledge, I decided to move to another spot that was a little more spacious but still exciting.

I pushed Darox away but batted my eyelashes at him as I took his hand and led him to one of the higher towers. I knew the guards' rotations by heart because my siblings and I had long ago mastered sneaking up to the towers. One part was especially tricky to get past unnoticed given Darox's size, but I turned us both invisible and we snuck past. I'd have to construct a bubble to hide the sound, but we would have relative privacy.

I had just started undressing him when I heard the hurried, uneven shuffle of guards running above us. I froze. Then I sat up to look out over the tower's ledge even as I sniffed the blood, instantly knowing it belonged to Xenon. I didn't need to see the three figures holding a fourth golden one between them as they flew back to know what was going on. I jumped up. "Go get Foxall right away. As fast as you possibly can," I commanded, popping the bubble and leaping over the ledge before taking my dragon form and flying up the tower to the next level, much to the guards' surprise.

*Alexius, stay in the Jade Room. Send Brixelle for towels and hot water. The Four are back and Xenon's not moving.* I didn't wait for a reply before issuing another order. *Jax, go get Xerus. Then meet us in the Jade Room. The Four are arriving. Xenon's unconscious.*

I pointed to a guard the second my feet touched the floor. "You, go wake my father and mother right away. Tell them we'll meet them in the Jade Room." Then I pointed to another. "You, when Darox returns, bring him and Foxall to the Jade Room."

Then I flew out to meet The Four. They looked tired—beyond tired. I flew beneath Xenon and helped them back, holding Xenon on my back. He was a big and old dragon, so he was long, not like us with our thick, squat bodies. He was more snakelike and easier to carry.

I directed them to the Jade Room's balcony. It was wide enough for us all to land on and big enough that Xenon could keep his dragon form. When we landed, we gently put Xenon on a long table that magically appeared. He was breathing, but it was labored.

"The idiot went out after we'd all gone to bed. Someone must have tipped him off and he went to explore alone. He was ambushed by fifty thugs," Yagaron said. They were all caked in dirt and blood of all colors.

"The North is in bad shape," Vadentia said. "Their king is ignoring the populace."

Alexius ran up in human form, and I popped back into it too, forgetting what I was wearing. Not even Talmaro commented on my barely there outfit though as we all went to work on Xenon.

Alexius came rushing over the moment we landed. He had the strongest healing magic in our family, and he'd studied anatomy extensively; he knew best what to do until Foxall arrived. Brixelle ran back a few seconds later with a team of people carrying towels and basins of hot water. She folded and tucked some of the towels around Xenon to make him more comfortable on the table, then threw the others into the buckets of hot water.

Alexius moved quickly as he took in Xenon's dragon form, pacing up and down the length of the ancient dragon and using his magic to look inside Xenon. My little brother kept his mind open to me, so as he assessed Xenon's injuries, I saw the list growing and Alexius prioritizing what needed to be done. We both made sure to keep Xerus's door shut. He was going to be upset enough when he saw Xenon.

I shifted closer to Vadentia, who eyed my attire—or lack of—with more appreciation than I expected. "When Xerus gets here, you might have to hold him back. Until then, we'll follow Alexius's orders until Foxall arrives," I whispered. She nodded and edged toward the door.

The doors burst open. Xerus looked angry at first, but the moment he saw Xenon, his anger evaporated and his scales paled. His knees buckled, but Vadentia joined Jax as he arrived, and they helped him to a chair near Xenon's head. Vadentia nodded to Jax. Then he came to join me as Alexius continued his evaluation. Jax's jaw tightened in response to Alexius's thoughts.

Suddenly, Alexius stopped in his tracks, right by Xenon's tail. He reached into a cut in Xenon's tail and pulled out a small rock no bigger than his thumb. But as his brows creased, he looked at us. *It's made of dragonsbane,* he said. *Jax, go get a container. There's more of it. That must be what's preventing Xenon from healing himself. Ouch!* Alexius dropped the little rock, looking at his burned thumb and finger. *We'll need it sealed. Keep Brixelle at Xenon's head.* He stared at his fingers; he was immune to the worst of dragonsbane's effects, as we were, but it looked now as though we weren't completely immune. This rock was something new.

I nodded and relayed the message to Brixelle, who was gently dabbing Xenon's forehead with a cool cloth.

So that's how something could take down a dragon as old and powerful as Xenon. I'd never heard of a stone made of dragonsbane. It would be lethal to most dragons. Only Xenon, the royal family, and maybe a dragonsbane farmer would survive exposure.

"The rocks in his body are dragonsbane. You need to stay back while Alexius removes them," I told the guards. I didn't know how dragonsbane would affect them. They nodded but never took their eyes off Xenon.

Alexius kept pulling more and more rocks out of Xenon's tail with the tips of his claws and dropping them on the floor. *They burn your flesh if you hold them too long,* he said. That was frightening. I counted the little lumps on the floor: eight so far.

Jaxon returned with a container and gloves.

Alexius turned and glanced at the jar. *You'll have to enchant the container to fully seal it. As soon as these touch flesh, it burns and burrows in.* Jaxon handed him a glove and Alexius nodded, continuing his extractions. As he did, Jaxon followed with the jar. Xenon started to shiver, so I used my magic to blanket him with warmth. When his shivering eased, I let the magic settle around him as I continued to watch Alexius pull more than twenty small stones from Xenon's tail. Alexius nodded at Jaxon then, who turned to pick up the ones on the floor with a gloved hand.

Alexius scoured the old dragon's body one last time, then returned to the tail, scanning it a second and third time, making sure there was no more dragonsbane buried in Xenon's flesh. That would explain how a dragon like Xenon had been taken down and unable to heal.

*When Foxall arrives, I need a jar of tar,* Alexius said.

Foxall ran in just then, and Jaxon relayed the message. Foxall immediately turned to the wagon the guards had flown up and placed on the balcony behind him. He donned a pair of gloves and grabbed a dark jar, trading it for the one Jax held. The apothecary held it away from him as he went through the process of sealing it.

Jaxon brought the jar of tar to Alexius. The dragonsbane must have had a lingering effect because as Alexius coaxed contaminated air out of each hole and drew the air into the tar, the tar bubbled with each addition. Finally, once Alexius had done that three times with each hole, I saw color starting to return to Xenon's body. The tarnished silver slowly became the brilliant argent that was his normal color.

Xerus jumped up with a start and leaned over Xenon. I supposed he must be awake then, or at least coming to. Alexius and Jaxon went to work on knitting the holes back together. Jaxon, always the observant one, had picked up on how Alexius was doing it so he could help.

I felt a strong desire to help too. *Here is some support, brothers,* I said as I sent some of my own magic to them, more for Alexius. Yet I was surprised to discover that Alexius was barely tired. He must have been practicing a lot lately to be able to keep his strength so.

Xerus took one of Xenon's claws, the look on his face telling me he was speaking to him through their oath. Alexius left Jaxon to finish knitting the wounds together as he moved up the dragon's body, still examining. His brow furrowed as he approached Xenon's middle. I looked in my brother's mind and saw internal bleeding. Alexius took a deep breath and started moving the blood back into the correct channels. His magic looked like light to me—magic looked like light to my whole family—and I watched with interest as he herded the blood back into Xenon's veins and arteries like he was scooping it back in with sun rays.

Alexius finally swayed, so I ran over and used my own magic to hold him up. He nodded in acknowledgment as he continued to fix Xenon from the inside.

Talmaro and Vadentia started to pace on the far end of the balcony, and Yagaron spoke in a low voice with Foxall. Foxall nodded then, finally finished preparing his draughts, and approached Xenon. Vadentia and Talmaro were about to object, but my parents—when had they even arrived?— reassured them of Foxall's credibility.

Foxall looked at Xerus, who moved to help. Xenon was indeed awake, and he opened his eyes when Xerus supported his head. Foxall slowly poured a dark-amber liquid into his mouth. Once Xenon had swallowed it, Foxall moved to stand across from Alexius, observing quietly.

"His wrist," Alexius said, and Foxall took Xenon's wrist, nodding. From inside Alexius's head, I saw Xenon had a few fractures too. It was mind boggling that he'd been so incredibly injured.

Jaxon approached Alexius too. *What can I help you with next?* Even Xerus heard it now that he had finally calmed down enough to join us in soxkendi.

*His collarbone. And get Foxall to work on the vertebrae just between the shoulders when he's done with the wrist.* Alexius was still busy working on the internal injuries, repairing things and coaxing the blood back to its proper places.

Xenon's breath came stronger now, but he closed his eyes again. The tension in the room had abated, but everyone still watched the ancient dragon closely. When Xerus had arrived, Brixelle had surrendered her spot to him and now popped her head out the door. A few minutes later, a few guards came in with food and water for everyone and put the trays on the table.

I suddenly felt a spike in Alexius's mind as he turned his attention to the last injury. He coaxed the last of Xenon's tissue back together, then scanned him with magic to determine how Xenon's blood was flowing. The moment Alexius finally finished, he let himself lean on the magical supports I was sending him. Brixelle was next to him in an instant and helped him to a grouping of couches that had appeared.

"You are the most amazing creature I've ever met. I love you," I heard her whisper, and I couldn't help but smile. I felt their love for each other, and I was truly happy for my little brother.

Foxall was labeling his draughts now, and Jaxon had gone to sit down, so we left Xenon and Xerus alone on the balcony. Now that Xenon was going to be all right, we all wanted to know what had happened.

My father held the magically sealed jar as he and my mother examined it. A moment later, Katsuro knocked gently on the far door and entered. He looked worriedly at Xenon lying on the table but nodded and smiled before turning to join my mother. The baku took the jar and twirled it around, making the little balls of dragonsbane roll around. "This is dragonsbane. The plant has been dried and crushed into powder, then mixed with a binder and pressed into these tiny spherical shapes," Katsuro said.

"Do you know what the binder is?" Jaxon asked.

"I would need to handle it to tell. But I assume you've sealed this jar magically for a reason?" He looked us questioningly.

Alexius nodded and said, "I couldn't risk anyone getting hurt."

I had my back to Xenon and Xerus, so I was surprised when Xenon, back in human form and with a thick robe around him, appeared beside me, Xerus supporting him.

"I'm sorry to have given you all such a scare," he croaked, not quite fully recovered. "I'm grateful to you, brothers and sisters." He nodded at each one of us, his stare lingering on Alexius long enough that I wondered if Xenon could communicate with just Alexius without the rest of us hearing.

"We're all glad you're all right—" Yagaron began.

Talmaro interrupted him. "What the Fates?!?"

Vadentia looked angry now. "Why didn't you bring one or all of us with you?!"

"Because I wasn't looking for trouble," Xenon whispered. "I just went out for a drink." Xerus closed his eyes in the saddest "I told you so" moment I'd ever witnessed. "I was looking for dragonsbane to drink. I'd run out of my own supply."

"Wait, you drink dragonsbane?" I asked.

"He enjoys the taste," Vadentia explained, rolling her eyes.

I shot him an incredulous look. Was that what he was always drinking in the evenings?

"I know. It's dangerous and I probably shouldn't. But I've built up an incredible tolerance because of it," he said.

"So what happened?" Alexius asked.

"Well, like I said, I went out for a drink. Sometimes it's tough to find my drink of choice, so I had to go to a seedier area. But up north, seedy is normal so I didn't have to go far. It seemed at first like some thugs thought they could take advantage of a well-dressed human, but they must have known what I was and targeted me on purpose because as soon as they cornered me in an alley, they shot a bunch of those little round pellets at me. I didn't think much of a few pellets at first, but suddenly, I felt them burning. The next thing you know, there were dozens more thugs in the alley surrounding me. I didn't stand a chance, so I tried to change back, but the pellets burned so much I couldn't. It wasn't until Yagaron and the others flew down and surrounded me that most of the miscreants ran off. Then they tossed me into the air to force me to change into dragon form. I was in so much pain, I think I only changed out of self-preservation."

Vadentia jumped in. "I felt something was wrong, so I woke the other two, and we flew over the city until we heard a commotion. I saw a flash of argent and knew Xenon was in the middle of the mass of thugs. So we flew down and protected him, killing those we could before they hightailed it."

"Cowards." Talmaro smirked. "When Xenon fell from the sky, we barely caught him before he hit the ground. We knew something was seriously wrong and flew him here directly."

"We didn't get much information up north. I heard rumors of dragonsbane plants growing in a field to the northeast of our position but didn't think much of it," Vadentia said.

Yagaron looked carefully at my family before his gaze rested on my parents. "The king of the North is not taking care of his responsibilities. The citizens are starving and turning on each other. Their streets are slums and thugs run the local villages. And the thugs are soldiers."

I watched my father's expression turn serious. "I haven't heard anything from the north in months, though Thaxton looked well enough at the ceremony," he said. "Now I wish I'd had time to meet with him."

"Oh, he's living well, for he's increased taxes three times in the last three years," Vadentia said, looking down at her feet.

"I will write to him," my father said.

"I don't think he'll confirm anything," Xerus said. "If he hasn't asked for aid in the last three years, he obviously knows what's going on and is choosing to ignore it," Xerus said through clenched teeth.

"Let us at least give him the opportunity," my mother, ever the diplomat, said. "He is, after all, our nephew," she said, taking my father's hands.

Of course they would feel responsible. Thaxton's parents had died while traveling, and Father had always felt responsible because they had been on their way to visit him. Later, my father had been the one to fly up and help Thaxton ascend the throne.

"If you don't mind, I think I'll go rest awhile," Xenon said, Xerus helping him to stand and head for the door. We all nodded, not that he needed our permission to go rest. Foxall followed them out, arms laden with bottles. He'd been quietly tending to his wagon of supplies during our conversation.

The rest of us were silent as we thought of all that had just happened. It seemed like the answer was too obvious. Was the North really in that bad a shape? Was Thaxton becoming rich on the backs of the citizens? And the dragonsbane being grown in the northeast, practically on royal property. Was it being grown with his knowledge or even on his orders? Was it all as easy as that? Were all our problems linked to this one individual?

"Sometimes, the easiest solution is the hardest to believe but the most obvious," Katsuro said.

I startled, forgetting he'd been here.

"Katsuro, what could bind the dragonsbane powder and create such small, solid shapes?" Alexius asked.

Katsuro looked serious. He furrowed his brows as he said, "There are many things that could bind it. It could be something as simple as dirt and water because to certain other creatures, it's as harmless as grass."

My mother rose. "Let us all get some rest tonight. We'll gather tomorrow morning and discuss the situation."

We all jumped to our feet immediately. The remaining members of The Four bowed, and we all filed out, my brothers and I heading back to our rooms. Xerus's rooms were quiet as we passed by, and we tried to be quiet too as we nodded to each other and returned to our rooms.

I started to peel off my dress, at first surprised that no one had commented before I realized I'd probably get an earful from my mother tomorrow.

A soft knock came at my common-room window, and even though I was partway out of my dress, I poked my head out of my bedroom to see what was going on.

I was surprised to see Vadentia, and I pulled my dress back on before going to open the window. "What's the matter?" I asked in a hushed whisper.

"Nothing's the matter. I'm just looking for a distraction. Besides, it would be a shame for that dress to not be properly enjoyed," she said as she climbed through the window and looked me up and down. "How are you feeling?" Her voice was soft, and I knew what game she was playing right away. Her hand moved to stroke my shoulder.

"I'm all right," I said, matching her stare for stare.

"What were you doing before our arrival?" she asked. "Was that you I saw with a guard in the tower?" she purred, her hand stroking my entire arm.

I shrugged, feeling the tingly feeling I loved so much along my skin. "Looking for a distraction, I suppose."

"Well, what do you know. Me too," she said, her hand trailing up my arm to my neck and face before she gently came closer and kissed my lips. I felt my blood rush through my body, suddenly picking up where I'd left off earlier that night.

# CHAPTER FORTY

## JAXON

THE MORNING SUN WAS trying to peek over the horizon and burn off the dawn's clouds as I sat in the conference room an hour before my family was to meet to hash out our strategy. More fires had been reported, and even though they'd been handled swiftly, it bothered me. I'd tossed and turned last night until finally giving up on sleep and starting my day a few hours earlier than usual. Thank goodness I'd asked my third, Felix, to oversee training this morning before I'd retired for the night. I'd passed him on his way to the barracks earlier, and he'd nodded. I'd absentmindedly returned the greeting, my thoughts still on the events of the previous night. Apparently, I hadn't been the only one who couldn't sleep. He'd looked somber, as if he knew something was coming. In fact, it felt as if the entire army knew. I'd heard murmurings and more whispers on my way here. It was dangerous to let the conjecture continue, but my family didn't have a solid plan yet, so they'd all just have to whisper a little longer.

I crossed my arms on the table and rested my head on my hands. The injuries Xenon sustained would have killed anyone else. Those pellets of dragonsbane were nothing to shrug off. Alexius, Foxall, and I were only the only ones who could treat a wound of that sort, and we were only three individuals. Even Aexie, who had trained some with Foxall, didn't have the magical skill. If a dozen of my soldiers got hit with those, they'd surely die before the three of us could get to them, and that was if they had some degree of immunity in the first place. How were we supposed to fight an enemy with no clear identity and weapons that lethal?

All they had to do was drop these dragonsbane balls from the sky and half my army would be dead. I made a note to ask my second—or my third now I guessed—to make a detailed list of every dragon's weaknesses and strengths. In truth, I needed to assess who was immune to dragonsbane. Could any of them keep fighting, or would my whole army be wiped out with one attack? Our only saving grace was that we had at least two creatures on each team that were not dragons; hence, they wouldn't be affected by dragonsbane.

Still, if two-thirds of every team was busy taking cover, then how would we ever overcome anyone on a battlefield? For that matter, if most of my army was vulnerable, we needed a way to protect them, or the loss of life would be catastrophic and the kingdom would fall in minutes.

I wondered if Xerus was thinking about that. Then I shook my head. If Xenon was safe and resting now, of course my brother was troubled by the same questions that had kept me awake.

The door creaked open, and Xenon gingerly stepped into the room with Xerus's help. I sat forward. "You sure you're up for this?" I asked Xenon.

He nodded. "You're going to need my information. Besides, this is my family now too."

I looked at my brother. He was worried and maybe even mad that Xenon wasn't resting. He looked like I felt, but worse.

"He was up all night thinking strategy," Xenon said as he thrust his chin at Xerus. He winced as pain shot through him.

"Maybe we should have paced together then," I said.

Xerus only helped Xenon to a seat, then sat and bounced his leg, trying to watch Xenon out of the corner of his eye. Clearly restless, he glanced first out the window, then to where the coffee tray usually sat. Seeing nothing there, he rose and went to stick his head out the door. "Could you ask someone to bring enough coffee for the whole family?"

He hadn't even had a chance to make it all the way back to his chair when a soft knock sounded, and Alexius eased in. Being a lot younger than us, he looked fresher than Xerus and I but still as if he'd been up all night. My insightful little brother turned around in the open door and rolled in a cart. "I figured if I hadn't slept, you two wouldn't have either. And by the looks of it, I was right to stop by the kitchen first." He rolled in a large pot of coffee and made us all a cup before pouring himself one.

As I watched him put two spoons of sugar and some cream in his coffee, I thought it was odd for him to add two since he normally only used one spoonful of sugar. And how was it that Alexius knew how the three of us took our coffee? We rarely dined together first thing in the morning. "Thanks," I said. I'd certainly missed a lot during that century I'd been angry and ignoring him.

Then we all sat there in silence, sipping our coffees and unwilling to open the conversation until everyone was present. Besides, if my brothers were of the same mind, our thoughts were consuming us. So, we stared into the air, into our coffees, or out the window, waiting. I let the coffee slide down my throat and warm my stomach. Despite my tension, sipping hot coffee early in the morning was cozy. So, even though the meeting was about to start, I put my empty cup down, laid my head back in my hands, and leaned back in my chair, closing my eyes. It felt so nice just to close my eyes for a little bit. Surely Aexie and my parents would arrive any minute to start our strategy planning...

I woke with a start. My head jerked up and I looked around. Alexius was curled in his chair, sleeping, and Xerus was rubbing his closed eyes as Xenon looked fondly at him. I looked away as they woke, feeling like I was trespassing on a private moment.

"What happened?" I asked.

"I asked Katsuro to put you all to sleep for a few hours." My mother rose from her chair beside the stone fireplace. She wound her yarn ball back up and stuck her crochet hook in it.

"What? Why?" Xerus asked.

Alexius stretched the sleep from his limbs and yawned. He furrowed his brow, likely just realizing he hadn't meant to fall asleep.

"You are my sons. I know you better than you think. Besides, I could practically hear you all pacing last night and knew none of you slept. So, I asked Kat to help you sleep when you all gathered in the morning." My mother drew herself up to sit tall as she usually did when she was taking charge.

"But what about the meeting?" Alexius asked.

"I rescheduled it until after lunch. Now that you've slept, you three will think even better once you've eaten," she continued.

"What about the coffee? Why didn't it keep us awake?" I asked.

"Baku magic is stronger than any stimulant you could ingest," Katsuro said as he stood up. He'd been crouched on the floor next to my mother's chair.

"Katsuro insisted he keep watch over you with me," she said. "Now, food first, then meeting."

I stood up, stretching my limbs. I definitely felt more rested, though some parts of my body complained about the sleeping position.

I wasn't particularly pleased as I entered the dining room and piled food on my plate, my stomach growling its displeasure at my late breakfast. I glanced at Xerus and Alexius and saw that they were grumpy as well. We all felt like we'd just been scolded like little dragonlings. Then I glanced at Xenon and realized he looked quite chipper as he too piled food on his plate—and quite recovered with not even a limp as he walked now. However, he put less food on his plate than usual, just enough to be considered breakfast.

"You didn't sleep like we did, did you?" I asked Xenon.

"What?" he turned to me, trying to hide his smile.

"You weren't asleep when I woke up," Xerus said, stepping away to better look at him.

Xenon threw his free hand up. "I slept through the night last night. I was deemed 'rested enough.'"

"Traitor," Xerus mumbled as he continued to pile food on his plate.

"It was for your own good," Xenon said, kissing Xerus's cheek and looking pleased as punch.

I sat on Xenon's other side and speared a sausage from his plate. "You already ate breakfast."

"What?" Xerus said, turning back again.

Xenon looked sheepish now, glowing a bit as Xerus looked at him expectantly. "I was starving when we woke this morning, but I didn't want to make everyone wait for me to eat. So when I realized Katsuro had put you all to sleep, I had breakfast," Xenon said.

"Then why are you eating now?" Xerus asked.

"I wanted to eat with you," Xenon said, trying to flash his most charming smile. "And I'm hungry again."

"He probably needs the calories. His body did rebuild a lot of tissue last night," Alexius chipped in.

Xenon threw Alexius an appreciative smile and looked back at Xerus, who shrugged his shoulders and focused on his own plate of food.

We ate quickly and silently, Mother watching us all carefully.

When we were all done, we waited for my mother to release us. I needed to get started, and as I glanced around the room, it was clear my brothers felt the same urgency I did. I don't know why it felt as if we were late, but it did. Finally she nodded, rising with us as we left and started to return to the conference room.

"Sorry, we moved the meeting to the Jade Room. We'll have a few extra guests," my mother said, forestalling us.

Xerus turned on his heel, not as slow now as he had been when he'd appeared with Xenon that morning. The rest of us followed and entered the Jade Room to find a large round table at its center and my father, Brixelle, Talmaro, Vadentia, Yagaron, and Aexie sitting there.

"Why didn't Aexie get put to sleep this morning?" Alexius turned to complain to Mother.

"She slept," she said, raising an eyebrow, which told us her patience at our questions was quickly coming to an end.

Brixelle stood up and went to Alexius. She gave him a quick hug and a peck before sitting back down beside him at the table. Katsuro and Foxall appeared through the still open door as we sat down, and they too took a seat.

We all turned expectantly to my father, who stood up. "Thank you for joining us this afternoon," he said. "We all have a vested interest in this realm and want to protect it from whatever danger is coming." He repeated Katsuro's warning so we were all on the same page.

Xenon already knew about it, but the other three of his crew looked concerned. They also kept glancing at Katsuro as if his presence made them nervous.

*Xenon says baku are very rare. It's the first time the other three have even seen a baku up close,* Xerus sent us. *Except of course, at our ceremony, but that wasn't this close.*

So that explained their anxiety at Katsuro's presence.

*Do you think Mom and Katsuro were intimate?* Aexie asked.

*Aexie!* Xerus exclaimed in our heads.

*Sorry. I know, gross. But look at how he looks at her. It's almost sad. Father looks at Mother the same way, but Mother only looks at Father like that. She looks at Katsuro like a little brother.*

*Focus on the task at hand please,* was all Xerus replied with. That didn't stop me from sneaking my own peek at Katsuro and how his attention constantly flicked to our mother. I was just glad that a baku was willing to risk his life for our mother's safety.

"I don't need to go over what happened to Xenon in the last day or so. But I would like to ask Aexie and Xenon to tell us what they know," my father continued.

Aexie stood and glowed a bit as she said, "I was at a tavern one night, and I heard that at least a couple dozen more dragonsbane plants on illegal farms had gone missing." She glanced briefly at Brixelle and Alexius. I pressed my lips together. I hoped Brixelle would be the forgiving kind if she ever found out Aexie had been trying to dig up dirt on her at that tavern.

"I didn't think the two things were related, but I suppose we can't deny it now, not with what happened to Xenon," Xerus added.

Foxall put the jar of dragonsbane on the table. We all stared mutely at the little pellets.

"Do we know for sure if it's all related?" Yagaron asked. "What if they're all separate events? Perhaps there's a rogue gang up north, and they stole the plants to control their own territory, gain power, or even overthrow the king? Do we know whether the thieves stole the dragonsbane specifically to use against us, or did they intend to use it against their own king?"

"You don't think they would come here?" I asked.

"Thugs attacked Xenon. Yes, they were dangerous, and this is a dangerous weapon. But how do we know everything is related? If I saw anything up north, it was that their king is very much detached from his people," Yagaron said.

"Their people do not like their king. That's for sure," Vadentia added before clamping her lips shut, probably remembering that the king was our cousin.

"How can you be sure of that?" I asked her.

"Well, besides the astronomical taxes, the thugs and gangs, and families living on the streets in filth, the walls around the palace were at least ten feet high. And that was just the stonework. Vines and trees nearly three times that height grow just inside the perimeter. You can't see anything beyond the walls. The trees and vines seem even to bow together to meet above the palace, enshrouding it in foliage," she said.

"What?" Father asked. "Trees taller than the palace? When I was there last, there were no trees at all. And no vines. Just stone walls."

"Even circling overhead, I still could not see past the trees to the palace grounds," Yagaron said. His brow was now furrowed as well.

"Well, we're certainly operating on some very dangerous assumptions," Alexius said.

"If indeed these are separate events, the dragonsbane and the coming attack, then we need multiple strategies. But if they *are* connected, we need to be prepared on multiple fronts. Either way, we need to find a way to fight the dragonsbane," Xerus said. "We need more information."

"We need to do some tests on those," I said, nodding at the dragonsbane pellets. "We may be immune to the effects of dragonsbane, but we're vulnerable to the initial impact of those pellets. We need to figure out a way to protect ourselves—and our army and citizens—from them. That we can do while we work to gain more information."

Everyone nodded. I went to the door and asked the guard there to run and bring me our three types of armor. This would be the first test: could the dragonsbane pellets penetrate the armor? If it could, that would hinder any plans and make things that much more difficult. If not, then we could at least protect ourselves and our people.

As we waited, Foxall and Alexius discussed different strategies for handling the dragonsbane.

"I can handle them for you," Vadentia said. As a minotaur, dragonsbane wasn't especially harmful to her.

"Right! Thank you, Vadentia. Now we need a dragon to wear the armor," Alexius said.

"I'll volunteer for that," Brixelle said.

"No," Alexius said.

"Look, you all need a dragon to test it on. The rest of you have to plan. I need to help somehow."

"It could kill you, Brix. You haven't yet developed the immunity to it after just a week of drinking the stuff," Alexius said.

"You're both right. So I'll wear the armor," Foxall volunteered. "I have the same immunity as the rest of you."

We nodded, and Alexius looked immensely grateful. Then the armor options arrived, and I went over to help Foxall put the horn armor on first. We only used a breastplate. Foxall laid down on the ground. We removed our magical seals from the jar, and Vadentia looked at us before she pulled on some gloves and fished out a few pellets. Slowly, she placed the pellets on the armor one at a time. Foxall breathed in and out deeply.

"Any pain at all, Foxall?" Xerus said.

"None. I don't feel anything at all," Foxall replied. At his nod, Vadentia pressed the pellets to the armor to see if they would burn into it.

When nothing happened, she put them back in the jar, and I helped Foxall up and into the second, softer leather armor. This was the one I was most worried about. Unfortunately, this armor was most commonly worn by soldiers, so if it didn't work, we'd have a lot of work ahead of us to gather and outfit the stronger horn armor. I stood nearby, as did Alexius, who had also pulled on some gloves, ready to pounce if needed. We all held our breath as Foxall took up his position on the floor again and Vadentia placed the pellets on the leather armor. We counted to five as I held my breath, but at the end of the countdown, I saw that the pellets hadn't moved.

"Nothing," Foxall said. Vadentia nodded in confirmation. Still we kept them on there, and Vadentia even pressed on them, then rolled them around to the weaker spots like the joints. Nothing happened.

Satisfied, she collected the pellets, and I helped Foxall up once again and into the last set.

"Wait," Alexius said. I paused. He grabbed an arm guard—this armor was made of shed dragon scale—and tossed it on the ground. "Try it without someone wearing it first. I have a feeling this one will fail."

Vadentia nodded and Foxall stood to the side wearing the oversized breastplate. We gathered around the arm guard, and Vadentia placed one pellet on it. Nothing happened at first, but then it started to fizz, and smoke rose in the air as the pellet burned through the armor.

*Plink!* The pellet hit the ground and Vadentia grabbed it before it could roll toward us.

"Makes sense," Alexius said.

I swallowed. Dragon scale was impervious to everything else. Many of our dragon soldiers wore little to no armor because their hides were resistant to everything. "I suppose we could outfit the dragon soldiers in leather armor," I said, wondering where we'd be able to find so much leather and how quickly we'd be able to outfit hundreds of dragons.

"We could all wear leather armor under dragon-scale armor," Alexius suggested.

Aexie stopped chewing on the inside of her cheek to speak. "The only problem is the pellets won't be nicely placed on us. They're going to come at us from all angles with velocity."

"No. You will all wear horn armor," my father decreed. "And leather under that."

We groaned. We all hated the horn armor because it was heavier than the others.

"We'll start training with it right away then," I said. Alexius and Aexie groaned again.

Currently, most soldiers could choose their preferred armor. Those with stronger hides like dragons often didn't wear any, and others just wore leather. Most though, had dragon-scale armor for the most dangerous of battles, rarely worn but carefully collected and crafted from their family's shedding. Our armory didn't contain much for horn or leather armor. We'd have to start digging into storage to determine exactly how much of each we had. And that left the biggest problem: how much more could we even make in just a few months?

"We're going to need to re-outfit most of the army," I said.

"We can ask the other creatures from the surrounding villages and towns to send their extra leather and leather armor, plus extra horn and horn armor, while we fashion new armor from our current supplies. The time it will take to make all that armor will be a problem though," Aexie pointed out.

Everyone was quiet.

"All right, well we have our first priority then," Xerus said as we all returned to the table.

Father had gone through an armory obsession a couple centuries ago, so we all had a complete suit of every kind of armor you could imagine. I made a mental note to get Xenon and Brixelle fitted for leather and horn right away. Personally, I looked forward to the new challenges that horn armor would present in training. It didn't move as freely as the other types, so we'd have some additional training with new tactics ahead of us.

"So, if we outfitted our dragon soldiers with leather and horn, they'd have a fighting chance against pellets?" Aexie asked.

I nodded. "Even at high velocity, it'll give them two protective layers, provided they wear the head gear too."

"What if we asked all our dragon citizens to start building their immunity to dragonsbane?" Alexius asked.

Xenon answered. "It would make treating some things difficult, but if we were to be attacked by those pellets, it might save a lot of dragons." He turned to the apothecary. "Foxall, how long does it take to build an immunity to dragonsbane?"

"It would take a good month to build a decent immunity to it but years to attain your level of protection," he replied.

Alexius's brow furrowed. No doubt he was thinking of Brixelle and her low immunity.

"Could we even make that many dragonsbane draughts?" Alexius asked.

"We should have enough plants if we call for harvest immediately," my father said.

Mother asked, "What about our own supply?"

"We have enough for two years, Your Majesty," Foxall said.

Xenon coughed. "Umm ... when was the last time you checked those stores?" He looked embarrassed as he tried to smile.

Foxall looked confused.

"Xenon enjoys dragonsbane recreationally," Xerus explained.

Foxall's eyes widened and he left immediately, bowing to Mother and Father.

Yagaron shifted in his seat and asked, "What if all this is for naught?"

"Then we've trained our soldiers to be faster and better protected our citizens from poisoning," Xerus said.

"And if everything is connected, and it rains pellets from above—" Alexius began.

"Then we'll be prepared, and our dragon citizens will have a fighting chance," I finished.

Aexie jumped in with another idea. "What if we evacuated those citizens near the palace?" Everyone turned to her, so she continued. "We can tell the dragons and whoever else would like to go to evacuate to a safer area. Maybe ask the griffins or pegasi to house them for a few months. Then they'll be out of harm's way. We wouldn't need nearly as much dragonsbane, and we wouldn't have to worry about as many folks."

My father nodded his head, and my mother beamed with pride. "That makes sense. Katsuro said the palace would be attacked, not the outlying areas. I'll send letters out to the various lands asking for their assistance in housing relocated citizens."

"I have a house among the minotaurs we can use. I'm barely there anyway," Vadentia offered.

"My wife won't be pleased, but I have enough space for a dozen at my place too," Talmaro said. He grinned. "The kids will love it."

I was a little surprised to learn that Talmaro had a wife and children.

Yagaron jumped in too. "My family has a large farm in the south. If they can make it there, I can house up to a hundred dragons."

I hadn't realized Yagaron had so much property. The things I didn't know about The Four.

My father nodded. "Thank you all." Then he glanced at Alexius. "Now, Alexius, what do you have for us?"

I had noticed Alexius disengage from the conversation and start to scribble. Calculations and pictures were all mashed up on the same page. How he made any sense of all that was beyond me. But he was our best strategist, so as long as he could make sense of it, that was all that mattered.

"We expect an aerial and an underground attack." he said, glancing at Katsuro.

Katsuro and I nodded.

"Then this is how we should set ourselves up," he said. We spent the next few hours listening to his plans, which he explained at length. Then we asked questions and adjusted his plans using our varied knowledge and experience. Katsuro was the most helpful.

I finally sat back in my chair, then stood up to move the blood around as we closed our strategy session. The rest followed my lead. Xenon yawned and wiggled his toes, Aexie stretched her arms over-head, and Alexius rolled his head around as Brixelle rubbed his shoulders. We'd eaten dinner as we'd spoken at length, and once we had a plan, we finished by assigning tasks.

"Now. If you would all humor an old woman and take a break, Brixelle and I have something special planned since you're all here." My mother smiled. She'd excused herself earlier to request our dinner, but now that I reflected on it, she had been gone overly long. Now, at her nod, the door opened to admit Roxana, Brixelle's mother.

"Roxana, welcome," my mother said.

Alexius looked from Roxana to Brixelle and tilted his head questioningly.

"Since you're all here, and because we all need a little injection of happiness, I'd like to invite you all to tonight's celebration of the union between my daughter, Brixelle, and His Royal Highness, Prince Alexius," Roxana declared, her smile so wide it filled her face.

I was stunned. My mouth even popped open. I knew they wanted to be united, but I didn't think they'd do it right away.

*When you know, you know*, Xerus said in my thoughts. I sealed the door between us a little tighter at that.

Alexius too looked stunned for a second. So even he hadn't known about Mother's plan. But finally, he smiled, his smile only growing as he looked at Brixelle.

"We will have a small interlude to allow everyone to change, but we'll meet here in an hour for the ceremony. Alexius and Brixelle had decided on a small ceremony on the balcony, and everyone present are those they'd like to witness their union, so I figured why not?" My mother explained. As she spoke, she opened the drapes and the balcony doors, and I saw a candlelit aisle and yet more candles lining the entire balcony railing. A small, raised platform made of purple flowers on green vines at the end of the aisle closed the bottom of a wide arch of matching flowers. The only other accents were the stars twinkling in the sky.

Wow, that's probably what Aexie and Brixelle and whoever else they could recruit to help had been doing this morning. Now I was glad I got to nap instead.

I clapped Alexius on the shoulder and made my exit with Xerus and Xenon as we returned to our rooms to change. And sure enough, as I approached my bed, an outfit had been laid out for me. Leave it to my mother to plan every detail. I bathed quickly, wanting the water to wash away the grime of being stuck in a room all day.

I put on the dark-green velvet suit waiting for me and noticed this one was a lot more subtle than the one I'd worn at Xerus's ceremony. I also wondered whether Alexius would also take the blood oath. Surely, he would have told us beforehand. I decided to just ask. *Hey, are you and Brix taking the blood oath?* I asked.

*No. Brixelle likes her independence. And if we have children, I don't want to chance orphaning them,* he replied.

Huh. Smart kid. I closed the door in my mind and inspected my outfit in the mirror. Orange stitching lined the edges of the coat, making me wonder if my siblings' outfits were also lined with their colors. Probably.

It suddenly occurred to me that Foxall hadn't returned that afternoon. I wondered if that meant that Xenon had used up all or most of our dragonsbane supply.

*Have you seen Foxall since he left?* I asked Xerus.

*No. I'll send someone to check on him. Are you wearing a green velvet suit with tails trimmed in your color?*

*Yes,* I said. So I'd been right. So what would Xenon be wearing? Would my mother have set out his outfit too? Or would he want to choose his own?

I shrugged and left my rooms. Xenon and Xerus were walking down the hall ahead of me. I coughed and they stopped to turn around and let me catch up. Xenon wore the same suit as Xerus and I but with gold embroidery.

"Your mother has wonderful taste," he said, smiling.

"I already apologized, but Xenon thinks it means Mother has accepted him as part of the family," Xerus explained.

I shrugged. "He's right."

We were about to head for the Jade Room when another cough warned us Aexie had come out of her room too.

I turned around to see what she was wearing, and of course she wore the dress version of our outfits. She looked spectacular in a long green velvet dress with bright green stitching outlining her silhouette and bodice. "Did you at least wear sensible shoes?" I asked.

"Nope," she said, lifting her skirts to show us the tall spikes she'd donned.

"That's my girl," Xenon said.

I rolled my eyes, offering her my arm so she wouldn't trip on the walk to the balcony.

"We should get Alexius," Aexie said, so we stopped at his rooms before heading off together. It seemed Aexie had been rather insightful because as handsome as he was in his suit, he was a quivering mess.

# CHAPTER FORTY-ONE

## ALEXIUS

I WAS NERVOUS. MY mother had just sprung this on me. Though we'd spoken of it earlier, this felt a little fast. Brixelle had explained that they had moved up the timeline given the danger we were facing, and I understood that, but I was still terrified at being the center of attention. So I just stood in my room, staring at the beautiful coat my mother must have had made for me. While Xenon and Xerus had worn flashy outfits of gold and silver, mine was a shimmery dark-green color. The back was embroidered in silver and red, telling my life story in swirls and sweeping stitches. Tiny red accent jewels caught the light when I picked up the jacket and swished it back and forth. Looking around the room, I realized Brix had moved most of her stuff in, and now it looked cheery. My empty dresser tops were now covered with little bottles and jars, and though I didn't know what any of it was for, I thought it all made the room look better, homier.

A knock on the door returned my attention to my jacket. "Come in," I said, taking the jacket with me to my sitting room. I hoped it was Aexie. I needed her help to do up the bow tie that my mother had left with the jacket.

Instead, I was surprised to see all my siblings and Xenon filing through the door. We all looked like a matching set. They each wore dark-green velvet the same shade as my own jacket. But where mine caught the light, theirs absorbed it. And of course, the stitching on their clothing matched their own personal dragon colors and their hair.

"Looking spiffy, Alexius," Xenon said.

"Wow, thanks," I said as I strode to Aexie. I could tell she was wearing spikes for shoes and didn't want her to fall walking across the rug in my room. She smiled and did up my tie without me having to ask. Jaxon took my jacket and examined the back of it.

"You look great, little brother," Aexie said as she patted my shoulders.

When she stepped back, Jaxon stepped around me and helped me into my jacket. "Like a fancy shmancy dragon," he said, grinning. I remembered when I was younger, I'd always made fun of the fancy evenings when we'd been stuffed into nice clothing for our guests. I'd always made a face, and Jaxon had always warned us that we had to be "fancy shmancy" dragons.

"Ready?" Xerus asked.

I took a deep breath, then nodded. Aexie took my arm, and we left my rooms to return to the Jade Room and its bedecked balcony.

I stopped at the doors to the Jade Room, and Aexie stopped with me, letting me take a few more deep breaths. While she and Xenon waited, Xerus and Jaxon went to open the doors but paused with their hands on the handles, waiting for my signal. I finally nodded, bracing myself for the stares.

They opened the doors, and Aexie walked through with me. My brothers followed close behind. I felt them there, the support, the stability. The candles glowed softly through the windows as we approached the second set of doors. Xerus and Jaxon again waited for my signal before they opened them. I nodded, and as they opened the doors, the balcony's soft candlelit glow eased some of the tension in my chest. The rest of The Four were standing near the doors, and Xenon moved to join them, directing them to their seats as my siblings and I made our way to the flowery platform.

My father stood with Foxall on the far end, speaking in low voices. When he saw us walk in and take our positions, he excused himself and Foxall grinned widely at me. I nodded in return.

Father approached me and straightened my already straight bow tie. "You look splendid, son. As do all my children," he said, clapping a hand on my shoulder as he looked at us all and stuck his other hand in his breast pocket. "Your mother told me you weren't going to take the oath, so I thought you might want these instead." He pulled out an exquisite set of intricately carved gold bands. "They belonged to my mother and father. Their story is much like yours and Brixelle's. They met quite young and as soon as they met, they knew." He looked down at the bands and added, "You wear these on your wrist, and the magic in them allows them to transform when you do. Do you remember how in some of the portraits of Grandma and Grandpa, he had that one golden nail when he was in dragon form?" I nodded. "This was it."

"They're beautiful," I said. I moved to pick one up and paused, looking at my father. He nodded and I picked it up to examine the engraving on the sides. It was an image of two ancient, intertwined dragons old enough to take the snakelike form instead of our bottom-heavy type.

"If you and Brixelle like them, they're yours," my father said.

Something soft welled up in me as I thought of the family history these bands held. "It would be our honor." I knew Brixelle would love it.

"Speaking of Brixelle," Jaxon said softly. My father and siblings took the hint and turned, then took their seats in the front. My mother snuck in and sat next to my father.

Katsuro silently appeared to my right. He smiled an uneven smile, and I realized that I quite liked the baku. Even with all his quirks, he was honest and well-intentioned. He must have heard my thought because he suddenly smiled even brighter. Then at his nod, everyone turned and stood as Brixelle and her mother stepped arm in arm onto the balcony. Brixelle looked exquisite in a sparkling, cascading, silver gown encrusted with purple embroidery and marquise-cut purple jewels that looked as if they too were cascading down her dress. For a second, I stopped breathing. My heart skipped a beat and I felt in my soul how lucky I was to have Brixelle in my life. My smile widened; I couldn't help myself. She smiled as our eyes met, and in just moments, she stood before me. What had I ever done to deserve this?

"Welcome everyone. We're here to celebrate and bear witness to the union and commitment these two dragons have chosen to enter into," Katsuro began. I held Brixelle's hands, grinning as I glanced down at the soft, shimmering fabric triangle adorning her hands where her sleeves slipped over her middle finger. I didn't hear the rest of what Katsuro said as I imagined for the first time what our future might look like: waking up with her nestled into my shoulder, a dragonling jumping onto the bed to wake us, dancing together and forgetting all the other dancers, wrangling three dragonlings as they hung off my body, dragonlings with my green eyes and her purple scales.

"Now, the bands, please," Katsuro said and I blinked and grinned at her. I was glad I had a chance to surprise her.

My father stepped forward, presenting the two golden bands.

I took them and somehow found the courage to say, "These belonged to my grandparents. My father tells me that their story is a lot like ours. Will you accept this golden band, forever worn and seen in all your forms, as a representation of our union and mating bond?" I asked.

She nodded enthusiastically as a tear slid down her smiling cheek. I caught it with my finger, then held her left hand and slipped the bracelet on her left arm.

She took the other bracelet and slipped it on my left arm, and we joined our hands in criss-cross fashion.

"Your union has been recognized and witnessed by all those present. May your future together be long, happy, and fruitful." Katsuro smiled and spread his hands out wide. A movement caught our attention behind him, and we watched a meteor streak across the sky. Katsuro winked at me, and I turned back to Brixelle, excited for us to start our life together.

"And now, we feast!" my father declared and led everyone inside. I held on to Brixelle so we could have a moment alone together. Xerus winked at me as he closed the doors, leaving Brixelle and me on the balcony.

"Do you like them?" I asked, glancing at the gold bracelet.

"They're beautiful. It was a wonderful surprise," she said.

"Really?" I asked.

"Really." She raised herself up on her tiptoes and pressed her lips against mine.

I felt that ribbon of a connection between us shine and glow, and I thought we might be lighting up the entire balcony as we stood joined at the lips for many minutes.

Someone coughed and I jumped back.

"Sorry to interrupt you two, but I wanted to let you know that we can see everything in here. Plus we're waiting for you to start the rest of the festivities." Aexie grinned as she pulled her head back inside.

I glowed at being caught but held my arm out to Brixelle. "Shall we?"

"We shall," she said, taking my arm and leaping off the platform.

"What kind of shoes are you wearing?" I asked, wondering whether Brix was just super agile on spiky shoes or if she'd chosen to wear something else.

She lifted her jeweled skirt to reveal her boots. They were much cleaner but still the same boots she always wore.

I grinned. "You know you can have other shoes now."

"I know. But these are the most comfortable. Though they barely look like my boots—they're so clean!"

I too was amazed at how shiny they were, and I chuckled. "I think you'll start a new fashion trend."

She lifted both sides of her skirts and strutted up the aisle to the doors, her shiny boots on full display.

I followed and opened the door. Then she grabbed my hand as we walked through it to the cheers and applause of our family.

I led her to the empty chairs at the end of the table and helped her sit down before I sat down next to her. Jaxon was on her other side, then Aexie, Xenon, and Xerus. On the other side were my mother and father, Xenon's three, Katsuro, and Foxall.

My father grinned as he snapped his fingers for dramatic effect and suddenly the tables were laden with a bounty of food.

In the back of my mind, a nagging feeling was pestering me. I'm not sure if it was the upcoming battle we might face or if it was something else, but I risked a glance at Katsuro. His expression didn't falter or change, so I ignored the feeling and joined Brixelle as she clinked glasses with Jaxon and drank from her cup.

I took her other hand and brought it to my lips, giving it a kiss as she turned and faced me. She leaned over to kiss me in return. The table erupted into cheers and clapping, and I glowed from the attention.

# CHAPTER FORTY-TWO

## AEXIE

ALL THE ATTENTION WAS on Alexius and Brixelle, and I was glad for it. They looked truly happy, even though Alexius glowed some from the attention. He deserved his own time to be the center of attention. In that moment, Katsuro's words crossed my mind. I ought to take it easier on Alexius. He'd had as hard a time—if not harder—as the rest of us since Danx had passed. She would have loved Brixelle. My little sister would have loved the union ceremony, and she would have adored Xerus and Xenon's ceremony too. I felt a weight in my chest as I thought of my lost little sister.

Vadentia caught my eye from across the table. She winked at me, and I couldn't help but smile. I wondered if she would come by my bedroom tonight.

"You didn't show up for training this morning," Jax said.

"I was busy helping Mother. How would you know anyway?" I whispered back, breaking eye contact with Vadentia and turning to my brother.

"Frinder told me," he said. "No matter our duties, you're still supposed to make time to train, Aexie."

I rolled my eyes at him. "Farzena's a tattletale. I'll be there tomorrow morning. I doubt Xenon and Brixelle were there."

"Actually they were. Now that you mention it, Brixelle spends double the time there than the rest of you," he said, glancing at the newest addition to the family.

"Oh, boo on her," I said, then hushed since it had come out louder than I'd meant it to.

"You should be pleased. She looks up to you," Jaxon said, turning to face me.

I swallowed my next comment. I should be kinder to them both, especially today.

The happy couple were so involved with each other that they didn't notice when I quietly excused myself and went back out to the balcony. The palace staff had already dismantled most of the ceremony's decor, but they'd left the candles along the railing and on the floor. I leaned over the rail and breathed in, closing my eyes and trying to fill my mind with happier and more positive thoughts.

The heavier footsteps weren't the ones I'd expected to hear. He joined me at the railing, and we just stood there, breathing in the fresh evening air and taking in the chill breeze of night.

"Do you think we'll ever find our mates, Aexie?" Jaxon asked quietly.

I can't say I was completely surprised by his question. I'd seen the envious looks that he'd tried to hide from Xerus and Alexius and the way he'd linger on the title of the book I was reading, probably wondering whether he ought to start reading it himself. "I think so," I said, "Look how long Xenon had to live before finding Xerus. It seems like an eternity, but given how happy Xenon looks, it's probably worth it." I shrugged. I wasn't sure about anything in that department.

"I guess so," Jaxon said. He looked out at the sky.

I wondered what he was thinking. Was Jaxon so desperate to start that part of his life? I just figured it'd happen when it did. Until then, I liked to enjoy myself as long as I could.

"Think they'll notice if I head off to bed now?" Jaxon asked.

"No. I don't think they'd notice."

Jaxon nodded. "Good night then, Aexie. I'll see you tomorrow for training, right?" He looked at me pointedly.

I nodded. "Good night, Jaxon." He turned to leave. "And Jax?" I added as he walked away. He stopped and looked over his shoulder. "Your mate is out there somewhere. I know it. You just aren't ready for them yet." I grinned.

He grinned back and waved as he left through the side door to sneak back to his own chambers instead of rejoining the party.

I watched him go, hoping he wouldn't ruminate on his sadness any longer than he had to. Then I turned back around to gaze at that evening's stars. I hoped for his sake he'd find his mate before I did.

"Is this seat taken?" Vadentia's voice was soft and quiet.

I shook my head, not turning around.

"Nice ceremony," she said.

I nodded. I wasn't quite ready for Vadentia's brand of fun. And after talking with Jax, I didn't know if I would be tonight.

"You know, from the day Xenon met Xerus as a dragonling until the day Xerus was old enough for Xenon to enter his life, Xenon was the foulest dragon you could imagine." She chuckled. "Once, in this mountain village where we were supposed to be laying low and scouting, Xenon burned down half the village just because this kid bumped into him."

"Half the village?" I thought of the damage that would have done and the cost to repair that many buildings.

"Everyone got out safely and the rest of us helped them rebuild. It didn't take long. But yeah, he was the grumpiest dragon in all the worlds for those centuries." I finally turned around to face her. She'd taken off her shoes and sat on a bench nearby.

"Xenon's the best of the best, and it took him ten millennia to find his mate. You never know when it'll happen," she said.

She must have thought I'd come out here because I couldn't stand seeing all the bonded mates. I suppose in a way I had. But not having found my mate didn't bother me as much as it did Jaxon. I didn't see the point of being tied down. Maybe I was selfish, but I liked having what little time to myself I did. Being part of the royal family gave me plenty of duties already. I didn't feel the need to start looking for more. And once you had found your mate, the focus turned mostly to dragonlings. I definitely didn't want that yet.

"I had a mate once," she said so quietly I thought for a second I'd just heard the wind in the nearby trees.

"What happened?" I asked, sitting down on the bench next to her.

"She was beautiful. Not as flashy as Xenon, but all light and cream-colored. She was a dragon from the East. But she was like a rope of pearls flying through the sky."

She smiled as she dove into the memory. "We found each other quite young. I hadn't even met those numbskulls in there yet." She waved at the Jade Room. "It's true what they say about bonded mates. You just know. I knew when we were younglings. And I suppose a part of her did too. We grew up together and when we announced our union, our parents celebrated for a century. They had been friends and were overjoyed that their children were together." She smiled at the memory, and I thought of how I knew little about Vadentia.

She continued her story. "I had always been good with weapons, making them, using them. It came naturally to me. But she couldn't have been more different if we'd tried. She loved painting. And flowers. She couldn't even bear to squish a bug. Every week I'd bring her new flowers from wherever I went, and she'd spend the next two days painting them carefully so she could always remember them." She chuckled. "Our entire home was completely covered, ceiling to floor, with paintings of flowers in various pots. You'd think we lived in a garden."

I kept quiet. If Vadentia wanted to tell me this story, then I'd listen carefully.

"One day, The Four angered one too many dangerous creatures, and instead of going after us, they went after our families. Yagaron's partner was a fighter, so when they tried to sneak up on her, she trapped them instead. Tal's wife had gone to visit his sibling with their hatchling while he was gone, so she wasn't even home. And Xenon didn't have a family, so no one could hurt him."

"So that left your mate," I said, gulping and bracing myself for the difficult part.

"Yes. I should have posted more guards at home, but she'd insisted more guards meant more trouble and more attention." She paused, then crossed her arms. "She'd been painting a portrait of us. I'm not sure exactly what happened, only that as I was flying, I suddenly dropped out of the sky and the boys barely caught me before I screamed her name and blacked out. I woke up in my own bed but with Xenon sitting in a chair next to me instead of my mate sleeping next to me."

"That's horrible," I said.

"It was terrible. And I chased every scoundrel even remotely responsible down and exacted my revenge. They shouldn't have gone after her. It was me they wanted. I wallowed in guilt for centuries after that."

"I'm so sorry," I said, not sure what else to offer.

She shook her head. "I've made my peace with it." She looked up and I joined her, leaning back on the bench to admire the stars.

Her next words came out in a whisper. "They say the next world is up there somewhere. So I just imagine she's watching me from there, painting all the flowers she can see around the world. I fully expect fields of flowery canvases when I finally get there."

We sat in silence, staring up into the sky.

The minotaur lay her bullish head in my lap then, and I gently stroked her hair as we watched the sky above.

I don't know how long we stayed there, but eventually, I led her back to my rooms, climbed into bed with her, and put my arms around her. She snuggled close, and we fell asleep. It was surprisingly pleasant to simply hold one another.

# CHAPTER FORTY-THREE
## XERUS

"I'M TELLING YOU, AEXIE needs to be more careful," I insisted.

Xenon just gave me a wry smile. "She'll be fine. So what if she likes to have a little fun? Vadentia's hardly dangerous."

The day-long strategy session, union ceremony, and celebratory feast had drained both of us, especially Xenon. He still had much recovering to do, so we had slipped out not long after Jax had disappeared. I'd spotted Aexie and Vadentia together on the balcony as we were saying our goodbyes, and it was niggling at me as I readied for bed. "Vadentia may not be, but what about the next one?" I pointed out.

"She knows what she's doing. It's not like she's getting her heart broken each time. She's just taking control of her own ... fun," he said.

I could tell Xenon was trying to find a balance between sibling and friend. It didn't make me feel better.

"You're not her parent, Xerus. You don't need to worry about it." Xenon sat on the bed naked.

"Really? Not even pants?" I asked, fully enjoying everything I was seeing but glancing at the doors. Surely someone was about to come in to get something or clean something or bring us something as always seemed to happen.

Xenon only wiggled his eyebrows at me.

"You're incorrigible," I said even as I smiled. I went over to give him a kiss, reaching behind him for a blanket to toss over his parts and dancing out of his reach when he tried to grab hold of me.

Right on cue, someone knocked on the door. "Come in," I said, turning to shoot Xenon a "Told you so" look as a messenger entered. Thankfully Xenon once again magically donned a loose shirt and pants. I rolled my eyes. He used magic way too readily.

"My apologies for the late hour, Your Highness, but this is marked 'Urgent.'" He handed me the letter and remained there until I nodded at him to leave. I opened the letter and read it.

"What is it?" Xenon asked.

I read it again and pulled off my nightshirt, trading it for the nearest decent shirt and pants. I hurried out of our bedchambers and through the main room to the door. Throwing it open, I called after the messenger.

He turned and came running back. "My apologies, Your Highness, I thought—"

"No matter. Who delivered this message?" I asked. I felt Xenon standing behind me.

"He said he was a messenger from the palace in the North. He bore the insignia and knew the current password, Your Highness."

"What did he look like?"

"He's a big fellow, broad like a blacksmith. Green hair and blue eyes. He's down in the kitchens getting a hot meal right now if you'd like to question him directly, Your Highness."

"Will you go fetch him? And bring his supper if he hasn't finished eating yet."

He nodded and rushed off.

I dashed back into my bedchambers and threw on some proper clothing. I hadn't seen him in years. How he'd even managed to get here was perplexing.

"What's going on?" Xenon followed me into our bedchambers and closed the door.

I tried to explain what I could while I dressed. "I went with my father once to the kingdom in the North to help my cousin when his parents suddenly passed. My father and I went to help him maintain stability during the transition between monarchs so he'd have an easier time of it. He had no one, no siblings, no friends, no advisers. I was still a pretty young dragonling, so I was mostly left to my own devices. Well, I befriended someone who worked in the palace there, and we became good friends."

I had edited what I was about to say. "Lovers" is what I should have said, but that was so long ago, I didn't want to open a can of serpents if I didn't have to. Xenon, however, must have caught a whiff of what I'd wanted to say because he raised his eyebrows, and I worked harder to keep my memories solidly in my own mind.

I hopped back into my boots, then took a deep breath with my hand on the door before entering the sitting room. Xenon followed closely enough behind me that I didn't have time to close the door before he entered the room too.

I'd never seen the burly blue dragon in human form before, and his brawny human form looked awkward on the fine couches in my sitting room.

"Max?" I asked.

He jumped to his feet, and his face lit up. "Xer, I mean, Your Highness. It's an honor." He bowed low.

"Max, it's good to see you. You should just have asked to come and see me directly," I said. I sat on the couch next to him, letting Xenon do whatever he liked.

"I didn't know if you'd remember me, Xer. I mean, Your Highness." He stumbled through around the unfamiliar title again.

"Please, you don't have to use the formalities when it's just us," I said.

"I mean no disrespect, Your Highnesses." He turned to nod at Xenon.

"None taken. Don't worry about it," Xenon said. He was unusually quiet, but I focused on my friend.

I smiled, glad Xenon was minding his manners. "What's happened?" I asked.

"My king, he isn't well, Xer. First, he grew all these giant trees to block the view of the palace. He cut the staff to the bare minimum. It's a big palace, Xer, too big for those of us left to take care of. And anyone still working there ain't allowed to live there no more either. We have to commute and are sworn to silence on pain of death."

"My cousin's always been a bit of a strange one," I said.

"There's more, Xer. It's not just the strangeness of it all. I knew I wouldn't have much of a case if I came to you with just that. We'd all be all right if he was simply a little strange, but he's been neglecting his citizens. Slum lords have taken over the city, and they deal in bribes and favors only. The whole realm is full of shady dealings, and truth be told, it's the only way to get anything done now. Everyone is afraid and hungry and desperate."

"You could just have sent a letter," Xenon said. His gaze landed on the letter I'd tossed on the table as I had gone to approach Max.

"I was gonna. But one night, I was closing the armory and saw one of the blades His Highness had sent down to be sharpened was done. So, I walked it up to his chambers myself as it was late, and I was one of the few still in the palace. When I knocked on his doors, he didn't answer, so I knocked again and waited. He didn't answer, so I pushed the door open just a crack to see if I could just leave the sword in his sitting room. I think he was bathing because I heard water splashing, so I decided to just leave the sword. But as I went to put it on the table, I saw the corner of a piece of paper sticking out from behind a tapestry. So—I know I shouldn't have, but some instinct said I had to—I went to peek and found a whole wall of drawings of your family. I took this one because there were dozens like it. I don't think he'll even notice it's missing there were so many. But this one here, I took it, ran straight back to my forge, packed up, and left that night. No one saw me leave. I just rode home, grabbed some supplies, and came straight here. On my way out, I borrowed a messenger's livery as a last thought so I could be sure I'd make it past your guards, you know, in case you didn't remember me."

He handed me the paper, and my eyes widened as I scanned the page. It wasn't a pleasant drawing at all. A bonfire occupied the middle of the page, and inside that fire, my whole family was burning, our faces all contorted in pain. He was a good artist because even I had to look away. I gave the paper to Xenon, shaking my head to get the image out.

"Thank you for bringing this to us and risking so much to do so, Max."

Max nodded. "I know," he said as he held Xenon's gaze. Xenon must have been speaking into his mind as only an ancient one could do. Finally, Max turned away from him and back to me. "I look back on our memories fondly, Xer, and I think your family is the only one that can help now. King Thaxton is dangerous," he said, glowing a bit as he said so.

"Do you know anything else? Did you ever hear anything? Whispers among the staff?"

Max shook his head. "He won't allow anyone in his private offices except Iyron, the cockatrice."

"His second?" I asked. I didn't remember an Iyron from my time there years ago.

Max nodded. "It was after you and your father left. Iyron showed up asking for work in the kitchens. He was hired, but in just a few years, he managed to work his way up to guard, then onto the advisers' council. Then somehow, he convinced His Majesty to fire the whole council but him."

"That's concerning," Xenon said.

Max only nodded. "The staff mostly gossip about how His Majesty stays in his chambers day in and day out. He almost never comes out."

I nodded. "Thank you, Max. If you'd like, we're in desperate need of armorers here. You'll be given a home, your own forge, and staff if you'd like. You aren't the first to bring concerns from the North, and we're preparing," I said, wondering if I should keep an eye on him.

"Oh, thank you, Xer. I'd like nothing more. Just being safe here would be enough. A job and a home too? It's too much really," he said.

"We're grateful for your swift action, Maxwell. Thank you." I led him back to the door and stepped out with him. I closed the door behind me to prevent Xenon from following, then walked down the hall a ways to have some privacy. "Max, you'll always have a special place in my heart. You were an important part of my life at such a critical time. I'm grateful for your kindness and the guidance you gave me. Please, if there's ever anything you need, let me know. And I hope you'll make a home in my realm. It's the least I can do for you," I said quietly so the guards wouldn't overhear.

He nodded with a half-smile. "You owe me nothing, but I thank you nonetheless." He swooped in grab my hand and press his lips to the back of it.

I glanced down and nodded in return. I relayed my wishes to a near-by runner, then left Max with him. Max turned before he rounded the corner and gave a brief wave. I doubted our paths would cross often, but I was happy to provide a safe home for him. I had instructed the runner to take Max back to the kitchens and put him in a guest room until permanent accommodations could be arranged, and I wondered now if Jax had space in the barracks. I thought Max might like living among the community of soldiers.

As I walked into my chambers, Xenon was smirking. I ignored him and headed into my office to scrawl a few notes before striding straight past the still smirking Xenon to our bedroom and changing into the loose nightshirt I always wore to bed. Finally, Xenon sauntered in, his smirk even more pronounced somehow as he snapped his fingers and slid into bed.

"I didn't realize you'd had other lovers, my darling," he said.

"Guess you don't know everything after all," I replied. I fluffed my pillows, willfully ignoring the look on Xenon's face.

"Do I need to watch my back for this special place in your heart?" So he'd been listening.

I turned to him then. "You may have known I was your mate when you met me, but you left me for centuries. I didn't know who my mate was, so I'm not about to apologize for having a past. Maxwell was nothing but kind and compassionate and sweet to me. I won't turn away from the opportunity to reward that kind of goodness in a being. Plus, he's one of the best swordsmiths I've ever met," I said.

"Whoa. Xer, I'm not angry, just amused. Maybe a little jealous, but not angry. You're right. How could I be angry when you didn't know I was your mate?" Xenon brushed a finger along my shoulder and down my arm. "You can talk about him, you know. You can talk about him and every other experience you've ever had. I love every part of you, including the experiences you've had with others. That's what made you, well, you."

I relaxed. I had been worried that Xenon would be the jealous type, and while his amusement annoyed me, it was sweet of him to be so accepting of my past.

I reached over and tapped my light globe, and Xenon did the same before we pulled the blankets up. I settled into my pillows, focusing on clearing my head so I'd be able to sleep, but then I felt Xenon shift closer until he snaked an arm across my chest and pulled me close.

"I love you," he said.

"I love you too," I whispered back. And like a wave, a calm sleepiness washed over me, clearing out all thoughts like waves wash away footprints on the beach.

I woke to pounding in my head. As I rubbed the sleepiness from my eyes, I realized it was just someone pounding on the door. I darted up like I'd been struck and squeezed my eyes as the pounding continued.

"Who's there? I mean, come in." I wasn't fully awake yet, but I wanted the pounding to stop.

"Xerus, no one's there. Go back to sleep," Xenon said.

I shook my head. So the pounding really was in my head. I opened the mental door and my brother burst in.

*Fires in the realm. Get up now! Jade Room. Squadrons deployed. Fight's arrived early.* Jaxon sent images from his own window.

"Get up," I told Xenon. I threw open our connection so he could see what I'd just seen. Fires in the realm, massive ones. I pinched myself to make sure it wasn't part of a nightmare. I'd just seen an image of fire too recently before sleeping.

Xenon snapped his fingers, and we were both suddenly dressed in the soft and flexible leather armor beneath the horn armor we'd had sitting aside in wait.

"Let's go." He led the way to our common room, then directly to my office and through the magic doorway to my father's office. How had he woken up so quickly? I was still blinking away the sleep, waiting for the adrenaline to kick in.

I peeked out a window as we crossed the room, and sure enough, I could see four distant fires, the plumes of black smoke rising. When we arrived in the Jade Room, I saw it had been converted into a war room with maps and desks in rows. The giant round table was now covered with a map of the realm.

I was the second to arrive; Jaxon was still buckling up his armor. Running footsteps told me the rest of my family was about to arrive.

On the way out of my room, I had snatched Max's picture, and I put it on the table now. "A friend gave this to me a few hours ago with a warning. I thought it could wait until morning but apparently not. His information told me nothing of a timeline, but it came directly from our cousin's bedroom," I said. My father's eyes went wide when he saw the drawing.

Alexius and Brixelle arrived next, and when Aexie arrived on their heels, she said only, "Vadentia will bring the others."

"All the fires started about twenty minutes ago. Apparently, from the reports coming in, they're just wagons filled with straw that were ignited," Jaxon said as he nodded to Aexie and I fastened his back buckle for him.

"What kind of wagons? And why?" I asked.

"Where are all the wagons?" Alexius asked as he approached us, buckling his own leather armor on and dragging the horn armor with him. Jaxon shrugged as he gathered papers in front of him.

Xenon didn't bother snapping his fingers as he usually would have; instead, he silently clothed everyone in their armor and fastened it all—magically of course.

"Large wagons, as big as a house," Jaxon finally replied. He went to the door then and coordinated reports as they came in. Aexie went to help him look them over.

"Uh oh," Aexie said. We all turned to her. "They aren't normal wagons. Someone's reported seeing a strange-looking plant in one, and by the description, it's dragonsbane."

Alexius scanned the map on the table.

"All the wagons have been placed in highly dragon-populated areas." Jaxon said as he read a report, then pointed to the locations on the map and used magic to create wagon figures.

"But didn't you evacuate everyone?" Aexie asked.

"We started. But evacuation takes time," I said.

"Burning dragonsbane. Everyone near the smoke will be affected," Jaxon said.

Alexius added, "It's the quickest way to achieve maximum casualties."

"What if it rains?" Xenon said.

We all turned to Alexius.

He nodded. "Rain would help. It would dampen the fires and slow the smoke."

Vadentia, Yagaron, and Talmaro walked in just then, and Xenon steered them to the balcony. Over his shoulder, he said, "We'll go to the roof and create rain to shower on the fires we can see." Moments after disappearing, he sent, *There are six fires. Two behind us.*

*Get out of harm's way if you have to,* I said, feeling the strangeness of Xenon's ancient magic combining with the others' as they summoned water from the nearby lake and positioned it over the fires. They worked seamlessly together, weaving their magic like pieces of a puzzle to make a whole.

I blinked to bring myself back to what was going on in the Jade Room.

"What are we going to do about the dragonsbane? If that really is dragonsbane in each of those wagons, we're about to have mass casualties," Aexie said.

"Well, each of us can go put out one fire. The dragonsbane won't affect us too badly, so we'll be able to save hundreds," Alexius said.

"There's only four of us..." Jaxon said.

"There are six in this family." My mother strode into the room in full battle regalia. I had never seen my mother as a Wild One, and now there was no mistaking the moniker. She hadn't had to fight since I was born because we'd enjoyed a reign of peace from the time of her union.

My father nodded, wearing his own battle armor as he took her hand in support. "I'll take the fire by the metalworkers' zone. Keep me in the loop."

"Are we leaving the palace undefended?" Alexius asked.

"I will keep the palace safe." Katsuro appeared next to me and I startled.

We divvied up the fires and all nodded. One by one, we took off from the balcony. I headed to the southeastern fire, thankful for the armor we'd decided to wear. I brought the swirling magic within me to the surface as I flew, gathering it as I beat my wings in the air. The fire was blazing as I landed near the wagon. Nearby buildings had already ignited, and soldiers surrounded it from a safe distance. Water creatures were throwing whatever water they could find at it while rain sprinkled down, but it wasn't helping much.

I called the magic wielders to me, and we formed a chain. I took the magic I had gathered in me and put a dome over the fire, slowly shrinking it so it became smaller and smaller, finally sealing it completely. Fire needed air to burn, so we closed off the air supply. As it started to slowly die out, I drew magic from the wielders at my side. Thankfully they were not all dragons, so they could support those of us that were as we stood farther back.

As my dome became smaller still, the dragonsbane burned hotter, and I felt it in my magic as if it were right on my skin. The magic holding the dome and sucking the air out of it wavered and shimmered as if the dragonsbane was burning right through it. I felt the dragon magic wane until it was only the magic of every other creature holding the dome together, so I dug down deep, turning my head to the sky and letting out a mighty roar. The fire was almost out, and I would be damned if I quit now and allowed the suffering and death of so many.

*What are you doing?* Xenon asked.

*Saving my citizens. It's almost out.*

Finally, the fire winked out and I opened my eyes again. My armor lay in shreds on the ground, and my scales had fallen off in patches with it. It was as if the dragonsbane had burned my scales off right through the magic despite my immunity and armor.

*I don't think I can fly back, though,* I said, bracing myself on a nearby boulder. As I panted, I realized I'd overdone it. I glanced at my wings, and sure enough, there were holes in the webbing. I folded them gingerly, not completely able to avoid a wince. *Keep up the rain though. I'm checking for hot spots,* I told Xenon.

I sent my siblings an image of my wings. They would take months to heal. *How are your fires? I hope you're in better shape than I am.*

*I'm about the same as you,* Jaxon said. Aexie and Alexius looked tired, but their wings were fine. My parents were covered in soot but thus far unhurt.

*I've been practicing my shielding magic, so I kept some of it to protect myself as I was putting the fire out.* Alexius said.

*Did you dummies really not shield yourselves?* Aexie asked.

I guess I'd have to start practicing that more often. Alexius, Aexie, and my parents could still fly back, but Jax and I started back on foot.

*An aerial attack is approaching. You might want to hurry,* Xenon warned.

I conveyed it to the others, but I could only get back so fast on foot.

*I'll take Jax with me,* Alexius said. *He's close.*

I watched as my family flew back to the palace as quickly as they could, just two specks against the orange of the early-morning sky. I turned then and saw rows and rows of an army we hadn't been expecting for weeks.

*I guess we should have known better,* Aexie said.

I started to run.

Our army had already lined the roof and every parapet as I limped in on foot. A healer placed a blanket around my shoulders, and it was cool and soothing like sinking into cool water after being in the hot sun.

I continued up to my assigned position on the tallest parapet. The enemy was coming; rows and rows of flying creatures filled the air as they appeared through the clouds, clouds that The Four had created to bring the rain. If Thaxton really was behind this, he'd thought everything out carefully.

The alarm bells peeled, and I was at least proud to see that the army had assembled quickly. They stood with bows pointed to the sky, and spying Jax on the ground with his troops, I shouted, "Release!" A sea of arrows bit into the first rows of incoming creatures, and the army on the ground finished off any creature that came their way. The enemy creatures in the air first targeted the army below. Jaxon gave the call to raise their shields just in time, creating a protective barrier as arrows rained down on them. Though we could all wield magic, my father was a believer in using the most primitive methods first. As much as I wanted to strike with magic, we couldn't always be sure of the cost of using so much of it. Magic used to harm another had unpredictable and expensive consequences, and the energy it required was enormous. I looked up then and enjoyed seeing the surprise on our enemies' faces when their arrows bounced harmlessly off the barrier. A few sizzling arrows had found gaps in the ranks below, but as we fired the second volley into the sky, more of our arrows hit their targets than theirs.

I realized suddenly that the enemy had been surprised because they had coated their arrowheads in dragonsbane. They'd expected the arrows to pierce our armor. I was glad we'd taken the time to wrap the shields in non-dragon leather.

Finally, the fires were out, and The Four removed their clouds so we could see the army approaching. I gulped as I saw how far they spanned. Why would my cousin do this? Why would he send so many of his people to die? For what? And why would he attack his family, the only ones who had helped him in his time of need? He couldn't possibly imagine he could usurp our throne. But then, maybe he did. Maybe he thought he could kill us all off.

I shook off the macabre thoughts and shifted my stance, feeling as I did the uncomfortable inflexibility of armor and looking down. Somehow, I was completely covered in horn armor.

*You're welcome,* Xenon said.

I looked down at Jaxon and saw he too was wearing horn armor.

*Thank you*, I said.

*They're my family too*, Xenon said. He and his companions were now at the palace's rear, keeping watch to ensure we weren't surprised from behind.

I was grateful for the armor as I saw the army above reach into their pockets with gloved hands and drop pellets on the army below. Jaxon gave the signal to overlap the shields together in a dome so the pellets would run down it to the trenches we'd dug. From there, the pellets would roll into a net. We'd planned for this possibility, and even if the army hadn't known why, they still knew the signals and resulting formations.

We continued to loose arrows from the ground and the parapets, and the enemy continued to fly above us, dropping more pellets as they went. Suddenly, on the next volley, the pellets froze about a foot from our heads and rained up instead of down, conveniently finding their way through the armor of those who had thrown them.

I felt a satisfied growl in my bond and knew that Xenon had been responsible for that particular action. Then, in the midst of the chaos, I heard a sudden and very loud *thunk* below us. I looked down to see the army had been scattered like popcorn. Again, another *thunk* came as the ground jumped. What had happened to the alert system we'd put in?

Something was trying to come up from underneath, and I was glad for the precautions we'd taken in and around the palace. *Alexius, where are you and your squadron?* I asked.

*We're a little busy fighting off one of those giant serpents to the west of you. Hey, Jax, any tips?*

*Yeah, don't let it open its mouth and spit acid. It'll fry you like fire,* Jax replied as he simultaneously ordered his troops to stay in formation despite the quaking ground.

Would the serpent give up eventually, or would it wear down the plates we'd put in place? All I could do was hope for the best because the aerial army came back for another round, refreshed. I ordered my squadron to release their arrows at will, and they did, taking down a few dozen flying creatures at a time. But this time, as the enemy dropped more pellets, they spun in the air to spray them in every direction. I brought my arm up to block my face yelling, "Shields up!"

at the same time. I heard a few screams, and my heart sank. This was surely only the beginning of the assault, and we were already stretched thin.

*Aexie, how are you doing?*

*We're almost there,* she said. We'd sent Aexie with her flying squadron into the air, but we wanted them to circle back around above the aerialists attacking us. I sent the message down the line to aim only at frontline enemies so they wouldn't accidently hit our own.

An arrow whizzed by my face, and I ducked out of the way, letting it harmlessly hit the rock wall behind me. Then a wild scream pierced the air and I smiled. Aexie and her squadron of warriors were making their move, so I gave the signal to halt so my sister and her crew wouldn't become friendly-fire victims. In their cream-colored leather armor, and Aexie also in her horn armor, they descended on our enemy, catching them off guard. Once my sister's squadron had encircled them, I ordered my archers to shoot at the middle of the cluster.

*Too easy. There must be something else coming. Surely, he would have foreseen our counterattack,* Alexius said.

Through his eyes, I saw his crew struggling with three serpents now.

*By the way, if you cut a head off, two more appear,* he said.

I almost laughed. Of course. I watched what Alexius was dealing with for a moment. One crew distracted the serpents while some other, very brave, soldiers attempted to sneak a rope around their tails to hold them in place.

One serpent turned its head suddenly and saw what was going on. But just before she could attack, Alexius used his magic like a giant hand to grab her mouth, simultaneously turning her head back around and muzzling it.

I fell to the floor as another arrow whizzed by my head. Leaving Alexius to do what he needed to, I notched an arrow and looked for a target. The cluster of aerial fighting was moving my way, and I shot my arrow into an enemy's thigh.

At least it was easy to see who was who in the air. Aexie had insisted her squadron be outfitted in cream leather, and now I could see why. It helped them blend into the clouds and the sky, but it also made it easier for the rest of us to differentiate the players.

For a time, it appeared as though we were holding the line, if not winning. I looked behind the palace and saw that The Four had engaged another serpent who had popped up quite far from the palace, outside the perimeter we had set up.

The serpent thrashed about wildly, and The Four danced around it beautifully. As much as I wanted to watch the golden body that danced and flew through the air, I turned my attention back to the front of the palace and my eyes widened. *We've got a problem,* I told the others.

*What now?* Jaxon asked. He was busy finishing off anything that fell from the sky.

*There's an army approaching, a big one. They're storming the castle on foot now,* I said. Rows and rows of the enemy gushed out of nearby homes, forming a formidable ground force.

*Ok, then I'm done playing,* Jaxon said.

I heard a *crack!* as he took his dragon form, completely covered in white horn armor, and started picking the enemy out of the sky as if they were apples. Even among dragons, Jaxon was larger and faster than most.

I popped into my dragon form too, now taking up most of the roof. The roof groaned, making me think perhaps I shouldn't be standing on the roof in my dragon form. Before I could move though, I saw a lone enemy soldier wave and walk to the front of the line. The enemy must have a message to impart.

*I'll meet them,* Alexius said. He was covered in something sticky, and even I could tell that he smelled horrendous. He had already been in his dragon form, but as he strode to the front lawn to hear what they had to say, a white cloth suddenly appeared in his hand.

*I can't have you getting killed, little brother,* Aexie said.

He nodded and left the door to his mind wide open so we could be part of the conversation directly. As he approached the opposing soldier, he popped back into his human form to match the human standing at the gates. Somehow, my brother was no longer covered in the sticky goo but was wearing clean leather armor. Then I realized he had hidden his horn armor with invisibility. He must have been practicing with Aexie.

Even without our soxkendi bond, I still would have felt Alexius's heart wrench as the messenger uncovered a wagon behind him. Brixelle sat bound and gagged within it, struggling against her bonds.

Shaking off my shock, I took a closer look at the messenger. It was no messenger. It was Thaxton himself.

*That's our cousin, Thaxton, not a messenger.* My siblings' distress radiated in my mind.

*How did they get Brix?!* I felt Alexius jump from scared to angry, and I hoped he wouldn't do anything rash even as Jax arrived and put a hand on his arm to hold him back.

*He's right. How did they get her?* I asked the others.

*We left her in the care of the queen. There should have been no safer place,* Xenon said.

*You have to stay calm, Alexius. Thaxton wants an excuse to attack. You can't give him one,* I reminded him.

*I'm fully aware of that, thank you, Xerus,* he snapped, barely containing his anger. I felt it rolling off him in waves. "Let her go," Alexius said.

Even from a distance, Thaxton didn't look particularly well anymore. In his human form, he was thin, shoulders crouched over his frame, his skin sallow and pale. "Well hello, cousin. It's good to see you too."

"She has nothing to do with this. She's an innocent. Let her go," Alexius repeated.

"Maybe ... or maybe not ... hmm. Tell you what, I'll give you a second gift before we even start this mess. You can have the contents of one wagon. You can have everything in it if you just give me this palace and this realm. I'm tired of mine. It's dark and cold and dreary," Thaxton said. "But before you choose, maybe you should take a peek at my other present."

He nodded and a guard uncovered a second wagon. The present was our mother. My heart plummeted. How was Alexius supposed to choose between his mother and his mate?

"Just so you know, it took a hefty dose of dragonsbane to catch my aunt." Thaxton smiled, but it was no normal smile. He'd really gone mad. Burn marks covered my mother's skin, and I gritted my teeth to keep my temper in check.

Alexius seethed. I'd never felt him so angry. Despite feeling all my siblings's anger, I tried to keep a cool head. There had to be another way out of this.

Brixelle kept wriggling with all her might until finally her gag slipped. "Alexius, you choose your mother. Do you hear me?! PICK YOUR MOTHER!" she shouted. "I will never forgive you if you choose me. She needs help right away. They threw pellets on her—" A guard slapped Brixelle hard enough that she flew back and hit her head on the wagon's edge.

Alexius growled. "If you touch her again, I'll skin you alive, family or not. I will use every method of torture I've ever read of on you and invent enough new ones to fill an entire book! Do you understand?!"

"Ohh, I'm so scared," Thaxton said. "You know, I'd be inclined to give them both to you if you'll hand over the palace. No big deal. Easy trade."

"Give me my mother," Alexius said, and I felt his heart crumble even as he said it. At our dastardly cousin's nod, Jaxon ran to help our mother. He scooped her up in his arms and ran as fast as he could back to the palace with her.

*I'm going to start working on Mother right away. From what I can see, she has about six pellets in her,* Jaxon told us.

Alexius took a step forward and raised his hands, palms up. I felt him swallow his anger and grief to try a new tactic. "Why do you want this palace? Your people hunger for a leader. You should go home and do right by them. You could be a revered leader," Alexius said. He was trying to pull Thaxton's attention away from Brixelle, to reason with him, but even I could see my brother's gaze kept darting over to her.

"Well, you see, I don't like my realm anymore. I think I'd rather have yours. I think it's much more fruitful. And warmer. I'm getting cold in that palace all by myself. Of course, when you surrender, I'll have both palaces, both realms. I'd be ever so much richer."

*His soldiers aren't healthy. They're all old or tired or sick. They won't last long. I have to wonder why this was the only army he could cobble together.* Aexie had gone invisible and was flying low over the army to take a closer look while Alexius engaged Thaxton. *I'm trying to make a wide loop to get closer to Brixelle. If you can all distract him, maybe I can snatch her.*

Thaxton pouted. "Why did they send me the youngest one? I was hoping to talk with the big boys." He looked over Alexius's shoulder, clearly hoping to set Alexius off. But as much as Alexius was seething, he didn't bother looking behind him. He knew we were here with him.

Besides, he'd known from the beginning his presence wouldn't please Thaxton. That's why none of us had argued when he said he would talk to Thaxton. I really needed to give Alexius more credit. He was an intuitive strategist.

Suddenly, I saw Brixelle open her eyes. Then she sat up.

Aexie saw it too because she said, *I'm going to make a go of nabbing Brixelle any minute now. Any chance you can send Yagaron to come help me, Xer? He can become invisible like me.*

*Honey, we all can,* Xenon said. I had opened the doors in my mind so Xenon had a direct line to my siblings. We needed to communicate as easily as possible.

It was obvious Brixelle knew someone was next to her because she moved discreetly to put her bound arms on her raised knees, while Alexius tried hard not to look at her.

"This is no way to repay all my father and brother have done for you," Alexius said.

"You mean how they abandoned me to run a whole realm all on my own?"

"They set you up with an army of help," Alexius said.

"All incompetent. If you really want to know a secret, I think your father wanted this, wanted me to fail so he could take my realm," Thaxton spat.

*Where's Father?* Alexius suddenly asked us.

*With me,* Jaxon said. *He's with Mother. We're removing pellets, Foxall and I. We've got four left.*

*You didn't honestly believe our cousin could have nabbed both our parents?* I asked Alexius.

*No. But I wanted to be sure he didn't have Father too. We didn't even realize he had Mother and Brix.*

Then in a blink, Brixelle disappeared. I realized The Four must have turned her invisible and were flying her away from Thaxton.

"So how could you rule two realms, Thaxton, if you couldn't handle one?" Alexius asked.

"Oh, that's my business. Summer palace, winter palace, maybe. I hear all the popular royals are doing it," Thaxton said. While he stood confidently, I noticed his thumb rubbing the edge of his armor back and forth. "So do you want to give it up or not?"

"Well, unfortunately, the palace isn't mine to give. But if you'd like to surrender, I can promise we'll show leniency." Alexius stayed stock still, giving The Four as much time as possible to move Brixelle to safety. I saw then that in a small corner of Alexius's mind, he was building a magical wall between him and Thaxton. So my brother suspected the usurper would try to kill him as soon as the talking was over. It seemed a likely possibility to me too.

"Well then, if we're all done here, may the best dragon win." Thaxton smiled, turned around, and almost skipped back gleefully. He had to have seen the empty wagon.

Alarm radiated to my siblings and I. *Why doesn't he care that Brixelle is gone?* Alexius asked. Thaxton spun around right then, sending six knives flying at Alexius, who deflected them with magic. One especially large harpoon arrow sped toward Alexius, but his training kicked in and he jumped back out of range. It circled back and I felt Alexius's consternation and instinctive reaction as he threw magic behind him, snapping the arrow midflight. It finally fell to the ground.

Alexius popped into dragon form and flew back to the palace, where The Four had taken Brixelle. Thaxton's army remained where they were, surrounding us, waiting. I remained where I was on the wall and watched Thaxton's army stand there, frozen like wooden soldiers waiting to be played with. What would the next phase look like? Could we prepare somehow?

# Chapter Forty-Four

## Alexius

I DIDN'T HAVE TO ask where Brixelle was as I ran through the palace doors and straight to her. I could feel her. A desperate panic gripped my heart, and it made me run faster. I bolted to the Jade Room, the tightness in my chest finally releasing the moment my eyes met Brixelle's.

We ran to each other. After a brief hug, I ran my hands all over her face and shoulders, reassuring myself she was here, and whole. Then, audience be damned, I gave her a kiss full on the lips.

"Are you all right?" I asked, using my magic to scan her before she even had a chance to say anything.

"I'm all right," she said, confirming my magical scan. "Go help your mother." Brixelle's eyes were filled with tears as she gripped my shoulders and turned me away from her. She led me to my mother, and I nodded at Jaxon. He and Foxall were still removing the pellets.

It was terrifying to see my mother unconscious on the table. Her head lolled to the side and her arms lay limply in the hard surface.

"Do your whole-body thing. Foxall and I are taking the last pellets out now," Jaxon said.

I nodded and shone my magic through her body, looking for anything odd. As I did, I noticed something strange. There was an invisible barrier between her body's most vital organs that even my magic couldn't penetrate, and while the barrier was formidable, it was also nearly indetectable. All I could see was a slight blue hue.

"Where's Katsuro?" I asked.

"Here," he said, suddenly appearing in a chair. My eyes widened when I saw he was also riddled with dragonsbane pellets.

Brixelle broke into a single sob before collecting herself. "We were waiting in the safe room, and then the door opened. We thought it was one of you, but it was Thaxton. He threw two handfuls of the pellets at your mother. But Katsuro moved so fast, he took the brunt of it, then vanished. We didn't know what had happened to him."

"When baku are injured, their first instinct is to take their gaseous form," I explained as I finished my mother's scan. She would be all right. Katsuro, on the other hand, was bleeding from every hole.

I summoned another table and gently guided Katsuro onto it. "I didn't realize that baku were also affected by dragonsbane," I said, starting another scan. Jaxon and Foxall were almost done with Mother by now, and I hoped they could help me with Katsuro.

He had curled into a ball, and I gently shone my magic in a warm wave as I untangled his limbs and took a look. A pellet was lodged in his chest, so I stopped scanning. If I didn't remove it quickly, it could go right to his heart.

I started drawing it out, pulling the pellet out of his flesh. Brixelle came up next to me wearing gloves and carrying a metal jar to put the pellets in. As soon as she saw the pellet break the surface, she gently took the pellet between her gloved fingers and put it in the jar. Then Jaxon and Foxall came and joined me.

"Xerus stayed on the wall. He says the entire army has frozen in place, perhaps awaiting our next move," Aexie said.

"I wonder how long they'll wait?" Jaxon asked, trying to pull another pellet out.

No one had an answer. We pulled pellet after pellet in silence, knitting Katsuro's flesh back together and closing veins and arteries as we went. Despite having veins and arteries, the fluid flowing in his veins and arteries felt like whisps of air instead of liquid. I hadn't studied much about baku anatomy and was discovering now that they were dragonlike in some ways but not many.

There were thirty pellets in total, so it took us most of the afternoon to finish. As we toiled, Xerus said, *I can't understand why Thaxton would wait so long. The smart thing would have been to attack us while we were seeing to injuries so we'd be weaker, less organized.*

"I think he wants us at full strength," I replied as I finished tending to the last of Katsuro's injuries.

"Why?" Jaxon asked.

"Because he wants to defeat us while we're at full strength. The victory would mean more to him," I said.

Aexie toyed with a fingernail. "That logic sounds pretty twisted."

"Thaxton isn't well," I said. "He's not thinking straight. His thoughts are twisted."

Aexie asked, "I still can't believe he thinks we abandoned him. Why?"

"He's been influenced by someone with their own motivations, and I think he's been losing his mind for some time," I said.

"Maybe I should have stayed longer," my father chimed in. He was sitting, cradling my mother in his lap. Her eyes were open, but she was very still.

"Did anyone ever consider he might have killed his parents?" Xenon walked in with Vadentia.

"It crossed my mind," I said.

"No. He couldn't have," my father said in disbelief.

Xenon put a hand on my father's shoulder. "Rixen. I knew them like you did. I spent a lot of time in that palace, and they were blind to their son's warped ways. They chose to ignore it instead of getting him help."

"How could he have taken down two old and powerful dragons?" Aexie asked.

"The same way he took down your mother and Katsuro. We're not the only ones who grow dragonsbane. It's common among the elite," Xenon said.

Jaxon turned to look at Xenon, raising an eyebrow. "But wouldn't they be immune to it?"

"Not if their son replaced their regular dose with something else for a long time and then gave them an extra strong dose," Xenon said.

"Great, we have a parricidal maniac trying to steal our kingdom," Aexie said. She had melted into a sofa and looked like she wasn't about to move unless she absolutely had to.

Now that I had removed all the pellets from Katsuro, who'd not once cried out while I'd removed them, I scanned his body more thoroughly. "Katsuro, is there anywhere that feels injured?" I wasn't sure what I was really looking for to begin with.

"My foot," he said. Katsuro being in human form helped anatomically quite a bit, but there were still oddities. I turned my attention to his foot and saw a few tiny broken bones. Taking a deep breath, I used my magic to guide the pieces back together. As I did, I came across an extra toe, and Katsuro said, "Like this," as he wiggled his other foot.

I scanned that foot more carefully to determine exactly where the extra toe should go. Then I returned my attention to the injured foot and guided that toe back to where it was supposed to go. When I was done, Katsuro sat up on the table, and I helped steady him. "Thank you," he said.

Suddenly, the balcony doors slid open behind him, sucking the curtains outside and allowing a giant ray of sunlight to pierce the room. I stepped between Katsuro and the light, weapons drawn—I hadn't even realized I still had my armor on—and heard my whole family do the same.

I squinted and finally saw two figures glowing so brightly, it hurt my eyes. As they stepped forward, I didn't know what they were or how to fight them.

"Maman, Papa, you must dim more. You are too bright," Katsuro said.

Suddenly, the light dimmed, and I blinked continuously, wondering what had just happened. My brain felt fuzzy, like it was difficult to connect two thoughts coherently or to think of any specific thing. The figures before me were like Katsuro, but not. In some ways, they looked much like him with their similar blueish hues, but their skin was filigreed with silver starlight as if they were made of the night sky itself.

"Katsuro." One of the figures rushed past me, or rather, she moved so quickly, I think I might have spun around a few times.

Suddenly the other figure stood before me.

"Young Alexius. You have my gratitude. If you ever need help, baku will answer your call," he said. But he—how did I know it was a he?—hadn't spoken with a voice, more of an understanding on a breath of wind.

Before I could even blink, they were gone. All of them. The two blue figures and Katsuro had disappeared, the balcony doors closed.

"What just happened?" Jaxon asked.

"That was Kat's family. They're even older and therefore less corporeal than Kat. They don't spend much time in their corporeal forms, so there's no practicing silly things like courtesy. They just ... are," my mother said softly.

My father looked at my mother. He still clasped her arm despite holding a sword in one hand. "That happen a lot when you guys were young?"

My mother smiled at that. "All the time."

"So strange to think of Katsuro as having parents and that there are beings even more powerful than him," Aexie said, sheathing her daggers.

"Alexius, you've been given a great honor. I don't know if I've encountered anyone who's received a favor of the baku, except your mother." Xenon nodded at my mother.

"Baku never bestow a favor unless they've seen how it might be used. I don't envy the individual who will come up against such enormous power that they need that favor," Talmaro said as he and Yagaron joined us, Xerus following close behind.

Vadentia stared daggers at him, as did Aexie. Jaxon looked sad and I couldn't bring myself to look my parents in the eye. None of that sounded good.

"So, little brother, what's our best move against that army out there?" Jaxon asked. He waved his arm over the makeshift operating table, replacing it with a table filled with little dots that represented a model palace and the soldiers outside.

I stepped up to the table. I'd never been asked my opinion on such an important matter. In all past altercations—few though there were—I'd been too young to play a truly active role. It was strange to see all my siblings turn to me expectantly.

Xerus raised his eyebrows. "Alexius, you spend more time than any of us in that library. I know you've read everything related to war and strategy. If anyone knows how best to use our resources, it's you."

"Wait."

We all turned to my father.

"Actually, it's time we made things official. Your mother and I are getting old now, and if today has shown me nothing else, it's that all I want is to spend more time with her. And you've all proven yourselves more than capable of taking up the reins." He looked at Xerus. "As the oldest, Xerus, I'm appointing you, Acting King."

Xerus began to shake his head in denial, but Father forestalled that. "Son, it's time. You're ready."

At that, Xerus stood taller and nodded instead. "Yes, Father. I'll strive to make you proud." Then he turned to my siblings and me. "We need to divide the work. Jaxon, will you accept the position of general? You already do all the work."

Jaxon nodded, his eyes misty.

"Aexie, I know you know everything about every part of this palace, and you're a whiz when it comes to organizing and planning. So, will you help me run the palace? And will you also officially command the aerial army that we will now divert more funding to?"

Aexie froze for an extra beat and leaped up to hug him.

He released her and turned to me. "And Alexius, will you accept the role of strategist and adviser? There's no one better at gathering information, and somehow in the last century, you've managed to become wiser than the rest of us."

He paused and I nodded, unable to find words. "And when all this is over, I'm going to want to found a school to teach the art of healing—" He glanced at Foxall then. "If you'll oversee it."

Foxall bowed deeply, then went back to cleaning and putting his instruments away.

I was touched and more than a little surprised. It was more responsibility than I'd ever imagined having.

"And The Four, if you'll accept, I'd like you to be our intelligence division. You'll have the freedom to move about as you wish and the discretion to do what you will."

Talmaro grinned wolfishly, but Yagaron nodded and said, "It would be our honor."

"Then let's get started," Xerus said.

I studied the model again, looking at the formations and numbers, thinking about our resources.

"What do you think Thaxton's waiting for?" Jaxon asked.

"Someone to arrive?" Yagaron suggested.

"Or night to fall?" Xerus asked.

"The perfect weather," Aexie scoffed.

"All of it," I said. They all turned to me. "You saw the chaos when the serpents and the aerial army attacked simultaneously. He meant to separate us, distract us, and test us. The aerial attack was to both test our aerial forces and get a better layout from above. The first serpents were also a test. Now they have a perimeter." I turned to Xerus. "Do you think Thaxton saw that we'd started evacuating the nearby villages and towns?"

"Maybe, but maybe not. They came in through just that one town, but everyone would have hidden in their homes even if they had been there. His army wouldn't have encountered anyone either way."

I turned back to the table. "He'll attack the villages then, with serpents probably, to get us to strain our resources. It takes too many of us to try and restrain the serpents. As much as I hate to say it, we need a quicker, more efficient way to neutralize them," I said. I didn't wait for agreement. "He'll attack again, at night, because we'll have limited vision. He's delusional enough to think that if he does nothing long enough, we'll continue about our normal business. I also don't think he'll send everything he has at once. He wants to see us struggle, so he'll send waves one at a time until we're overloaded, and then send more."

I started moving the pieces around on the table. It was tough to jump into the head of a delusional dragon, but if I had to guess, he would attack the nearby villages, expecting to separate us. Then he'd send his ground forces to take the palace, followed by his aerial army, then another set of serpents at the perimeter of the palace grounds.

Xenon filled the silence. "We might have a better way to restrain the serpents."

"You want to go into their minds," Xerus said without even looking up.

"If we take control of their minds, not only does that reduce our enemies, but we can attack Thaxton's forces with their own weapons, reducing our casualties significantly," Xenon explained. Yagaron nodded behind him.

"What you're suggesting is unethical," Xerus said.

"As unethical as your own cousin attacking you?" Xenon asked.

Yagaron added, "As unethical as a king who has turned his back on his people and controlled the minds of serpents for his own use?"

Xerus turned to my father, who furrowed his brow before speaking. "We don't know what the serpents' current mental states are. It could be worth exploring. If we could get into their minds, maybe we could calm them or destroy their link to Thaxton or whoever wields them. They might come back to themselves and gladly leave the battlefield."

"I have a plan," I finally said. It had come together right as I'd spoken. I just had to hope that my assumptions were correct. I explained my strategy and the signs we needed to look for. We'd also have to be ready to adapt in seconds, depending on Thaxton's first move.

That night after I'd outlined my plan, we set up a watch with one sibling always on the wall, unseen but watching carefully. We didn't have to wait long.

I had just woken, donned fresh leather armor, and taken my turn on watch when I saw a blob moving in the dark. Someone was going down the lines of soldiers waiting on the ground. Then I spotted another, then another. I looked for Thaxton's flag, but it was nowhere to be seen among the shadows.

*I think something's about to happen,* I thought. Within moments, I felt my siblings were awake and ready. Xerus crept up to join me, and we watched in silence.

And then it happened. Fires started to spring up in three directions, far away from the palace. I could smell them before I could see them. Then, even at a distance, I saw the writhing bodies of the serpents because they had been painted in bright colors and the fire light shone on them, making them look like writhing flags.

I glanced at Xerus. He wasn't pleased about his mate's part in this, but he nodded as he gave the signal for Xenon to go forth. Xerus, like me, was wearing plain leather armor. To a passing stranger, we would look like any other soldier waiting for the action to start.

I'd sent my squadron to follow Talmaro as he was the closest in body shape to me. Yagaron wore Jaxon's armor and led his forces, and Xenon wore Xerus's. Vadentia had taken up Aexie's post, though the minotaur had needed quite a bit of magic to hide her true form and fly.

The fake Xerus, Jaxon, Aexie, and Alexius flew out to the serpents, making a great show of looking organized and forging ahead without turning back. I waited, peeking over at the soldiers looking up at us. I felt like we were waiting forever.

"It worked," Xerus suddenly whispered. In my mind, I saw what Xerus was seeing through his bond with Xenon. A serpent had calmed.

"No. Keep them going. Keep them flailing so Thaxton thinks we're still struggling," I whispered back. Xerus nodded and I heard a distant whistle. I hoped it wouldn't give them away.

A horn blared and then I heard the rumble of several thousand feet on the ground marching toward the palace. So I'd been right. He was sending his ground troops in first.

Xerus nodded at me, and I made my way back inside the palace as he handed leadership of the archers to his second. Then my brother took his lieutenant's place in the protected alcove, where he could see above in all directions. Xerus would protect the soldiers on the ground from attacks from the sky. His personal guard was disguised as soldiers and loosing arrows by the dozens as the enemy approached.

I ran to the Jade Room and saw Jaxon pacing back and forth in his armor as he waited. There was no way to disguise the bulky Jaxon as his much smaller second, so he had to wait while she carried out his orders for him. His forces would be in the thick of the fight, and his hands twitched as he itched to dive into battle. He knew, however, that as the royal second, he had to stay safe, especially with Xerus out there.

"How is it out there?" Jaxon asked.

"As expected," I said. My gaze darted around nervously. We were now waiting for the enemy's aerial army and more serpents to attack, and Xenon's crew was waiting for our signal to stop pretending and return to the palace.

"I think more serpents will come next," I said. And as if waiting for my cue, we felt the thump of a serpent hitting the protective barrier. It was a little unsettling knowing a great serpent was just a few meters below our feet as it railed against the plate in the ground below us.

"Jaxon, Father, you go handle the serpents," I said, sending them out. Aexie was waiting with the rest of her aerial army near the roof, ready for action.

Minutes later, Jaxon said, *This is easier than I thought*, as he took hold of a serpent's mind and released it from its bond with Thaxton. I wondered briefly if my cousin would realize it, and more importantly, what he'd do about it.

*Father is now racing me to get to all the serpents. There's a lot,* Jaxon said. He started counting and I was surprised when he counted over a dozen. However Thaxton was controlling them, it was astounding how many he could control at one time.

A shock laced through my shoulder then, and I shot my hand to it. I wasn't injured. So I dove into my mind and found that Xerus was in excruciating pain. I raced toward the roof.

*No. Alexius, you stay there. His troops are bringing him to you. If there's dragonsbane, you'll have to help him. I'm coming back,* Xenon said, and I froze where I stood.

A heartbeat later, Xerus was rushed in on a makeshift pallet.

"I never should have let you take the roof," I said. I had just endangered the heir to the throne. The arrow had pierced his leather armor, and the arrowhead itself was buried in his shoulder. From the amount of pain Xerus was in, I guessed that the arrowhead was made of dragonsbane. "This is going to hurt," I said. As Xerus opened his mouth to reply, I grabbed the shaft and shoved it through his shoulder, ripping through flesh as I did so.

Xerus roared in pain, and it took six guards to hold him down. I winced as the roar echoed in my head.

*Yes, it was necessary,* I said to the others as I scanned Xerus's wound. Brixelle soaked some towels in warm water and tried to comfort him as best she could. I furrowed my brow in concentration as I put protective filters around his heart, letting blood through but protecting it from the dragonsbane that coursed through his veins. Then I followed his circulatory system, expanding outwards to protect what I could from the poison. When I finally found traces of it, even the light of my magic wanted to shy away from it. I didn't let it slip through, though, and coaxed it back to its origins, slowly drawing more and more together as I got closer to the source. When I was finally back to the wound, I asked Brixelle for assistance.

"Brix, I need you to dig it out. You'll see it. It looks like black sludge. The rest of you will have to hold him down as best you can," I commanded. I needed all my magic to hold the protective barriers inside Xerus to make sure nothing else slipped by, so Brixelle worked quickly and scraped what she could out with a wooden spoon and dumped it in a bucket. From the moment the tool hit his wound, Xerus roared in pain, balking and bucking against the six guards sprawled across him.

"Every last drop, Brix. Use the fabric," I said as I pushed a small black strand of poison back toward the wound. Most of it was gone now, but Brixelle took the cloth and held Xerus's shoulder as she went in to absorb blood and the lingering poison. Though Xerus roared again and again, she went back in repeatedly, with a fresh cloth each time, to get what remained. Xerus finally passed out from the pain, and she went in one last time to make sure it was all gone.

She looked up at me. I examined Xerus with magic and nodded. She had gotten all of it. Brixelle nodded then, a curl of hair falling endearingly over her eye before she blew it away. I turned to focus on Xerus as Brixelle stepped away and tossed all the contaminated clothes and the spoon away.

I scanned my brother carefully. Now that he was unconscious, the guards stepped back, and Brixelle went to handle the bucket of black goo.

Xenon flung the doors open and rushed to Xerus, taking his hand.

"He'll be all right," I assured the ancient one. "He just passed out from the pain of us digging into his wound. We got all the poison, but I want to check him once more before I wake him," I said.

Xenon nodded and continued to hold his mate's hand. I moved carefully around Xerus, combing through his body before finally moving to his wound and knitting the flesh back together. When I'd finished, Foxall handed me a jar of smelling salts, and I waved it over Xerus's face. He blinked slowly at first, then faster until he finally opened his eyes. He looked around before sitting up. Something wasn't right.

*Xerus.* When I got no answer, I looked in my mind and realized that Xerus had closed the door. I glanced at Xenon, whose eyebrows furrowed. He glanced at me, and I gave the smallest shake of my head. So he couldn't get to Xerus either. I waved a hand behind me to usher everyone else out, and they pretended to calmly leave the room as if they were being called somewhere else.

"Xerus. How are you feeling?" I asked, pretending to reach for his injured shoulder.

He pulled violently away as if afraid of me touching him.

"I'm just trying to check your injury," I said. He stilled then and allowed me to touch his shoulder, but his face took on a very non-Xerus look. He looked darker somehow.

As soon as I finished bandaging an injury that didn't need bandaging since I'd already knitted the flesh back together, Xerus sat up and made to stand.

"Sweetheart, let's not upset your injury. Stay here with me. You need to rest," Xenon said. I'd never heard him call Xerus "sweetheart." I wondered if he was testing him.

"But my kingdom needs me," Xerus said stiffly.

"We risked too much putting you on the roof. You're the heir. You need to stay hidden and safe. I won't risk our realm's future again," I said. Xenon gave me the smallest of nods.

If Xerus was not himself, we wanted him out of harm's way until we could figure out how to get the true him back. Xerus stood and nodded, going over to our strategy table. There was nothing too revealing there, and the battle raged on outside anyway. Nothing he saw would come as a surprise.

*Something's wrong with Xerus. He's not himself. Xenon and I will handle this, but that means you're all on your own.*

*Ugh. Of course,* Aexie said.

*Let me know if you need my assistance,* Jaxon said. I could tell they were both locked in combat, and I pushed a little strength their way. We were spread pretty thin now with Xerus not being himself and Xenon and I both occupied with a new problem. I wondered what could have happened while my brother had been unconscious, especially with so many of us close by watching him constantly.

I briefly wondered if he would wake up as himself if we knocked him unconscious again. I wasn't sure, but I had a pretty good idea who was controlling Xerus. It was time to play his game.

So, I made myself walk nonchalantly over to the table as if nothing was amiss and leaned on it as if we were going to discuss the next move. "What do you think? Should we move our forces over here to meet him? Or should we watch the back?" I waved lazily at our current setup.

"I think ..." He looked over the contents of the table carefully. "We need to keep forces at our back in case something happens there. We wouldn't want to be surprised," Xerus said. This was definitely not our Xerus. He would not have deviated from our plan.

I watched Xerus pick up one of the little black dots and rub his thumb back and forth over it as he continued to study the map. I had seen that same motion not long ago. Thaxton definitely had control of Xerus.

Brixelle was the only soul who hadn't left the room, and I wanted so bad to tell her to go, but she came over to me, knowing something was wrong but not understanding the severity of it. I felt panic rise in my throat just realizing how close Thaxton was to my beloved again.

I didn't want to risk Thaxton knowing what we knew, but I had to warn Brixelle. I just didn't know how. As intuitive as ever though, Brixelle took my hand, and I used my thumb to spell out his name in the palm of her hand.

She stayed perfectly calm. "Should I get some drinks? Or food? You boys must be hungry after all that?" She didn't quite sound like herself, but I didn't think Thaxton would notice.

I nodded. "That would be wonderful, sweetheart."

Brixelle turned to leave the room. But just as she approached the doors to freedom, Xerus said, "Wait. Bring me tea. Please," he said. I almost breathed out audibly and noticed how he'd thrown the "please" at the end as if remembering that Xerus might be more polite than he was. Brixelle nodded and closed the door behind her.

"So when did you know?" Xerus-Thaxton turned around, smirking at Xenon and me.

"Know what?" Xenon said.

Xerus-Thaxton crossed his arms. "When did I slip up?" He knew we knew.

"When you showed so much interest in our strategy," I lied. "Xerus would have moved at least one squadron to the main battle. We might need to protect our back, but our front needs it more," I said.

If I never saw Xerus smirk again, I would be forever grateful. He drew up one side of his lip and said, "So now that I'm the ruler of this realm, what are you going to do about it?"

The door opened again and Brixelle came back, carrying a tray with tea and some biscuits. Why had she come back? We'd have to have a serious conversation about signals and not endangering herself when this was all over.

"I know you're probably tired, so I went to the extra effort of making this turmeric-infused tea to help boost your energy," she said, smiling at us all. The moment she'd walked back into the room, Xerus had wiped the smirk off his face. Xenon and I still stood between Brixelle and Xerus. She poured the tea, facing us, and then mixed in some sugar before coming over and giving Xerus a cup. He took it gently, nodding at her.

"Wait right there for me, will you?" he asked before she could retreat behind us.

He took a sip of the tea, still wearing his pleasant face. He started to motion for her to go away as he took a second sip. His wave became a slash, and Brixelle didn't have enough time to move away. Three large gashes appeared in the back of her clothes as she screamed and fell. I caught her in my arms and saw that her back had been shredded to ribbons, her blood flowing profusely.

Xerus clutched his head and crumpled to the floor. Xenon ran to hold him as he started panting on all fours. Xenon put Xerus's forehead to his own and closed his eyes.

I took another look at Brixelle's back and the deep gashes. Without thinking, I blanketed her back with my magic and started to knit the flesh back together. Her hands gripped my arm and her nails dug in. My heart hurt as if it too were being gashed to pieces. She looked up at me, then squeezed her eyes shut.

"It hurts so much," she said through gritted teeth.

I nodded, closing my eyes, and squeezed her hands tight with one hand. After taking a steadying breath, I gently lifted the cloth away from the gashes with my free hand. Brixelle flinched, but she didn't cry out and I kept squeezing her hand with my own.

I put my hand over the gashes; they were so deep, I could see bone. All I could do was try to knit the flesh back together, so I started with the deepest one. Once it was no longer life threatening, I moved on to the next gash.

When the last gash was finally fused together, I poured my magic into her in hopes of helping her renew all the blood she'd lost. I didn't let myself think, I just did. Finally, I felt her grip slacken as she slipped into unconsciousness. Not caring if I overused my magic then, I flooded more magic into her and checked the rest of her body in case I'd missed an injury. Then I couldn't think of anything else to do, but

I was comforted by her beating heart. I scooped her into my arms and held her to me.

Xerus and Xenon came up behind me, and they each put a hand on my shoulder.

"Thank you, Alexius," Xerus said. "I owe Brixelle my life."

Before I answered, I peeked in my mind. His soxkendi door was open again. I nodded and breathed a sigh of relief. At least I had my brother back again.

Xenon was grim but content. He nodded at me.

"We're going to join the fight, but I want you to stay with Brixelle. You're too important as a healer. We can't risk you getting injured," Xerus said. He closed his eyes, and I felt him infusing some of his magic into me.

"I love you, Alexius." The words, in my favorite voice, floated softly into my ear.

"I love you too." I held Brixelle even closer. Xerus and Xenon made their exit then, leaving Brixelle and me alone in the Jade Room. I secretly wished we weren't. Being alone felt so much like a goodbye that I prayed someone else would come into the room.

"I didn't know life would be so exciting with you. I thought I'd fallen in love with the bookish prince." She smiled weakly, and her laugh turned into a cough.

I smiled against her hair. "You make me brave," I said.

"Alexius, I'm so tired. Can I sleep yet?"

I nodded against her head. I had examined every inch of her body, and she was healing. She had lost a lot of blood, but she was producing more now, and I kept monitoring it carefully.

She closed her eyes, and I magically scanned her body again, carefully inspecting all her organs and making sure they were working properly, that I hadn't missed anything. I put her down gently on the wide couch and then slipped in next to her. In her sleep, she curled up against me, and I covered her with a blanket of warmth magic.

I couldn't sleep though. I continually scanned her body, noting any small changes. *Everything is working fine*, I reassured myself. It would all be fine. Everything would be fine. We would win. Brixelle would recover. My siblings would come back without a single scratch on them. Xerus would continue to be himself. Thaxton would leave us alone. No. Maybe Thaxton would fall off a wall and die. Katsuro would return to protect my mother. My father would rule for a long time yet. Jaxon would find his mate. And Aexie would find her mate—begrudgingly maybe—and she'd be happy. Brixelle would get better. Brixelle had to get better. We had just started our lives together. Brixelle would get better. Brixelle would get better, Brixelle would ...

# CHAPTER FORTY-FIVE

## JAXON

I COULD FEEL ALEXIUS's despair as he wished and hoped and prayed that Brixelle would live. He hadn't started bargaining yet, but I knew it would come soon. I'd seen it before with my soldiers' spouses. He'd eventually promise the universe anything if only she lived.

I used his despair to fuel my battle rage. I sharpened it to a point, and like my blade, it sliced through our enemies. But it didn't seem to be making a difference. It didn't look good for us. We had been fighting all night, and with my night vision, it was easy to see that we were outnumbered. We'd taken down maybe a third of the enemy. But Thaxton had been preparing his army for months, maybe even years. It seemed he'd sent his weakest soldiers in first to tire us.

Light slowly started to fill the sky, and as the sun came over the horizon, I thought I heard ringing in my ears. I sliced through two more opponents before glancing to the east. Silhouettes lined the hill. The ringing in my ears had been a call to arms, and I watched with relief as a griffin-led army came charging down the hill. The enemy turned to meet them, so with renewed energy, I charged ahead. I didn't know who had mustered them, but at the moment, I didn't care.

*Are those griffins?* Aexie asked.

*Yes. And minotaurs.*

Aexie had been flying and fighting the aerial army that continued to arrive in waves, with Talmaro and Yagaron eventually joining her, while Vadentia stood with Xerus and Xenon, shooting arrows into the mass of combatants.

A boom sounded above me as if the sky had ripped open. I strove to take down two more enemies, but between strokes, I looked up. White, winged, four-legged bodies filled the sky.

*Pegasi have come to join us in the skies,* Aexie said. I glanced up when I finished yet another enemy to see the great, widespread wings of pegasi as they descended to meet the enemy in the western sky.

Suddenly, also from the west, manticores joined the fray. With them were a multitude of creatures from the kingdom of the West. It was a mish-mashed army, but it gave us the better numbers. We just might stand a chance.

*Where did they all come from?* Xerus asked.

*I don't care. They're here, and we need them,* I said before leaping back into battle with renewed energy. We could win.

The soldiers next to me cheered as more of their own kind joined the fight and bolstered their spirits. They fought to get to each other, crushing the enemy in between. The battle turned quickly, and like waves crashing to meet each other, our new forces crashed into the enemy's rear, and for once, we could see friendly faces past the enemy. I hollered and hooted, feeling refreshed as the sun finished rising and I cut my way toward our friends. I was impressed by the bravery of the farmers and citizens around me who had taken up arms. They weren't trained warriors, but they charged in with weapons high, making up for skills they lacked with an unnamed energy.

*It's called pride,* Aexie said.

Time slowed then, and all the action around me seemed to slow with it as I moved swiftly through the roiling mass, taking care of the enemies who loomed before me. As I struck down a particularly large creature with great pincer-like claws, I felt something pierce my heart, as if with an arrow. But when I looked down, my armor was whole. I turned inward and realized I had felt a shadow of what Alexius was feeling. Oh no. Brixelle.

*I'm on it.* Xerus took off and I heard the ringing of his footsteps in the empty palace halls as he ran back to the Jade Room. My soldiers had pressed on beyond me, and I stopped for a moment to see through Alexius's eyes. Brixelle had been sleeping peacefully, and Alexius must have fallen asleep at her side. One of her arms was crossed over her body like she'd been reaching for him, but her chest was still, her eyes glazed over in death.

Through Xerus's sight, I watched him burst into the Jade Room to see Alexius crumpled on the floor, Brixelle's motionless hand on his forehead.

"Cover me!" I yelled, and when my soldiers nodded, I turned to fly back to the Jade Room. Aexie was making a similar beeline, and when I ran through the doors, I saw that Xerus had coaxed Alexius into a chair.

Foxall was with Brixelle now. "She fought with all she had. But she just didn't win. She lost too much blood," he said. I saw the tears in his eyes, and I looked over at Brixelle. Her body was motionless. I thought she had been healed and would get better. I had felt Alexius's meticulous healing, his continuous inspection, his infusion of magic. I was confused. Even though she had been a new addition to our family, I had already seen the sunny afternoon laughter we'd share, the teasing I could unleash on her while she doted on my little brother.

Foxall folded her arms—the glow of her skin now just a papery gray—over her chest, then covered Brixelle with a black sheet.

I went to my brother. I'd never seen him so pale or immobile. He had mentally checked out and locked himself away in a place where he didn't have to acknowledge the world and its realities. I could sense how far he'd shuttered himself away from our soxkendi bond.

*Alexius?* I tried knocking at his door in our shared space, but there was no response, just a dark expanse.

Xerus was whispering to Alexius out loud, too quietly for me to hear. But I found myself glad that Alexius had not taken the blood oath. As devastating as it was to lose a new friend, I didn't know if my family could handle losing another child.

While Xerus took care of Alexius, Aexie rushed in. We hugged each other. Then she looked at Brixelle, suddenly welling up with tears. "Two sisters," was all she could say before bursting into sobs. I hugged her tighter, supporting her whole body in all her armor as her sorrow shook her small frame.

Foxall joined Xerus and spoke to Alexius in a low voice. But even without using the bond I could see that Alexius was not capable of much besides a nod here and there. I wondered if he even heard what they were saying. He just kept staring into the space straight in front of him, not really seeing anything.

*Jax, you need to get back out there. Xenon says it's almost done. They'll need direction,* Xerus said.

*All right,* I replied.

Aexie's sobs had slowed. She wiped her eyes one last time and nodded at Xerus before turning away. I wondered what Xerus had asked of her. I too turned away and left the room, returning to my squadron on the ground. Everyone was celebrating, cousins and neighbors hugged each other. My squadron was already stacking the dead in funeral pyres to be set aflame.

As I walked toward my squadron, they all stopped and turned to me, looking for words to mark the occasion.

"We thank you all, each and every one of you from every corner of our realm, for coming to our aid. Without your assistance, we would not be celebrating this victory. But before we can celebrate properly, I ask that we somberly mourn the dead. For this morning, we not only mourn the death of our fellow soldiers, but also Princess Brixelle, who died of the vicious injuries King Thaxton inflicted," I said in a loud, clear voice that carried across the battlefield. Tears welled in my eyes as a lump rose in my throat. I let what I had said sink in, both for the fighters and me. She had reminded me so much of Danx, and it felt like she had been ripped away from us again.

Many of the soldiers stood in shock, some covering their mouths and faces with their hands. The atmosphere went from celebratory to somber.

I threw myself into the remaining work needed to clear the battlefield. Somehow, at some unknown point, Thaxton had disappeared. I hoped he would get eaten by a sea serpent.

It was late afternoon before I was able to return to my family inside the palace.

*Father asks that you and Aexie bathe before returning to the Jade Room,* Xerus said.

I felt like I was dragging my feet through mud as I returned to my room, especially when I passed Alexius and Brixelle's room. I peeled off my armor, leaving it on the floor where I stood, and walked to the bathing room. I stripped naked by the tub and climbed in, letting the warm water wash away the horrible things I'd experienced today.

I was no stranger to blood and death and other battle atrocities, but somehow, the sorrow I felt through Alexius made the horrors worse, the hope for the future Brixelle had brought our family erased.

I eventually scrubbed and soaked myself clean, pulled myself out of the water, and automatically went to my wardrobe to pull out the dark colors of mourning. Then, my heart heavy, I made my way to the Jade Room. It was candlelit and Brixelle's body had been dressed beautifully and placed upon an altar.

All but Alexius, Aexie, and Xerus—who I assumed were all together getting ready—had arrived. My mother was weeping into my father's shoulder as they stood nearest Brixelle. My father looked terribly sad, hopeless almost. I spotted Brixelle's mother, Roxana, with Yagaron, who comforted her, and Talmaro, who offered her water.

Then silently, Xenon approached me. Without words, he put his arms around me and embraced me, rubbing my back three times before pulling away slowly. I felt the tears prick the backs of my eyes.

Then the doors opened and Aexie came through, swathed head to toe in black, as did Xerus in his usual long coat and tunic also all in black. Alexius was between them. Aexie had his arm, and Xerus hovered nearby to support him. Alexius's gaze moved to the altar and stayed there as if he was praying and hoping she would show some sign of life, that it had all been a mistake. Maybe he was hoping she'd wake up and say, "Just kidding!" and then we could celebrate our victory properly. From my bedroom window, I'd heard cheers from taverns nearby. Despite the dark cloud of death lingering over the festivities, it would be a late evening of celebration for many in the realm. Tomorrow, Xerus, Aexie, and I would have to acknowledge the victory and honor our allies and citizens for their bravery and sacrifices.

But tonight was about Brixelle. So, I went to Alexius and embraced him in the fiercest hug I could manage without snapping him in half. My shoulder moistened as he shed some of the tears he held onto so tightly.

Aexie and Xerus came over and each took their turn embracing him before clasping his arms and accompanying him to the altar. He climbed the few steps and kneeled at its base. He reached gently under the dark cloth to hold her hand, now cold, then pressed it to his forehead. I could see him whispering something, but I didn't want to intrude, so I stayed where I was. He continued murmuring for long moments, so Aexie and Xerus slowly backed away from Alexius. They joined me, Aexie taking my hand and Xerus's.

*I can't believe she's gone,* Xerus said.

*Alexius healed her,* Aexie said, still in disbelief.

*She must have lost too much blood. Or maybe she was too close to death to bring back with healed tissue and knitted muscles,* Xerus said.

*How's Roxana?* I asked, looking again at her and Yaragon.

*In shock but proud that Brixelle defended what she loved,* Xerus said.

I nodded gently. *The additional forces have elected leaders to come speak with you tomorrow morning,* I told Xerus before I could forget.

*All right.* I could feel him holding back a barrage of emotions. Xenon was next to him in a second, and I saw how tightly they held each other as they moved to sit on the couch. I stood where I was, just to the side, watching Alexius. Aexie took up her own post, flanking Alexius and standing like me: legs apart and hands together behind our backs. We would stand vigil for my brother. For Princess Brixelle.

From my angle, I could see the shadow of Alexius's profile outlined in the candlelight against the black cloth. He continued to murmur words, and I wondered what he spoke of. Perhaps he was making promises to universes and gods, hoping they would bring her back to him. Or perhaps he was telling her everything that he'd wanted to and not yet had the time to. Or perhaps he was talking about the future they were supposed to have had, the many dragonlings they would have raised, the many moments of laughter and fun they'd have had together, the many decisions they would have made together. Whatever he spoke of, he spoke quickly and quietly, his eyes closed as he continued to press her hand to his forehead.

I felt his grief and sorrow as it permeated through the room. Alexius had always been the most cautious, and lately, the most dedicated to learning and reading. He had always quietly stood to the side, learning what he could. When Danx was torn from our lives, he might as well have become an armchair. He'd been silent for nearly a century before starting to participate in his own life again, though much of that was our fault. For his mate to be ripped away from him so soon after they'd found each other could be disastrous. He would need time, but we would have to watch him. We needed him more than he realized, more than we had realized when we'd shunned him after our sister's death. My whole family was better with him. He had even been the original reason we had created soxkendi.

On that night all those years ago, Xerus and I had been fighting. I couldn't even remember why. Some military strategy maybe. I'd been about to leave and not come back, to abdicate my position in the family so I could travel and live among our relatives. But that night, Danx had dragged me to the library. Seeing little Alexius nervous to speak to his own siblings, I realized I had been neglecting him. He shouldn't have been afraid to speak to us. When he told us the story of the guard, I looked to Xerus and knew that my plans had changed. I had to protect my family. Xerus and I had to protect our family and this realm. That night in the library, my siblings and I established soxkendi and swore vows to each other. If a guard had found an opportunity to lash a royal prince, then we were all failing, so Xerus, Aexie, and I had vowed to lay our differences aside and respect one another so we could work together. Alexius was the reason we had bonded, the reason for soxkendi—until Danx had died. Then we'd pushed him away again. Looking at him now, knowing I was useless while he suffered so much agony and sorrow was difficult for me to swallow. I glanced at Aexie from the corner of my eye and saw her staring at Alexius, likely making the same promises to help him I had moments ago. We would get through this together.

# Chapter Forty-Six
## Xerus

W E'D ALL SPENT A sleepless night in the Jade Room, standing vigil in Brixelle's honor. I couldn't believe what my little brother was having to go through. I'd felt his sorrow and the only thing I'd secretly wanted was to hold Xenon tight. He'd felt it too and had been at my side since.

I felt like I was walking through fog as my father, Jaxon, Aexie, Xenon, and I walked down the hall to the public receiving room. My mother had stayed with Alexius.

The leaders of the creatures who had come to our aide wished for an audience with us and then we could go back to mourning. Kind of. We'd have a thousand more things to do now that the battle was over. Paperwork was stacked up to the ceiling probably. Maybe I could rope Aexie and Jaxon into helping me.

We entered the lofty room together like a sweeping wave. My father sat on the dais, and I was grateful for the other chairs someone had brought in for the rest of us. My father's throne was on a raised platform, and Aexie and Jaxon sat to his left, Xenon and I to his right. My mother's throne was empty. None of us would risk leaving Alexius alone right now. He had stood—or knelt—vigil in the same spot all night and continued to whisper to Brixelle's cold hand even as we'd left. I pushed aside the thought, not wanting to bring more tears to my eyes, and Xenon squeezed my hand.

A griffin, a minotaur, a manticore, a pegasus, and a cockatrice were introduced as they walked up to meet us. They all bowed deeply.

"Your Majesty, Your Royal Highnesses. Please accept our deepest condolences on the loss of Princess Brixelle. Even now, our lands mourn our princess." The griffin spoke on everyone's behalf.

My father nodded. "Thank you for your condolences. It is a difficult time for my family, so please excuse the absence of my wife and Prince Alexius. He is too deep in sorrow to be present, and my wife refuses to leave his side." They all bowed again, obviously not at all surprised. "We also must thank you for coming to our aide. We did not think to call on our citizens and are immensely grateful for your commitment and dedication to this realm," my father continued.

They bowed their heads. The manticore stepped forward. "We have heard of the King from the North and how he treats his people. We were all too ready to come not only to your aid, but the aid of our own. We wish for your reign to be long and prosperous and would like to avoid His Majesty Thaxton's rule." The manticore bowed and I wondered why he'd glanced over at me.

"We're grateful for the sacrifices of all our people, and if there is anything we can do for you, please name it. If it is in the realm of possibility, we will do it for you," my father said. I could tell he was nervous about what they might ask.

They all glanced in my direction, and suddenly I was nervous.

"May we speak with Your Majesty in private?" the manticore asked, glancing at me again.

"My son is the heir to the throne. It would be wise for him to hear your words and witness our meeting." My father stuck out his chin, and I knew he was easing back into his position as king and away from being a grateful friend.

The manticore nodded. "Very well then." He turned to my father after glancing at me yet again.

Xenon squeezed my hand. *I think they've been looking at me, not you,* he said.

*What do you think they want?* I asked.

*I have an idea, but let's see what they say.*

"We, the citizens of your realm, were thrilled to hear of the union of the late Princess Brixelle and Prince Alexius as she was one of the realm." I felt a stab of pain lance my heart on my brother's behalf. "And we are also glad the heir to the throne, Your Highness, Prince Xerus, has found happiness." They nodded at me, and I held my breath as I waited for the other shoe to fall. "But the proximity of the ancient and honorable Xenon makes us all uncomfortable."

Xenon squeezed my hand, holding me back from jumping up and shouting at them.

"And how does he make you uncomfortable exactly?" my father asked.

I glanced over at Jaxon and Aexie. Jaxon's posture was rigid, and he stared at our guests' feet while Aexie's head tilted questionly as she watched our guests carefully. I looked at my father, wondering what was going on.

"Please, speak plainly," my father said.

"We wish for Xenon to leave the realm," the manticore said.

"I'm sorry, what?" I said before I could stop myself. My father shot me a look, and Xenon reeled me back in as he squeezed my hand.

They pointedly ignored Xenon and me sitting to my father's right. But they continued to explain. "Your Majesty, Xenon is an ancient. They were never given lands or realms to rule for the simple reason that it would be too much power to allow any one ancient. Prince Xerus and all your children have been raised to rule the realm, and we're grateful for this, but it worries us that an ancient could have influence over our future king."

I wanted to stop listening. I wanted to crawl back into my bed with my beloved Xenon and hide under the covers. I wanted to go to sleep and wake up and go back to normal. I even wanted to go back to my duties. I'd never complain again about the boring days of stacks of paperwork.

"As you know, Xenon has accepted the role of prince consort. He has no role in the hierarchy. My son, Jaxon, outranks him in the line of command, as do all my children," my father said.

It sounded like an echo in my ears.

The manticore still refused to look at me or my siblings. "We understand that, but there are other ways to influence a person. How will you know if Prince Xerus is himself or if Xenon has taken over his mind?" the manticore almost pleaded.

"My children are bonded. They know when one is not well or not themselves. That you can be sure of," my father said, looking at my siblings then resting his gaze on Xenon.

"Still." The manticore puffed out his chest and stood taller. "You have asked us what we would like in repayment for the lives lost and the resources used to protect your palace and your place on this throne, and it is this: that the ancient, Xenon, not reside in this realm."

I would have to leave. I would have to leave the position I'd been training for my whole life.

My father sighed, gracefully somehow. Then in a blink, he became more authoritative. "We will consider your request. But we make no promises, and we will be the ones to decide. We thank you for your services." He dismissed them and as they walked out, I could feel the panic rising in my stomach.

When they had left and the doors had closed, my father turned to Aexie and Jaxon. "What do you think?" he said.

They looked at each other, then at Xenon.

"Xenon's family now. He fought next to us. To rip him away is cruel," Jaxon said.

"I see their point though," Aexie said. She waved her hands quickly. "I'm not saying I agree, but they're worried this realm becomes a tyranny with Xenon at the helm. They don't understand soxkendi, and they're worried that those training to rule won't be autonomous," she said, shrugging. Her shoulders drooped and she stared at her feet.

That did it. I'd made up my mind. I didn't want to have to choose between my realm and Xenon, but here it was anyway. "I will abdicate. Xenon and I will move to another realm. We will be there to aid you as you wish." I nodded at Jaxon, the next in line.

"No, no, no. I will not be king. Not in a million centuries," Jaxon said.

"Don't even try," Aexie said.

"You will do no such thing," Xenon said. He turned to my father and siblings, then back to me. "You have worked your whole life to become king. And as much as I've come to love your siblings, they are not you. They have trained to help you, not be you," he said.

"So what are we going to do?" I asked him.

"I will live in another realm," Xenon said.

"But what about us?" I asked. The panic rose anew.

"They never said I couldn't visit. I will come to you. This realm needs you," Xenon said.

"But I need you," I said.

"You have me. I'm all yours. And you will always have me," he said, taking my hands and bringing them to his lips. "I do not want to come between you and your family or your realm. You need each other. And

Alexius needs you, Xerus. I can't take that away from him. Not now that he's lost his mate."

"But what about what I want?" I asked him.

"You'll still have me. I just won't live with you. We'll always be connected, up here," he said, pointing to his head, his other hand over his heart. "But you're the future king, and your wants come second." Xenon embraced me. "Alexius just lost his mate. I won't risk losing you. This isn't ideal, but it's better than a realm torn apart. I don't want more battles, more war. I will live in another realm, and I will visit. And we will always be able to speak to each other."

"But why do we have to give them what they want?" I asked. I looked to my father, who wore a serious expression but let us talk it through without interrupting.

"Maybe it's not for forever. Maybe they just need more time to get to know me and see that I'm no threat to them," Xenon said.

"How am I going to do this without you?" I asked.

Xenon smiled. "Like you always planned. With Jaxon and Aexie and Alexius." He looked over at my brother and sister, who looked sadly at us. And just like that, it was decided without my agreement. Xenon had decided for us.

⁕

Xenon had said he didn't want to disrupt the peace anymore, so The Four stayed only a week more and then they left, going to live on Yagaron's estate as it bordered the realm of Korsel. It was far enough away to satisfy the citizens who had demanded it. I started working later and later into the evening. Paperwork always had to be done, and my rooms were too lonely, too sad without Xenon's presence filling them.

We spoke often, but he refused to hear anything of official matters, so we started having less and less to talk about. The realm became my whole life. The realm and Alexius. He'd stayed at Brixelle's side for over a hundred days, immobile, just whispering for the first seven days. Then he was quiet. He kneeled at her hand for a hundred days before finally standing up, kissing her forehead, and lighting the funeral pyre.

Then he spent the next few years going through the motions, not truly being present, but moving on with his body's needs and his old routine. I often found him in the library when I was up late. In the wee hours, he read. He too couldn't seem to spend much time in his own chambers. Sometimes, I'd set up my paperwork in the library just to keep an eye on him.

Many nights, we sat silently in the library together. At least we weren't alone. It was less daunting to get through the wee hours of the night if we mourned together. He read and I read or signed papers. Every once in a while, I flicked my gaze up to check on him and would catch him staring out the window, just staring straight out for minutes at a time. But then he'd shake his head and turn back to the book he was reading. I knew what he was thinking. *Had it been real? Is this really my new life? What happened? What did I do wrong?*

Aexie and Jaxon tried to cheer us up, or beat us up, but it would take time, time to smooth the sharp edges of our pain into rounded corners.

To see a bonus scene where Xenon meets Xerus, click https://geni.u s/YearoftheDragon or scan the QR code below:

# Note from the Author

I initially wrote this during a NaNoWriMo (National Novel Writing Month). I remember a friend asking me on November 1st if I was planning to do Nanowrimo and it occurred to me that I wanted to explore the backstory of a specific character. I also like to take Nano as an opportunity to try something new. This was my attempt at a first person, multiple points of view story. Plus, who wouldn't want to find out more about a family of dragons?

I'm sorry if Brixelle's death came as a surprise. This book does stand alone. But if you've read of Thali's adventures in publishing order, then you were hopefully more prepared for it. I don't enjoy making people sad, and perhaps you will take comfort in that I cry every single time I read it.

This book came about because Alexius popped into Thali's story and I knew that he had lived a life full of many adventures in a fantastical land before he meets Thali.

I intended for this story to stand alone. But as this is being published, Jaxon and Aexie have piped up to let me know they're ready to share some of their stories.

# Acknowledgements

Thank you, dearest reader, for choosing to spend your precious time with this story. I'm forever grateful and hope you were entertained.

I'm so grateful to my early readers. This story didn't go through the normal early channels, so there is much appreciation to Charity, Paul, and Char for their care.

Always and forever, I'm so grateful for my editor, Bobbi Beatty, of Silver Scrolls Services. You made this story better and you push me to be a better writer, thank you.

Equal gratitude to my proofreader, Lorna Stuber. Besides your amazing attention to detail, it comforting to have an author bestie to share the trials and tribulations with!

MiblArt has always done fantastic work and not only was I stunned to see they could fit all four dragons on here, but so beautifully too! Thank you!

Much gratitude, always, to my family, my friends, my communities. Your enthusiastic support means more to me than I can fairly express.

It just so happens that during the editing of this novel, this story became representative of a difficult time in my life in more ways than I could have predicted. There are no guarantees in life, and I'm grateful for what I have, but I hope, if you've ever wanted something pretty badly but couldn't have it, you buckle up your bravery when you're ready and have adventures afterwards. To those who share their stories so openly on the internet hoping to help someone else, thank you.

# About the Author

C AMILLA IS A LOVER of many mediums of storytelling. She loves to write strong heroines who can kick butt and find the love of their life. She always has projects on the go and loves to consume stories of all kinds—books, shows, movies, plays, amongst many others.

When she is not writing, Camilla is often found exploring animal behavior, crafting, drinking a hot beverage, and clicker training her animals.

Come visit her at CamillaTracy.com or on instagram @camilla_tracy or sign up for her newsletter by visiting: https://geni.us/CamillaTracynewsletter

# Thali's Adventure Continues in...
## Of Spools And Billows

C LICK HTTPS://GENI.US/OfSpoolsandBillows TO BUY now, or scan this QR code:

## Or start at the beginning with

## Of Threads and Oceans.

Buy now at https://geni.us/OfThreadsandOceans or

Manufactured by Amazon.ca
Bolton, ON